FRESH
ERS

A MESSAGE FROM CHICKEN HOUSE

My first week at uni was like a kids' birthday party gone mad: dressing up, weird games, food fights – but with the helpful addition of lots of booze . . . It's nice to know that nothing has changed!

In FRESHERS, Tom Ellen and Lucy Ivison have written an unmissable account of this defining rite of passage, in all its crazy glory. Our protagonists discover friends for life, embarrass themselves and figure out who they want to be – and who they really are. As well as being hilarious, FRESHERS is full of wisdom, offering heartfelt insights about respect, friendship . . . and even love.

BARRY CUNNINGHAM
Publisher
Chicken House

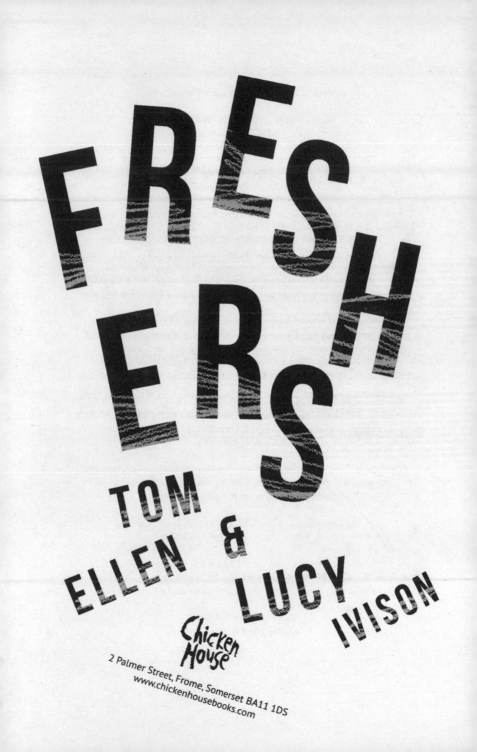

FRESHERS

TOM ELLEN & LUCY IVISON

Chicken House

2 Palmer Street, Frome, Somerset BA11 1DS
www.chickenhousebooks.com

First published in Great Britain in 2017
Chicken House
2 Palmer Street
Frome, Somerset BA11 1DS
United Kingdom
www.chickenhousebooks.com

Cover and interior design and illustration by Helen Crawford-White
Typeset by Dorchester Typesetting Group Ltd
Printed and bound in Great Britain by CPI Group (UK) Ltd,
Croydon, CR0 4YY

First line of 'You're' by Sylvia Plath, from *Collected Poems* (Faber, 1981),
copyright © 1960, 1965, 1971, 1981 by the Estate of Sylvia Plath,
is used by permission of Faber & Faber Ltd.

The paper used in this Chicken House book is made
from wood grown in sustainable forests.

1 3 5 7 9 10 8 6 4 2

British Library Cataloguing in Publication data available.

ISBN 978-1-910655-88-7
eISBN 978-1-911077-45-9

For Cassie Cooper, Louise Geoghegan,
Nell Booker and Vicky Clarfelt –
I'll keep your secrets if you keep mine – L.I.

For Carolina – T.E.

Also by Tom Ellen and Lucy Ivison

Lobsters

Never Evers

PART 1

CHAPTER 1

PHOEBE

Luke Taylor was right there and I did not feel prepared.

I kept dancing but the sight of him had kind of electrified my insides. The boy he was with passed him a pint of something green; Luke took a sip and grimaced. The klaxon went off and everyone started shrieking.

'Jutland College, make some noise!' the DJ yelled. 'And don't forget to introduce yourself when you swap clothes!'

A girl bopping next to me gave me a big smile and said something I had absolutely zero chance of hearing. I nodded and shouted 'Phoebe' as loudly as I could before taking the Yoda ears she handed to me and giving her my mirrored waistcoat. The song changed and she started dancing like she was at a rave.

I needed to compose myself. And share the hysteria. I needed to call Flora. I dodged my way off the dance floor but got stuck in front of a T-shirt with a picture of Princess Diana on it that said 'Queen of Hearts'. A head emerged from it – that girl Negin from my corridor. The one in the room opposite me.

'Hey.' I smiled really widely.

She said something, but the music was too loud.

'A really weird thing just happened to me,' I yelled.

She pressed her finger in her ear and leant towards me. 'Sorry?'

'I just saw someone—'

She kept shaking her head. In a weird moment of madness I grabbed her hand and started to weave us between people. We stumbled out into the bar area and I realized I was still gripping on to her hand, which was a bit bonkers, as we had only met a few hours ago. But now it felt like I couldn't just randomly let it go. I led her into the toilets and inside a cubicle.

'Are you OK? Are you going to be sick?' She sounded mildly concerned, but mostly grossed out. 'I'm not really a hair-holding person.'

'No, I'm fine. I'm just—'

'Sorry, it's just I actually hate puke.'

'I thought you were doing medicine?'

She frowned. 'You don't have to *love* puke to study medicine.'

'Sorry, obviously, yeah.' I went to sit on the toilet but it had no lid. 'I'm not gonna puke, anyway.' I was bobbing up and down on the spot, peeling my shoes from the sticky floor. 'It's not a *physical* problem.'

Negin's eyebrows disappeared slowly into her fringe. 'You are having an *emotional* problem.'

It was actually ridiculous. I snorted, which must have made

me seem mental. 'Sorry, I snort sometimes. I can't control it. Anyway, yes, it's an urgent emotional problem.' I took a deep breath. 'Basically, a boy that I went to school with . . . *is here*.' I whispered the 'is here' bit, and pointed at the floor.

The eyebrows dropped back down again. 'That *does* sound emotional.' There was a hint of a smile at the side of her mouth.

I didn't know how to explain it. I couldn't think of a way to describe the last seven years of nothingness accurately. I tried again: 'OK, this boy I have wanted – to different levels – for, like, my entire existence, is here.' I was waving my hands about insanely.

'Oh.' Clearly, Negin had no idea how to respond to my declaration. 'Did you not know he was coming to York?'

'No, I totally did.'

'Right . . .'

'I'm not explaining it well because I'm drunk.'

'O-*kay*.' She nodded solemnly. She was actually pulling the same face as Princess Diana.

'I just feel like I need time to prepare myself for seeing him, you know? Like I need to regroup and get my game face on.'

Negin didn't sound that convinced. 'I would hug you,' she said, 'but I'm not really a hugger.'

She wasn't a hugger. She wasn't a hair-holder. What *was* she? I really needed Flora. Flora could hug and hair-hold at the same time, as expertly demonstrated on my seventeenth birthday. Ugh – I needed to stop rose-tinting my old friends and focus on my potential new ones. It was Flora who gave me

5

those tequila shots in the first place now I thought about it.

'Do you want to go and talk to him?' Negin said.

'NO! Oh my god. No.'

She looked at the door again and took a deep breath. 'OK. So, what *do* you want to do? We have been in this cubicle for like . . . a while. I mean, I'm not that into the crazy first-night-of-Freshers' thing, but, I was hoping for more than . . .'

We both stared down the bowl of the toilet.

'What the fuck? Are you lot dead in there?' a girl shouted from outside.

'Not dead.' I shouted back. 'We're just . . . one second.'

Negin tucked her hair behind her ears. 'My brother told me this story about how a girl he knew went to uni and the day she got there, she tripped up putting her duvet cover on, hit her head and knocked herself unconscious. And because her door was shut, no one knew she had even arrived. They found her, like, six days later.'

'What . . . dead?'

'Well, she hadn't just been trapped in her duvet for six days.' Negin smiled awkwardly and I burst out laughing.

'I'm sorry, that is the most awful thing I have ever heard.'

She shook her head. 'It's probably not even true. My brother probably just made it up to freak me out even more about going away.' It made me feel better to hear that someone else was nervous, too. She opened her bag and got out a tin of Vaseline. She had a black bob with no hair out of place, almost like a Lego person. Apart from the faded Princess Di T-shirt, she looked neat. Black jeans, Converse, no make-up. Like if a

6

newsreader fronted an indie band.

'Either way,' I said, 'I'm never shutting my door again. Or changing my duvet.'

Negin carefully dabbed Vaseline on her lip. 'Don't worry, we can just check on each other every night. You know, just in case the other person is dead.'

'Yay,' I said. 'Death pact.'

What was *wrong* with me? I hate the word 'yay'. 'Yay' is the worst. It's so cheerleader-enthusiastic. It's not something I even say. The stress of Luke Taylor was making me nuts.

The girl outside banged on the door again. 'If you're not dead, then maybe let some other people piss, yeah?'

'OK,' Negin shouted, and then turned back to me. 'All right. Are you ready to go out there and face . . .'

'Luke,' I said. 'I don't think I'll ever be ready to face Luke Taylor. I feel like if you saw him you would understand.'

I got my phone out and searched for a picture of him. 'See?'

Negin looked down at the photo. It was from two weeks ago. Luke Taylor holding up his L-plates after passing his driving test. He was wearing a white T-shirt and his hair had been bleached really, really blond by the sun. It almost looked dyed because there were dark roots coming through. He looked a bit sheepish, like someone had made him pose for it. I pressed the phone into her hands and she dutifully leant in to look closer. She didn't say anything.

'That's him,' I hissed.

She nodded. 'I got that.'

I waited for her to speak. She must have realized she was

supposed to say something else. 'He looks . . . like a standard hot boy.'

My seven-year loyalty to him bristled. 'His hair looks better longer.'

'Where is he?' she asked.

'At the driving test place, I guess.'

'No,' she sighed. 'Where is he *now*?'

'Oh. On the side bit next to the dance floor.'

'OK, well, we'll walk past and if he sees you, just casually say hello.' Negin sounded confident so I went with it.

'OK.'

We opened the cubicle door and the girl outside huffed and barged straight in past us. We washed our hands, even though neither of us had actually been to the toilet. I tried to arrange my tutu, sweatbands and Yoda ears. Negin offered me some of her Vaseline.

'I wish I looked a bit less . . . random,' I said.

'It's a clothes swap party,' she said. 'You'd look *weirder* if you were wearing a matching outfit.'

'Yeah, you're right.'

I took a deep breath and we walked out. But Luke Taylor had vanished.

LUKE

I was doing my best to focus on what Arthur was saying, but the buzzing in my pocket kept distracting me.

If I'd counted right – and I was pretty sure I had – this buzz was the eleventh buzz since we'd got down to the bar. The *eleventh*. A sudden rush of anger cut through me. Did she really expect me to spend the first night of Freshers' stood outside talking to her? Wasn't the whole point of this week to talk to *new* people?

The buzzing stopped as Arthur pushed a luminous blue shot and a pint of lager along the bar to me. He was wearing a bright-red bathrobe over a sleeveless denim jacket, his sweaty black hair just about tucked into a yellow swimming cap. I had on my mum's 2007 Bon Jovi tour T-shirt under a massive, multi-coloured Mexican poncho. We both looked absolutely ridiculous. But then, so did everybody else. Even the barman was wearing a kimono.

I realized Arthur's mouth was moving again, so I leant in and tried to concentrate.

'I was supposed to be off-campus this year,' he was shouting over the music. 'Me and some mates had a house sorted and everything. Even put the deposit down.'

'So, what happened?' I yelled back.

'It got fucking *condemned*. Like, literally, two weeks ago. Asbestos. So that's why I've ended up back in B Block next door to you.' He did his shot and winced. 'Still, could be worse. Most second years don't get to do Freshers' Week again, do they?'

I nodded and drank my shot. It tasted like vodka-flavoured toothpaste. 'What is asbestos?' I shouted.

Arthur necked half his pint in one go. 'It's this sort of invisible presence that lives inside your house.'

'A bit like Wi-Fi.'

9

'A bit, actually, yeah.' He nodded. 'But Wi-Fi that silently kills you in your sleep.'

'Right. Shit.'

The klaxon went off, and he shrugged off his bathrobe while I gave him my poncho. The barman started lining up more blue shots on a tray as Beth came over with Barney. Or maybe it wasn't Barney. Was it Tom? Tom also had red hair. It could be Tom.

'Beth! Barney!' Arthur yelled.

'Just seeing if you guys needed a hand,' said Barney-Not-Tom, cheerfully. He was short and skinny with a strong Dorset accent and tons of orangey freckles. Beth was almost a foot taller and had a sort of strict, 'head girl' vibe about her that was being nicely accentuated by the Harry Potter robe she was wearing.

'One, two, three, four, five . . .' Arthur clamped the shots one-by-one between Barney's fingers.

'I'd rather have a gin and tonic than another of those shots, to be honest,' Beth said, sharply. 'They're like drinking Listerine.'

'No worries,' said Arthur. 'One G&T coming up. We'll bring it over with the rest of them.'

'Thanks.'

Arthur leant in to me as they walked back to the table. 'You wanna watch that Barney, by the way.'

'Why?'

'He's a labeller. I saw him putting a Post-It note on his Nutella. We had a labeller on the corridor last year. Total nutjob. Got kicked out in the second term for shooting a squirrel with a BB gun. He was a chemist, too.'

'Barney's doing Geography, isn't he?' I'd only managed to remember that because me, him and Arthur were the only ones *not* doing Chemistry on our corridor.

Arthur finished his pint and slapped the plastic glass back down on the bar. 'Yeah, well, it's all the same *Big Bang Theory* ballpark, isn't it? Except that Geography is basically just colouring-in. What are you doing again?'

'English. You're Philosophy, right?'

'Yes, mate.' He ran a hand across his patchy black stubble. 'I'm wrestling with the big-boy questions: what is the nature of truth? How can we find meaning in a godless universe? *How* hot is that girl chatting to the DJ?' I looked at the girl in question, who was indeed hot. He picked up the tray, which was now dangerously overloaded with drinks: 'Shall we get back, then?'

My pocket started buzzing again. Number twelve. I pulled my phone out. 'I'll be there in one sec, sorry man, just need to quickly get this.'

I slipped out of the main door and the cold hit me hard. I pressed the phone to my ear. 'Hey.'

'Hey.' Her voice sounded wrinkled and far away. The way it'd sounded pretty much all summer.

'Look, I'm sorry I didn't pick up, it's just—'

'I know,' she said. 'I know you're busy.'

'I'm not *busy*, it's just . . . It's the first night. Obviously everyone's out.'

11

'I know.'

Silence.

'So, maybe I'd better go back in.'

'OK. Have you met anyone nice?'

'My corridor are all right. They've pretty much just talked about chemistry so far, but they seem nice. And this one bloke Arthur seems cool. He's a second year, though.'

'That sounds good. Cool. I . . . I just wanted to check everything was OK. It felt like we didn't really sort stuff out properly this morning before you went. I didn't want you to leave when it was weird between us.'

I sighed. 'It's been weird between us all summer.'

More silence. That was the first time either of us had actually admitted that out loud. For some reason it felt easier to say knowing she was 200 miles away.

She still wasn't speaking, so I kept going; the booze and the pocket buzzing and the 200 miles making me spill stuff that had been locked up firmly in my head until now. 'And, I mean, the thing is, it's not gonna get any less weird now that I'm here, is it?'

'What do you mean?' she said, quietly.

'I mean, I'm here and you're there. We won't see each other that much.'

'Yeah, but you said, at Reece's party, remember, you said we could make it work.'

'I know, but . . . if this is us making it work, then maybe it won't work.'

I heard her inhale sharply, but I carried on. 'Like, I'm

supposed to be working at other stuff, too, y'know? Meeting people. Making friends. But instead I'm standing out here talking to you. Do you really want me to spend the whole three years on the phone to you?'

'You're being a dick, Luke,' she muttered.

I was a bit. But I was also *right*.

'Look, I'm sorry. It's stupid to speak now,' I sighed. 'I'm a bit pissed. I'm wearing a bathrobe. I'll call you tomorrow.' I wasn't quite sure why I'd added the bathrobe information.

'I don't want to talk about this tomorrow,' she said, her voice getting lumpy with tears. 'I want to talk about it now.'

'Well, I don't.'

'If you've got something to say, then just say it. Have you met someone else?'

This actually made me laugh out loud. 'Of course I haven't fucking met someone else, Abbey! I'm out here talking to you! How *can* I meet someone else?'

'Do you *want* to meet someone else, though?'

'I *want* to go back inside.'

I hung up before she could respond. But my pocket was buzzing again as soon as I stepped back in.

PHOEBE

'You were terrified of seeing him, but now he's gone you're gutted.'

I groaned. 'I know. He's ignored our subliminal instructions. What a bastard. We just planned the whole scene out and he hasn't even bothered to turn up.'

13

Negin nodded. 'The same thing happens when I argue with my mother. I rehearse this whole speech in my head and go downstairs and start it and then she interrupts and I'm like, Mum, stop' – she held her hand up – 'you are ruining my epic comeback.'

I had been daydreaming my Luke Taylor meet-cute all summer. It was part of my uni prep. I had also discussed it with Flora in detail. The only part of it I had actually managed to execute was buying an oversized scarf, which I took off in the car on the way here when my mum said it was twenty degrees and I would look strange and potentially terminally ill.

We bought another drink and found a spot on the edge of the dance floor. There was a girl up on stage with rainbow-dyed, bowl-cut hair, chatting to the DJ. I'd watched her arrive earlier, through my window. She was still wearing the same tracksuit bottoms and crop top, but now she also had a gold crown that was sort of hanging jauntily to one side, like she was in some kind of fashion shoot.

'How is that girl a fresher?' I said. 'Seems like she knows everyone.'

'I saw her earlier and she was writing in marker pen on this boy's stomach.' Negin didn't seem to have an opinion about this, just delivered the information matter-of-factly.

'What, like her phone number?'

'No, I think it was a line from a song or something.' Negin rolled her eyes. 'Deep.'

'I saw her arrive this afternoon. She didn't have any stuff at all. Nothing. She just walked into her halls carrying a *colander*. Like, she is so cool, all she needs for the next three years is multi-coloured hair and a *colander*.'

'Like she fell from space.' Negin nodded.

'Exactly. She just sauntered in with the belly and the colander. She hasn't even got changed. I genuinely think those are the only clothes she has.' How do you even *become* a person who is brave enough to get a rainbow bowl cut and wear boys' trackies on a night out? What does your life preceding that point even look like?

We kept staring at Bowl-Cut as the DJ gave her his headphones and she started waving her hands out to the crowd.

We found the rest of our corridor and all started dancing together. You could tell we were all from the same halls because of the luminous glitter the Scouse girl, Liberty, had enthusiastically doused on us before we came out. Negin was dancing in her reserved way and the really shy girl, Becky, was hardly dancing at all. Every time the klaxon sounded she looked panicked. Liberty oscillated around the group, hugging us all and breaking out into random and unexpected stripper moves every so often.

The klaxon sounded again and Connor, the boy in the room next to me, jumped into the middle of the circle, took his T-shirt off, and started swinging it round his head like a lasso. None of us was in danger of forgetting his name, as he had 'Kiss me I'm Connor' written right across his forehead. His boom was so loud that you could hear his 'First night of Freshers'!' war cry reverberate around the room.

The exaggerated lasso-swinging was making everyone jostle and my Yoda ears fell on the floor. I bent down to get them, and stood up face-to-face with Luke Taylor. He had come out of nowhere, just as I had forgotten about him for one second.

'Hey.' I tried to smile demurely.

'Hey,' he shouted over the music. The klaxon went off and he handed me his bathrobe. 'It's . . .'

There was this moment where I didn't know what he meant. And then I did and it was like a stone had appeared in my stomach.

'Phoebe,' I said.

'Yeah, of course.' He smiled. 'Phoebe. I'm Luke.'

I could feel my face getting red and tight. 'Hey.'

Negin was trying not to seem obvious and was sort of half dancing next to me, her back slightly turned the other way. Her being there made it worse. I wanted to replay the night from the beginning and not have blabbed on about him like some desperate idiot.

I handed him the Yoda ears and he put them on.

'So random we're both here,' I shouted brightly.

'Yeah, I kind of . . .' He felt in his pocket for his phone and then glanced down at it. 'Sorry, I . . .' He didn't finish the sentence, just looked across the room and started to shuffle away. He didn't even say goodbye. If I'd seen someone from school, even if I didn't really know them, I would have made an effort. We were 200 miles away from home. We had known each other to look at since we were eleven. It was like he actively

16

didn't want to be associated with me. Like he didn't want anyone here to even know that we were connected. I took a deep breath and turned to Negin.

'So . . . that was him, then?' she said, cupping her fingers around my ear so I could hear her over the music. I bit my lip and nodded.

She shrugged. 'He's not all that.'

'It was a big school,' I said. 'So not everyone knew each other.' I felt ridiculous. Like some psychotic weirdo. We *had* only directly spoken, like, five times in seven years, but I thought he knew my name at least. I felt like someone had let the air out of me. I made a conscious effort to pull myself together and smiled at Negin really widely. 'I feel like such a loser.'

She shook her head. 'My aunt still calls me Leila. That's my sister's name.'

'D Block squaaaaaaad!' Liberty shimmied over and hugged us both and made us smile for a selfie. We cuddled together and she took it.

'I'm gonna go to the loo,' I mouthed. I pushed through the dance floor to the toilets. I took some deep breaths and caught myself in the mirror. I was bright red and had glitter smeared all over my face.

I suddenly felt a bit tearful; the Luke thing had caught me off guard, made me feel small and exposed. Everything had been going really well and then I had ruined it all by banging on and on like Luke was some *thing*. I took a deep breath. It was only midnight. I sat on the toilet and got my phone out and

17

there was Luke Taylor. Smiling up at me from a pre-drinks picture he had been tagged in. Friends already with a whole group of new people, looking self-assured, even in a Bon Jovi T-shirt and Superman cape. I shoved my phone into my bag. Maybe I was just drunk. I washed my face and managed to smear glitter into my hair.

I walked out of the toilet and back on to the dance floor, but Negin wasn't where I had left her. I scanned the room. I couldn't see a single person I knew. Not Connor, not Liberty, not Becky, not any of them. I danced on my own for a second and then made my way back to the bar. I scrutinized the room again and again. I was going to have to go back to the corridor.

But then I saw Josh, our second-year contact person, waving at me from across the bar. He was tall and kind of stacked and had a shaved head, like he was in the marines or something. I walked across. He was on the edge of the dance floor with some boys, playing table football. He had been so nice earlier: spent twenty minutes showing my mum where the outlet shopping centre was on the map, and labelled each of our doors with stickers with our name on and a picture. Mine was a panda, which was weirdly appropriate as my behaviour was sort of suggesting I deserved to become extinct.

'I've kind of lost everyone.' I glanced around the room to prove it.

'Don't worry.' He grinned. 'You can totally hang out with us. I'm your second-year rep. It's basically my duty to make sure you have fun. These are my housemates, Will and Pete.'

Will was classically good looking. Tall, with boarding-school floppy hair and the kind of smile that only comes from knowing you're attractive. He leant over and kissed me on the cheek to say hello. Pete was smaller and less chatty and had somehow ended up wearing so many clothes he was almost drowning in them.

Some hip hop song came on that they all liked and we started dancing. Me and Will started doing that thing where you look at each other and then look away. With every song that played, we moved a bit nearer. He was smiling at me, almost shyly, and I could sense Pete and Josh tactfully shift away. Me and Will were dancing closer and closer, and then we were getting with each other. He was a good kisser, but I couldn't really get into it because I kept wondering if the people from my corridor were somehow watching. Or if Luke Taylor was watching. Not that anyone, least of all him, would exactly care. The whole night had already descended into a bit of a meat market, anyway. And even kissing a good kisser gets a bit awkward when you don't really know the first thing about them, and you're wearing a dressing gown.

'I better try and find my friend,' I said, finally. 'She might be on her own.'

The whole night felt a bit out of control. Like I needed to sort myself out and concentrate on making friends – not being rejected by Luke Taylor, getting lost and kissing randoms. I still couldn't see Negin anywhere, so I walked out of the main doors and into a hall area with vending machines. There was a darkened room labelled 'COMPUTER LAB'. At first I couldn't work out what the noise coming from inside was.

I creaked open the door. Gradually my eyes got accustomed to the dark, and I matched the low, gentle sound with the shape in the corner. Facing the window and shuddering every so often. Someone crying.

Luke Taylor crying.

CHAPTER 2

LUKE

I hadn't meant to say it. It just sort of . . . came out.

It was like she was pushing me, almost. Daring me to say it. 'If you don't want to speak to me,' she'd hissed, 'if you don't want to work at this, then maybe we should break up, Luke. Maybe we should just fucking break up.'

And I'd said, 'Yeah. OK. Maybe we should.'

And then there was only the gentle hum of her crying in my ear, and this terrifying, exhilarating feeling, like I'd jumped off a cliff with no clue if there was water or concrete at the bottom.

I just sat there, listening to her cry, feeling the panic and the toothpaste-y vodka fighting for space in my chest, surging up into my throat and pressing against the backs of my eyeballs.

Then the phone went dead. And I thought: *Is that it?* Are we actually broken up? Can three years of your life really come to an end, just like that, in a dark computer room in the middle of the night? I covered my face but the tears wriggled out

21

between my fingers. What the *fuck* was wrong with me? Half a day away from home and I was already falling apart.

I caught a glimpse of my reflection in one of the screens. This sweaty, moony, tear-stained face with a pair of green Yoda ears on top of it. It was so ridiculous I actually started laughing. Which, if anything, made me look more insane. I took the ears off and dropped them on the table in front of me.

Suddenly, I heard a noise from outside. I looked up but there was no one there. I wiped my face and checked the corridor, which was empty except for that Phoebe girl from school, who was getting some chocolate out of one of the vending machines.

A little shiver of anxiety ran through me as I realized she might have seen what I was doing. Even if she hadn't seen it, she was probably still wondering what sort of maniac sits alone in a computer room at midnight.

'Hey,' I said, trying to sound casual. She smiled and said 'Hey' back. Her cheeks were flushed from the heat of the bar and she had purply glitter smudged all across her forehead.

'You having a good night?' I asked, and she nodded.

I suddenly panicked that my eyes might be red and watery, so I blurted, 'I just took my contact lenses out.' She nodded politely, and I realized that, if my eyes *weren't* red and watery, this might have seemed like *quite* a random statement.

She then said something I missed completely, because the bar doors burst open behind us and a blast of music and shouting filled the hall. A girl wearing bright-orange dungarees and Pikachu earmuffs stepped out. She wobbled on the spot for a second, and then sort of slumped down on to the steps in slow motion.

'Are you OK?' Phoebe asked her.

The girl blinked a few times and squinted at us, as if she was having trouble focusing. She smelt strongly of tequila and sick. We helped her up.

'Where are your friends?' I said.

'I don't know . . .' she slurred. Then her face fell. 'I mean, I've only just met them . . . Do you think they *are* my friends? Do you think they *like* me?'

'Definitely,' Phoebe said.

'Do *you* like me?' she asked, and I nodded. 'Yeah, of course. We're both huge fans of your work.'

Phoebe laughed, and the girl seemed satisfied by this, because she draped an arm around each of our shoulders. 'OK, well at least *we* made friends. We can be each other's friends, can't we? First-night Freshers Friends.'

'First-night Freshers Friends,' Phoebe and I repeated, grinning at each other.

The girl took a deep breath and examined us more closely. It seemed like every change of facial expression required massive effort. 'What're your names?' she whispered.

'Luke and Phoebe,' I said.

She nodded. 'Hi, Lucan Phoebe. I'm Stephanie Stevens.'

'Nice to meet you, Stephanie Stevens. Are you going to be OK getting back to your corridor?'

Stephanie Stevens sighed and shook her head violently, like a grumpy six-year-old. 'Noooooooo.'

'Where do you live?'

She screwed her eyes up tight in concentration. 'Seventeen Belmont Road, Sunderland, SR1 7AQ.'

'No, I mean *here*, in Jutland, where do you live? B Block? C Block?'

'Oh. I'm not in Jutland,' she said. 'I'm in Wulfstan.'

Phoebe looked at the campus map that was pinned up next to the bar doors. Wulfstan was the next college along from Jutland. 'OK . . . Wulfstan College . . . This way.'

We all linked arms, with Stephanie Stevens in the middle, and started trooping slowly down the covered walkway. A few ducks waddled up out of the darkness of the lake, and started quacking along behind us.

It was mad to think me and Abbey had done this exact same walk less than a year ago, on the campus tour. Trailing our guide from college to college around the huge, murky lake, we'd talked about whether people swam here in the summer, and taken photos on the grassy banks. We'd even had a winter picnic by the main bridge, with all the most random foods we could find in the 'international' aisle of the supermarket. We'd sat there, chewing on biltong and weird German Haribos, and talking about all the things we were going to do here next year. The memory of it now seemed so detached from reality it was like it wasn't even mine. I shook it out of my head, and turned to Phoebe.

'So, how's your corridor?' I asked.

'They're pretty . . . mental,' she said. 'We've got this one guy, Connor, who was a rep in Ibiza over the summer, so he's

24

basically taken it upon himself to force us to have as crazy a time as possible.'

I nodded. 'There's nothing better than enforced fun.'

'Yeah. Although I drew the line when it came to drinking tequila out of a washing-up bowl.'

'Please don't mention tequila,' muttered Stephanie Stevens, darkly.

'What about your corridor?' Phoebe asked me.

'Pretty much the exact opposite of yours, by the sounds of it,' I said. 'No, they seem nice. Quite quiet, but nice. They're pretty much all doing Chemistry, though, so they basically spent the whole of pre-drinks talking about polymers and matter. What are you studying?'

'English.'

'Ah, nice one. Same as me. Maybe we'll be in the same tutor group.'

There was a pause, and Stephanie Stevens stopped and said, 'I'm doing French and Hotel Management.' Then she threw up in a bush.

By the time we got to Wulfstan, the ducks had abandoned us. By some miracle, Stephanie Stevens managed to remember the code to her block, so we all staggered up the stairs, still arm-in-arm. In the corridor she fumbled for her key, opened the door, murmured 'OK, then . . . night night, First-night Freshers Friends' and collapsed face-first on to her bed. Her room looked exactly like mine; same tobacco-yellow walls, same scratchy, Brillo Pad carpet, same weird little brown cupboard that opened to reveal a sink and mirror inside it. She even had the same brand-new Ikea desk lamp.

'Do you think she's OK?' Phoebe whispered.

'Well, she's snoring,' I replied. 'That's got to be a good sign.'

Phoebe winced. 'Not if you're the person next door. Listen to her. She sounds like a didgeridoo. And these walls are really thin.'

I laughed. 'We should probably put her in the recovery position, right? Just in case.'

We gently rearranged her on the bed while she mumbled, 'I love my First-night Freshers Friends,' over and over again.

'I'm a bit worried about leaving her like this,' Phoebe whispered.

'Yeah. Let's have a cup of tea, and then come back and check on her in a bit?'

'Um . . . yeah,' she said. 'Yeah, that sounds good.'

We went into the kitchen. She boiled the kettle and I found mugs and milk, then we walked downstairs, taking our teas with us. There was a little red bridge stretched across the lake, and we stood together in the middle, leaning against the edge, watching the steam rise from our cups.

It was freezing, and I could feel the cold and the tea starting to rub away at my drunkenness. I thought about Abbey and the phone call and all the utter, utter shitness of the past few months. I'd spent the whole summer thinking that uni would magically solve everything. I'd go to York Met, she'd go to Cardiff, and we sort of wouldn't even need to have the maybe-we-should-break-up conversation. Ten hours into university and I was already learning important life lessons: don't be so fucking naive.

'Oh my god, *yes*.' Phoebe fished into the pocket of the bathrobe I'd given her back at the bar and pulled out a Twix. 'Totally forgot I'd bought this.' She opened it. 'One finger each?'

'Nice one.' I took the chocolate off her. In spite of everything, I couldn't help wondering why I'd never noticed how pretty she was. Masses of brown, curly hair and an amazing smile.

I must have walked past her a million times at school. She couldn't have changed that much in ten weeks. Maybe I was just too hung up on Abbey to notice any other girls. But, no, that wasn't it. I'd definitely noticed Isha Matthews. And Lauren Green. And Katie Reader.

But I'd never noticed Phoebe.

PHOEBE

The whole thing was beginning to feel like an out of body experience.

This was exactly the kind of shit fourteen-year-old me was always daydreaming about. Well, maybe not Stephanie Stevens vomming everywhere and feeling like the pre-drinks 'Freshers' punch' was kind of creeping ominously up my oesophagus, but the Luke Taylor part. The part where I was now alone and kind of matey with him. Like a weird *Doctor Who*-type thing where I had jumped back into my own Year Nine fantasies. I focused on looking unfazed and generally breezy and not babbling. Flora says when I'm drunk I over-touch people, so every time I got within thirty centimetres of

27

him I took a step back.

Luke took a sip of his tea, then sat down and let his legs dangle over the edge of the bridge. I followed suit. Sort of. I followed suit forgetting how my mug was much fuller than his and also that when it comes to smooth physical movement, I am a dud. For a split second I thought I might just tumble underneath the iron railing and into the lake. I made a kind of squawking sound and then just fell on to my bottom with a thump, like some sort of geriatric penguin.

I looked up and saw that Luke was shaking his hair out over the lake and tea was dripping out of it.

'Oh my god, are you OK? I'm so sorry.' I *almost* reached out and touched him, but managed to stop myself in time. 'I prioritized the tea. I'm sorry.'

'"I prioritized the tea."' He started full on laughing, which made me laugh, too. 'Good to know you value me less than some tea.'

A part of me wanted to get out my phone and actually text that as a direct quote to Flora.

'Clumsiness is one of my defining features,' I said. 'My parents made me do disco dancing for three years to try and like, train it out of me. But all it did was give me even more of a complex. There is a picture in my house where I am wearing a turquoise unitard. I mean, that is only going to give your kid more problems, not less—' I pinched my thumb to try and physically stop myself babbling. At least I hadn't snorted. Snorting is probably the *least* sexy of all mannerisms.

Luke smiled. 'My mum made me do flamenco dancing for a

term because my sister did it and she didn't want to pay for a babysitter.'

'How old were you?'

'Old enough to know I was the only boy,' he said. 'They had to get me a special frilly shirt with red and black dots. I did an exam in it and everything.'

'How did you do?'

He shrugged in mock modesty. 'Oh, I can't remember. Distinction. No big deal. Just a distinction.'

I laughed. 'I cannot imagine you flamenco dancing.'

'I was all right at it, actually. Do you want some of my tea?'

'No, like I said, I prioritized the tea. I still have some left.' I showed him my mug. 'I feel a bit bad. These mugs have never been used. Look, they still have the label – £2.99, Robert Dyas.'

'I'm sure they won't mind,' Luke said. 'And more to the point, they won't even know. Plus, we can always blame Stephanie Stevens.'

'Yeah, we could leave them a note that says "Stephanie Stevens did it".'

We sat for a bit, just drinking our tea and staring at the lake. It made me realize how exhausted I was.

Luke sighed. 'I really feel like today has been one of the longest days of my life. Waking up this morning feels like weeks ago.'

I wondered if it felt longer for him because of what had happened to make him cry – whatever that was. Did it have something to do with Abbey Baker? Surely not. They were our year's golden couple. Out of nowhere, an image of them at the leavers' prom popped into my head. They looked like they belonged on the Oscars red carpet, not in the reception of the Kingston Holiday Inn.

'Yeah, but we made it.' I held my mug up. 'Cheers. To making it through the first day.'

He clinked his mug against mine and nodded. 'Yup. Me, you and, if Stephanie Stevens isn't dead, then her too. We made it through the first day of uni. And we both made a friend. *Two* friends actually, if we count Stephanie Stevens. If she's dead we can definitely count her, cos she won't be able to contest it.'

I shook my head. '*Seriously*, why are people so obsessed with dying at uni?'

'I don't know. Do you know Reece Morris?' Of course I knew Reece Morris. He was Luke's best mate.

'Maybe . . .'

'Anyway, he told me this story about this boy who fell in a skip on the first night of Freshers', knocked himself unconscious and then got tipped into a landfill site.'

'What? Random. And it's not just dying. It's dying in weird ways. My friend from my corridor, Negin, is obsessed with it too.'

'Oh, you've already *got* a friend, have you?' he said, raising an eyebrow. 'That's awkward. I thought me and Stephanie Stevens were your First-night Crew? Anyway, if this Negin's your friend, then where is she?'

I actually had no idea where Negin was. Would she be angry that we had got separated? I pointed vaguely out across the lake towards Jutland. 'Over there somewhere.'

'That's a duck, Phoebe.' It started swimming towards us.

'Look, it wants to be our friend.' I threw a bit of Twix into the water.

'OK, fair enough,' Luke smirked. 'It's you, me, Stephanie Stevens, this girl Negin – whoever the hell she is – and that duck. That's it for first night of Freshers'. Any more friends is overkill.'

'It's weird, cos everyone says you don't speak to the people you make friends with in Freshers' ever again, but I actually do really like Negin.'

He held his mug up. 'Cheers. Me and Stephanie and the duck haven't made the cut. We don't care. We've got each other anyway.'

Luke was actually funnier than I imagined. And less confident. He was quite softly spoken, really. He stared down blankly at the water. 'I wonder what will have happened between now and like, three years' time'. He said it like he'd almost forgotten I was there.

'We'll be twenty-one,' I said. 'That feels so far away. What do you *want* to have happened?'

He didn't look up. 'For everything to feel less complicated, I guess.'

It was the first time he'd said something that wasn't just banter. It was like his real voice came through. I didn't know what to do. So I just stayed silent.

He swung his feet underneath the bridge like a kid. 'Shall we go and check on our First-night Freshers Friend?'

He got up and held out his hand to me. 'Try not to fall in.'

Even as it happened, I simultaneously imagined describing it to Flora. It was the first time I had ever touched him. I took his hand but didn't want to put my whole weight on him in case I ungracefully pulled him over and into the lake. We walked back into the block and up the stairs. In the kitchen, we washed our mugs carefully and put them back in the cupboard. Then we looked in on Stephanie Stevens like new parents checking on their baby in its cot. She was snoring so loudly her bookshelf was shaking.

We wandered back over the bridge and along the walkway. Music was still blaring from Jutland Bar, but the lights had come on now.

We were walking side by side and every so often our arms brushed. I could feel my heartbeat upping its rhythm. Even though my Year Nine phase of stalking the hell out of Luke Taylor was just an embarrassing memory now, I still really, really fancied him. More than even Max and Adam, the two people I'd *actually* slept with. A part of me didn't even have the guts to look at him, in case he could tell.

We stopped outside Jutland Bar. We were facing each other and not far apart. My tummy flipped over a few times. We were in a classic kiss position.

'See you tomorrow, then, yeah?' he said, and reached forward to give me a hug. It was just a quick, see-you-later, cursory one; the kind you would give someone you were going to see right after the next lesson. But it woke my whole body up.

I wandered back to D Block in a bit of a daze. I kept replaying the hug in my head. I messaged Flora, saying, LUKE TAYLOR BREAKING NEWS: EVERYTHING YOU CAN IMAGINE HAS ACTUALLY HAPPENED.

Negin's door was closed but I could see her light was still on.

I knocked gently. 'It's Phoebe,' I said softly. 'Just checking you're not dead.'

'Not dead,' I heard her say. Then she opened the door in her pyjamas and smiled. 'Sorry I lost you. I was waiting up to check you weren't dead either.'

LUKE

Jutland Bar looked like a bomb site. The lights had come up and people were staggering about, broken and sweaty and blinking at each other like ridiculously dressed moles. Five lads in ripped bedsheet togas were on the dance floor, punching the air to 'Build Me Up Buttercup'. There was a girl wearing a full-length banana costume crying underneath the table football table, while a girl in a Justin Bieber onesie comforted her. Two pissed blokes were playing an aggressively competitive game above them, apparently unaware the girls were even there.

I felt empty. Not in a stupid, over-the-top, dramatic way. Just sort of . . . numb. And exhausted. I tried to let the phrase 'We are broken up' sink in properly, but it was like entering the wrong password. It wouldn't compute. It felt unreal, somehow. The phone call and the computer room meltdown seemed like days ago. In a weird way, the whole thing with Phoebe and Stephanie Stevens had been the best part of the night. It had taken my mind off everything, at least. There was no way I should have been able to enjoy myself after what had happened, but Phoebe's sunniness was infectious. She was just so easy to chat to.

I couldn't see Arthur or anyone else from the corridor, so I headed back to B Block. Even though it was nearly 2 a.m., I didn't feel like sleeping. I didn't want to give my brain the chance to properly process what had happened. I heard the soft thud of music coming from Arthur's room next door, so I tried knocking. His voice came through muffled: 'Hang on . . . Who's that?'

'It's Luke.'

There was a pause. 'All right . . . Come in, then. It's open.'

For a second, I thought I must have heard wrong, as there didn't seem to be anyone inside. Over the music, I could hear a watery tinkling sound, like a burst pipe somewhere in the walls. But then, suddenly:

'Where'd *you* get to, then?'

From behind the open door of the sink cupboard, I spotted Arthur's trainers.

'Oh, sorry,' I said. 'Didn't see you. You OK?'

'Yeah, man. Nearly finished.'

Before I could ask him what he was nearly finished doing, I suddenly realized what the watery tinkling was.

'Sorry, are you . . . y'know? Weeing? In the sink?'

'Yeah. Obviously. What do you think the sink's for?'

'Well . . . not for weeing in, I wouldn't have thought.'

'Look, mate, just cos we're not rich enough to get an en suite, like those posh fucks up in Gildas College, doesn't mean we can't *improvise*, if you know what I mean.'

I saw the trainers bob up and down, and the tinkling stopped. Arthur stepped out from behind the door, grinning. His face was red and shiny, and he was wearing the Superman cape I'd started the night with.

'All right! How—' He raised his forefinger, stopping himself mid-sentence. 'Sorry, forgot to flush.'

He reached back inside the cupboard and turned the taps on. My feelings about this must have been reflected pretty accurately in my facial expression, because he smirked and said, 'Don't you worry, my friend, you'll be weeing in the sink in no time. I mean, the toilets in this block are literally *at the end of the corridor*.'

He switched on his Xbox and pulled a little bag of weed out of his trouser pocket. 'Go on, then, I'll have a cup of tea if you're making one,' he said.

I laughed. 'All right.'

'See if there's any food as well,' he whispered. 'My mum bought me fuck all this term. Just cos I'm not a first year any more, she apparently thinks I don't need to eat.'

'My mum got me *ingredients*, but no actual food,' I said. 'I've got, like, flour and salt and olive oil, but nothing I can actually *eat*.'

Arthur raised an eyebrow mischievously. 'We could always crack out Barney's Nutella . . . I'm sure he won't mind if we have a *tiny* bit . . .'

Three spliffs and ten slices of chocolatey toast later, we were lying nearly comatose on the floor. Arthur scooped out the last splodge of Nutella and examined the now-empty jar.

'They shouldn't make this stuff so fucking delicious,' he groaned. 'Having something *this* delicious is clearly going to cause problems within a communal living space. It's fucking *irresponsible* is what it is.'

'What we gonna do?' I mumbled stickily.

He yanked open his bedside drawer and pulled out a Sharpie. 'Fuck, I've only got a black one. If I had a brown one, we could just colour the jar in, and he'd never know the difference.'

'Until he decided to actually eat some,' I said. 'Which we've got to assume he will do at some point.'

Arthur just shrugged and chucked the jar back at me. 'Just dispose of the evidence. He can't prove it was us, can he?'

I went out into the kitchen, but just then Beth's door opened and Barney stepped out, wearing what was presumably Beth's T-shirt, since it said 'LANCASTER GIRLS HOCKEY' and stretched all the way down to his knees. Beth poked her slightly dishevelled head out behind him, and the three of us just stood there, staring awkwardly at each other.

And then Barney said, 'Is that my Nutella?'

After I'd apologized and promised to buy him a new jar in the morning, I went back to Arthur's to find him snoring loudly on the floor. I switched off the Xbox and headed back to my own room.

I lay down on the bed, surrounded by unopened suitcases and untouched Ikea bags, and stared at the dirty yellow ceiling. My phone had run out of battery, and I decided, for once, to leave it that way.

CHAPTER 3

PHOEBE

I feel like how cool you are is in your DNA. Cool people naturally sleep until their sleep is interrupted – it's the mark of the effortlessly rock 'n' roll. I wake up at seven most days. Maybe earlier, if I've been drinking.

I forgot where I was for a second, and reached over to push the thin brown curtain to the side and look out of the rickety window. It felt weird. I wasn't on holiday. I actually *lived* in this strange little room now, hundreds of miles away from home. Across the road was a little village green and an old church with some ducks waddling about, like a card you would buy for an old person you don't know very well. A postcard of quiet English countryside life, but with a few thousand teenagers living stage left.

I was sort of acting being myself, *to* myself. But the performance involved a lot of faffing. I made my bed, which I never do. I folded up my pyjamas and put them under my pillow – never done that in my life. And then I looked through my drawers of perfectly folded clothes and put on my *loungewear*. Because, now I am a student, I have a knitted tracksuit thing from ASOS, specifically for lounging.

I had got dressed just to go to the toilet. Was that what you're supposed to do? I opened my door slowly and peeked down the corridor. It looked like a hospital. Plastic floor tiles and walls that weird shade of yellow that classrooms are always painted. It was dark, apart from the lit-up fire exit signs. It's weird that I *live* somewhere that has fire exit signs.

I padded down the corridor in my new flip-flops and wondered if anyone else was awake inside their little box. It was so silent in the toilet that I put loads of paper down first and leant forward to wee to try and make it quieter. I wouldn't say I'm precious about who hears me wee. Quite the opposite, really. I'm liberal with my wee if anything . . . I've weed in front of loads of randoms at parties. But the version of myself I was acting isn't really me. It's Sandy from *Grease* when she wakes up in the morning and the birds put her dressing gown on. Her *loungewear*.

In the kitchen, every single surface was covered in stuff. Mugs and pans that still had their plastic labels on were piled up in the sink, some still full of food. On the table there were plates with burnt crusts of toast and about twenty mugs half filled with tea. And there were bottles everywhere. It smelt like burnt cheese and stale alcohol. There was a washing-up bowl on the table that still had some red punch at the bottom and a few Doritos floating around in it. I walked over and picked up the kettle, but there was so much in the sink I couldn't fill it up.

I didn't really know what to do, so I just went back to my room and got back into my bed with its new cardboardy duvet cover. I scrolled through pictures of last night. Flora had posted one that looked like some arty album cover. She was sitting on the steps of some grand building in Leeds wearing a ball gown, battered up trainers and a feather boa. Her bright peroxide bob lit up the black and white picture, all moody and messed up. On one side of her was a girl wearing a black dress with a slit and a *Breakfast at Tiffany*'s tiara, and on the other a boy in a dishevelled tux. She had just captioned it 'ball'. She felt far away. With people I had never met, in a place I had never been, wearing a dress I had never seen before. It scared me a bit. Like she was slipping away from me. Even two weeks ago, if I had spent the evening with Luke Taylor I would have literally banged her door down at 2 a.m. to tell her about it.

She still hadn't read my message from last night, so I started composing a long, rambling essay about what had gone on:

'Luke Taylor TOUCHED me' – *scream emoji, scream emoji* – *'He is so fit I wanna die . . . We drank tea, I think he actually is THE ONE. He used to FLAMENCO dance'* – *flamenco dancer emoji* – *'He is actually funny, oh my god, he cried . . . Luke Taylor CRIED'* – *cry emoji*.

Then I realized the cry emoji made me a terrible person, so in the end I just deleted everything and wrote 'WAKE UP, CALL ME'. *What* would make Luke Taylor cry? *Who* would make Luke Taylor cry? Luke Taylor *cry*. Luke Taylor crying had made him hotter. Sensitive, intense, troubled and achingly enigmatic.

There wasn't really anything else to do except lie there, listening to the creaking sounds of the building, wondering if anyone was ever going to wake up.

The evening with Luke had re-cast him as the lead in my daydreams. In a non-weird-stalker way. With a bit of weird stalker thrown in. I wonder if boys ever lie back and daydream scenarios about girls. I wonder, if they were projected on to a screen, would they look the same as ours? It is a bit skank that I've been dreaming about Luke Taylor for all these years but never actually considered what he is really like. Him crying and speaking and making tea and being a real person had given me a lot of material.

Not that I've *needed* material in the past, obviously. He just morphs into whatever I feel like him being at the time. In Year Seven, when I was on the football team, I always imagined us going on football camp together. Later it was seeing him at a gig, and then it was him joining model UN and us both representing Swaziland, or whatever. He's like the face of the life I want, whatever that is at the time.

No wonder I've never been in love, I'm too busy daydreaming about it.

I ate some Minstrels and watched a video of a boy being friends with an elderly otter. And then I got up for the second time, put my flip-flops back on and got my sponge bag. I tiptoed down the corridor, opened the door to the shower and was immediately overwhelmed by how awful it smelt. There

41

was a giant mound of red sick in a solid clump like a cowpat right in the middle of the cubicle. I decided to just shut the door again. I got my Fairy liquid and Cillit Bang and did the washing-up. It felt like time was moving really slowly as I scrubbed each plate. I sent Mum a picture of the gleaming counter: 'That's right, I cleaned something!'

I got dressed and wandered out into the unknown. I felt like a grown-up; in charge and independently up and off to buy food.

The whole campus was deserted. I couldn't see one single person and it was kind of scary, but turning back felt silly and defeatist. I walked along the path, following the signs, trying to work out the way to the shop. It was zombie-movie freaky, being in this concrete jungle, totally alone, but knowing there were actually hundreds of people, sleeping in buildings all around.

The shop was closed, which felt like an anti-climax. It was cold, even in my new duffle coat. And I was hungry. And then I couldn't remember which way I had walked. Or where Jutland was. I went back to the lake and tried to decide which way to go.

And then, out of one of the towering grey walls, a door swung open and a boy walked out.

So, it was me and this random boy in the post-apocalyptic York Met University. The boy looked back at the doors he had come out of as if he wasn't quite sure where he was or how he had got there. I realized I was staring at him. And then I realized I *recognized* him. He was wearing the 'Queen of Hearts' T-shirt, but it had various liquid stains and a footprint on it now.

'Phoebe!' Josh said, and hugged me. 'You look lost.'

'I am. No one on my corridor is awake and I thought I would come and buy some food.' I sounded so square. *I* hadn't got shitfaced and woken up in an unknown's bed. I purposely stopped myself looking behind him to the door he had come out of. 'But the shop is shut and now I have absolutely no idea how I even got here.'

'And just like that your rep appears, like a genie, to save the day.' He looked like the hero in a Thomas Hardy novel. Tanned and solid and kind of open and honest looking. He had soft blue eyes that seemed out of place under his shaved head. He bowed ever so slightly, 'You summoned me?'

'Yes. Clearly you are sneaking about campus in last night's clothes because *I* summoned you.'

'I'm not sneaking,' he said. 'I don't sneak.' He laughed like a kid who has done something naughty and then took a deep breath and closed his eyes and groaned. 'I have to go to work.'

'What? Now? It's 8.45.'

'Not till eleven, but still.' He yawned and stretched his arms above his head. 'I'm starving. Come on, I know where we can buy food.'

We walked across the bridge I'd sat on with Luke. A duck quacked at Josh and he waddled after it, quacking back. A woman passed, wearing a bright-red suit and matching heels. She smiled. 'Josh, it's still late. Today is the last day. *Last day*.'

'Avril, that's why I'm up so early. I'm going to the library to do it right now.'

43

'The library is over there.' She pointed in the opposite direction.

'I've got to eat, Avril. Even boys with late essays have to eat.'

She shook her head but carried on walking, smiling to herself.

'She's the lady who works in the English office. She's like my best mate, Avril. She's who you have to talk to if you are gonna hand something in late.'

'Sweet talk, you mean?'

He shrugged. 'I'm not even that subtle, I literally bring her cakes from my work and lay them out and am like "Avril, here are some cakes, save me."'

'Smooooth.'

'Not the only one, am I?' He put his arm around my shoulder. 'So, you and Will looked friendly last night.' His eyes twinkled.

'Yeah, he's really nice.' And also really fit. I should have messaged Flora about that, too. The Luke Taylor interlude had knocked it to the back of my brain. Josh carried on smiling at me. 'Stop. You're making me embarrassed. He's really nice.' I had already said that. *Oh god.*

We wandered over another bridge. We were walking right by the side of the lake now. The ground was frosty. 'Aren't you freezing?'

Josh shook his head. 'Nah, I'm a warrior.' He jumped up and down on the spot. 'An extremely cold warrior.'

'Do you want my hat? It's a bit girly but—'

'Yes, I was wondering when you were going to be chivalrous and offer me one of your many winter garments.'

He pulled the red bobble hat right down over his ears.

We came out into a little village square. We went into the shop and Josh picked up a basket. 'Shall we make breakfast for everyone?' he said. 'I feel like that's what a good rep would do.'

I nodded. We got hot chocolate and milk and eggs and then Josh put icing sugar and sprinkles into the basket. 'Are you gonna bake them a cake for breakfast?' I asked. 'I thought you had to work . . .'

'Trust me,' he said. 'I have four younger sisters; I know how to do a good breakfast picnic.'

D Block was still quiet when we got back. 'Wow, your kitchen is *tidy*,' he laughed. 'Ours never looked like this last year.'

'I was so bored I cleaned it,' I snorted.

He got a bowl and started mixing the icing. 'Do you think I can use this frying pan?'

I nodded. 'It's mine. What are you making?'

Connor walked in as Josh cracked an egg. Connor was not concerned about appropriate corridor dress; he was wearing fleece shorts and a T-shirt that said 'LET'S GET MESSY'. He walked straight into the wall before ricocheting down on a chair.

'Do you want a cup of tea?' I asked.

He laid his head on the table and groaned a kind of yes, then Liberty walked in wearing a silk romper and knee-high woollen socks.

'Are you cooking?' she said.

Josh nodded. Connor laughed into the table. 'The way you say 'cooking'. *Coooo*-king.'

Liberty had the strongest Scouse accent I had ever heard. '*Coooo*-king. *Coooo*-king.' She said it loudly in Connor's ear and sat down next to him.

I started buttering a big pile of bread. Josh picked up the bowl of icing mixture.

'What are you doing?' I looked over his shoulder. 'Are you gonna ice the egg sandwiches?'

'That looks disgusting,' Liberty said.

'Dis-gus-tin',' Connor mimicked, and she kicked him gently.

'When it comes to egg fairy-bread you need to get over what it is in your head and just let your heart lead you.' Josh shovelled an egg on to a piece of bread and sandwiched it.

'That's way too deep for me, mate,' Connor said, and took a sip of tea. 'Sounds like some *Lord of the Rings* shit.'

I peered over the bread as Josh poured the icing on top of it, and then covered it in sprinkles.

I ran over to my cupboard and took out the cookie cutters I had made my Mum buy even though I have never baked a biscuit before, ever.

I got a duck one and plunged it into the bread.

'Did you really bring cookie cutters to uni?' Josh smirked.

'Do you *really* make egg fairy-bread served with poetic life mantras?'

Negin and Becky wandered in. They had both got fully dressed.

'None of us died overnight.' I smiled.

'I almost did,' Negin said. 'My room is freezing.'

Becky lingered by the microwave. It was like she didn't

know if she had permission to sit down.

'Becky –' Josh pulled a chair away from the table – 'are you prepared to have your life changed?'

'Do you want a cup of tea?' I smiled as encouragingly as I could.

'Thanks,' she almost-whispered, and sat down next to Liberty.

Josh laid the duck-shaped iced egg sandwich in front of Connor.

Connor sat up and looked at it, and then shoved the whole thing in his mouth. He chewed, swallowed and then got up and put his arms around Josh, picked him up and walked him around the kitchen. 'That is the most beautiful thing I have ever eaten. That is all I am gonna eat for the next three years. I love you.'

'Negin, there is a rocket. It matches the rocket on your name sticker.' I picked the cookie cutter up, plunged it into the sandwich and handed it across.

'I don't think we should use plates unless we *absolutely* have to. Or knives and forks,' Connor said. 'If you can eat it with your hands I think you absolutely should. D Block policy.'

Negin didn't look convinced by the policy or the iced egg sandwich. She smelt it and then took a tiny bite.

Josh cut Becky a dinosaur and I took a picture to show my Mum that the cookie cutters had actually been a good investment.

Then Josh downed the last of his tea and stood up. 'OK, I have to go to work. And you lot have to go to Freshers' Fair.'

'Do you wanna borrow my jumper?' I said, and then looked

47

down. It was white with a purply glitter outline of a rabbit's face. 'Or . . . I can lend you another one.'

'Don't worry.' He smiled. 'I reckon I can pull that off.'

LUKE

It looked like a cross between a car boot sale and a circus. Hundreds of tables strewn messily across the huge hall, all surrounded by brightly coloured, hand-drawn posters advertising every kind of sport, hobby or society you could think of, and presided over by wackily dressed, wide-grinning, way-too-hyperactive-for-this-time-of-the-morning people. Everywhere you turned, someone was yelling at you, or waving you over, or shoving a leaflet or a pen or a cookie in your hand.

Me and Arthur weaved our way through the madness, chain-eating cookies, both still heavy with last night's hangovers.

It had been beyond weird to plug in my phone this morning and see no new messages, no missed calls. All summer, I'd thought I'd feel relieved by that sight, but if anything it made me more ill at ease. Like the guilt and the worry had suddenly been amplified.

I just wanted, so badly, for her to be OK. To be happy again. I'd sat on the edge my bed, trying to actually, properly process what had happened, but then Arthur had pounded my door down, and the idea of missing Freshers' Fair to sit alone in my room suddenly didn't seem like an acceptable option.

Arthur pocketed yet another novelty biro offered by a psychotically jolly random, and glanced around the hall, anxiously. 'I should be keeping my head down, really,' he muttered. 'After last year's Freshers' Fair.'

'Why?'

'When I turned up, I was still pissed from the night before. I signed up for all sorts of random shit and I haven't been to a single meeting since.'

Right on cue, a figure stepped into our path wearing a baggy, full-body white boiler suit, with a black mesh mask totally covering its face. It was carrying a fistful of flyers that proclaimed: 'YORK MET BEEKEEPING SOCIETY: A GREAT WAY TO MAKE FRIENDS . . . AND HONEY!'

'Hello Arthur,' said the figure, in a stern northern accent. 'Haven't seen you at any of the meetings. You seemed so keen last year.'

Arthur looked at his feet. 'Yeah, sorry about that, man. I just, erm . . . I prefer to beekeep by myself, to be honest. Just me and the bees. It's more of a private, personal thing, for me, bee-keeping.'

The figure didn't move. 'You've got your own hive, then?'

Arthur nodded. 'Yep. Keep it in the bath.'

The figure flinched. 'You shouldn't keep hives in damp places, Arthur!' it snapped. 'Bees *cannot* cope with damp. That's the *first* thing we would have taught you at Beekeeping Soc if you'd ever *bothered* to show up to a meeting.'

Arthur flapped his hands apologetically. 'Yeah, no, sorry. What I meant is I keep it in the oven. Or the microwave. I rotate it between the two.' Then he added, 'I don't know why you're so bothered about me, anyway, Martin. I'm sure you've got

49

tons of recruits. Where's the rest of Beekeeping Soc?'

'He's over there,' said the figure.

'Right, well, we should be off,' Arthur replied, dragging me away by the arm. 'I'm just showing Luke here around.'

We moved away, and Arthur shook his head. 'This is a fucking nightmare,' he said darkly. 'The bloke from Fencing Soc will probably stab me in the face if he spots me. Trust me, man, you should only sign up to shit that you're actually, *genuinely* interested in. Once they've got your email, they own your soul. They'll never let you go.' He kicked at a bit of loose carpet. 'I'll still be getting the minutes from those fucking beekeeping meetings on my deathbed.'

Across the hall, we noticed Rosie, Tom, Beth and Nishant from our corridor signing up for 'Chemistry Soc'.

'They're already *doing* Chemistry,' groaned Arthur. 'Why the hell do they have to sign up for Chemistry Society as well?'

A bloke on stilts wobbled by, yelling 'COME JOIN STILT WALKING SOC!' and Arthur reached up to fist-bump him. 'Yes, Danilo!' He turned to me. 'That's Danilo. He's on my course. He's bang into stilt walking.'

And then, from a speaker somewhere in the hall, a girl's voice boomed out in a low monotone, like an airport announcement: 'Arthur Watling, report to the Singalong Stand immediately to perform "Some Day My Prince Will Come". Once again, Arthur Watling, to the Singalong Stand, please.'

Arthur's face split into a grin, and he looked around wildly in search of the voice's owner.

'Arthur Watling, you should be wearing your glasses,' the

voice deadpanned. 'Arthur Watling, I'm quite clearly in the corner, next to the Warhammer stand.'

We walked over to the corner, past the shaggy-haired vikings of Warhammer Soc, where a good-looking girl in a red woolly jumper was sat by herself at the Singalong Soc desk. She was waving a glitter-covered microphone at us, which was hooked up to a speaker on a rickety-looking stage.

'Yes, Reets!' Arthur said. 'Since when are you bossing the York Met karaoke squad?'

'I'm not,' said the girl, undoing her top-knot and letting her curly black hair explode out in all directions. 'Never done karaoke in my life. I'm just minding the table for Liz while she gets some crisps.' She tied her hair back up again, then waved the mic at us. 'I'm supposed to be trying to get people to sing.'

'No chance,' Arthur grimaced. 'I know people in here.'

'You sang last year,' said the girl, arching an eyebrow.

'Shit. Did I?'

The girl laughed. 'Yeah. "Single Ladies",' if I remember rightly. Then you went and signed up for Warhammer.'

'Fuck's sake. No wonder they all look so pissed off.'

'No, I think that's just how they look generally.' She turned to me and smiled. 'I'm Rita, by the way. Me and Arthur were neighbours in halls last year.'

'I'm his new neighbour, Luke. Nice to meet you.'

She frowned. 'Oh dear, poor you. Has he enlightened you on the virtues of sink weeing yet?'

'He's outlined the basic argument for it, yeah.'

'Yes, I got that spiel on the first day, too. Thing is, weeing in a sink's not quite as easy when you're a girl. Oh, thank god, here's Liz.'

Liz – who was wearing a bright green SINGALONG SOC hoody – reclaimed her microphone, and Arthur and Rita went off to get a coffee. They didn't ask if I wanted to come with them, which was a bit gutting, and I didn't ask if I could, so I ended up wandering round by myself for a bit, feeling my hangover start to dissolve slowly into a ravenous hunger and trying to put off thinking about Abbey.

I went and signed up for the football team, which was by far the busiest and noisiest stall in the hall. The blokes at the table seemed to recognize me straight away as one of their own; they all nodded and smiled and one guy called Will shook my hand and said, 'Nice one, mate, see you at trials, yeah?'

I suppose I *am* one of their own, really. Obviously, the whole point of uni is to broaden your mind and try new things, or whatever, but surely there's no harm in also sticking to what you know. And I *know* football. It's the one thing I really like that I'm actually, definitely good at. That's got to count for something.

I was starting to feel self-conscious about walking around on my own so I went to join the queue for free chips at the Nando's stand. But then I finally saw a face I recognized. Across the packed hall, Phoebe was standing at one of the tables, signing a form, while a pig-tailed girl jabbered away excitedly at her.

Feeling lighter suddenly, I waved and walked over. 'All right?'

'Hey! Luke. How's it going?' Her cheeks flushed a bit. She seemed genuinely pleased to see me. 'I've been on the lookout for our old friend Stephanie Stevens, but no sign of her yet.'

'I know, I feel quite protective of her now. Though she blatantly won't even remember us. What are you up to, anyway?'

'Just signing up for Feminist Soc.' She flicked the big bunch of purple balloons that was attached to the table. 'They've got balloons and everything, so they must be legit. Have you put your name down for anything?'

'Erm . . . football, and that's about it so far.'

'Ah yeah, of course, football.' She snorted a laugh, and then covered her mouth. 'Sorry, that's my main memory of Monday assemblies – Mr Weale's match reports.' She adopted a surprisingly convincing Mr Weale voice. '". . . And Luke Taylor scored an exceptional hat-trick on Saturday. Well done, Luke."'

'Well, I'm going to sign up for other stuff, too,' I said, probably a bit too defensively. 'I'm just not sure what yet.'

'Yeah, me too.' She nodded.

'So, come on then. What shall we do? We could sign up to something together.'

She went quiet for a second. 'Er, yeah, OK . . . What?'

We both looked around us. 'Maybe Caribbean Soc?' she suggested, pointing at a table with a huge Jamaican flag behind it, where a small white guy with matted blonde dreadlocks was nodding his head to a Bob Marley track.

'Do you think that guy is actually Caribbean?' I asked.

'I've spoken to him already,' she said. 'His name is Jeremy, he's from Guernsey. He told me that coming from a small island gives him a "Caribbean mentality".'

'Right,' I said. 'Well, I think we'll pass on Jeremy. What else is there?'

'I dunno . . .'

I picked a balloon out of the Feminist Soc bunch. 'OK, tell you what: I'll flick this balloon and whichever table it lands nearest, that's what we'll sign up for.'

She smiled. 'OK.'

I sent the balloon spiralling up into the air, way above the forest of heads and hands. We followed it, and watched it descend slowly on to a table surrounded by broomsticks and cheerful-looking people wearing long, flowing black robes.

Phoebe raised her eyebrows. 'Woah. That looks quite . . . intense.'

'No, come on!' I said, mock-sternly. 'We said whichever one it landed on, we had to sign up for.' It was weird. I suddenly felt this massive urge to prove to her that I wasn't just some boring, one-dimensional football player. That there was more to me than that. Even though, to be honest, I'm not entirely sure there is.

'Yeah, I know we said that.' She nodded. 'But . . . Quidditch?'

'The balloon has spoken, Phoebe.'

'Balloons can't speak, Luke. Not even in Harry Potter.'

'The whole point of uni is to try new things, you know.'

'You sound like my mum,' she scoffed.

'Well, your mum's clearly a legend. Let's do this.'

We wandered over to the quidditch table and I scribbled

our names down on the form. A bloke with a Ron Weasley wig on told us there would be an 'informal meet-and-greet' this afternoon.

'We've got to go,' I told Phoebe. 'We can't just sign up and then wuss out.'

'Well, technically, we could do that . . .' she whispered.

'No, we've put our names down now. We've *got* to go at least once.' I stuck out my hand. 'Shake on it?'

She grinned. 'OK, OK. I'll be there.'

We shook hands. Then we swapped numbers, but as I put my phone back in my pocket, I felt it buzzing again. I took it out and, with a little flutter of relief, saw that it wasn't Abbey. It was a landline.

I answered it. 'Hello?' said a woman's voice. 'Luke? Luke, this is Sally.' There was a pause. 'Abbey's mum.'

CHAPTER 4

PHOEBE

It wasn't a date. That's what I kept telling myself. We were just randomly joining the Quidditch Society for a laugh.

But then it also sort of *was* a date. We had made an *arrangement* to see each other. And that led to lots of questions and mass internal hysteria. From 'Should I wear my hair up?' right through to 'If it came to it, would I actually skank Abbey Baker and get with him?'

Obviously, yes. Although I *would* feel bad about it, because in Year Nine she let me join her group in dance when Flora was away and stuck up for me when Maud Evans tried to give me the role of a toothbrush in 'Shake It Off'. Plus, she cried when Mrs Renchanova left. So I know she is nice. And she is so good looking that she blatantly doesn't have to be.

In my head, she had definitely made Luke cry by cheating on him with her fit corridor neighbour at uni. Flora had kind of scattered that idea about and it had taken root in my mind and become the only logical chain of events.

The fact Luke had even suggested doing this whole quidditch thing had changed him in my eyes. In seven years of observing Luke Taylor it never occurred to me or Flora that he might have a sense of humour. He cried *and* was funny. He actually might be my perfect man.

I readjusted my tracksuit bottoms. I had tried to channel cool as a cucumber Bowl-Cut Girl, but without the actual bowl cut it hadn't quite worked.

'It's here.' Negin looked up. We were standing a few metres away from a very long, low shed-like building. There was a small clump of people standing near the door, all talking to each other. Luke wasn't there yet.

'OK,' Negin said. 'See you later.' She put both hands on her rucksack straps like a hiker and turned. I didn't want her to leave me alone, awkwardly waiting for one of the quidditch clump to talk to me.

'Are you sure you don't want to come?'

She looked into the distance like she was having extreme contemplative thoughts. 'Yes.' She nodded slowly. 'I'm one hundred per cent sure I do not want to join the Quidditch Society.'

'I'm not actually joining it either.' I lowered my voice mid-sentence. 'And you really like Harry Potter.'

'Yes, but I am Ravenclaw and I don't think anyone in Ravenclaw is actually into physical exercise.' She rolled her eyes. 'OK, I'll wait until he gets here.'

'Are you guys waiting for Quidditch Soc?' A really, really

tall girl with a really, really posh voice was standing in front of us. 'Can I walk in with you so I don't look like an *actual* weirdo.'

She didn't wait for us to say yes, just smiled really broadly. 'Mate, it's so small, I probably won't even fit in it.' She walked over to the shed building and stood with her back against it like she was being measured at primary school. Her head almost reached the roof. 'No, but literally, look.'

She lolloped back over. 'I'm Frankie.'

'Phoebe.'

'Negin. I'm not actually joining.'

'Oh my god, *why* not?' Frankie said. 'You literally have to come for like ten minutes because this is going to be *massive banter*.' She reached her arms out as she said 'massive' to physically show us how much banter it was going to be. Without waiting for Negin to respond she took her arm and started walking her to the shed door.

'Are you both in the same halls?' she asked.

Negin and I nodded. Negin had kind of been swept up by Frankie against her will. I looked for Luke but I couldn't see him.

Frankie made a really loud groaning noise and the other people waiting all looked at her. She spoke to them as well as us. 'No, don't. Genuinely. I actually might cry if I start talking about halls.' She didn't look like she was about to cry at all. 'Basically, it's all my own fault. Right now, I'm actually supposed to be in Costa Rica at a sloth sanctuary.'

I smiled. Negin looked a bit dazed. Frankie was bat-shit mental.

'No, I know,' she carried on. 'I actually do love sloths. I love *all* animals. Even mosquitos. Because you know, they are just trying to *live*. Like, in my next life I am going to be a vet because I love animals so much. But I am too thick to be a vet in this life. But I am still considering being an animal psychologist.'

'So, why didn't you go to Costa Rica?' Negin chose to bypass any animal psychology chat.

'*Such* a good question. My best friend Tiggs is also massively livid. Because she wanted to go to Thailand and Australia but I was all like, "No, no, the sloths *need* us." But then when results day came I just really wanted to go to uni. Also, I found out that in Costa Rica they have spiders the size of schnauzers. Miniature, but still.'

I laughed. 'Had you paid for your flights?'

'Yeah, so my dad also hates me. They wouldn't buy me *any* new clothes.' She lifted up her leg. 'That is why I am wearing these gash leggings. They can, like, stop a snake biting you in the jungle.'

I stared at them. She nodded. 'Honestly, these are like Bear Grylls-endorsed leggings. Try and bite these bitches, because you won't get through. I have no uni clothes. Only jungle survival gear. But if there is a zombie attack I also have a mosquito net, a head torch and a £300 non-returnable monogrammed travel journal.'

Negin still looked a bit shell-shocked by Frankie. 'What subject are you doing?' she ventured politely.

'Archaeology. They are quite jokes for letting me scab on to their thing. But because I'm not with the sloths I got put on a corridor with all these old people. And they are not interested at all. I slept for a week straight before I came to prepare for Freshers' and so far all they have done is eat some cheese together.'

'Like mice,' I said.

She laughed so loudly the whole clump stopped speaking to each other and just stared at her.

'They are *actually* mice,' she sighed. 'But actually they are OK and they feel sorry me and one of them gave me a toasted teacake. And one of them is doing a PhD in Archaeology so hopefully she will tell me what the hell is going on with all the archaeology shit. I thought we'd be cruising round Cairo like *The Mummy* but you don't even go to Egypt apparently, which is budget, right? They are well upping the drama by making us wait outside, I mean it's Baltic out here, especially in tropical wear.' She started doing star jumps on the spot. 'Quick warm up. Why are you here then? Not at uni obviously, I mean here at Quidditch Soc.' She puffed. 'I think I'm a natural chaser, TBH.'

'I'm just here as a supportive friend,' Negin said. 'Phoebe is waiting to meet . . . someone.'

Frankie star-jumped forward almost straight into Negin. 'What, like a *date*?'

Negin nodded at the same time I shook my head. Frankie lit up.

'It's definitely not a date,' I stuttered. 'It's just this . . . boy.'

'Please tell me,' Frankie hissed. '*Please*. I live for stuff like this. Even more than animals or Harry Potter. This is my actual *life.* Don't freeze me out of the gossip.' She put her face in between me and Negin. 'Tell me,' she whispered again.

I scanned the whole campus as far as I could see and there was no sign of anything Luke Taylor shaped. 'OK,' I said. 'There's this boy here that I kind of fancied at school . . .'

'What's his name?' Frankie snapped.

'Luke Taylor.'

'OK, go on.'

'Well, I saw him at the fair and we both decided to join Quidditch Soc.'

'We decided, or he asked you?' Frankie's eyes narrowed.

'Well, he definitely wanted to join something : . . together.'

'Done deal.' Frankie clapped her hands. 'Book the church because you are in the *luuuuurve* business.' She started jumping up and down again. 'I would actually pay money to see how this plays out. Not loads, but like, maybe five pounds.' She clenched her fists together and made an excited yelping sound. She looked at Negin. 'Front row seats for us.'

The door swung open and a ginger girl dressed head to toe in pink, including her shoes, flung her arms above her head and squealed, 'We're ready.'

'When Luke Taylor comes in do this signal.' Frankie looked at the sky and let out a loud howl. The clump all turned around. 'Just a subtle pack-howl, no big deal. Keep it caj.'

The long, low-ceilinged room was totally empty. One entire wall was filled with pictures of extremely happy looking people. Happy at *The Cursed Child*, happy on the Warner Brothers Tour, and very, very happy playing quidditch. Above the photos were various ribbons and cups and house scarves. Along another there were some brooms lined up and, at the very end, one mop.

A boy was almost dancing around the room, offering people Freddos from a plastic bowl.

'I don't think anyone here is Slytherin,' Negin whispered.

'Oh my god. Chocolate frogs,' Frankie yelled and took three, handing me and Negin one.

I looked at my phone and then at the door. No sign of Luke and it was already ten past. The longer he didn't come, the more nervous it was making me. I couldn't concentrate properly on what was going on. I kept re-tying my hair up.

A girl in army fatigues strode into the middle of the room and clapped her hands incredibly forcefully. She had the stance of a bouncer and an expression to match. She looked like she could take down The Rock. Next to her was a small, incredibly thin boy wearing a Gryffindor knitted jumper and trousers that were almost leggings.

'This is legit my fave society already,' Frankie said in her stage whisper. 'I mean, *come on*.' She unwrapped another chocolate frog and shoved it in her mouth, whole.

Negin saw me looking at the door again. 'It's not even quarter past,' she said.

'It's not a big deal.' I smiled and she smiled back reassuringly.

'Welcome to Quidditch Soc,' said the incredibly thin boy. 'I'm Brandon, I'm the co-captain, and this is Misty, the other co-captain. We decided not to have a vice because we are both equally important.'

'Misty and Brandon,' Negin mouthed.

I nodded. 'Brandon sounds like someone who rides dirt bikes in California. And Misty, Misty sounds like . . .'

'A stripper.' We all whispered it at exactly the same time and in unison it became audible. Frankie coughed loudly to try and cover it up.

The door creaked and I finally felt my tummy relax. I turned to speak to Negin so it didn't look like I had just been waiting for him. But after a few seconds I turned around and realized that none of the people who had just walked in were Luke. I clamped a smile back on my face and tried to look normal.

'Sorry, we didn't know whether to come in,' a girl with long blonde hair was saying. Next to her was a stunningly attractive boy with glasses and masses of black curly hair. He was really tanned and was wearing a black polo neck.

Frankie made a quiet howling sound. 'Luke Taylor is *insanely hot*. Well done you.'

'That's not him.' I tried to sound offhand but my voice came out flat.

'Well, would he do?' Frankie whispered. 'Because oh my actual god.'

We all looked at the curly-haired boy and he smiled. 'I'm gonna slouch to look smaller.' Frankie bent her knees slightly. She shuffled closer to me with her knees still bent. 'Are you OK?' she asked. Her face softened and it was like for the first time she wasn't joking around. 'Whoever this Luke Taylor is, he obviously doesn't appreciate the importance of quidditch.'

'Or punctuality,' Negin said, darkly.

He wasn't coming. Whichever way you looked at it, it was a dick thing to do. I felt like such an idiot.

'It's fine,' I said. 'It's just weird because this whole thing was *his* idea. He seemed really into it.'

Frankie put her extremely long arms around me. 'I find boys in general *very* perplexing,' she said, matter-of-factly. 'From now on, sisters before misters. But obviously if Luke Taylor turns up late you can ditch us.'

I laughed, and the skinny boy at the front started talking again.

'You are all now part of our quidditch family,' he said. 'We are the York Boggarts.'

Negin couldn't suppress a smirk, but Frankie whooped loudly.

'Right,' said Misty, and everyone went quiet. 'Firstly, I can't emphasize enough that the real-life sport of quidditch differs vastly from the sport of quidditch you have encountered in the Harry Potter novels. We do not *actually* fly in this version of the sport. The York Boggarts are part of the Varsity league. Last year we finished bottom of the first division, which, I won't lie to you, was a blow. It is really encouraging to see so many new faces here this evening. The Leeds Obliviators are our main threat this season. But I am confident that with regular attendance at training we can turn into their worst fear, and *obliviate* them.'

There was a beat where Misty almost smiled to herself. It was like she was riling us all up to go over the top.

'This is extremely surreal,' Negin murmured in her perfunctory way.

'Right.' Brandon smiled. 'Shall we do a quick warm-up game?'

We all got in a circle and introduced ourselves and told everyone what Hogwarts house we were in. Then we started playing catch with bean bags. I stopped looking at the door when we started playing ladders, accompanied by Harry and the Potters.

Quidditch was basically lots of running round with a broom between your legs and trying to dodge flat volleyballs. At one point, I was laughing so hysterically that I had to stand at the edge and compose myself. As we left I realized I actually wanted to come back.

As soon as we were a few metres away from the hut, Frankie started shaking her head. 'I'm sorry but how jokes was that whole thing? And also, LOLs that we actually tracked down the fittest boy at this whole university on the second day. I mean, maybe one of the fittest people in the whole *world*. And also he is foreign, so he probably doesn't know anyone here. Vulnerable and in need of a tall woman to show him a good time.'

'He really was unexpectedly fit,' I agreed.

Negin nodded. 'Even you must be able to see that he was fitter than Luke Taylor.'

'I actually can't believe he didn't come,' I said.

'Luke Taylor is dead to me,' Frankie announced. 'I mean, I know I've never met him but, still, he's dead to me.' She stopped suddenly in her tracks. 'Maybe he *is* dead. And that's why he didn't come. I mean, you know loads of people die in Freshers', right? Like, *millions.*'

LUKE

'We just think it's best if she doesn't go.'

That's what she'd kept saying. And then she'd added, 'Obviously, no one's blaming you.'

But the thing is, if no one really *is* blaming you, they don't need to say it, do they? Not ten times in one phone call.

Obviously, everyone blamed me. Because obviously it was my fault. I had stopped loving her. It was as simple, and ridiculously complicated, as that.

I don't know when it happened. It wasn't like a wake-up-one-morning epiphany. It had taken me all summer to realize it. After results day, the whole of August and September had merged into one long, tearful conversation about how it didn't matter that she didn't get in to York Met, and we could still make it work long-distance. And then, at some point, it had dawned on me that maybe I didn't *want* it to work any more. Does that make me a massive prick? I don't know. Probably.

In fact, no. *Definitely.* Because now she was missing out on uni. Her whole life was broken in half. And it was all my fault.

'We just can't let her go to Cardiff like this, Luke,' her mum had said. 'She's had one bad knock already with the results, and now, after what happened last night . . .' She sighed, heavily. 'I just don't want her getting any more knocks, you know? She was in such a state this morning, saying she didn't want to

66

go next week. And I think for once that she's right. You've got to be in a certain . . . frame of mind, to start university. And with everything that's gone on, she's just not ready right now. So, we'll wait a year, and . . . see what happens.'

I hadn't really said much. I'd just let her talk. She'd said they were going away for a week or so, as a family, and that maybe it would be best if me and Abbey didn't speak for a bit.

I'd walked back to the corridor in a sort of numb daze. I thought about calling one of my mates. Reece or Harry or someone. But what would they say? It's not like I could talk to them about the endless missed calls or the constant nagging guilt or the crying in the fucking computer room. I wouldn't even know how to start that conversation.

I got three missed calls in quick succession from my parents, making me one hundred per cent sure that Abbey's mum must have phoned them, too. It suddenly felt like I was treading water in a thunderstorm, beginning to sink.

I just wished I could understand what had happened. What had changed inside me. I mean, surely, if you don't feel the way you used to feel, isn't it better to be honest? To actually own up to it? Or should you spend the rest of your life pretending, just to keep everyone else happy?

I bought two Twixes, went back to my room and fell into a lumpy, half-hungover sleep.

When I woke up again, it was dark. I stared around at the empty walls, with the two unopened suitcases still sat grumpily on the carpet. Outside, I could hear people bustling between the blocks, plastic bags clinking with pre-drinks bottles.

To take my mind off the call, I unpacked and started putting some pictures up. I'd brought my tatty little red folder with me, where I keep everything of any emotional value – pictures, cards, letters, that sort of thing. But that hadn't really helped, because most of the stuff in it was Abbey-related. She was in pretty much every photo. All the letters and cards were from her. Who else would send me a letter? Her name was written right through my life, like in a stick of rock. Who the hell was I without her?

There was a knock on the door and Arthur didn't even wait for a reply before kicking it open. He stood in the doorway, yawning stickily and blinking at me, the sickly sweet smell of weed wafting in with him.

'I will have a cup of tea, then,' he said. 'If you're making one.'

I laughed despite myself. 'I'm not making one. And we're out of milk anyway.'

'There's two pints in the fridge!'

'They're Barney's. They've got Post-Its on them.'

Arthur made a face. 'Fuck's sake, milk is communal. Everyone knows that. Certain things are beyond Post-Its.' He started holding up fingers. 'Milk, butter, beer, chicken kievs . . .'

'Did *you* eat his chicken kievs? He was going on about that earlier.'

Arthur shrugged. 'Like I say, they're communal. Clue's in the name: Kiev. Russia was the birthplace of communism.'

He walked into my room and started picking through the stuff in my folder, snorting at random photos of me and Reece in fancy dress. Then he held up a card that said, 'Life

68

begins at 40!'

'Why the hell have you got this?' he laughed.

'Oh, it's just a stupid thing,' I said. 'Private joke.'

Rita poked her head round the door. 'Aw. Are you two decorating? I had to get a book from the library, so I thought I'd come and say hello. So weird being back on the old corridor.'

'Reets, you're doing Law,' said Arthur. 'Tell Luke that chicken kievs are communal.'

'We've haven't covered chicken kievs yet,' Rita said. 'That's not till third year.'

Arthur dropped the card on my bed and walked out. 'Well, Rita will have a cup of tea with me. Rita's a real friend.'

They left and I stared down at the card. It wasn't a stupid thing, really.

I pulled the others out of the folder. As well as 'Life begins at 40!' there was 'Good luck in your new job!', 'Happy Chinese New Year!' and 'To The World's Best Granddad!'

It had started on Abbey's sixteenth birthday. We'd only been going out a couple of months, and I was coming back from holiday when I realized I hadn't got her a card. The card shop at the airport had a pretty rubbish selection, and the only vaguely birthday-related one said 'You are 8 today!' and had a big colourful badge on the front. I gave it to her later that night, and she'd cracked up laughing.

After that, it snowballed: every Christmas, birthday and anniversary, we competed to see which of us could give the most random, obscure, inappropriate card. I remember us both snorting tea out of our nostrils as she opened my personal masterpiece: 'Congratulations on Becoming an Uncle!' last Valentine's.

That had only been, what . . . seven months ago? Back then, there was literally no part of me that could imagine life without Abbey. I was totally, completely convinced we would be together for ever. How the fuck can you just . . . lose that feeling? Why had I lost it and she hadn't?

I lay down on the bed again and tried to trace it back, properly. It had definitely started around A-Levels. Our parents had both agreed we should spend less time together, so we could concentrate on revising, and I remember noticing after a while that it was almost a relief to not have to see her every day. To have more time to myself. It was like this murky, guilty secret I carried around with me, and every time we were together, it got heavier.

And then, after exams had finished, there was Tenerife. That was when things had really started to go wrong. Me and Harry were the only ones with girlfriends, so we used to head back early every night while the rest of them got off with randoms on the dance floor. And on the last night, I'd just thought: fuck it, and stayed out. And that Naomi girl had kept smiling at me, and dancing nearer and nearer and nearer. And nothing had happened, obviously, but the truth was . . . I had wanted something to happen. And that felt just as bad, somehow. I remember lying in bed that night, listening to Reece mumbling drunkenly in his sleep, and feeling like I'd properly betrayed her. Like things could never go back to how they were.

When I got home, I swore she could tell. She could tell

something was up, anyway. And it was like the more I backed off, the more tightly she clung on. I started calling less and less; she started calling more and more. And slowly it was like all the fun was being strangled out of the relationship, and we were just spending time together because . . . that was what we did.

And then results day came, and she opened that envelope, and as she crumpled down on to the bench in tears, it was like our whole future crumpled with her. We wouldn't be spending the next three years together at York Met. And that seemed big and scary and terrible, but deep down it also seemed exciting. Because for so long, it was like me and Abbey were almost the same person. Or, maybe, just that we were completely defined by each other. To half the school I was just 'Abbey's boyfriend', but now, for the next three years, I would be . . . me.

I should have told her, right there on that bench, how I felt. But I didn't. I just held her and kissed her and promised we would make it work.

I felt the tears start to prickle under my eyelids. It was ridiculous; this was supposed to be the most exciting week of my life, and I was pissing it away, crying in my room. I could hear Arthur and Rita's muffled laughter through the wall. I sat up, took a deep breath and tried unsuccessfully to calm the frantic whirring guilty panic in my stomach. I washed my face, stuck a few photos up on the wall – all Abbey-less – then stuffed the cards back into the folder and pushed it under my bed.

I went and knocked on Arthur's door and he shouted 'It's

71

open!' The room was thick with weed smoke. Arthur was slumped at the foot of his bed, playing Xbox, while Rita sat cross-legged on top of the duvet, drinking tea and reading a book the width of a house brick.

I took the spliff off Arthur, had a drag and offered it to Rita.

'Oh, no, thanks,' she said. 'I don't smoke.' She smiled down at Arthur, who was staring blankly into the TV. 'I just come here for the sparkling conversation.'

I took another drag.

'So, how was Freshers' Fair then?' she asked, folding her page over and putting the book down. 'Did you sign up for anything?'

'Yeah, football and . . .' It hit me. 'Oh fuck!'

'What?' said Arthur. 'Tell me you didn't sign up for the fucking Caribbean Soc?'

Rita laughed. 'Poor old Jeremy. He's always trying to get me to join that. I keep telling him: my *mum*'s from Trinidad, I'm from Luton.'

'No . . .' I moaned. 'It wasn't that. It was quidditch.'

Arthur frowned at me. 'What, the Harry Potter thing? Do people *really* play that?' He looked at Rita. 'People can't *actually* fly, can they?'

'We don't cover flying till third year either,' she said.

'I was supposed to go to this quidditch thing this afternoon,' I muttered. 'I completely forgot.' Phoebe and the balloon and the handshake all suddenly swirled into my head.

'You dickhead,' Arthur scoffed. 'I told you not to sign up for anything you weren't genuinely interested in!'

'I *am* genuinely interested. Like, I was going to go, honestly. It's just . . . Something came up.'

Everywhere I turned I was fucking things up. I'd only just met Phoebe properly and already she probably thought I was a total prick. I suddenly felt I had to go and see her. To say sorry for not being there. Her block was only a minute's walk away. She'd be doing pre-drinks there right now. I stood up.

'I'm just going out for a bit.'

Arthur paused the game. 'Oh, great, well get some more booze while you're out, yeah?'

He dug into his pocket for a wrinkled £20 note. 'There you go. Just get as much beer as that will buy. And maybe some crisps. Quavers.'

I headed out towards Phoebe's block, feeling the weed start to take effect in the form of a fuzzy warmth behind my forehead. I walked across the grass to D Block and looked up to see her through the first-floor kitchen window. She was talking to a tall blonde girl and a bloke with a shaved head. They were all drinking and laughing, throwing robot dance moves to some hip hop track I could hear thumping through the glass.

I had a weird sort of moment of clarity. Why the hell did I think she cared whether I was at the quidditch thing or not? Who was I to her? No one. Someone she used to walk past in the corridor at school.

I sat down on a bench and rubbed my eyes. Every window of every block was full of noise and people, and I suddenly felt tiny and invisible and completely alone.

I stood up to go, feeling the scrunched-up £20 note in my pocket and wondering how much cheap booze it would buy. I needed to try and get my head straight. To think a bit more clearly. And the best way to do that, I decided, would be to get really, really pissed.

PART 2

CHAPTER 5

PHOEBE

'None left,' Frankie shouted from the other side of the fancy-dress shop. She groaned before disappearing. Me and Negin found her splayed out on the floor, wailing dramatically. Her height meant she covered almost an entire aisle.

'Shame,' the woman at the front of the shop said half-heartedly. 'We've been that busy.'

Above the empty section where Frankie was lying was a label that said 'ghost robes'.

'This is *effort*,' Frankie whined and closed her eyes as if she was going to fall asleep on the shop floor. 'I swear the last five nights have broken me.'

I kicked her gently. 'Come on, last night of Freshers', mate.'

'All right, *Connor*, calm down.' Negin shook her head and then peered at Frankie. 'And what's happened to you? This morning you were so emoji party obsessed you wanted to make a papier mâché lychee with a yoga ball.'

'No, but *such* a good idea.' Frankie opened her eyes. 'If someone bowls in papier mâchéd up as the lychee I'm gonna be *livid*. Same with the duck coming out of a cardboard-box egg.'

Negin picked up a random scythe. 'The ghost is so obvious.'

'What about the moon?' I said. 'We could all go as the moon at different stages of its development.'

Frankie snorted from the floor. 'You're supposed to take an emoji and sex it up. Like, sexy crocodile, sexy satchel, sexy loaf of bread.' She flung her leg in the air and pouted. 'Sexy the *moon* in different stages of development.' She howled with laughter.

'Sexy bread,' Negin repeated slowly. 'Sexy. Bread.'

Frankie held a finger up. 'Mate, trust me, there will be at least one sexy loaf of bread there. Probably two or three.'

'If you wanted to be sexy you would go as the bunny girls or the flamenco dancer or the . . . I dunno . . .' I got my phone out.

'Sexy bread,' Frankie shouted.

The woman behind the counter glanced over at us. 'I've got no Playboy bunnies left,' she said. 'And no sexy senoritas either.'

'See?' I said to Frankie. I looked at the woman: 'How many bread costumes have you got left?'

'None. We've got a Heinz beans?'

'I don't think there's a Heinz beans emoji.' I looked down at Frankie. 'We just need to find any old thing now. It's three o'clock. We just need to buy whatever.'

'It's the last night of Freshers' Week,' Frankie said. 'We'll remember it for *ever*.'

78

Would we though? It was impossible to know. There's *always* a chance that tonight is going to be the night you remember for ever, but then it never is. I've randomly never forgotten me and Flora sneaking out of our houses in the middle of the night in Year Eight and cycling round the empty town centre. Not the whole night, just this snippet, this moment of it, really. I don't know why my brain chooses to remember *that*, out of all the nights that ever happened. Maybe tonight would be burnt into my brain for ever. Maybe tonight is one of those nights. Maybe.

Over the past five days, me, Negin and Frankie had started to feel like a little team. We messaged each other when we woke up and went shopping together and checked we were all not dead before we went to bed. It was a relief to have found people who were nice and who seemed to like me. They weren't Flora, but then how could they be? That's what's weird about the whole thing; how you're expected to be so insanely close to people you've only just met. I was still careful with Negin and Frankie; I tried to pick up on what kind of people they were, and mirror it, to not do anything that would rock the boat of our five-day friendship. Maybe we were all doing that though? Maybe we'd all talk about it one day.

I picked up some mouse ears. Maybe the mouse was a good middle ground between sexy and fun.

'Is there a nun emoji?' Frankie asked, clambering to her feet. Her and Negin were still buried in their phones. 'I swear there is.'

'Who would need a nun emoji?' I picked up a plastic

corncob and held it up to Negin.

'The Pope?' said Negin. 'The Pope's on Instagram.'

'Yeah, well, if there *is* a nun emoji I'm going as that. I am *literally* the Nun of Freshers'. I need to turn things around tonight.'

'Nothing says *get with me* like corn on the cob.' I held it in front of my mouth and smiled.

'There are *no* tall men,' Frankie wailed. 'I thought there'd be Dutch exchange students. I *hate* my height.'

'Can you hate your height *later*?' asked Negin. 'We've got, like, two hours. We need to focus.' She went back to scrolling through her phone and me and Frankie dutifully followed suit.

'Shut. Up.' Frankie poked me in the arm and looked out the window.

It was Josh and Will, crossing the road. My whole face flooded with heat.

'I can't see Will,' I hissed. 'Not now. Shall I hide? I've never even seen him in daylight.'

'Like a vampire!' Frankie yelled.

I had never seen him when we were not in a bar and either about to get with each other or getting with each other. I stared at the floor. We had been together for ages in the club last night. Only a few hours ago really. But in the daytime, everything was different. I picked up a skirt labelled 'rock and roll sweetheart' and pretended to be examining it intensely. Frankie and Negin acted 'browsing with intent' too.

'This looks weird,' Negin whispered as the door swung open, and they walked in.

'Hey,' I said, and waved. Hard. Almost to the level of flagging someone down in the street. I tried to tone it down by tucking my hair behind my ears and sort of shrugging. Which obviously looked quite mental. Will smiled at me lazily. It was ridiculous how he still managed to look hot on three hours' sleep. I couldn't think of anything to say.

'There are no ghost robes.' Thank god Negin was there.

'And no bread. There was never actually any bread.' And Frankie.

'If Connor was here you know what he'd say.' Josh smiled.

'Last night of Freshers'!' we all chimed in a Connor-esque cheer.

'Exactly.' Josh nodded. 'How are you feeling?'

'We're all going to have a group disco nap to prepare,' Frankie said. 'And I've bought Crunchy Nut Cornflakes and two bags of giant chocolate buttons.'

She offered them the open box of cereal we had been eating on our way around town and they both took a handful.

I was desperate to say something so that the situation wasn't weird. 'We don't know what to go as,' I blurted out, slightly manically.

Will smiled at me. 'Nor do we. You haven't got any huge cartoon eyes have you?' The woman at the front of the shop shook her head. Will nodded and grimaced. 'Stuff like this is not easy on a hangover.' The fact he had even half-referenced last night made me blush even more. We were facing each other and I felt like he was nervous too. Negin and Frankie and Josh were talking to the woman. I shuffled my feet.

'They don't really give you much time to sort out what you're going to wear and . . . stuff.' I sounded like a mum.

Will nodded. 'Yeah, but no one really cares when you get there. Loads of people will just wear a hat or paint their face or something. Honestly, it's nothing to stress about.'

Oh god, it was so cringe. We had kissed for so long last night and it was just there, splodged between us, this giant mountain of unsaid physical contact. Even accidentally brushing against his sleeve would feel like an invasion of personal space now. I kept not looking directly at him. Like he was the sun or something. This tiny moment of silence passed and in it we both looked at each other. And it was like making eye contact kind of acknowledged the kissing all week on various dance floors. And then we both smiled at the same time and then it turned into a laugh. And we were both just laughing together, both knowing why but not saying anything.

Then he looked at his phone. 'I've got to take football trials in like an hour, so we better go.'

The mention of football made Luke Taylor pop into my head. I hadn't forgotten about the whole first night. Although now I couldn't really remember what actually had or had not happened between him being *The One* on the bridge and *The One* who stood me up at quidditch. Frankie had taken to calling him 'Luke Taylor, Quidditch Bailer', which, to be fair, was quite catchy.

I had seen him a few times over the week but we had basically just blanked each other. Which in any other situation would have been the major drama of my existence, but in this

Freshers' haze, with Will chucked in, it had just become a weird thing I blocked out of my mind. I think Luke Taylor is destined to be one of the enigmatic mysteries of my life. It's like we belong on different sides of a Venn diagram and the first night of Freshers' was a strange crossover that should never have happened.

'Ready?' Josh said, and Will nodded. 'See you later,' he smiled at me. 'Hope you find something. I'm sure, you know . . . you'll look nice whatever.'

And then they left.

Frankie cackled so loudly the woman in the shop jumped. And then she was laughing so hard she could hardly breathe. She was doubled over. '"You'll look nice."'

'Stop.' I put my head in my hands. 'Stop.'

'You'll. Look. Nice.'

Negin was laughing in a more genteel way. 'I think it's sweet. Cringe. Cringe-sweet.'

'You'll look nice,' they chanted, while we bought mouse ears and cat ears and a plastic turtle and the corn. And after every time they said it they burst into even more hysterics until it just started to feed on itself and none of us could really breathe.

'Why is everyone always having sex except me?' Frankie wiped away tears.

'I'm not having sex,' Negin said.

'Yeah, and I haven't even slept with Will,' I added.

'*Yet.*' Frankie handed me the box of Crunchy Nut Cornflakes. 'I think you need to carb load. You know . . . for later.'

LUKE

I was in the kitchen, nursing a hangover so horrendous I could literally feel it in my *bones*.

The past five days had basically snowballed into one long, hazy night out. It had been a weird drunken cycle of going out to whatever party was happening down at the bar, then coming back up to Arthur's room, getting stoned, waking up on his floor, having breakfast, getting stoned again, playing Xbox, going out again, coming back, getting stoned . . . And so it went, on and on and on.

I had been making a concerted effort to block out all thoughts of Abbey, and the best way to do that seemed to be to just keep going: keep drinking and smoking and partying, so that my brain didn't have a chance to settle on her for longer than a few minutes. Occasionally, though, lying wasted on Arthur's floor at five in the morning, she'd float into my head, and a hot wave of guilt would sweep right through me.

I speed-ate a Nutella sandwich over the sink, keeping one eye on Beth's door, as I could hear her and Barney whispering and giggling inside. Then I went into Arthur's. He and Rita were playing what looked like a fairly intense game of Scrabble; she was sat cross-legged on the duvet, hunched over the board, while he was kneeling on the floor, his elbows propped up on the edge of the bed.

'Yes, Luke,' he croaked, not taking his eyes off the board. 'Man, I'm fucking feeling it this morning. We should *not* have done those last Jägerbombs.'

'Gherkin,' said Rita cheerfully, laying down some tiles. 'Fourteen, plus a double letter score on the K, so that's . . . nineteen. Quite pleased with that. Hey, Luke.'

'Hey, Rita.' I sat down on Arthur's wheelie chair. 'Gherkin. Good work.'

'Cheers. Your go, Arth.'

Arthur exhaled slowly and pinched the bridge of his nose. 'Er . . . What words are there? I feel like I've forgotten all the words.' He turned to me. 'What are some words, Luke?'

Rita smiled at him like a nurse might smile at a patient. 'You've got an "s" there, Watling. Just do "gherkins".'

Arthur nodded, and laid the 's' down. 'Gherkins. Genius. This game is really fucking difficult when you're hungover.'

'I'm quite enjoying it,' Rita said. 'It's like I'm playing against myself.'

'You got your outfit for tonight, then?' Arthur asked me, shaking out a new tile from the bag.

'Yeah,' I said. 'Well, I just printed out a thumbs-up in the computer room. Gonna glue it to a white T-shirt.'

'Classic,' Arthur smirked. 'You've really pulled out all the stops there.'

'What you going as, then?'

'Oh, you'll see, my friend. I've got this emoji thing locked down, trust me.'

'What time are we doing pre-drinks, then?' I yawned.

Arthur snorted. 'We can have our own pre's in here. The chemists are being boring as fuck, as usual. And I haven't seen Beth or Barney all day.'

'I think Beth and Barney are shagging each other, actually,' I said. 'I forgot to tell you, I saw him coming out of her room on the first night.'

Arthur spun round to look at me. 'Fuck, you're kidding? I'm surprised he hasn't stuck a Post-It on her.'

Rita threw a tile at his face. 'Oi. You misogynist knobhead.'

Arthur took his cap off and ran a hand through his scraggly hair. 'I definitely need a Twix after that bombshell. Who's going to the machine? Nominate Luke.'

'You can't nominate me.' I stood up, stretching my arms out, painfully. 'I've got to go to football trials.'

'What, seriously?' Arthur looked appalled. 'Can't they post-pone that? It's Freshers' Week. You can't make people do ex-ercise when they're hungover. It's a human rights violation.'

'Yeah, well. It'll probably make me feel better in the long run.'

'I highly doubt that,' Arthur muttered.

Rita laid some tiles on the board, and he squinted down at them. '"Can't"? You can't have "can't", Reets! Even I know that. Where's your apostrophe? There's no apostrophe!'

'It's "cant",' Rita laughed. 'It means, like, "hypocritical bullshit".'

'*This* is hypocritical bullshit,' he huffed. 'You can't just make words up.'

Rita climbed off the bed, and patted him on the shoulder. 'All right, Watling. You google "cant" and I'll go and get us both a Twix, shall I?'

Arthur jumped up and hugged her tightly. 'Maurita, I love

you, man. You are literally the greatest person that's ever lived. Have I ever told you that?'

'Yes,' Rita said. 'Yes, you have. Now give me some change for the machine.'

Me and Rita stepped out of B Block into the mid-afternoon breeze. 'How you finding Freshers' Week then, Luke?' she asked, as we trooped along the covered walkway towards the munchie machines.

'Yeah . . . It's good. I mean, it's pretty . . . mad. But good. I dunno. How was your Freshers'?'

'Not great, to be honest,' she said. 'It's like, there's so much pressure to have fun that you can't really . . . have fun. You know?' I nodded. 'Plus, I was splitting up with my boyfriend,' she added. 'That was pretty grim.'

Something I had learnt about Rita over the past few days was that she didn't really do small talk. She came out with big, meaningful, surprisingly honest statements in the same way most people came out with comments about the weather. It made me really like her.

'Was he at York Met, too?' I asked. 'Your boyfriend?'

'No, Jack's at Edinburgh. We both went off to uni, thinking it would be OK long-distance, and then three days into Freshers' Week he just called me and said it wasn't going to work.'

'Shit, really?'

'Yeah.' We got to the munchie machine, and she started feeding a thick block of 20p pieces into the slot. 'I mean, it's fine. And it's definitely for the best that it happened. He was actually a bit of a knob, to be honest. He used to wear a flat cap. And you can't really get away with that unless you're a farmer or a 1920s gangster.'

'And he wasn't either, I'm guessing?'

'Unfortunately not, no. So, yeah . . . I guess my memories of Freshers' Week aren't that great on the whole. I mean, it's good that you're having fun and everything, but it does get better than this, trust me. Contrary to popular belief, this is *not* the best bit of university.'

She smiled at me as the Twixes spiralled off the shelf and clattered noisily into the machine's belly. For a split second, I considered telling her about Abbey. Just spilling everything that had happened from results day to right now, and asking her what she thought. I wanted to talk to someone about it so badly.

But if I couldn't get it straight in my own head, how was I supposed to explain it to anyone else? The truth was, I didn't know how to describe it without it sounding like I was the bad guy. Like I'd ruined Abbey's life. Which seemed to pretty much confirm that I *was* the bad guy. That I *had* ruined her life.

We said goodbye and I headed over to trials. The pitches were all the way across campus, so I followed the covered walkway right around the edge of the lake, exchanging nods with people I vaguely recognized from drunken nights out. The grass was still shimmering with dew and the ducks were out in full force, quacking their heads off. It was bitterly cold, but the sun was glaring down in the blueish-white sky, making my hangover scratch angrily at my temples.

All the football lads greeted me enthusiastically, even when

I told them I might genuinely throw up at any minute. 'Don't worry, mate, we're all suffering,' said one bloke called Toby. 'I haven't slept in four days.'

The captain – a posh, floppy-haired guy called Will – gathered everyone together in the middle of the pitch. 'All right, boys. Thanks for coming. I know it's not easy in Freshers' Week. But we're just going to do a few drills, and play a quick match – just take it easy and have a laugh, basically.'

I'd seen Will before – most nights this week, actually – in various clubs, usually getting off with Phoebe on the dance floor. I'd tried to go and chat to her a couple of times – mainly to apologize for bailing on quidditch – but she'd either been surrounded by people or attached at the lips to Will. It seemed weird to me that we hadn't even spoken since Freshers' Fair.

Will carried on: 'Anyway, if you make the cut, we'll have initiations in the next couple of weeks, so be afraid . . .'

A third year called Dempers, who was short, stocky and red-faced, added, 'Be very, *very* fucking afraid.'

An uneasy laugh rumbled around the first years, but Will just waved it away: 'He's fucking with you, don't worry. We're not *that* bad.'

In the end, the trials were actually quite fun. My team lost the match – due largely to having Toby in goal – but I still scored twice, and I could tell I'd done OK by the way Will and a few of the others thumped me on the back as we left the pitch. For the first time all week, I actually felt happy and vaguely in control. Football's always had this weird effect of blocking everything else out; giving me something real and physical to focus on that means I literally can't focus on all the other shit swirling about in my head. At the end of a match, I feel battered and sore and tired, but I also feel *better*. Like I've been rebooted, or something.

As we were all stumbling back to the changing rooms, I got caught behind Will and Dempers and a couple of the other lads, who were huddled around Will's phone.

'Mate, have you seen the wall today?' Dempers was whispering, excitedly.

'Classic Wicks,' laughed Will.

'She was seriously fucking hot, actually,' said another bloke.

They suddenly realized I was behind them, and Will dipped the phone back into his pocket and grinned at me. 'Good game, Luke, mate. See you tonight, yeah?'

CHAPTER 6

PHOEBE

'You look amazing.' She really did; I couldn't stop staring at her. Liberty had really gone for it in the sexy cherub department. She was wearing kawaii-type frilly white knicker shorts, white over-the-knee socks, a white vest and giant white feathery wings. Unbelievably, she still seemed to have copious amounts of glitter left, and had lathered herself in it head to toe, giving her a slightly oily, celestial sheen. She had brought her GHDs into my room and was curling her white-blonde hair. Negin was meticulously drawing whiskers on to Frankie's face and Becky was wrapping giant pieces of brown fur around her ankles.

'I don't think I look like a monkey.' Becky jabbed a giant safety pin through some fur. 'I look like a shire horse, if anything.'

'No, but do the shy face,' Frankie shouted. Becky put her brown furry hands over her monkey-painted eyes. Frankie burst out laughing. 'Let me take another picture, honestly, it's immense.'

Negin had threaded her corn through some string and was wearing it around her neck. 'I look like someone from the Depression.'

'They would have eaten their corn, not fashioned it into a necklace,' I said.

'I played Lennie in *Of Mice and Men*,' Frankie screamed, putting her hand up like she was in a lesson. 'Just saying.' And she started shouting the word 'alfalfa' again and again in a strange American accent.

'What *is* alfalfa?' Negin asked.

'No one knows, it's one of the great mysteries of the book,' Frankie replied, still in character.

I looked at myself in the mirror. Negin had done a good job of my whiskers – I just had to remember not to rub my face and smear them everywhere.

I was wearing jeans and a white vest top and I had threaded a Babybel on some of Negin's string and hung it round my neck. I adjusted my ears. I wasn't gonna stop traffic with a runway entrance, like Liberty, but I felt good.

'My ears keep getting lost in my hair,' I said.

'I like it. You look like a Pre-Raphaelite mouse.' Frankie started making the plastic turtle walk along the floor.

'I was going to cut all my hair off before uni,' I told her. 'But the hairdresser said cutting it would make it lighter and it would spring out sideways.'

'I think that would look cool,' Negin said. 'I cut mine the

week before I came.' She got out her phone and showed us a picture of her with poker-straight, waist-length black hair.

'You look *so* different,' we all chimed. She did.

'Do you think Bowl-Cut Girl did all the colours right before she came here?' I asked.

'I think she was born like that.' Frankie shrugged. 'I think she came out of her mum with a multi-coloured bowl cut. I *must* find out her name.'

'I heard it was Persephone.' Liberty had still only curled one tiny bit of hair.

'You said it was Ariel,' Negin said to Frankie.

'Yeah, but I think that's just because she reminds me of a mermaid, and I got confused.' Frankie was throwing the turtle in the air and catching it.

'Persephone is a cool name. It probably is that.' I gave up trying to flatten my hair around the ears.

Becky's phone flashed, and she smiled at us apologetically. 'Sorry, it's Aaron. Won't be a second.'

She picked up her monkey tail and walked out.

'Becky and Aaron are one hundred per cent goals,' Frankie sighed. 'You know he sent her flowers on the first day. They were literally at reception when she arrived.'

'Ah, that's lovely,' Liberty cooed. 'The most romantic thing my ex ever did was piss my name in the snow.'

Frankie shrieked with laughter, then added: 'That's actually quite impressive, to be fair. You *have* got a long name.'

We trooped out into the kitchen, where the boys were all already assembled, drinking. All of them had painted their faces with thick yellow paint and Negin had drawn various emoji expressions on each of them with black eyeliner.

Connor was wearing a sombrero and a fake moustache and seemed even more excited than usual. When Liberty started rinsing the washing-up bowl to make the punch, he stopped her.

'Got a better idea!' he shouted. 'To the bathroom!' He picked up a bag of bottles and a tub of Nesquik and charged off.

We all squeezed in to see him perched with one foot on either side of the bath, simultaneously pouring out a bottle of wine and a bottle of tequila. 'We can turn this into a *giant* punch bowl!' he said.

I saw Negin wrinkle her nose slightly. The bath was absolutely *disgusting*. There was a dark-grey tidemark around the top and some long black hairs coming out of one of the taps. Even after Connor had poured in everyone else's contributions, plus two litres of Coke, a bottle of Ribena and the Nesquik, the liquid inside barely covered the bottom of the tub. It looked like grainy, purple handwash with a weird shiny film across the top.

Connor scooped a glass into it and handed it to Negin.

'I don't drink,' she reminded him, politely.

'Oh, yeah, course,' said Connor. 'So is that, like, a religious thing, then?'

She shrugged. 'In this case it's more a not-wanting-to-get-gastroenteritis thing.'

Connor necked the glass himself. Then he leapt into the bath and lay down, knocking his sombrero off in the process. 'Come on, team!' he yelled. 'Bath of booze!'

Josh came in wearing a donut rubber ring around his middle and his normal jeans and T-shirt. He looked at Connor. 'That might not be totally cool with health and safety, but whatever. It's the last night of Freshers'.'

'Last night of Freshers'!' Connor bellowed.

'Right,' said Josh, 'quick round of I Have Never and then head to the bar.'

We all went back into the kitchen and started arranging the chairs into a massive circle around the table and I noticed Connor, still dripping with bath booze, position himself next to Liberty with one deft move.

'Guys, before we start, I just want to say thanks so much for adopting me,' Frankie announced. 'Honestly, I actually feel emosh. I love the old people because obviously they share their pâté with me. But you guys *actually* saved me.'

'You're an honorary D-Blockite,' Josh said. 'So you can start the game.'

I looked around the table. I had been really lucky; everyone was so nice. Even people like Phillip and Nathan, who never got that involved, were here. We had formed a random but solid little group.

'I have never felt attracted to anyone in this circle,' Frankie said proudly.

A murmur rippled around. Connor, Liberty and Josh all drank.

'Do you know by the time you leave uni there is an eighty per cent chance that the telephone number of the person you are going to marry is in your phone?' Frankie nodded exaggeratedly as she said it.

'Have you got Will's number in your phone yet? That's the question.' As Liberty screamed it, everyone made cooing noises at me.

Will and me had somehow become a *thing*. I got nervous when I saw him walk into a room, and giddy when he smiled at me. So far, in the bloke stakes, uni was definitely delivering.

'I read that too, about the phone numbers,' Negin said. 'I'd like to see the evidence.'

Frankie put her hand up again. 'My parents met at uni.'

'It's just more stress,' I said. 'By third year we'll all be scrolling through our phones hysterically.'

'I have never vomited in the shower,' Connor bellowed, and then stared at Liberty.

'It wasn't *me*,' she wailed, and pulled her angel wings around to cover her face.

'I have never had sex outside,' Josh said, and took a big sip of beer.

You had to be so on your guard in these games; come across as grown-up and experienced and fun. They felt exposing. I didn't really care, but for people who were really private – like Becky – they must feel like torture. I suddenly wondered if that was why she was still in her room.

Things progressed until there was no punch left in the bath, so Connor pulled a quarter-full bottle of vodka out of the cupboard.

'We need to go soon,' Josh said. 'Last round.'

'I have never wanked!' Connor shouted, and burst out laughing.

All the boys drank. Every single one. Even Nathan and Phillip. They all did. None of them looked the remotest bit shy, not like they had done with some of the sex questions. I felt my face go ever-so-slightly red and I stared down at my glass. I glanced sideways to look at Frankie but she was just talking to Negin as if neither of them had really heard. Liberty giggled to herself but kept her glass in her hand. I felt like between the girls it was suddenly awkward, even if between the boys everything had got more jovial. *Wanking.* Even the word is a boy word. Boys *wank*. Maybe none of the girls drank because they didn't even associate the word with themselves.

For a second I thought about drinking, but I wasn't brave enough. Even Liberty the sexy cherub wasn't brave enough. It's weird how so many things in the world are unsaid.

Connor turned the empty bottle upside down. 'Let's go,' he shouted.

LUKE

Arthur opened his wardrobe to pull out what appeared to be a large, puffy, brown dress, held up by brown braces. Then he twirled it round and I saw the dress had two big googly eyes painted on it.

'It's the pile of poo!' he said, cheerfully.

'Yeah, I can see that,' I said. 'Are you really wearing that?'

He downed the dregs of his lager and chucked the can at the bin, missing by a fair distance. 'Yeah,' he said. 'I wore it last year, too.'

'I thought you said you got off with three girls at the emoji party last year?'

'I did.'

'What, dressed as a massive turd?'

'Yeah.'

'Impressive.'

'Cheers. Who knows? I might even beat that this year.'

'What, really?' I said, genuinely surprised. 'I thought you were . . . You know? You and Rita?'

Arthur laughed. 'I wish.' And then his grin dissolved for a second, and he blinked down at his shoes. 'I mean, I *do* wish a bit.' He caught himself and snapped straight back into banter mode. 'But anyway . . . Come on, let's get on it!'

We rounded up our corridor from the kitchen and headed down to the bar. Beth had glued a hockey stick emoji to her sweatshirt, Barney was wearing a wink-smiley beanie and the chemists all had specially made T-shirts featuring the cry-laughing emoji in protective science goggles.

The bar looked easily the maddest it had all week. Every-where you turned there were ballerinas doing shots, giant bunches of grapes dancing and tons of people wearing those big ball-shaped lightshades on their heads, sloppily painted yellow with random emoji faces.

Arthur spotted his second-year mates, Dan and Hassan, at the bar, so we headed over. As I ordered some beers, I felt a damp plop on my right shoulder, and looked down to see that a clump of stringy spaghetti had fallen on me.

'I'll have a pint and a shot, Fresher,' said Will, picking the pasta off my shoulder and putting it back into the plastic bowl he had strapped to the top of his head.

'Pasta emoji,' I said. 'Like it. Very niche.'

'Cheers, mate, I thought so.' He thumped my shoulder and leant in. 'Listen, we're not officially sending emails till next week, but I might as well tell you now. You made the first team.'

PHOEBE

'I feel like they are having a heart-to-heart.' Frankie took a sip of her drink. 'Will keeps touching Luke Taylor meaningfully.' We were all just stood in a row on the dance floor, watching them. Frankie grabbed my cheese necklace, pulled me towards her and stared into my eyes.

'"Touching him meaningfully,"' Negin repeated, and shook her head.

'I know, when he's supposed to be doing that to Phoebe.' Frankie burst out laughing at her own joke and sprayed me and Negin with blue WKD.

'Stop staring. Can we all go and dance or just do something else?' I pleaded.

Negin and Frankie ignored this and carried on looking at them, so I did too.

'Your greatest love sprung from your greatest hate.' Frankie put her arm around me.

'Will hasn't sprung from him,' I said. 'And I don't hate Luke.'

99

'Are you saying you *love* Will?' Frankie took another sip with her arm still around me, putting me in a kind of headlock.

'Will is obviously trying to pump Luke Taylor for information about you,' she boomed.

'Luke Taylor doesn't *know* anything about me.'

Frankie ignored this completely. She put her hand to her ear like she was reporting live. 'Now Luke is saying, "The biggest mistake I ever made in my life was bailing on quidditch. I just couldn't face Phoebe's beauty. I was intimidated. I was a pathetic excuse for a man. But now my heart burns for her. It yearns for her. I would literally die for her. She is my first, my last, my *everything*."'

Negin frowned. 'Bit creepy.'

Frankie squeezed my shoulder hard. 'Oh my god, and that hand movement Luke's doing now, see that? That means, "I will fight you to the death for her, Will." That basically means, "Meet me by the vending machines at dawn, bring a pistol and the victor shall have Phoebe's heart."'

'Are they going to *eat* her?' Negin said.

'Stop!' I yelled. 'They're gonna see us looking.' I was laughing so hard I could barely hold my drink.

Frankie was still in full flow. 'Now Luke Taylor is saying that Phoebe makes him insane with love. He is saying he would eat his own face just to be close to her.'

'Funny how he never indicated that all through school, and he probably still has a long-term girlfriend he is madly in love with.'

Frankie unwrapped her arm from my shoulder and looked

at me. 'If you had to marry Will or Luke Taylor Quidditch Bailer right here, right now, or you'd be put to death, who would you marry?' She held her bottle up to my mouth like a microphone.

'Will,' I said. 'Obviously Will. Because I really like him and he actually fancies me and he is actually really, really nice.'

LUKE

'Honestly, mate, fucking good effort today,' Will said. 'Not that many freshers get straight into the Ones.'

He handed me a shot and we clinked glasses and drank.

'Cheers,' I gasped, just about managing to keep the minty vodka down.

I was having to concentrate fairly hard on not being sick, and my right shoulder was literally heaving with spaghetti, but I still felt amazing. Even Reece hadn't managed to get straight into the Ones at Nottingham.

'Oi, mate!' Will called to the barman. 'Two more, yeah?'

He passed me a pint, and I paid. 'So, where are you from, then?' he asked, taking a sip.

'Kingston,' I said. 'What about you?'

'London, mate. Fulham. I swear we're pretty much the only Londoners in this whole uni. It's fucking wall-to-wall northerners up here.'

'Well, we are in the north, to be fair.'

He shrugged, like the idea had just occurred to him. 'So, what you studying?'

'English'.

'Oh, mate!' He took a big swig of his pint, landing a massive dollop of spaghetti on to the bar behind him. 'Fucking good ratio. So many girls do English. You'll be well outnumbered in the seminars, trust me.'

'Oh, OK. Right. What are you doing?'

He frowned and wrinkled his brow. 'PPE.'

'What's that?'

'Philosophy, Politics and Economics. My dad's choice. And he's paying for all this, so . . .' He swept his hands about grandly, as if 'all this' literally meant Jutland Bar. 'Still,' he carried on, 'at least I'll get a decent job after uni. Unlike you, who'll be stuck in a skip, writing poems.'

'That's the dream,' I sighed. 'Although you don't walk straight into a gig like that. I'd probably have to intern in the skip for a few months.'

He laughed and finished his pint just as Dempers came bustling over, looking even more sweaty and red-faced than usual. He was wearing a pretty horrendous gold T-shirt with a bright-green dollar sign scribbled on it; maybe the only person here who'd made less of an effort than me. A couple of the other third years from trials were with him, and he introduced them as 'The Ox' and 'Geordie Al'. They were both dressed in tiny black leotards, which was particularly distressing in the case of Geordie Al, whose thick, wiry body hair was poking out from every available corner.

He laid a furry hand on Will's shoulder. 'Mate, when I said we need to find some freshers tonight, this wasn't exactly who I had in mind.'

Will laughed. 'Chill out, I was just telling Taylor he made the Ones.'

Al clinked his pint glass against mine. 'Nice one, mate. Now if you'll excuse me, I'm off to locate some freshers of the *opposite* gender.'

'As if you're getting anything tonight dressed like that,' Dempers smirked. Al shrugged and smoothed his leotard down. 'It's a conversation starter, innit?'

'You shouldn't need a conversation starter on the last night of Freshers',' Will murmured, scanning the dance floor. 'It's always carnage.'

Dempers nodded. 'If you can't get some on the last night of Freshers', you might as well chop it off.'

'Oh, really?' Will nodded towards the dance floor. 'On you go, then, Dempsey . . .'

Dempers rolled his eyes. 'All right, watch.' He huffed off, and as we watched him go I spotted Phoebe and her mates by the speakers, all three of them staring straight at us. They clocked me looking and suddenly spun round and started dancing really energetically. Phoebe's tall blonde mate was doing a weird kind of robotic chicken move. I decided right then that at some point tonight, I'd finally go over and say sorry to Phoebe. End the awkwardness.

'What you saying for this evening, then, Taylor?' Will asked. 'Any hotties on your corridor?'

'Er . . . Not really, no.'

'Well, come on, then,' he said, scanning the bar again. 'Who d'you want introducing to?'

Geordie Al whacked him on the back, spilling more pasta everywhere. 'Barnes has got himself sorted, so now he's trying to sort out everyone else. What a fucking legend. What a gent.'

Will shrugged, modestly. 'I'm not *definitely* sorted . . .'

'You've got with her pretty much every night this week,' said The Ox, and I suddenly knew who they were talking about.

'She's fit.' Al shrugged. 'Hair's a bit mad, but still. Fit.' I wondered if I should tell them I knew her, too.

'Yeah, well, we'll see what happens,' said Will. Then he turned back to me. 'But come on, Taylor. You're a fresher, for fuck's sake. You can't *not* get laid this week. That's, like, illegal.'

'Ah, yeah. Well, the thing is . . . I've sort of got a girlfriend.'

It came out of nowhere, like a reflex. I wasn't even sure why I said it. But the thought of Abbey had the instant effect of sobering me up slightly.

Will nodded wisely. '"Sort of" being the operative phrase, there. Can't see that lasting long in first term, mate, no offence. I had a bird when I started last year, too. That lasted all of about four hours.' He laughed loudly, then finished his pint and slammed it back down on to the bar. 'Cheers for the drinks, anyway. We'll email about initiations and stuff next week.'

Geordie Al leant in to me and started a long monologue about some drinking game he'd just played, as I watched Will walk right on to the dance floor, right over to Phoebe.

CHAPTER 7

PHOEBE

Will turned his key in the lock. He pushed open the door and felt for my hand as we walked in.

'OK, there's no bulb in the hall and a lot crap, so go slowly.'

I reached my other hand out and tried to feel for the wall but felt bike handlebars instead. The floor felt uneven underneath my feet and I kept treading on random shoes.

'OK.' He let go of my hand and patted the wall for the switch and we both blinked as the living room lit up.

On one side it had a depressed-looking little red sofa that was missing one of its cushion covers. Opposite it was a wall with three bikes stacked up against each other. Various items of football kit and some T-shirts randomly hung off them. Behind the bikes the wall was covered in some sort of fantasy football scoring system that had notes written in green marker with points next to names. Josh and Will were up there and then 'Pete' and 'Lolly'. I think I had met Lolly, he had a strong

Northern Irish accent and had started a conga line round the dance floor earlier. The flat smelt strongly of rotting fruit.

There had obviously been some pretty heavy pre-drinks going on, as the whole of the living room floor was covered in empty beer cans. There were also four polystyrene boxes lined up by the sofa, some still with kebab and chip remnants in. The carpet was covered in so much pasta that it was unbelievable that there had been any left for him to wear on his head. He shrugged. 'This house is disgusting. My mum won't even come in. She just waits in the car.' He didn't seem embarrassed or anything.

'OK.' He smiled at me. 'Now I'm going to prove to you that I wasn't bullshitting about the midnight feast. Do you want a cup of tea?'

I nodded and he disappeared into the kitchen. Usually I go for intense, creative types. Well, I think the main reason I fancied Adam was cos he was in a band for about seven minutes in Year Ten, and Max's final art piece was a painting of a girl with a tear on her cheek and I thought it meant he was deep and understood women. I suppose Luke Taylor doesn't really fit the troubled thinker mould. But then did I even actually fancy Luke Taylor, except to look at?

Will was just hot. No one could look at him and say he was unattractive. You could say you weren't into posh boys with floppy quiffs and perfect teeth and canvas shoes, but you couldn't say he wasn't hot.

The more I got to know him the hotter he was getting, too. Over the course of the week Will had gone from random hook-up to my kind of steady person. It would feel weird now to get with anyone else. We were in a week-long exclusive thing. Well, in my head we were.

I pushed the various games controllers and some tracksuit bottoms out of the way and sat down on the sofa. The night had passed really quickly. As soon as Will had come over, pasta flying everywhere, everything had got more fun. He was one of those people that everyone seemed to know and everyone seemed to love. Him and Josh and their mates were always at the heart of everything. Will was so relaxed. He didn't care about making a fool of himself. He would dance to cheesy songs and at the end he got in a line with me and Liberty and Frankie and Negin and did the Macarena. And every so often we would make our way to the edge of the dance floor and he would tuck my hair behind my ears and cup my face in his hands and start kissing me.

At one point, we were by the bar and they played 'Jump Around'. He grabbed me and started bouncing me round and then picked me up and kind of carried me to a space so we could keep dancing a weird kind of polka together. And I just couldn't stop laughing. Boys who make you laugh are everything.

I made the decision in my head then that I wanted to go home with him. Because why not? I'm at uni; it was the last night of Freshers'. I'd never had a one-night stand. And it wouldn't even *be* a one-night stand. And who cares if it was anyway? Isn't the whole point that you're allowed to go a bit mad?

Will reappeared, holding a white box in one hand and two mugs in the other. 'We've got no plates and no cutlery so we'll just have to eat it with our hands.' He handed me a mug half filled with clear brown liquid. 'We've got no milk either, sorry.'

'I actually dread to think what that kitchen looks like,' I said, smiling.

'It's best that you never ever go in there. We try and go in there as little as possible, to be honest.'

He sat down next to me, on top of a heap of crap. He rested the box on his lap and started to open the sides gently.

'I feel like there's a kitten in there or something. You are being really careful.'

He pushed the lid back to reveal four perfectly formed little cakes. There was a fox, a hedgehog, a mouse and a badger, all carved delicately out of marzipan.

'Wow. We can't eat them, they're works of art. Why do you even have these? I feel like they don't even belong in this house, no offence. Did you buy them?'

Will laughed. 'Obviously not. Josh works in Bettys in town. He gets, like, untold amounts of cake.'

'I hope he *can* get me a job there if this is what you take home.'

'Is he actually sorting that?'

'Well, he's got me a trial shift next week, so hopefully. Are you sure he won't mind us eating these?'

Will shook his head. 'He's probably already eaten about twenty-five of them this week.'

I carefully picked up the badger.

'I knew you'd go for the badger.'

'How?'

'I don't know. Because it's the weirdest one.'

'Oh right. Saying I'm weird, are you?' I leant sideways and bumped him with my shoulder.

'No, I'm saying you're awesome.' He smiled at me and reached down and picked up the hedgehog.

'What does the hedgehog say about you?' I said.

'That I'm a pie. It's the biggest one.'

'Oh my god, it's so nice inside, it's full of cream.'

He nodded and we both sat, just eating. And then the atmosphere changed that tiny bit. Like we both knew that we couldn't just sit there eating fondant fancies. They weren't really the main event; they were the reason we both latched on to so we could come here. Obviously neither of us thought I was going to get up and leave after tea and cake. But it would feel random to just start kissing on the lumpy sofa. For the first time I felt nervous, because it was almost getting awkward; I just wanted it to be the next bit.

And then it was.

He leant over and kissed me and then we were kissing on the sofa for ages.

'OK,' he whispered. 'So my bedroom's through the kitchen. I don't want you to faint before we get there so let's just run through with the lights off.'

I started to laugh and he jumped up and grabbed my hand and started to actually run, dragging me along with him, through the dark kitchen and into his room. We fell with force in a heap on the bed and started kissing again, even though we were both still laughing. But we kissed our way out of the laughter.

I find moving from stage to stage really weird. He was on top of me but we were both fully dressed still. Which one of us was going to instigate getting undressed? I pushed him away gently and took my top off and then reached over and half helped him get his T-shirt off, too. Our skin was against each other. His chest felt kind of hard. More built than anyone I had ever been with for sure. I knew he wouldn't be able to take my bra off, so I reached behind my back and unhooked it. We kept kissing and kissing and then he reached down and tried to unbutton my jeans. I did it for him and wiggled out of them. I was naked except for my pants. It was pitch black so he wouldn't even see the bright blue lace set I had worn, just in case.

'Do you want to?' he whispered.

I kissed him and said yes and he took his jeans off. And then Miss Hay popped into my head.

I wonder how many people's heads Miss Hay has popped into just before they have sex. Miss Hay and her penis facts: 'Any time you are naked near a penis, sperm can go astray and just get in you and impregnate you.' Any time. It can go on his hands and then on your hands and then just end up in there. It can be on the bed and just swim up you. Miss Hay and her terrifying penis knowledge designed to ambush you just when you were supposed to be focusing on something else.

We started kissing again and he reached down and put his

hand inside my knickers and then suddenly he just stopped and moved away. Neither of us spoke for about five seconds.

'I'm so sorry,' he said through the darkness.

I wasn't sure what was going on. I was glad it was dark because it suddenly felt truly, horribly awkward. 'Why?' I whispered.

'I shouldn't have drunk so much.'

I had absolutely no idea what he was talking about and the silence just permeated the darkness. Did he expect me to say something?

'We might have to wait,' he murmured. 'Until I'm a bit less pissed.'

And then I felt awful for not realizing what he had been trying to say. I panicked. I wanted to make it better but I didn't know what to do. I crept across the bed and put my arms around his neck and kissed it.

'Honestly, it doesn't matter at all.' I tried to make it sound really offhand but in the silence it didn't feel like that.

We lay back on the bed next to each other and I wondered if it *was* because he had drunk too much. Maybe it was because he wasn't that hot for me? I pulled the covers up over me. I suddenly felt self-conscious about it. Like I might have caused it. I wanted to text Flora. Or google it. My phone was in my bag in the living room. I hadn't even texted the girls to confirm I wasn't dead. The house still felt empty. We hadn't heard anyone come in.

I could tell from the way Will's body relaxed next to me that he had fallen asleep.

LUKE

Arthur was either out, or passed out. He wasn't opening his door, anyway. I messaged him and he messaged straight back:

'In town with Reets. My room's open if u wanna play Xbox. Help yourself to Twiglets on the bed.'

I went into the kitchen, where the remains of last night's emoji pre-drinks cans were still scattered across most surfaces. Rosie, Tom and Nishant were stirring a massive pot on the hob and having a lively conversation about something called 'covalent bonding'. They broke off when I came in, and smiled at me.

'Hey, Luke,' said Tom.

'Hey. You guys all right?'

'Yeah.'

'What you making?'

'Well, it was supposed to be tuna mayo pasta,' said Nishant. 'But Tom forgot to buy the tuna . . .'

'And the mayonnaise . . .' Rosie added.

'So, basically, it's my speciality . . . Extremely Dry Pasta,' Tom said.

Rosie rolled her eyes and smiled at him. 'That Jamie Oliver book your mum bought you is really coming in handy, isn't it?'

They all laughed. It was mad to think they'd only known each other six days. They were already like a little family.

'Are you all starting labs tomorrow, then?' I asked them.

Tom nodded, and Rosie said, 'Do your seminars start tomorrow, too?'

112

'Yep. Should do some reading for them, really.'

A silence descended, which Nishant burst by reigniting the covalent bonding chat. It felt a bit awkward to shuffle around them, cooking my own dinner, so I just made some toast and took it back to my room. I found Barney out in the corridor, knocking on Arthur's door.

'Just tried it,' I said. 'He's out.'

'Oh, right.' Barney stiffened, slightly. 'It's just that I had some Twiglets, but I can't seem to find them at the moment. I was wondering if Arthur . . . knew anything about that.'

'I'll ask him when I see him.'

'Thanks, Luke. I'll be in Beth's room.' He cleared his throat. 'Studying.'

'OK, cool.'

I sat on my bed and ate my toast and wondered if I was the only person on campus currently sat on their own. Beth was with Barney, Arthur with Rita, the chemists with the chemists, everyone with someone else.

Freshers' Week was basically over, and what did I have to show for it, except a series of increasingly bad hangovers? The only properly enjoyable bits had been playing football and making sure Stephanie Stevens didn't die. I hadn't really made any friends. Not proper ones, anyway. Dad had met Ryan – my godfather – on his first night at Manchester. Reece was constantly posting mad pictures of all his new mates at Nottingham. Was it bad luck or was it just . . . me?

I chewed my toast and tried to convince myself that it was just because football hadn't started properly yet. Football was how I'd meet people. It was how I'd always met people. Or maybe I'd meet them in seminars and lectures. But it was like the terror of not making friends was stopping me actually making friends. Like, how can you relax and be yourself when you're constantly wondering if every conversation might be the beginning of a life-long friendship?

I finished my toast and started reading the first chapter of *Modern Romantic Poetry* for tomorrow's seminar. And, then, after about three paragraphs, I gave up and watched *Rick and Morty* on Netflix.

When I went back into the kitchen an hour or so later, the chemists had relocated to Tom's room to eat their dinner, and Arthur was there instead, unwrapping something on the counter.

'Where d'you get to?' I sniffed the air. 'And what the fuck is that smell?'

He turned around, his eyes sparkling with excitement. 'I have found the bargain of the century here, man. I mean, literally, the supermarket Holy Grail. Only fifty quid . . . for this.'

He stepped aside flamboyantly to reveal a massive wheel of brie, about the size and thickness of a car tyre. It was wrapped tightly in cellophane, but it still absolutely reeked.

'Didn't they have any edible stuff?' I said, pinching my nose.

He ignored this question and patted the cheese proudly. 'Look at the fucking size of it! I'll literally be able to live off this beast all term. I won't have to spend another penny on food.'

'You can't just eat brie for ten weeks, Arthur.'

He raised an eyebrow. 'That sounds like a challenge, Luke.'

'It's not a challenge. You'd die. Probably. Plus, won't it go off at some point?'

Arthur snorted. 'Cheese can't go off, Luke. It's already off. That's the great thing about cheese. I could literally still be eating this in 2050. My kids could be eating this.'

I opened all the windows as wide as they'd go while Arthur tried to jam the monstrous cheese into the fridge. But it was way too big. So he chopped it into six smaller, smellier, chunks, then labelled each one with a Post-It. 'Don't want Barney getting any ideas,' he muttered. 'This is definitely not communal.'

He straightened up and dusted his hands off. 'Right, that's that sorted. I'll see you in a bit. Going out to meet Dan and Hassan and that.'

'Oh, OK.' I nodded. 'Cool.'

He stopped in the doorway. 'I mean, obviously, come if you want.'

I shook my head. 'Nah, you're all right. I need to be up early for this safety briefing thing anyway.'

'Oh yeah. I remember that from last year. Massively boring. Bring a book, or something. Anyway, see you later, man.'

I went and sat on my bed again and stared lamely at the wall as I listened to the muffled chatter wafting across the corridor from Tom's room.

I thought about calling Reece but decided against it. When have I ever called Reece just 'for a chat'? Then, suddenly, without realizing it, my finger was hovering over Abbey's number. For some reason, I wanted to hear her voice so badly. To talk to someone who actually knew me, who actually cared about me.

Before I could make the decision, though, my phone exploded into life on its own.

'Hello? Will?'

'You all right, mate?' he said. 'You in Jutland?'

'Yeah, just finished dinner. Why?'

'I had to come to campus to hand something in. Just wondered if you fancied a beer. They'll have *Match of the Day 2* on in the bar.'

'Yeah. Nice one. Sounds good.'

A few minutes later I was down in the bar, which was by far the most deserted it had been all week. Will brought two bottles of lager over to our table, then flopped down dramatically into his chair.

'Fuck, mate.' He took a long swig from his bottle and wiped his lips. 'Hungover essay writing. Never, ever fun.' He swept a hand through his hair. 'I miss being a first year. No pressure. Except to get fucked-up every night.'

I picked a sticky piece of spaghetti off the chair next to me. 'They're going to be cleaning up after you all year in here.'

He laughed. 'I might make the pasta a regular thing. No matter how pissed I get, I'll still be able to tell where I've been.'

'Did you have a good night last night, then?' I asked. I'd watched him leave around 1 a.m. with his arm draped round Phoebe's shoulders.

He raised his eyebrows and grinned. 'Yeah. Good, mate. *Very* good.' He picked carefully at the label on his beer bottle, and left it at that.

'So, how's your corridor, then?' he said.

116

'Yeah, they're all right. I don't have that much in common with them, to be honest.'

'Translation: they're boring geeks.' He laughed, and I laughed along with him.

'No, no, they're nice,' I said. 'We're just not that similar, I guess. I dunno. I mean, it's just luck who you end up on a corridor with, isn't it? Some people get lucky, some people don't.'

Which was about as close to 'I'm fucking lonely here and I don't know what to do' as I could manage.

But it was almost like Will got what I meant. His smile dropped and he scratched harder at his beer label. 'Yeah, well ... You're in the Ones now, aren't you, mate,' he said, not quite looking at me. 'I mean, you've got us lot, haven't you?'

I nodded and smiled, as if that made me feel better. Then I realized it actually did.

Will's phone buzzed and he checked it, snorting a laugh at whatever had just come through. He dropped it back on to the table and stood up. 'Just going for a slash.'

I watched him walk off, then stared down at his phone, which was just lying there, unlocked on the table. In the split second before the screen went dark I caught a glimpse of a photo – what looked like a girl's face, asleep on a pillow.

I went to pick up the phone but it had already locked. So I just sat there, sipping my beer and watching the football flicker silently on the massive TV.

CHAPTER 8

PHOEBE

Frankie looked like a medieval king, her duvet dragging along the grass behind her.

'Too early,' she was wailing. 'I didn't even know it could *be* this early.'

Me and Negin traipsed alongside her and on to the walkway. 'What if Will's there?' I asked them. 'Like, with Josh?'

'He won't be,' Frankie yelled. 'Who the hell would go to an 8 a.m. safety briefing *by choice*?'

'Well, you,' Negin said. 'You're not even in Jutland. You don't technically have to come to this.'

'What?' Frankie stopped dead and stared at her. 'Why are you telling me this *now*?' She turned and looked at D Block. 'Just when I've come too far to turn back.' She carried on trudging slowly behind us, wailing intermittently.

I really didn't want to see Will. I didn't think I could cope. It had been a full twenty-four hours now, and nothing. As

Frankie had acknowledged, *no one* can be offended by a guinea pig doing the Macarena.

Negin said Will probably didn't know he was supposed to respond to it, and that I should just chill. But I hadn't told them about the awkward sex thing. It was too embarrassing to admit to myself, never mind them, and even if I could face it, I didn't know them well enough for *that* level of humiliating awkwardness. I kept wondering if *the incident* was why he hadn't replied. I had told Negin and Frankie that I went back for a bit but that nothing had happened. Which was true. In terms of *stuff*.

Will's room didn't have any curtains and I had woken up at seven, like always. There wasn't even a bottom sheet on the bed. I felt like my mother, lying there, wondering how he could not mind sleeping on the bare mattress. I needed a wee really badly but I didn't even know where the bathroom was. I crept out and tiptoed about, but all the doors were shut and I didn't know which one it was. Will woke up as I was getting dressed and offered me a no-milk tea. We cuddled and kissed goodbye and it had felt natural and couply. When I got back I had tucked in with Frankie – who'd already crashed in my room – and sent him the picture of the guinea pig wearing a birthday hat doing the Macarena, and fallen asleep.

And he just hadn't messaged back.

We followed the walkway over a bridge towards Gildas College, and the Central Hall building hoved into view. It was huge and oval, and almost totally made of glass. It looked like a giant UFO. Frankie was still moaning on about the earliness.

'To be fair, Frankie,' I said, 'out of everyone at this uni, you are probably the one most likely to fall in a river.'

'Or start a fire.' Negin nodded. 'They probably heard you were coming and organized an emergency health and safety briefing. This whole thing is probably specifically tailored to you.'

She ignored us and squinted at the crowds of people heading into the hall. 'Is Josh holding a clipboard?' He was at the main door, ticking people off as they walked in. I wondered if he knew I had been in his house. It's weird that I went there and he was probably asleep in the next room not knowing I was downstairs. I wondered if Will had said anything to him about me.

Josh's jean pockets were filled with pens and he was trying to count people. He smiled at us, but he looked a bit overwhelmed. He was wearing a massive neon-yellow tabard that said 'York Met'. 'You look like a teacher,' I said.

'I look like a twat,' he laughed. 'It's like the one important thing the rep has to do. Basically, if I tick you off this list, and you die in a fire, no one cares. If you jump in the lake, that's fine. As long as you are ticked off this list.' He smiled at me. 'Phoebe Bennet. Tick.'

We shuffled into the hall and sat down. Frankie's duvet was so massive it covered her and Negin entirely.

'This is immense,' Frankie said. 'It's like going to the aquarium. I love the aquarium. I even went there as my family thing for my eighteenth and we all dressed up as sea cows. *Look*, though. Literally *everyone* is here.'

There was a kind of electric buzz being transmitted from person to person, getting more intense as it was passed along. There must have been a thousand people squeezed into the hall. Everyone from the past week was in the same room. *Everyone.*

Frankie held the duvet across her face and me and Negin leant in. We all peered over the top. 'I think this is drawing *more* attention to us, not less,' Negin whispered.

A man got up on stage and started speaking but no one paid any attention to him.

'There's the boy you got with,' Negin whispered triumphantly to Frankie, pointing with her forehead across the other side of the hall. 'I *told* you you got with someone. He's even wearing the exact same red jumper. Red Jumper Boy. Look.'

'This is the thing about you not drinking,' I said to Negin. 'You remember everything. You're like this teetotal elephant, keeping the Domesday Book of Freshers' regrets.'

Frankie slumped down into the duvet until she disappeared. '*Don't* let Red Jumper Boy see me,' she hissed. 'My face is falling off.'

Negin rolled her eyes. 'You've got dry skin round your nose.'

'Literally all the greats are in here.' I started pointing discreetly. 'Beautiful Eyes Boy, Hot Quidditch Marco, Interesting Thought Boy, Afraid-of-Sex Phil. So many hot boys we might marry.'

'None of whom we've actually spoken to,' Negin added.

121

'*I've* spoken to Afraid-of-Sex Phil,' Frankie said. 'How do you think I know he's afraid of sex? I spoke to him at the quiz. I told him about my height, he told me about his fear of sex. We bonded.'

'Interesting Thought Boy is so enigmatic,' Negin whispered.

We all looked at Interesting Thought Boy. He was wearing a loose-knit woolly jumper with holes in the sleeve, and scratching his chin while sort of gazing dreamily into the middle distance.

'Yeah, good old ITB.' Frankie nodded. 'He's probably philosophizing about what to have for breakfast.'

The man on stage started demonstrating how to use a fire extinguisher and then they played us a painfully bad *Crimewatch*-style re-enactment of a girl wearing a bodycon dress falling in a river. I just kept scanning the room, looking at all the people I had seen over the last week, penned into the same space.

I somehow missed Luke Taylor on the first couple of sweeps, but then he came into focus. At school, he had always been surrounded by people, but he was on his own, politely paying attention to the video. He was so good-looking he seemed out of place. Like a Hollywood film star who had been plonked into *EastEnders*.

The man was pointing at the screen and telling us how you're only ever one Bacardi and Coke away from river death.

'Look –' Frankie jabbed her elbow into my ribs – 'there is Quidditch Bailer himself.'

'Already clocked him,' I whispered. 'He looks amazing

today. Like, *amazing*.'

We all looked over at Luke. His white T-shirt and tan easily identified him on the row. He ruffled his hair, leant back and yawned.

'I feel like we're observing a lion in a documentary,' Negin said.

'When I was little I had to go and see an educational psychologist because all I drew was lions.' Frankie mimed drawing manically. 'I had, like, a mania for drawing lions.'

'Can we just all appreciate Luke Taylor for a second?' I said. 'I know he is an up-himself arse, but just push that to the back of your mind and you know . . . objectify him.' I could feel Negin and Frankie rolling their eyes. 'Come on, you can't deny it, he is insanely beautiful.'

'I think he looks like a Ken doll,' said Frankie. 'He is very square. His face, I mean. And his hair.'

'When did you stop drawing lions?' Negin whispered.

They showed us a final clip of a boy getting an STI test and then we all filed out of the spaceship. 'I'm going back to bed,' Frankie yawned at me. 'In your room. I'm also really hungry.'

'Me too,' said Negin. 'Me and Becky are meeting early to get breakfast.'

I left them and wandered towards the English department, which looked like a dilapidated block of flats covered in tattered old Drama Soc posters. Everyone says making friends with people on your course is important, so you know more people than just the ones on your halls. I gave myself a mental pep talk about speaking to everyone but not seeming too eager-beaver. But then I got lost trying to find the seminar room.

When I did get there, it was already almost full. The only person I recognized was Bowl-Cut Girl, who was wearing a low-cut, electric-blue vest dress thing and no bra. The dress was kind of draped over her and looked like it could just fall off at any time and leave her completely naked.

I did a jolly smile at everyone and said 'Hi' as I walked in and took an empty chair. They all said an awkward 'Hi' back.

Then Bowl-Cut leant across and said, 'You're in Jutland, right?'

I nodded.

'I've seen you around,' she said, and smiled.

I felt sort of honoured. Bowl-Cut knew who I was. I smiled back but didn't really know what to say, so I just said 'Great!', and then felt a bit stupid.

I got out my pencil case and notebook and laid them out on the table in front of me. Bowl-Cut was directly across from me and I could not stop staring at her. She had a tattoo that went from just underneath her boob right around her back. What did it say? I kept trying to make it out. She had scraped her rainbow hair back and was wearing no make-up but she still looked amazing. She didn't seem nervous at all. She was sitting cross-legged on her chair like a kid waiting for story time, like she had done this shit a million times before.

Another person came in and sat down. I'd been half wondering if Luke Taylor would be in my seminar group, but clearly not. More awkward small talk about whether we had all read the books.

And then a bloke walked in and sat down. He was wearing jeans that were covered in white paint and a faded red T-shirt that said 'The Velvet Underground'. He had thick black hair that stuck up all over the place and was also splattered with globs of paint. He looked foreign, with that kind of tan that is hardened every summer and never goes away. Like the frontman of a band that sings about being heartbroken in black and white.

'OK.' He nodded to himself and smiled at all of us. 'The literature of memory. That is a kind of crazy thing, right?' He was French, maybe Spanish. Some incredibly fit kind of accented nationality. He was the . . . what is it even called? It's definitely not the 'teacher'. The seminar leader? The professor? He definitely couldn't be a professor. He was like, twenty-five, max.

Bowl-Cut looked me dead in the eye and mouthed 'Hot tutor'. *Tutor*, that was it.

I smiled in agreement. It is a wonder that I have only slept with two people, because I fancy so many people at a time. If I was Bowl-Cut and wore artfully draped boob curtains I would probably have slept with a hundred people already.

He took the lid off his board marker. 'Just say anything, guys. When I say memory, what do you think about?'

'The past.' Bowl-Cut didn't even put her hand up. Were you *supposed* to put your hand up?

Hot Tutor nodded and wrote it on the board. 'What's your name?'

125

'Mary,' she said.

I could not believe it. Mary. And I could not wait to tell the others. How is anyone even called Mary now? Mary, the most boring Bennet sister. Mary, the mother of God. Mary, the woman who used to babysit me after school when my mum went to Slimming World.

Hot Tutor tapped the board with his marker. 'So, what else do you think about when I say memory?'

'Nostalgia,' said a girl with French plaits.

And then Luke Taylor walked into the room. Just like that. On cue.

'Sorry. I got lost.' There was no chair for him to sit on. I had a wild thought about offering him mine, then realized just how insane that would be. Hot Tutor went and got him one from a stack at the side, and everyone shuffled up to make room for him. Bowl-Cut Mary smiled at me again as if to say, 'Wow, all this hotness in one room,' which made me instantly feel both terrified and certain that she was going to get with Luke Taylor, and also made me want to message Frankie and confirm that fancying Luke Taylor was a universal thing, not just confined to me.

'What's your name?' Hot Tutor asked.

'Luke.' He looked slightly flustered. Had I ever seen Luke Taylor flustered? Luke Taylor looked attractive flustered.

'What do you think of when I say the word memory, Luke?'

Luke seemed slightly alarmed. 'Erm. I don't know. Maybe extremes? Like things that are good enough or bad enough to stay in your head?'

126

Hot Tutor wrote it on the board and I copied it down, word for word, slowly. We wrote down our earliest memories and the colours we associated with them and then a memory of school and a memory of a holiday. We talked about whether you can manufacture memories and why so many of us remembered the same things.

Bowl-Cut Mary re-tied her hair and I saw that her tattoo said, *I love, I have loved, I will love.* Bowl-Cut Mary had fucking *lived.* How had she had time to *have loved*? And how could she be so confident about the *will love* bit too? I needed to get on with things.

I started to wonder whether Luke would talk to me at the end and whether he would mention the quidditch. And then Hot Tutor said we could take a five-minute toilet break. Some people got up and left. I got my phone out. Luke was sitting across from me studiously copying things down from the board. I thought about speaking to him, saying some jaunty ice-breaking thing, but I couldn't think of anything. He had typical, scrawly, boy handwriting.

I opened my camera and slowly shifted my phone up, trying to look natural. And then I pressed the button and quickly put the phone down. I copied out the same sentence I had already copied out and then picked up my phone again.

'Up close indisputable proof. Luke Taylor is the HOTTEST BOY ON EARTH.' I made the o's with a pair of eyes for effect and sent the picture to Frankie.

Hot Tutor walked back in. Luke checked his phone and then put it away before copying one last thing off the board.

'You and someone else might both experience the same event,' said Hot Tutor. 'But the memories you form might be entirely different. Your memories are not about what actually happened, but about *you*. Who you are and how you experience the world.'

I thought about Flora and the night with the bikes and whether she remembered it, too. I suddenly wanted to ask her. Things were turning quite deep. People were talking about their earliest memories.

'Me and my sister had this teddy called Norvin,' Bowl-Cut Mary said. 'And it's weird because she swears he was orange but I know he was purple. And we are both one hundred per cent sure.'

Hot Tutor smiled. 'What does that memory say about each of you?'

Bowl-Cut Mary shrugged. 'That one of us is wrong?'

He nodded. 'Let me tell you something. The night Ted Hughes met Sylvia Plath at a party at Cambridge, they both went straight back to their rooms and wrote about this amazing, intense, explosive connection. It was so important to both of them that they immediately documented it. The beginning of a love affair. Hughes writes about the blue velvet ribbon Plath was wearing in her hair, and she writes about the red velvet ribbon she was wearing.'

'She must have known what colour her ribbon was,' Bowl-Cut said. 'It was hers.'

Hot Tutor nodded. 'Maybe. You would think. You know, in all Plath's poetry she associates herself with the colour

128

red. And in all Hughes' poetry he associates her with the colour blue.'

'What does it mean?' another boy said.

'I don't know.' Hot Tutor shrugged. 'That he always saw her one way, but that she saw herself another. What do you think, Luke?'

Luke still looked a bit flustered. 'I don't know. That sounds scary. Like no one is really seeing anyone else.'

Hot Tutor nodded and we read a Ted Hughes poem called 'Red' and because I get emotional about everything I almost started to cry. When Hot Tutor turned to write something on the board I sneaked a look at my phone.

And then I had the most intense physical reaction I have ever experienced. My whole body seized up and saliva flooded into my mouth. For a second I thought I might faint or be sick.

'Memory and writing cannot exist without each other,' Hot Tutor was saying. I could barely get a grip on what was happening.

I stared down at my notebook and curled my hands into fists to stop them trembling. I looked at my phone again to make sure, and it was like a knife twisting in my chest.

The worst moment of my life had happened. And I was still living in it.

I had sent the message to Luke.

I had sent the picture of Luke . . . to Luke.

It was like everything suddenly tripped into slow motion. I almost felt like I'd floated up out of my body, but then I realized my left leg was literally shaking under the table, and that brought me back down to Earth.

It took everything I had not to look at Luke. To see whether he was checking his phone. Maybe he'd already checked it. I felt simultaneously boiling hot and freezing cold. I needed to get out. Not just of the room, but of the entire uni.

I looked up at the clock. There were still thirty-seven minutes of the seminar left.

I could hear a weird buzzing in my head, and my cheeks felt like they were on fire. If I said I was ill it would draw more attention to me. I tried to breathe evenly and keep copying stuff off the board but my brain wasn't communicating properly with my hand.

And then I realized Hot Tutor was staring at me. Everyone was staring at me. *Luke* was staring at me.

'Phoebe?' Hot Tutor said, smiling. 'What do you think makes a moment stay in your head for ever?'

CHAPTER 9

LUKE

Phoebe was up and out of the room faster than I had ever seen a human being move.

As soon as the tutor bloke said, 'See you all next week,' she just snatched her bag off the table and bolted out the door. I'd barely even noticed him saying it. But then, I'd barely noticed *anything* he'd said once I'd looked at my phone and seen that message staring up at me. My first ever university seminar and I learnt practically nothing because I was obsessing over a twelve-word text.

As far as I could see, there were two possibilities. One: it was a joke. Quite a weird, inexplicably harsh joke but, still, a joke. She was winding me up. She wanted to embarrass me. Or maybe she thought I'd find it funny. Whatever, Possibility One meant that she was *clearly* mental.

Then there was Possibility Two: that it was a *genuine* message, *genuinely* meant for someone else, *genuinely* saying that

Phoebe Bennet thought I was 'the hottest boy on Earth'.

I much preferred Possibility Two.

I re-read it over and over again as I walked back down the covered walkway to B Block. I dodged the ducks and nodded at randoms I recognized from Freshers' Week, and slowly let the whole concept of Phoebe shift and transform in my mind.

It was weird. It was like the message had suddenly lit her differently in my brain. I wondered why I hadn't seen it before. She was definitely hot. She was really funny. That hour we'd spent together on the first night was one of the only times I'd felt relaxed and easy here. She had this openness and positivity about her that sort of drew you in, made you feel more open and positive, too. Even the occasional rush of Abbey-guilt couldn't stop me smiling as I thought about her. By the time I was back at B Block, punching in the entry code and clambering up the echoey staircase, I officially fancied Phoebe Bennet.

The corridor was totally empty. The chemists were all in labs from nine to five and a knock on Arthur's door revealed he was out, too. I braved the socks-and-sewage brie stink and went into the kitchen to make a cup of tea. There were three sides of A4 propped up on the table, addressed to Arthur, with the heading: 'UNACCEPTABLE CHEESE SMELL'. I started reading and had just got to the final paragraph about 'missing Twiglets' when Rita walked in. She immediately heaved and covered her nose.

'My god, that cheese is not messing about, is it?'

I waved Barney's essay at her. 'He's already had a formal written complaint about it. Do you want a tea?'

'Yeah, that would be nice, cheers. Just sat through an incredibly boring lecture, so I need one. Is Arthur in?'

'Don't think so. I've just knocked.'

'Oh.' She frowned and looked around at the cold, sticky, pasta-sauce-spattered kitchen, still holding her nose. 'Well, we can't very well have a nice cup of tea in here, can we?' She unpinned the laminated fire safety sheet from the notice board and inserted it carefully into the crack of Arthur's door.

'Er . . . Rita. What are you doing?'

'It's fine,' she said, biting her lip in concentration. 'I used to do it all the time last year when Arthur wasn't in.'

'Is that definitely legal?'

'I'm a law *student*, Luke,' she said, as if that somehow answered my question. She jiggled the laminate gently and tried the door handle at the same time. Suddenly there was a soft click, and the door swung open. 'Ta-da,' she said, flopping on to Arthur's bed. I followed her in, and as we sat sipping our tea, I decided I had to tell someone about the text.

'Bloody hell,' she murmured, reading it with raised eyebrows. 'She's not very subtle, this girl, is she?'

'So do you think it's for real, then? Like, she actually means it?'

'Well, she clearly didn't mean to take a photo of *you* and then send it to *you*, but, yeah. I think it's safe to assume that she wants your body.'

I laughed and felt a little flickering glow inside me, like someone had switched on the central heating in my stomach. 'Do you reckon I should message her back?'

Rita rolled her eyes. 'No, obviously don't message her back, Luke, you idiot. The poor girl's probably mortified. She's probably buried under three duvets, crying her eyes out as we speak. And what would you say, anyway?'

I thought about it. 'Dunno. "Thanks for the message" or something.'

Her eyes rolled back the other way. '"Thanks for the message". Brilliant. You might as well punch her in the face and be done with it.' She took a sip of tea. 'How do you know this girl in the first place?'

'Well, we went to school together, actually. But we didn't really know each other then. We met properly last week. I sort of said I'd go to that quidditch thing with her at Freshers' Fair.'

'Oh yeah. Why didn't you go, again?'

'I just . . . forgot.'

She made a face. 'Right, well . . . You should probably apologize. And make up a better excuse.'

'Yeah. I guess.'

'Do you actually even like her?'

'I mean . . . I hadn't really thought about it before. But now . . . yeah. I sort of think I do.'

Rita groaned loudly. 'So when she's just a random girl from school you don't give her a second look, but as soon as she accidentally informs you that she wants to jump your bones, you're suddenly in love with her. Men are such predictable twats, honestly.'

I didn't bother arguing with that, because, to be fair, she had a point.

She finished her tea and plonked the mug down on Arthur's bedside table. 'Well, this has all worked out perfectly for you, hasn't it? You like her, she thinks you're the hottest boy on Earth . . . I mean, it's all good by the sounds of it. You've not got a girlfriend or anything, have you?'

I thought about Abbey, who I hadn't heard from in more than a week now; the longest silence between us in almost three years. 'No,' I said. 'I haven't.'

Rita shrugged. 'There you go, then. Say sorry for being a dick about the quidditch, and then, I dunno . . . Ask her out, or something.'

Suddenly we heard the tinkle of keys outside, and the door was kicked open. Arthur stood in the doorway, holding a massive cheese sandwich and frowning hard at us.

'You know I could report you to the police,' he said, chucking his keys on the desk. 'You have broken into my property. You are *literally* criminals.'

'Oh, come on, Watling,' said Rita. 'Your room's like the living room. It's a communal space.'

'It is *not* a fucking communal space!' Arthur yelled, jabbing his stinking sandwich at us. 'This is my actual, private, personal room! What if I was in here doing something actually private and personal?'

'What, like weeing in the sink?' Rita smirked.

'*No*. Like romancing a girl, or something.'

Rita clicked her tongue against her teeth. 'You won't be romancing anyone now that you constantly stink of brie.'

'Wrong, *actually*, Maurita. I'll be romancing sophisticated

135

French women who appreciate once-in-a-lifetime supermarket deals.'

They grinned at each other, and not for the first time I wondered why they weren't a couple. They seemed pretty much perfect together. But then, me and Abbey had seemed pretty much perfect, too. How the hell are you *ever* supposed to know if you're right for someone?

I stood up. 'I'll leave you two to it.'

'Are you going to initiations?' Arthur asked, eagerly. He'd become weirdly obsessed with the football initiations. He thought they'd be some kind of mad combination of freemason ceremony and Satanic ritual. Maybe he was right.

'No, they're next week. I'm going back to my room. Need to do some reading.'

'Are they all right then, that football lot?' Rita asked.

'Yeah, they seem cool,' I said. 'Why?'

'No, nothing. Just, we had that Will Barnes on the corridor below us last year. Do you remember, Arth? He seemed like a bit of a . . .'

She tailed off and just let the sentence hang there, unfinished, in the air.

'He seems all right to me.' I shrugged.

She smiled. 'No, yeah. I'm sure he is. I don't know him, to be fair.' Arthur flopped down in his swivel chair and she said: 'By the way, Arth, you're not gonna believe what Luke just got sent.'

Arthur turned to look at me but I headed for the door. 'You can fill him in, Rita. I'd better do this reading.' I clapped Arthur on the shoulder as I left. 'You got a note about the cheese, by the way. First of many, I reckon.'

'That cheese is the best thing that's ever happened to me,' he said, stiffly.

I went back to my room and tried to read Ted Hughes' *Collected Poems*, but I couldn't stop my brain flicking back to Phoebe. Rita was probably right: I probably was a predictable twat. But knowing that Phoebe liked me had made me feel totally different about her. Maybe I'd even liked her all along, but I hadn't realized it. Maybe I'd forgotten what liking someone new actually felt like.

To be honest, it felt pretty good.

PHOEBE

'Honestly, this is the worst thing that's ever happened to me.'

I genuinely couldn't think of anything more awful. I couldn't think of anything else full stop. I was trapped in it, like a hamster, running away as fast as I could but not realizing I was stuck in the plastic wheel.

Negin reached out and touched my arm gently. 'Phoebs, do you know you're rocking?'

'It's probably PTSD setting in,' Frankie said from the kitchen floor. She had crumpled into the foetal position when I'd showed her the message, and oscillated between sympathetic nods and helpless laughter ever since.

Negin reached over to my phone. 'Don't touch it,' I screamed, and snatched it off the table.

Frankie dissolved again. Her whole body was convulsing in

hysterics. 'You know Negin touching your phone isn't gonna make it worse, don't you? I mean, let's be honest, nothing could make . . .'

I let out a loud groan–wail hybrid. 'It is the *second week* of uni. How can I have done this? Oh *god*.'

'You are pretty epic.' Frankie threw her legs in the air above her. 'Your love life is like fucking . . . dynamite.'

'I don't have a love life,' I shouted.

'You do. Luke Taylor bailed on you. And then guinea-pig-gate with Will and now . . .' Negin kicked her quite hard and she trailed off. 'Sorry. I mean, better to have loved and lost than to have loved and then . . . accidentally confessed your love via text message.'

Negin tried to fake-cough her way out of a laugh, and kicked Frankie again.

'This is your fault anyway,' I yelled at Frankie. 'You were the one who said Luke Taylor wasn't hot.'

Frankie sat up straight and screamed back at me: 'Yes, but at no point did I make you send a photo of him . . . *to him*!'

I took a deep breath. 'I still feel sick. My whole body is boiling and my face is really itchy.'

Negin leant in and squinted. 'Yeah, I didn't want to mention it but you have got a kind of . . . rash.'

'What?' I jumped over Frankie and looked at myself in the toaster. My face was covered in massive red blotches, and they were spreading down my neck.

'Accidental Text Rash!' Frankie bellowed through her fingers.

'You need to calm down,' Negin said. 'It's just stress.'

'My face is burning,' I screamed, and started jumping up and down.

'OK, OK.' Frankie sprang up, ran over to the sink and started chucking the dirty pans out on to the floor one by one. The crashing reverberated around the kitchen. She turned the tap on.

'What should I do?' I turned to Negin.

'I don't know.'

'Are you a doctor or not?' I screeched.

'As I have said a thousand times, I won't be a doctor for seven years.'

Frankie was beckoning me to the sink. 'OK, the plug is fucked so just do it quickly.'

'I feel like I'm on fire.' I stared at the water.

'Just do it,' Frankie shrieked.

I put my face close to the sink, took a deep breath and closed my eyes. 'I can't,' I shouted, just before Frankie plunged my whole head into the freezing cold water. The shock of it hit me hard but it felt kind of calming. I couldn't really hear anything except my heartbeat and the water in my ears.

I gasped from the shock as I pulled my head out.

Frankie threw her arms around me. 'I feel like I fucking baptized you.'

'Er . . . What are you lot doing?' Connor was standing at the door looking very confused.

Negin handed me a tea towel with old bits of pasta stuck to it.

'We're just . . . daring each other to . . . dunk our heads in water,' she coughed.

'Nice one.' Connor ran over to the sink and plunged his face into it. Then he stood up and shook himself out like a dog. 'Yes!' he roared.

'This is one of the strangest days of my life,' Negin said, and put the kettle on. Becky walked in. If she thought it was odd that there were two people drenched in water she was too polite to say.

'Tea?' Negin said to her, and she smiled.

'Do you want to get dunked in water, Becks?' Connor asked amicably.

Becky shook her head. 'I've got loads of work to do, and I'm going out later.'

'Fair play.' Connor nodded.

'Can I tell them?' Frankie said. 'D Block circle of trust.'

'You're not even in D Block!' I screamed. I was starting to shiver uncontrollably but I didn't feel like my face was burning quite as much.

'Phoebs took a picture of a bloke and wrote underneath it that he is and I quote . . .' Frankie made speech marks with her fingers. '"The hottest boy on earth." Then she sent the picture to him by mistake.'

Connor held his hand up to high five me. 'Phoebs. You are a banter legend. I think that is fucking brilliant. If he doesn't like ya, who cares, move on, and if he does, he'll make a move now for sure.'

'He has a girlfriend,' I said.

'We don't *know* that,' Negin pointed out.

'Anyway, whatever, I know he doesn't like me.'

'How?' said Connor. 'You're hot, Phoebs, and you've got good chat. Trust. I don't shit where I eat, but if I did, I'd be well up for it.' He winked at me. Weirdly, it made me feel a bit better.

'When did you send the message?' Becky sounded genuinely concerned.

'Like, two hours ago,' I said. 'Honestly, this is the end for me and blokes. And technology. No men, no technology. Full stop.'

Becky took a sip of tea. 'Well, he might message you back.'

'Seriously,' I wailed. 'What am I actually going to do?'

'Isn't it obvious?' said Frankie. 'Just avoid Luke Taylor *at all costs.*'

CHAPTER 10

LUKE

Campus was so weird. It was like a really annoying alternate dimension. You were constantly bumping into all the people you *didn't* want to see, but the people you *did* want to see were never around.

I'd spent a whole week trying to 'accidentally' run into Phoebe. We'd had two lectures together; she'd been sat right across the other side of the hall both times.

I'd even tried skulking around the entrance to D Block, pretending to browse the munchie machines for longer than was strictly necessary, on the off chance she happened to walk out. But no luck.

On the other hand, as I shuffled down the walkway that led off campus, I realized that this was the fourth time in as many days that I'd seen Caribbean Jeremy. He was sat on the grass next to the lake, a big bag of Doritos at his feet, knocking out a fairly appalling rendition of 'No Woman, No Cry' on an acoustic guitar. Because he had his eyes shut, he hadn't noticed there were two ducks with their heads buried in his crisp packet, cheerfully snaffling away.

I left campus and walked up the ring road, past the massive oak trees and the weird little bungalows where the PhD students lived. It had been a week of nothingy limbo – just Netflix, microwaved lasagne and the occasional spliff with Arthur – but I felt like tonight would be the proper start of uni. This was where the next three years would actually begin. Football initiations.

They were happening in a slightly grubby-looking flat-roofed pub just off campus, and when I arrived there were about five other freshers bumbling about nervously in the car park.

'They told us to wait outside,' said one lad called Trev, who I'd spoken to a bit at trials.

He grinned sheepishly from under his floppy dreads. 'You nervous?' He was quite short, with a sharp northern accent – Manchester, maybe.

'Not really,' I lied. 'You?'

'Probably the most I've ever been in my life, mate, yeah.' He nodded. 'I mean, second most, actually, now I think about it. My brother was on *Pointless* last year, and that was the most nervous I've ever been in my life. It sounds bad, but I wasn't even nervous for him, really. I was more nervous for me, like, that he'd say something stupid, and then people would take the piss in school the next day. "Oh, saw your brother on *Pointless* last night, he made a right dick of himself." That sort of thing.

But in the end, he did quite well. He didn't win or anything, but he got a Pointless Answer. It was on flightless birds.' He stopped talking and breathed out. 'Sorry, man. When I get nervous, I chat shit. It's a medical condition.'

I laughed, and felt some of the tension in my stomach dissolve. 'Yeah, well, I'm bricking it as well, actually. When I get nervous, I lie and pretend I'm not.'

A few other people arrived, including one bloke who was easily a head taller than the rest of us. He had a stubbly beard and a huge, dirty-blond cloud of hair, and could definitely have passed for a *Game of Thrones* character if it wasn't for his bright-green rain jacket.

Drunk Toby from trials arrived just behind him, clutching a half-empty bottle of Schnapps. He started offering it round.

'Mate, you do know they're gonna be, like, plying us with booze for the next five hours?' Trev said.

Toby shrugged and took a swig. 'Settles the nerves.'

Trev gave me a look as a third year finally opened the doors to let us in. He led us into the back room of the pub, where there was one long, banquet-style table laid out in the centre.

'Maybe they're just gonna cook us a really nice meal,' Trev suggested.

We all took our seats, and I spotted Will milling about, as well as a few other second and third years I recognized. Dempers pulled a chair out at the head of the table and stood on it.

'Right, freshers, shut up and listen,' he barked, in his plummy public-school accent. I could easily see him as a red-faced, sweaty politician in twenty years' time, shouting across the House of Commons. 'If you do exactly as we say,' he continued, 'you will escape from this pub unscathed. However, if you disobey, you will be punished . . .' He left what he probably assumed to be a dramatic pause, and then slammed his fist into his palm. 'Severely punished!'

Trev leant in to me. 'This bloke,' he whispered, 'is a fucking tool.'

Dempers reached down into a cardboard box and pulled out a load of metal handcuffs. There was a genuine gasp of either surprise or horror or both from the freshers. All the older lads cracked up.

'Don't worry, this isn't some sick *Fifty Shades* shit,' Dempers laughed. 'You will all be handcuffed to one of your superiors –' he gestured at the second and third years – 'and you will have to drink double whatever they drink. So, for example . . .'

He plonked himself down and clicked the handcuffs on to Game of Thrones and then himself.

'This is probably not a good time to tell you,' Thrones said. 'But I don't actually drink.'

'Fuck off,' Dempers snorted. Someone passed him a pint of Guinness, and he downed it, spilling most of it on his T-shirt. 'Right,' he gasped. 'Now you. Two pints.'

Thrones shook his massive curly head, sadly. 'Like I said, pal. I don't drink.' He had a deep, booming Yorkshire accent.

'Are you fucking kidding me?' Dempers spat. 'Then you can fuck off, you faggot.'

I felt myself flinch inwardly, but Thrones didn't bat an

eyelid. He shrugged, nodded, then stood up suddenly and walked off, yanking Dempers to the ground behind him. Dempers hit the floor with a loud smack, and a few people laughed.

'You fucking dick!' he bellowed.

Thrones took no notice; just carried on walking across the room, dragging the wriggling Dempers behind him.

'Oi! Fucking stop!' Dempers was screaming.

Thrones finally turned and looked down at him blankly, like he was a stone that had got stuck in his shoe. 'You might want to undo these handcuffs, pal, because I'm not dragging you all the way home.'

Everyone was laughing now, even the older lads, and Dempers was almost purple with anger as he fumbled to undo the handcuffs. 'Good fucking riddance,' he shouted, as Thrones walked out.

Will didn't look quite so convinced. Clearly, having someone Thrones' size on the team could only have been a good thing. He cleared his throat and waved his hands for quiet. 'OK, OK, chill. You always get one walkout. Wouldn't be a proper initiation without it.'

Dempers chucked the handcuffs out and everyone got partnered up, and started drinking. I was cuffed to Geordie Al, who for some reason was insisting on calling me 'Swift'.

'That's four tequila shots you owe me now, Swift.'

Between the third and fourth I asked: 'Why Swift?'

'Cos you drink like a fucking girl, mate. Luke Taylor . . . Taylor Swift.'

'Oh, right. Bit tenuous.'

He downed a gin and tonic. 'That's two G&Ts, Swift. Go.'

After a while, Drunk Toby had puked so many times he was literally coughing up air, and Trev had just given up altogether. He was sat groaning with his head in hands while Dempers cackled and took photos of him. I was trying to stop the room spinning, but my head and stomach were both pulsing mercilessly.

'Some of you are drinking slower than others,' Dempers bellowed. 'We need extra nominations.'

I felt a hand clap me on the shoulder and looked round to see Will standing over me, smirking.

'I think Taylor could do with a more experimental drink order.'

'Yeah,' I slurred. 'If you like.'

Will reeled ingredients off the top of his head: 'Whisky, Pot Noodle, mayonnaise, absinthe, mustard, Guinness.'

Trev winced next to me. 'Fuck's sake, man.' Will grabbed a glass to prepare this lethal cocktail, but Dempers stopped him.

'No. He has to drink it . . . out of his shoe.'

The second and third years all cracked up laughing. I looked at Dempers to see if he was serious, and his pinched, unsmiling face told me he was. The mood seemed darker suddenly, more violent. But being massively off my face, I couldn't tell for sure.

'Get your shoe off, Fresher,' Dempers snapped.

'I'd rather not,' I said.

He leant down so his face was almost touching mine. He

was so close I could smell his tangy, chicken-korma breath. 'Did you not hear me, Fresher?' he spat. 'I said . . . Get. Your. Fucking. Shoe. Off. Now.'

A flash of anger momentarily sobered me up, and I felt like shoving his face away. The second and third years started chanting 'Shoe off, shoe off,' and the other freshers were just laughing nervously. I looked at Will, vaguely hoping he might step in and veto the whole thing, but he was chanting along with everyone else.

I took my shoe off slowly to a massive cheer, and watched as Dempers proceeded to fill it with the lumpy, greenish-black cocktail. He handed it back to me and I thought about the *Game of Thrones* bloke. How could he be that confident to just walk out? How he could be so sure he'd find other mates?

'Do it,' Dempers barked. I could see blobs of mustard bobbing up ominously near the laces. I put it to my lips, feeling the noise in the room rise and rise around me, and hoped the drink would just knock me flat out, and put an end to the whole evening.

But it didn't.

It just made me throw up, quite violently, on my other shoe.

The rest of the night happened in stop motion. One minute we were in a taxi into town, streetlights fizzing by in a blur, fresh air billowing through the window. The next, Toby was gabbling apologies and the taxi driver was shouting: 'Fucking students! Who the hell's going to clean up this sick?'

Then we were in some club somewhere, and I was trying to

stay upright, as Will yelled in my ear over the music.

'Don't mind Dempers earlier,' he was saying. 'He gets a bit carried away.'

'It's all right.'

'Sure you've seen it all before, anyway.'

I nodded, but the truth was, football drinking at school had always been much tamer than this. More of a laugh. Probably because me and Reece were in charge, and we weren't exactly going to force anyone to drink out of their own footwear.

Will got his phone out. 'I'll add you to the group chat so you'll know about training times and that. Plus, y'know . . . some extra stuff.' He handed me another Jägerbomb. 'Some bonus material.'

I've no clue how I got back to the corridor. I staggered into my room, opened the sink cupboard, and tried to focus on my face in the mirror. But it kept dividing at the nose and swimming into two separate faces staring back at me.

I lay down on the bed and looked at my phone. The football group was already buzzing with pictures of me and Trev and Toby and everyone else throwing up. Most of them involved me and the shoe.

I scrolled up a bit and suddenly had to squint harder at the screen to make sure I wasn't seeing things.

In among all the puking photos there were three pictures, one after the other, of three different girls. Each was asleep in bed, their eyes closed, their hair messy on the pillow. Underneath the last one, Dempers had written: 'Wall of Shame Top 3 from last year. Gauntlet laid, freshers . . .'

I felt my skin prickle. It was like pressing your eye to a peep-hole; seeing something totally private that you knew you shouldn't have access to. I don't know why, but at that moment, for the first time since I'd got here, I really, really wanted to go home.

I closed my eyes to try and sleep, but the next thing I knew I was hearing voices.

'Hello?' someone was whispering. 'Luke?' I looked down at my phone.

'Abbey?' I slurred.

'Luke . . .' she mumbled. 'Do you know what time it is?'

'No . . . What's going on? Are you OK?'

'You called me.'

'Did I?'

She sighed. 'You sound pissed.' She sounded tired. She sounded like home.

'I'm not that pissed. How are you? I've been wanting to call you. All week.' I watched the ceiling spin faster and faster above me.

'Why?' she whispered. It felt *so* good to hear her voice.

'Because . . . I don't know. Because I miss you, I guess. I was . . . Maybe I shouldn't have said what I said on the first night. I wasn't really thinking.'

'You're not thinking now.'

'No, I am . . . I just . . . Uni's not how I thought it would be. I don't know if I'm fitting in here. I don't know if it's working out.'

'So you thought you'd just call me and we'd get back

together and everything would suddenly go back to how it was.' She sounded tearful. 'It's not that easy, Luke.'

'No, I know. It's just . . . Maybe I'm not over you.' The words seeped out of me before I could think about whether I really meant them.

'I'm not over you, either,' I heard her say.

'Well,' I said. 'OK, then.'

And then the ceiling stopped spinning, and I fell asleep.

CHAPTER 11

PHOEBE

I was irrationally nervous.

In the worst case scenario I wouldn't get a job at a cafe. It wasn't A Levels, losing your virginity or skydiving; just another situation I had to walk into, not knowing what the hell I was doing, and hope for the best. I had tied my hair back into a tight ballet-dancer bun and it was making my ears ache so I kept trying to wiggle them free.

I gently pushed at the door but it was locked. Josh was behind the counter neatly laying out a row of giant scones. It was weird seeing him doing something so precise and un-blokish. The last time I had seen him he had been right in the middle of the dance floor of a club, really going for it. He was wearing a white shirt and it made him look younger than he normally did, like he was in school uniform. I knocked gently and he looked up, beamed and came over to let me in. Josh hugs you properly. Not a formality hug, but one like he has been waiting for you at the airport for hours. You don't really get those kind of hugs at uni; huge, tight confidence-giving squeezes.

'Nice Bettys bun, Bennet. You OK?'

'Yeah, I'm fine, apart from the fact I'm knackered cos Frankie has shared a bed with me for three nights and she's a massive wriggler.'

'That girl is an absolute nutter. Last night she got behind the counter at the kebab shop and begged the bloke to let her serve the chips.' He shook his head. 'Negin had to trick her to leave by saying there was a tall man giving out pâté in the street.'

'I went home at midnight because I'm taking this trial shift seriously.' I was, I needed the money, and working at Bettys tea rooms seemed slightly more romantic than Pizza Hut.

'Bettys are serious about people taking it seriously.' He walked back over to the counter and handed me a box of scones and some gloves. I started to lay them out in a row next to his.

I wanted to say something about Will. I didn't want him to be this awkward thing in me and Josh's friendship. I had enough awkward things with people at York Met to last me the next three years, and it'd only been three weeks.

Even though I had now taken a solemn vow of chastity, including text message chastity, in front of Frankie, Becky and Negin, I was already notorious in the D Block love-life stakes. I'd seen Will out a few times since Freshers', and he'd just acted like he didn't know me. I'd seen him get with people in clubs, and I didn't really care. Well, I did care. I mean, I cared that I'd had this weird thing with him that included that first week of Freshers' and the weird night at his and the guinea pig. But apart from that I just wanted to be able to go out and not have to *worry* about seeing him. Especially when I was already on high alert for Luke Taylor sightings. I'd had to hide twice in toilets this week, waiting for the all clear, and I was planning to just completely avoid eye contact with him in all future seminars.

'Are you wiggling your ears, Bennet?' Josh laid out his last scone.

'Yeah, I went a bit militant with the bun. It's giving me a headache.'

'You look different with a bun. I can't believe all that hair can go so small.' He leant towards me. 'Right, so Sandra will come up in a minute. When she does, just be super smiley. Like you're in a cult. Round here it's like, you've got to smile all the time. That's the main thing. You can be a murderer as long as you are smiling hard.' He looked down. 'Excellent Battenberg arranging.'

'I'll be the judge of that.' A stern-looking woman, actually wearing what looked like a *Downton* servant's uniform, came round the corner.

Sandra took me downstairs to the staff room and handed me a neat pile of clothes in a clear plastic bag. I went into the staff toilet and pulled the shirt over my head and fixed the little brooch that came with it in the middle, where a bow tie would go.

'You OK?' Josh shouted from outside.

I opened the door.

'Yeah, I look ridiculous. And I don't know what this is.' I held it to my waist. 'Do you have to be really skinny to work here?'

'It's the hat thing,' Josh said.

I looked in the mirror and put it on my forehead. 'I don't get it. How does it go on?'

'I don't know. Blokes don't have to wear them.'

'That's the patriarchy for you.'

'Hold on, turn around.' He gently took a couple of pins out of my bun and my hair fell down. Then he gathered it into a ponytail and rewound the bun slowly, pinning it again, but more loosely. He held up each end of ribbon below the bun and tied them together with the hat thing on my head.

'I feel like you're getting me ready for school,' I said.

'Four sisters. I can do fishtail plaits, Dutch plaits, French plaits, those weird bun things on the side of your head, glitter partings.' He patted my bun and we went back upstairs. There were lots more people there and we had a team meeting where Sandra spoke a lot about specials and clearing tables and keeping the queue happy. I was still a bit nervous. She kept saying words I had never heard before and everyone was nodding knowingly.

'You'll be fine,' Josh whispered.

I was on the counter for the morning and it wasn't that bad. I didn't have to work the till, just get the scones and cakes and biscuits and put them in boxes and hand them to a lady called Julie who seemed to have an encyclopaedic knowledge of every single thing Bettys had ever sold: 'Do you have the Lady Betty Peppermint Creams?' 'Only at Christmas, my love. Give it a few weeks.'

Just when I felt like it was all going well, Sandra appeared behind the counter.

'That Laurel is ill again so I'm afraid I'm going to have to put you on the floor, Phoebe.'

My stomach churned. I had never waitressed before and waitressing at Bettys seemed to be the Olympics of waitressing. Silver cake forks and tea strainers and lots of very white table-cloths. I thought about the words 'silver service waitressing' on my CV, which referred to pouring champagne at my gran's seventieth.

I just kept getting hotter. People kept asking me questions I didn't know the answer to and everyone looked too busy to help. The quicker I took people's orders the quicker more people seemed to sit down. I couldn't remember the table num-bers and I couldn't remember all the teas and I couldn't seem to input the orders without taking so long that people started trying to wave at me to come over and see them.

I knocked over a tiny vase on one of the tables with a red tulip in and Sylvia Plath popped into my head. And that made Luke pop into my head, and I got a horror wave that I was getting my accidental text rash back, and then I couldn't re-member what I was supposed to be doing. I had needed the toilet for so long that the pain just began to feel normal. How can people get paid so little to do something so complicated? The panic was making my mind go completely blank. I couldn't remember what had happened three seconds ago.

Four women at one of my tables kept looking at me. I took a tray of sandwiches over to a group of Americans and they shook their heads like I had done something wrong. I could feel sweat dripping down my back. I looked through the millions of little pieces of paper I had stuffed into my apron pocket. I found their one. I had definitely taken their order.

'Sorry honey,' one of them said. 'We've been here for a half hour and we haven't even been given our tea.'

'I'm so sorry. Let me just go to the kitchen and check on your order.'

'Just the pot of tea would be good,' another said, and gave her friend a look as if to say I was a complete idiot.

Panic was rising inside me. I went downstairs and into the staff toilet and looked over the slips again. I hadn't put their order through. And if I did it now it would go to the end of the orders and it would be another half an hour until they got anything.

I couldn't think properly. I needed to just own up to it, find Sandra and tell her what had happened. I took a deep breath and walked out. Josh winked at me from across the room. I shook my head trying to indicate what had happened.

He smiled and said something that made the whole table laugh and then walked over to me.

'I think I've totally fucked it up,' I whispered. 'I forgot to put an order in.'

'Don't worry,' he said. 'I can sort it.'

But then Sandra appeared. 'Are you all right love?' she

asked. 'You're supposed to be upstairs.' Her voice had an edge to it.

'Sandra.' Josh wrinkled his nose. 'I said to Phoebe I would put an order through for her, but I totally forgot. Don't blame her. I said I would do it, cos she had that many tables and we were quieter down here.'

She shook her head. 'Right, go and sort it.' And then she walked away. I wanted to throw my arms around him, I was so relieved.

'Your hat's coming off.' He grinned.

'Thank you so much.' I was acting like he had pulled me out of the water after *Titanic*. I needed to get some perspective on this trial waitressing shift.

'Well, I want you to get the job.' He smiled. 'So I have a mate here. I mean, I do like having twenty-odd mothers about but, you know . . . It would be a right laugh with you.'

We got the tea and cakes for the table and served them together. Josh definitely had a way of talking to people that made them just like him, even before he had really said anything.

Once the lunch rush passed, things got quieter. Josh and me re-laid all the tables and played Shoot/Snog/Marry in whispers between serving customers.

Four o' clock came around really quickly and I got changed and tried to fold up the uniform into the same neat pile it had been handed to me in.

'You keep it.' Sandra smiled. 'Welcome to Bettys.'

Me and Josh walked out together, and when we got to the corner he gave me another one of his massive hugs. He hugged

161

me so tight he lifted me up without even realizing.

'Thanks for getting it for me.'

'I didn't,' he said. 'You got it for yourself.'

It was getting dark. People were finishing their shopping and going back to their cars. We wandered along the cobbled street towards uni.

'Do you want to come to mine for a cuppa? It's on the way back.'

I pulled a face. 'Um . . . Dunno.'

'You mean cos of Will?' He sounded almost concerned. 'Are you OK? About all that?'

I nodded. I didn't really know what to say. I wondered what he knew about that night. What exactly Will had said about it, and what Josh thought.

We both looked in a toy shop window. 'What would you go for?' Josh pointed. 'I reckon you would go for the squirrel Sylvanian Family.'

'I already have that family, obviously. It's the classic family. I would go for the light-up hula hoop. I mean, when did they invent those?' I peered through the window. 'I reckon you are a Nerf Gun kind of boy.'

He crinkled his nose. 'What? That's a massive insult. I would go for the teddy bear. I love a good teddy bear.'

We kept walking in silence. 'I am OK about it,' I said. 'The Will stuff, I mean. I just feel like . . . I just don't want it to be weird.'

Josh nodded. 'Yeah. Well, Will's . . . He's a bit . . .' He trailed off. 'He's great in loads of ways, but . . . I dunno.'

'I thought you two were really good mates?' I said.

He dug his hands into his jacket pockets. 'I mean, yeah. We were on the same corridor last year and we both played football and it seemed really obvious from the start that we were gonna live together. And then his dad literally bought a house in York, so . . .'

We stopped outside a kitchenware shop. 'The living thing freaks me out a bit,' I said. 'People are talking about it already. Like, getting houses together.'

'Honestly, Bennet, do not give in to the pressure. You don't have to decide straight away. I kind of . . . wish I hadn't.'

'Do you still play football?' I wondered if he'd met Luke.

'No, I stopped at the end of second term. I played at school and everything, but up here, those lads are all quite . . . dunno. Can't describe it really.' He shook his head. 'Like I said, I've got four sisters, so I guess I'm a bit more sensitive to all that sort of banter.'

I waited for him to say something more but he didn't. 'Well, you can always join quidditch with me, Frankie and Negin. There's a social next week.'

He smiled at me. 'You never know, Bennet, might take you up on that, actually.'

I peered through the kitchen shop window. 'Look, they have a whole wall of cookie cutters. I can spend all my wages stocking up for fairy bread egg sandwiches.'

He nodded. 'Yeah, we need to keep adding to our collection.'

There were loads of them, in the shape of literally every

object you could think of. I turned to Josh. 'OK, which do you reckon's my fave?'

He narrowed his eyes. Then after a second, he said: 'I'm going for the train one.'

'Yes! That actually is my favourite.'

'I know you so well, Bennet.' He pointed. 'Is that a phone-shaped one?'

I started walking again. 'We are not buying that one. Phones are the root of every single problem in my life. Do you actually, really want to know what happened with Will?'

'Well, how graphic is it? I mean, will I see you in another light, Bennet?'

'I sent him a picture of a guinea pig doing the Macarena. And I never heard from him again.'

Josh stopped still and then burst into laughter so loud that a woman crossed the street.

'Stop.' I pulled my hat over my eyes. 'Please. It's still raw.'

He linked arms with me. 'Don't worry. Trust me, guinea pig Macarena is amateur stuff. On Valentine's, when I was sixteen, I wrote my girlfriend a cheesy love poem. And then accidentally texted it to my mum.'

I pulled out my phone. 'OK. That's bad, but this blows everything out of the water. If I show you this, we have to be friends for life.' I found the message and handed it to him.

He squinted. '"Luke Taylor is—"'

I whacked him on the arm. 'Don't read it out loud. It's horrific enough as it is.'

'And you sent this to . . .?'

I shut my eyes and nodded.

'Wow.' Josh stopped and ran a hand over his shaved head. 'I mean, yeah, there's no beating that. That's the Usain Bolt of embarrassing texts. That's made me feel a lot better, actually.'

'Oh good. Great. Glad my shit-show of a life could be of service.'

He sighed. 'I feel like life is always manageable until you get girls involved.'

'Or boys.'

'People. Basically, you shouldn't get people involved.'

'Or technology,' I said. 'Especially phones. Phones have caused all my uni dramas to date. You wouldn't catch Elizabeth Bennet sending a comedy guinea pig picture to Darcy. She'd have to paint it and then send it by horseman.'

Josh shrugged. 'Maybe she did do that, it just didn't make the final cut. It's probably in the bloopers.'

'You know it's a book, too, right?'

'You know I do English, too, right?' he shot back.

I sighed. 'Maybe we should just throw our phones away and live like people from the olden days.'

'Agreed, you stay away from phones and I'll keep living like a monk.'

I scrunched my face up. 'You don't live like a monk. What are you talking about?'

'An emotional monk. I have vowed to be an emotional monk. I'm not gonna fall in love with anyone again.'

'Who were you in love with? Are they here?'

He shook his head. 'Nah, she's at home. We broke up last

year. She broke up. Broke up with me. Broke me.' He sounded really serious.

I wanted to ask him more but his face sort of told me not to. I feel like everyone has had some great love except me. Like, maybe it will never happen to me. Maybe I'm immune or something.

'I think we'll both be all right.' He smiled at me. 'And you're a Bennet, Bennet, so it is inevitable that one day, someone will tell you how ardently they admire and love you.'

CHAPTER 12

LUKE

Will was muttering like a maniac and jabbing randomly at the quiz machine's buttons.

'Krypton . . . 1968 . . . The Diet of Worms . . .'

But he was getting every answer right. It was genuinely quite impressive.

'How the hell do you know all thi—'

'Shut up,' he hissed. 'We're one off the money.'

He squinted at the screen. 'Who wrote the 1925 novel *The Trial*?' He spun round to face me. 'Come on, English. This is all you.'

I pressed the 'Franz Kafka' button, and a few pound coins clattered out of the machine. 'Fucking yes, mate!' Will beamed, reaching down to collect the money. 'Dream team.'

He squeezed past the pool table and I followed him up to the bar. 'Played that machine so many times last year that I still remember pretty much all the answers. I might be fucking my

LIBRARIES NEATH PORT TALBOT

degree up, but I could definitely get a first in pub trivia.' He waved the barman over. 'What d'you want?'

'Nothing. I've got a seminar. Got to go back to the block and get my stuff.' Will shrugged and ordered a pint, and I wondered if I should maybe try and talk to him about Abbey. About what 'I'm not over you' might actually mean.

Did it mean we were back together? It definitely didn't feel like we were. Mainly because I hadn't actually heard from her since the night we'd said it. It had been more than a week, and nothing. Not one single message. I'd been so pissed at the time, I was starting to doubt whether the conversation had even happened.

Will sipped his pint, and asked: 'Your corridor still boring as fuck, then?'

'I don't see them, really.' I shrugged. 'They're all doing Chemistry so they're usually in labs all day.'

He nodded. 'Cool. It's just . . . I dunno what you've got sorted for houses next year, but we might have a spare room at my place.'

'Oh, right. Really?'

It sort of knocked me sideways. The chemists were already talking about getting a house together next year, and in my head I'd been working up to asking Arthur and Rita what their plans were. But, then, they had their own mates and their own lives. They never actually messaged me, or arranged to meet up with me, like Will did. Arthur had only ended up next door to me because of asbestos and random chance. It wasn't like we'd somehow bonded and found each other. The truth was, Will was probably the closest thing I had here to a proper mate.

'Yeah, I'd be up for that,' I told him. 'Sounds good.'

He started counting the quiz machine winnings out on the bar. 'I mean, nothing's definite yet, mate. I need to see what Josh is doing.'

'Of course, yeah.'

I said goodbye and went back to B Block to get my bag, where I found Beth and Barney in the kitchen furiously spraying air freshener to cover the stink of Arthur's cheese.

I headed up the walkway to my seminar, pulling my jacket collar tight against the bitter wind and thinking for the zillionth time about that Abbey conversation.

The hardest thing was that I had literally no one to talk to about stuff like this. Last night, I'd got so sick of all these doubts and fears nagging at me that I'd even called Reece. But all we'd ended up talking about was how shit Arsenal were this season. I couldn't get beyond the banter and pointless small talk. I couldn't ever find the space to say what I really wanted to say: that I was starting to freak out. About everything; friends and football and not fitting in. But mostly about the idea that I'd broken something in Abbey, something that couldn't ever be fixed.

It was like I was on edge all the time. Like I was slowly sinking, surrounded by people, and I couldn't shout for help.

My phone buzzed, and my heart did its usual mini drum roll, but it wasn't Abbey. It was someone on the football group; a fresher called Murf. I opened the message, which was another photo of a random sleeping girl – about the fourth this week.

You had to keep checking the group in case it was about training or a match, or something, but that meant you basically couldn't avoid these photos. Dempers called it 'The Wall of Shame': whenever anyone in the team slept with a girl, they put a picture up. But the thing was, the pictures weren't even the worst of it. It was the comments underneath that really gnawed at me. People rating the girls out of ten, saying horrible shit about the way they looked.

I looked at my phone again. Dempers and Geordie Al had already commented: '3/10 . . . Rough as fuck m8' and 'Any hole's a goal . . .' I put it back in my pocket and kept walking.

When I got to the seminar, everyone was already sat down. Phoebe was on the other side of the room, getting her books out of her rucksack. She looked particularly pretty today; her masses of curly hair were all pulled up neatly into a bun at the back, so you could see the whole of her face.

I tried, and failed, to make eye contact with her as I walked in. We didn't even nod hello these days. As weirdly great as it had been to receive that text, I was starting to wish it had never happened. What was the point of fancying someone if they were too embarrassed to ever speak to you?

The idea suddenly occurred to me that I could even things out right then and there by sending her a text telling her how hot she looked. But I dismissed that pretty quickly as one of worst ideas anyone's ever had.

Our tutor, Yorgos, came in, and dumped his bag on the desk.

'Right,' he announced. 'I'm afraid I've got some bad news for you all today. Presentations.'

Someone groaned and Yorgos laughed. 'I know, I know. Literature is supposed to be about sitting and writing, not standing and talking. But your essays will only make up seventy-five per cent of your mark this term. The other twenty-five per cent will come from this presentation.'

There was a louder groan this time, and Yorgos smiled again. He looked a bit like a younger, skinnier, less terrifying Javier Bardem. 'Don't worry,' he said. 'You won't have to go through this humiliating ordeal alone. You'll do it in groups of three.'

He scanned the room. 'And don't just grab hold of your two friends next to you. Let's mix things up a bit.'

He flicked his fingers like an orchestra conductor, picking out groups of three at random. On the last flick, he took in me, Hot Mary with the ridiculous hair, and Phoebe. 'You three.'

Hot Mary grinned at me, and I grinned at Phoebe, but Phoebe just stared down intensely at her notepad.

As soon as the seminar was over, Phoebe bolted for the door, but Hot Mary blocked her off.

'I was thinking we could grab a coffee, or something?' she said to both of us. 'Chat about the presentation?'

A few minutes later, the three of us were sat in Wulfstan Bar, drinking grainy lukewarm cappuccinos, and Phoebe had *still* not made eye contact with me. In fact, neither of us had actually said more than about five words. Hot But Ridiculous Mary seemed quite happy to do all the talking.

'Like, I was thinking we should do the whole thing about memory, right?' she was gabbling. 'We could put Ted and Sylvia at the heart of it, obviously, but we can also bring in shitloads of other memory stuff: Joyce, Nabokov, Proust . . .' She banged the table suddenly, causing half my coffee to bail out into the saucer. 'Oh my god, we could make it a Proust-themed performance piece! Like, we could all sit at the front of the class, dunking bits of cake into cups of tea, talking about our earliest memories!'

She stopped speaking and stared at us, and I realized that she was finally expecting one of us to say something. She was wearing a green top with a sort of lightning-shaped split up one side. I could see a gothic-lettering tattoo snaking down into her jeans, but I couldn't work out what it said.

I was focusing so intently on this that I momentarily forgot about the silence. Luckily, Phoebe didn't. 'Well . . . I like the memory thing,' she said. 'We should definitely do that. I'm just not sure about the performance piece bit.' She smiled softly. 'I'm not that much of a performer.'

'Oh, don't worry about that.' Mary flapped her hands, dramatically. 'You can leave the performance stuff to me. I could maybe even read out some of my poems. I've got one called 'Winchester Casts No Shadows' that deals heavily with the theme of memory . . .'

She reached down to get something out of her bag, and I saw that the tattoo said *I love, I have loved, I will love*. Out of nowhere, a memory hit me – a memory I didn't even know I had – and it was like stepping on a landmine.

I looked at Phoebe. 'You *are* a performer,' I said. 'You were whatshername in *Grease*. Frenchie.'

Mary stared at me. So did Phoebe. Mary was smiling a confused sort of smile, but Phoebe's face was literally impossible to read.

'I don't know why I just remembered that,' I carried on, feeling a weird rush from looking into Phoebe's blue-green eyes for the first time since Freshers' Fair. 'It was Year Ten, wasn't it? In the dining hall. You were great. I remember Annabel kicked her shoe off into the crowd and you ad-libbed a joke about it.'

Phoebe smiled, then looked down at her coffee. 'Yeah, Year Ten, you're right.'

I'd only gone to see it because Abbey had been Sandy. She'd looked ridiculously hot in the end scene with the leather trousers and blonde wig. I'd actually thought about auditioning for one of the bloke parts, but Reece had laughed so hard when I told him that I'd chickened out.

'What the absolute fuck are you two on about?' Mary demanded.

'Me and Phoebe went to school together,' I explained, and her eyes widened.

'Oh, shit, this is perfect. So, like, maybe we can weave that in? I could do my poems, and then you two can, like, reminisce about sitting next to each other in double Physics, or whatever.'

This made me and Phoebe catch eyes again and smile.

Mary looked at her phone. 'Oh fuckbags, I'm late for band

173

practice.' She stood up, artfully messing her multi-coloured hair with both hands. 'You guys should totally come to our gig next week, by the way. We're called Fit Sister. We do Electro Tuesdays in Gildas Bar.' She slurped the rest of her coffee, and slammed the cup back down. 'Anyway, chat later. Awesome brainstorm.'

Then she bounded off. And just like that, I was alone with Phoebe.

PHOEBE

The thing about Frenchie had totally freaked me out.

I'd basically been aiming to just keep my head down, not look at or speak to Luke, and then get out of the bar as quickly as humanly possible. But him mentioning *Grease* had dredged up all this random stuff I'd completely forgotten about.

That play had been right around the same time Luke and Abbey Baker had started going out. Every night, I'd come out of rehearsals to see him kicking a football against the wall, waiting for her. And then I'd go home and daydream point-lessly about what it'd be like if he was waiting for me instead.

Now that Bowl-Cut had disappeared, being alone with Luke definitely felt like too much to handle. It was like the text was flashing in front of me every time I looked at him. It was all just way too humiliating. I grabbed my bag, and was about to make an excuse and leave, when he spoke.

'So, Mary's quite . . .' He raised his eyebrows. 'Isn't she?'

That made me laugh, in spite of everything. 'Yeah,' I said. 'She is.'

He mopped up some of his spilt coffee with a napkin. 'I mean, there's no way I'm sitting at the front of the class, dunking biscuits in tea and talking about my earliest memories.'

'Yeah, I'm not really into that either.' I still had one hand on my bag, ready to jump up and leave whenever the conversation stuttered or broke down. But it didn't. It kept going.

'Have you seen her tattoo?' Luke asked.

I nodded. '"I love, I have loved, I will love." *Pret*-ty deep.'

'Yeah,' he said. 'Although it also sounds a bit like GCSE verb conjugation.'

'True. Can you imagine what her poems are like?'

He raised his eyebrows again. He looked so fit. I tried not to think about it, as thinking about how fit Luke is tends to be what gets me into trouble. 'I know,' he said. 'It might actually be worth sacrificing twenty-five per cent of our first term mark just to hear them.'

We both laughed, and I thought, Is this what being a grown-up is? Can proper adults accidentally text someone confessing their undying love, and then just have a friendly coffee with them afterwards? Is that really how the real world works?

'I don't want to be mean about Mary,' I said. 'I actually quite like her. To be honest, me and my friends are kind of obsessed with her.'

He nodded. 'I'm kind of obsessed with her too. I sort of fancy her, but she also sort of terrifies me.'

Hearing him say he fancied Mary was definitely too much. I grabbed my bag handle a bit tighter, and Luke must have spotted it because he reached for his bag, too.

'Well,' he said, 'we're both agreed that we're mildly obsessed with Mary, so that's good. You heading back to Jutland?'

We finished our coffees and started wandering slowly back together. It felt like we were walking on ice. Feeling our way carefully back into normality. Every time it started to feel natural and easy between us, I remembered the text and imagined him reading it, and wanted to dissolve into the ground again. I prayed we didn't bump into Frankie and Negin, as that really would send the awkwardness levels off the chart.

'So,' Luke said, 'what actually is all this Ted Hughes and Sylvia Plath stuff about memory? I sort of missed all that in the first seminar.'

He didn't add: 'I missed it because I was laughing my arse off at a message you'd just sent me calling me the hottest boy on Earth.' But he must have been thinking it. It was the first time either of us had mentioned that seminar, and I felt my neck getting red. The text rash was following me. I pushed my scarf up to hide it.

'Well, basically,' I said, 'what happened was, Ted Hughes and Sylvia Plath met at this party, and it's like one of the most epic and intense meetings in literary history. She bit his cheek and it bled.'

'What? That's a bit harsh.'

'No, I think she just fancied him. Or it was like some kind of expression of . . . something. I don't actually know. But she definitely bit him and from that moment they both knew that for better or worse they were tied together. Like they were meant to meet. And they both really believed in that kind of fatalistic moment.'

'Right.'

'But it's just weird because they both wrote about it in their diaries, but one of them got this insignificant detail wrong. The blue or red ribbon thing. So, Yorgos was saying it means a lot because they are poets, and colour and imagery is significant, I suppose.'

Luke nodded slowly. 'So, it's like, either the ribbon was blue, and he really did see her clearly, like the person she really was . . . Or it was red, and he never really saw her. He just projected on to her what he wanted to see?'

'Yeah, exactly,' I said. 'I agree with Mary, to be honest. It was her ribbon, she must have known. So, it was like he misread her from the very start.'

I could feel Luke looking straight at me. 'OK, right,' he said. 'I get it.'

LUKE

I didn't get it.

Was that what had happened with me and Abbey? Had I misread her from the start? Or had she misread me? Maybe she'd thought I was calm, steady blue, when really I was fiery, ruin-your-life red.

Thinking about Abbey made me suddenly feel guilty about liking Phoebe and even finding Mary hot-yet-terrifying. And then I felt guilty for thinking about Abbey and Mary when I should have been focusing on what Phoebe was saying. And then I got so frustrated with it all that I booted a conker off the walkway, scattering a bunch of squirrels.

'Poetry's too complicated,' I muttered.

Phoebe laughed. 'What do you like, then? Like, who's your favourite writer?'

'I dunno. I like John Fante and Ken Kesey. I like Hemingway a lot.'

'Luke!' She looked at me in what seemed like mock-horror, but could just as easily have been actual horror. 'Hemingway was a violent drunk.'

'I don't mean I like *him*,' I said. 'I'm sure he was an absolute dick. But I do like his writing. I like how you can feel he's really burning to find some sort of meaning from life. All these obsessions with shark fishing and bull fighting and big game hunting – like, doing mad, dangerous stuff to feel more alive.'

'So, basically, loads of innocent animals had to die just for one drunk guy to "feel more alive"? I think I'll stick to Jane Austen.'

We strolled past Jutland Bar and the computer room and the munchie machines. It was weird; it was like we were slowly finding a rhythm again. Nowhere near back to the easy banter of the Stephanie Stevens night, but not a million miles from it.

'I've got a good book on Ted and Sylvia, actually,' Phoebe said. 'It was my mum's – she was really into them. I can always lend you that if you want. Especially if we're gonna be doing this whole presentation on them.'

'Yeah, that'd be great, actually. Cheers.'

We were now right at the end of the walkway, where the

path split, with D Block to the left and B Block to the right. We both stood there for a second, fidgeting with our bags and not looking at each other.

'Well . . .' Phoebe let the word hang in the air between us. I really didn't want her to go. I wanted to keep hanging out with her.

'Maybe . . . I could get it now?' I tried. 'The book, I mean?'

She fiddled with her massive scarf, and looked up at her window. Then she said: 'Yeah. OK. Cool.'

D Block looked exactly the same as B Block, but the absence of Arthur's headachey cheese smell made it seem more welcoming somehow.

Their kitchen was in a much worse state than ours, but Phoebe's room was way tidier and nicer than mine. She'd actually bothered to decorate properly, for a start. There were pictures Blu-Tacked up all over the walls, and little, multi-coloured fairy lights strung over the sink cupboard. She reached up to get the Ted and Sylvia book from her shelf, and I squinted at some of the photos.

'No way,' I said. 'Is that . . . Book Day?'

Among all the shots of Phoebe and her mates, there was a group picture of our whole school in Year Nine, with everyone dressed as different characters.

'Yup'. She knelt on the bed next to me, and smiled as she looked at the picture. I peered harder at it, rocking forward on my knees. 'Found you,' I said.

'The hair's a giveaway,' she sighed, taking a fistful of it and smoothing it out along her shoulder.

'Are you . . . what?' I looked closer, but I still had no idea. 'A cloud?'

She laughed. 'I'm the mouse.'

'Oh, right, I get you: the mouse.' I nodded. '*The* mouse. The generic mouse of literature. Which mouse?'

She rolled her eyes. 'The Gruffalo mouse. Look.' She pointed at the girl next to her, who appeared to be dressed as the devil. 'Flora is the Gruffalo. Do you remember Flora?'

I did remember Flora, but I didn't know she was called Flora. 'Yeah, I remember her,' I said. 'Gruffalo and Gruffalo Mouse. That's a bit . . . niche, isn't it?'

She shrugged and handed me the Ted and Sylvia book. 'The niche stuff is the best stuff. Are you even in this picture or were you too cool for Book Day?'

'Of course I'm in it,' I pointed at tiny, spiky-haired, fourteen-year-old me, squashed in between Reece and Harry on the back row. 'I'm the greatest literary character of all time. Boy in an Arsenal kit.'

Phoebe made a face. 'You wore an Arsenal kit to Book Day?'

'Yeah, someone, somewhere, in the vast expanse of world literature has definitely worn an Arsenal kit. The bloke out of *Fever Pitch* for a start.'

'The bloke out of *Fever Pitch*,' Phoebe scoffed. 'Classic.'

'It *is* a classic, thank you very much'.

'Whatever. You're just crap at dressing up. Admit it. What did you wear to the emoji party? A smiley face, or something, wasn't it?'

'Thumbs-up, actually.'

'Well, you could've made more of an effort,' she laughed. And even though I knew she didn't mean anything by it, it still made me think of the quidditch bail. And Abbey. And all the other fuck-ups I was leaving in a long trail behind me.

Could've made more of an effort. That would probably be written on my fucking gravestone.

I sighed and slumped down from kneeling to sitting on the bed. 'Yeah, it's true. The thing is, Phoebe, I guess I'm just, y'know . . . a bit of a prick, really.'

I smiled at her, but she didn't smile back. She just stared at me hard. Which was quite disconcerting, as we'd only really been making nervous, fluttering, two-second eye contact since we got into the room.

'You're not a prick, Luke,' she said slowly. Then she scooched away from me slightly, and started looking at the other photos. 'Do you remember Zoe Kenney's seventeenth?' she asked. 'In her dad's massive house?'

'Er . . . yeah,' I said, although I had no recollection of Phoebe being at that party at all.

'Well, you remember when Chris Isaacs and Alex Paine and that lot showed up? They were really pissed and they started giving Justin all that shit? Going on about how his long hair made him look like a girl?'

The memory started to defrost in my head. It was a horrible moment. They'd pushed Justin Hader on the floor and Chris had grabbed a pair of scissors, telling him they were going to give him a proper haircut. A boy's haircut.

'Yeah,' I said. 'I remember.'

181

'You were the one that stopped that,' Phoebe said quietly. 'You pulled Chris off him. You got them to leave him alone.'

'Chris Isaacs and Alex Paine were the biggest twats in the whole school.'

'Yeah, but they listened to you.'

'Only cos I was on the football team with them.'

'Yeah, well, either way . . .' She looked at me again, right in the eyes. 'That awful thing didn't happen because of you. And I remember thinking, at that moment . . .' She tailed off, and then shook her head gently, like she was embarrassed or something. She smoothed out another fistful of her long, curly hair. 'Well, I remember thinking Luke Taylor's not a prick, anyway.'

I tried to laugh, but it got stuck in my throat. It was like she'd shaken me awake suddenly, reminded me there was more to me than what had happened with Abbey. I sat there in silence on the bed next to her, pretending to look at the photos, and for the first time in for ever, I actually felt OK.

CHAPTER 13

PHOEBE

'I can't believe how *long* your hair is,' Liberty said. Every time she clamped the straighteners near my head I jumped a bit, internally.

'Yeah, but does it look *good*?' I asked.

'I have never in my life seen anything like it.' She said it totally sincerely.

'Liberty, that is not a reassuring answer. "I have never in my life seen anything like it." That's what people say about nuclear explosions or those people who have plastic surgery to make themselves look like cats.'

'No, it's just, you look *so* differe—'

Frankie crashed in and did a sort of over-exaggerated double take. 'What the *what*? Mate, *what* is happening?'

She bent over next to me so her face was right in front of mine. 'Mate, I *literally* didn't recognize you. As in, this is freaking me the fuck out.' She was shaking her head. She leant back out into the corridor and shouted: 'Negin! Negin!'

I jumped up and looked in the mirror. Straightened, my hair reached all the way to my bum. I actually did look like a completely different person. Frankie held her phone up and took a picture. Then she banged on my wall. Liberty had dissolved into laughter. 'Connor! Connor!' Where *is* everyone?' Frankie stood in the middle of the room and just started shouting. 'Becky! Nathan!' She walked over to my bed and opened the window. 'Anyone, please? I can't experience this alone.'

I cut her off. 'OK, let's focus. I have to see Luke in an hour.'

Frankie made a face. 'You've seen him, like, every day this week.'

'I know, but today is the actual presentation.' I looked at Liberty. 'Should I wash it out?'

Frankie picked out a piece of my hair and peered at it. 'No way, I mean firstly, it could create a whole new beginning for you and Luke. As in, you could literally pretend to be another human being. Like, "Phoebe had to leave but I am – Horatia, the new person in your presentation group. I will never send a photo of you to you because I am Ho—"'

I ignored her and turned back to Liberty. 'Seriously, I know this represents an hour and a half of our lives, but should I wash it out?'

Liberty shook her head. 'No way. It's like red lipstick, you just have to get used to it.'

'What should I wear?'

Frankie opened my wardrobe. 'What would Horatia wear? That is the question.'

Liberty jumped up and down. 'I'll lend you some of my clothes.'

'Liberty, me and you have very different styles.' Liberty's style was unashamedly sexy. More 'Ibiza VIP lounge' than 'romantic poetry seminar'. 'I think the hair and then me turning up looking so glamorous might make people think I was—'

'Horatia,' Frankie shouted. 'She's like Sasha Fierce. Like, Horatia wouldn't pretend the Luke Taylor text never happened. She'd just be all like, "Yeah, that is how I test my men. Do you wanna stroke my long straight hair or not?"'

'Can we stop talking about the text?' I pleaded.

'I will *never* stop talking about the text,' Frankie said, crossing her arms. 'It's literally the most hilarious thing that's ever happened to me. And it didn't even happen to me.'

I laughed. 'Yeah, well, I can only cope with seeing Luke if I do this weird mental exercise where I convince myself I never sent him that photo.'

It was true. Me, Luke and Bowl-Cut Mary had met up in the library every day for the past three days, and I'd only managed to get through it by burying the text somewhere deep inside me. Just literally pretending it had never happened. But the truth was, the more we hung out, the less weird and awkward it was starting to feel.

'I reckon Luke probably keeps that message as his screen saver,' Liberty said. 'Has he honestly never mentioned it?'

I shook my head.

'So weird,' she sighed. Then she turned to Frankie. 'Can I

have a Sasha Fierce name, too?'

Frankie shrugged. 'You don't need one, mate, but yeah, OK. What about Hercules?'

'Ooh, Hercules, I like tha—'

She was cut off by Connor's boom from the kitchen. 'Waffles!' I knew he was beating his chest as he said it. 'Waaaaaaaaffles.'

The kitchen door opened and Connor poked his head through. 'We have made waaaaaaaffles.'

We walked into the kitchen, where he and Nathan were standing over a machine.

'You bought a waffle maker?' I said.

'Woah, you look totally different.' Nathan seemed genuinely shocked.

Frankie held up her phone. There was a picture of me spliced next to Cousin It. Underneath she had written 'Freaky Friday'.

'We've melted Smarties, Chomp bars and Honey Nut Loops together,' Connor said proudly. 'Although the Honey Nut Loops aren't really melting.'

'Connor, do you think I look ridiculous?' I said.

'She means do you think Luke Taylor will think she looks ridiculous?' Frankie corrected.

Connor shook his head. 'I would like to say he won't notice the hair, but you do look like a child from a Japanese horror film, so he probably will.' The waffle maker started smoking and he flapped at it with a tea towel. 'But, then, y'know, that's the beauty of fancying girls, isn't it? Never knowing what mad shit they are gonna do next. Like, wearing those wedge shoes, or having nails like Wolverine or making you take the same picture millions of times. I, personally, love it.'

Frankie was still cuddling me so I shuffled over and we added Connor to the huddle. 'Strangely, you've actually made me feel better.'

I went and got changed into the most boring outfit I could think of; jeans and a white T-shirt. The hair was enough of a statement without Liberty's over-the-knee boots.

I tucked my hair into my duffle coat and packed my bag. Even aside from all the Luke stuff, I was actually a bit nervous about the presentation. It was the first thing that properly counted. As I walked to the seminar, I tried to retract tortoise-like into my hood to take attention away from my hair.

I thought Luke was late at first, but then I saw him on the grass outside the English block, on his hands and knees.

'What are you doing?' I stood on the path looking at him.

He smiled up at me. 'I forgot the leaves.'

'Mary will kill you,' I laughed. 'The leaves are like . . . the whole thing.'

'Yeah, but the thing is, now that I actually need some leaves, there are none. The whole place has been covered in them and now the wind has blown them all away or something.' He looked genuinely quite stressed.

'It's because you are looking at a patch of grass where there are no trees. Why would there be leaves when there aren't any trees?'

He stood up. 'Oh yeah, right. That makes sense.' I swear he went a tiny bit red.

I pointed at the trees on the other side of the lake. 'Hurry up, we've got time.'

We rushed across the bridge, and I realized it was the same bridge we'd sat on back on the first night. When I looked at Luke, he was staring right up at Stephanie Stevens' block, but neither of us said anything.

We paced about picking up random leaves. 'They're a bit damp,' he said.

'OK, well, you find them and I'll dry them with my coat.'

He handed me a leaf and I started wiping it dry.

'I mean, this whole thing is ridiculous,' he moaned. 'Why did we let Mary lead us down this damp-leaf-ridden path of madness?'

'Cos neither of us had any ideas whatsoever.'

He handed me the last leaf and I smoothed it out. 'They look a bit budget, but they'll have to do.'

We met Mary outside the seminar room. She was wearing tons of mascara and had a silver star stencilled just underneath her eye. Plus her usual baggy trousers and crop top. Was she so hot she was actually immune to the cold?

She hugged us both. 'Luke, have you got the leaves?'

He nodded. 'Yeah, of course. Got them yesterday.' I shook my head and mouthed 'twat' at him. Then Mary did a kind of overly dramatic double take as she properly took in my hair.

'Shit, Phoebs. So much hair. Such good hair. Phoebe with the good hair.'

Luke nodded. 'Yeah, I meant to say, earlier. It looks really different. Like, good different. I mean, it looks nice curly, too.

But, like this, it also looks really . . .' He sort of puttered to a stop as he saw Mary biting her lip. 'Nice,' he finished.

Mary whistled. 'Smooooooth. Save that silver tongue for the presentation, Taylor.'

LUKE

I should've said something about the hair earlier.

Obviously, I'd noticed it straight away. With Phoebe, the hair is always the first thing you notice. And it did look really good. But I never know what to say in those kinds of situations. Like, if you mention it, it's like you're making a big thing of it. But if you don't mention it, you're a twat. You literally can't win.

We all sat down in the seminar room. Yorgos arrived and started telling us how excited he was for our presentations. He picked Martha and Scouse Paul and Katie first. They got up and opened their PowerPoint. They had a PowerPoint; we had a bag of damp leaves. I was starting to get very nervous.

Mary looked like she literally didn't have a care in the world. She even looked slightly bored. I nudged my notebook towards Phoebe and wrote 'Are we fucked?' on it. She wrote 'POSSIBLY YES' underneath in block capitals.

Scouse Paul finished his monologue about Chaucer and everyone clapped. Then Yorgos started talking about how vital good research is. I had the sudden feeling that I was about to fail my first proper piece of university work.

'OK,' Yorgos said. 'Mary, Phoebe and Luke. Let's see what you've got.'

Mary was straight out of her chair, handing out the leaves with a kind of smug look on her face. 'Our piece is experiential,' she announced, and I saw Phoebe wince slightly.

She handed Yorgos a leaf and then walked over to the door and turned off the lights. 'Everyone close your eyes,' she said in this slightly GCSE drama-type voice.

Me and Phoebe stood either side of her at the front of the room. 'We want to take you on a hypnotic journey . . . through memory,' she continued. 'Through your own memory but also into the collective memory of everyone who has come before you.'

The side of Phoebe's mouth twitched. Even though it was our presentation, and I was stood at the front, it was like I couldn't concentrate on it. I just looked across the not-that-dark room at everyone with their eyes closed, holding a mouldy old leaf.

'Feel the veins,' Mary was whispering. She had a way of whispering that was actually louder than her normal speaking voice. 'Think of how they reach out to one another. Think of your mother's hand reaching out for yours on your first day of school. And think of the hand reaching out behind her, and the one behind that. And all the hands that came before you, reaching out into the darkness. Reaching back and back and back.'

People were actually feeling their leaves. 'Think about the love you have felt,' Mary said. 'Think about single moments of time that have changed your – or someone else's – life for ever.'

I tried very hard not to think about Abbey.

'Think about the secrets you keep inside you,' Mary continued. 'Feel the veins connect and think about the secrets other people hold in their veins too.' She was holding her hands out like Gandalf and speaking in a slow, kind of dream-like voice. Me and Phoebe both looked down at our sheets.

'You were blue,' I recited.

'Clownlike, happiest on your hands,' Phoebe said.

'Think of your ancestor, walking in the snow to find food,' Mary whispered.

'When you can no more hold me by the hand,' Phoebe read.

'Nor I half turn to go, yet turning stay.' I tried to match Mary's sombre tone, but didn't quite nail it.

Mary shuffled to the back. She shouted, 'Speak, memory!' then switched on the light.

No one said anything for a few seconds. They just sat there, blinking and holding their leaves. There was just this long, awkward silence. Then Phoebe cleared her throat and launched into her short, non leaf-based analysis of 'Ariel' by Sylvia Plath, which was scarily impressive and eloquent, and I bumbled through my bit about Ted Hughes' 'Last Letter', most of which I'd nicked from the book Phoebe had lent me.

And then Mary beamed around the whole class, and said: 'Yeah, so . . . That's it, basically. Keep the leaves. Remember us every time you look at them.'

Everyone clapped and Yorgos shot us a big smile, and got the next three up. And I had absolutely no idea whether it had gone well or not.

*

Mary definitely seemed to think it had. She literally danced out of the room when it was all over.

'I totally respect everyone else's approach, but ours was obviously the best. I mean, the fact that Yorgos actually took his leaf with him when he left . . . Like, I actually think it made him see stuff differently. I hope so.'

She linked arms with us both and we wandered down the hall.

'I feel like I might sleep with Yorgos at some point, y'know,' Mary said, as if she was mulling over what to have for dinner. 'Like, I know it's a cliché to sleep with your tutor, but when they're that hot . . .'

'Yeah, seconded,' Phoebe said. 'I think his hotness makes him impervious to clichés.'

'Thirded,' I said, and they both laughed.

Mary stopped. 'You guys are coming to Fit Sister later, right?' She said it like it wasn't actually a question, more a statement. And in the third person, like she wasn't even in Fit Sister.

'Definitely, yeah,' I said.

'Cool. I'll see you there. Just need to go pick up the smoke machine . . .'

PHOEBE

I spent two hours pulling every single item of clothing out of my wardrobe, before deciding I didn't own anything cool enough to wear to a Fit Sister gig. I settled on classic wallflower jeans and a plain T-shirt and vowed to buy an electric-blue vest dress just in case this ever happened again.

I met Luke outside Gildas Bar, and as soon as we walked in I felt self-conscious.

The whole place was full of people who looked like they were one hundred per cent part of the Bowl-Cut tribe. People with bright aqua hair tied in buns on top of their heads. A girl wearing a Run DMC vest top and a sequin skirt, and another one wearing baggy combats but also a wedding veil. She was just randomly wearing a full-length wedding veil. The boys were all good looking in a cool, alternative way.

Me and Luke, sitting with our drinks at the side, looked like a mum and dad who had accidentally walked into the wrong tent at a festival.

'I do not feel cool enough to be here,' he whispered.

I wanted to say, 'You are, but I'm definitely not.' But I just said: 'Me neither.'

The lights went down and a few people cheered, and suddenly Mary was up on stage, standing behind a massive keyboard and a microphone. Under the black light you could see she had UV stars painted all over her stomach.

Next to her was a hot bloke with shaggy hair and a moth-eaten jumper. He was also stood behind a keyboard and mic stand. It took a couple of seconds for me to place him, but as soon as I did I whipped out my phone.

'Such a groupie.' Luke shook his head as I pressed 'record'.

I covered the clip in hearts and sent it to Frankie and Negin: 'Interesting Thought Boy is performing LIVE before my eyes.'

'We are Fit Sister,' Mary yelled into the mic. 'You guys aren't ready for us yet . . . but your kids are gonna love us.'

She and ITB both started whacking their keyboards, making a kind of music I have literally no idea how to describe. It sounded a bit like a computer game playing underwater, with Mary's distorted singing over the top. She actually had a really good voice.

People at the front started dancing. Or, not really dancing dancing, but sort of swaying and nodding and jerking about wildly.

'D'you think that bloke's all right?' Luke nodded at a guy in a Sherlock hat who was flailing his arms about by the speaker. 'He looks like he's having a seizure.'

'Everyone here is mental, but in the coolest possible way. Like, treading the line between headlining-at-Glastonbury and being-committed-to-an-insane-asylum.' I took a sip of my drink. 'I'm definitely the geekiest person here.'

'Geek power.' Luke raised his fist in salute.

'You are so not a geek. You're one hundred per cent pure jock.'

Luke actually looked offended. 'I hate that word. It's like you're just a dumb knobhead who's not interested in anything except football.'

Negin and Frankie had sent a photo back; they were both in their PJs, drinking hot chocolate. Frankie had written, 'Can't BELIEVE you wouldn't let us come. As if we really would have embarrassed you in front of Quidditch Bailer. Tell ITB that Negin is his ONE TRUE LOVE.' Negin had just written: 'Do NOT tell ITB that. How's the date going . . .?'

On stage, ITB was now holding a small bell up to his microphone and ringing it gently in time to the drumbeat. I took another picture.

'I'm sure you're interested in other stuff,' I said to Luke. Then, because it was dark, and I was half-drunk and feeling brave, I added: 'Just not quidditch, obviously.'

He turned to look at me, and shook his head. 'Honestly Phoebe . . . I have wanted to talk to you about that for ages. Something just . . . came up, and I felt so, so bad about it and I actually really wanted to go and—'

'It's fine. It is actually really fun.' We both glanced at a couple exaggeratedly waltzing next to us.

The song ended, and Mary jabbed her finger at me and Luke: 'Yes! Big up my leaf memory seminar bredrins!'

A few people whooped around to us, and we both grinned at them. Then the music started bubbling and squelching again, with Mary wailing all over it, and Luke said: 'Come on, we've got to at least try to dance after she basically dedicated the gig to us . . .'

We made our way down to the front, and started copying the Sherlock guy. It went from awkward to really, really fun in the space of about five seconds. After three songs, we were both laughing and sweating so much we had to go back to the bar.

'Honestly, can I come to the next thing?' Luke shouted into my ear as we ordered more drinks. 'Quidditch, I mean. I really, genuinely want to.'

He stuck his hand out.

'We've shaken before, Luke Taylor,' I said. 'You are not a man of your word.'

He pulled a leaf out of his pocket. 'I swear on the rotten leaf of memory.'

'OK.' I shook his hand.

Then the lights came up, and Mary was bouncing down into the crowd, hugging people. She came over to us, with a few other girls in tow – including Sequin Skirt and Wedding Veil, who had now taken her wedding veil off.

'You guys came,' Mary howled, hugging us both.

'Of course.' Luke smiled.

She thumped the bar. 'I demand to have some booze.' The barman appeared and she started ordering.

I pointed at the 'Feminist Soc' badge on Wedding Veil girl's lapel. 'I feel bad, I still haven't been to any meetings,' I said. 'I signed up at Freshers' Fair.'

'You should totally come.' Wedding Veil smiled at me, and then Luke. 'You too.'

'Yeah, I'd definitely be up for it,' Luke said.

Mary handed him a shot. 'Luke's on the football team, so he's more into oppressing women than emancipating them, aren't you, Luke?' She clearly meant it as a joke, but the girl with the sequin skirt bristled a bit, and stared at him hard. 'Are you really on the football team?'

Luke nodded.

'So, is all that Wall of Shame stuff true, then?' she asked, and suddenly everyone was looking at Luke.

'What's the Wall of Shame stuff?' I said.

'They take photos of girls they sleep with and then rate them out of ten, and shit,' said Sequin Skirt. 'It's fucking Donald Trump-level wankerdom.'

'Yeah, and it's only a rumour, Jen,' frowned Wedding Veil. Then she turned to Luke. 'Right?'

I felt myself getting hot. What if it was true? Had Will taken a picture of me when I was asleep? He might not have messaged me back, but he wasn't that much of a bastard, surely? Panic started to rise up in my stomach. I hadn't even slept with Will. I had just slept *with* him.

Luke downed his shot and winced. 'Yeah, it's not true,' he said, wiping his lips.

Mary punched him on the shoulder. 'See? If my man Taylor says it's bollocks, then that's good enough for me.'

Luke smiled at me, and I felt relief cooling my whole body as I thought, *Me too.*

CHAPTER 14

LUKE

It freaked me out how quickly it was happening.

How quickly I'd gone from fancying Phoebe in this vague, daydreamy, nothingy way, to fancying her in solid, this-might-actually-happen concrete.

When I was around her, I was constantly on edge. I felt that weird, unexplainable electricity you get when you like some-one new. I hadn't felt that since Abbey sat down next to me at the start of Year Ten French, and it made me scared and guilty and excited all at the same time.

Just thinking about seeing her made me pick up my pace as I left the pitches. It was a weirdly warm morning for late October, and me and Will were strolling back through Jutland after an early five-a-side. We'd played our first proper match last week – against Chester Uni – and lost 4–2, so Will was in-sisting we all practise at every available opportunity.

I hadn't really been able to focus on today's game, because

I was so caught up in Phoebe thoughts. We'd arranged to meet at our poetry lecture, and then head straight over to the quidditch thing afterwards.

'You coming for a pint, then?' Will asked, looking at his phone.

'It's not even half ten.'

'Is that a yes?'

'I've got a lecture.' I considered telling him about quidditch, but instantly decided against it. Firstly because I was fairly certain he'd take the piss, but also because I still wasn't sure what had actually happened between him and Phoebe. I'd seen him get with tons of girls over the past few weeks, so he couldn't have been that into her. But I still wondered what he'd think if he knew I liked her. And I wondered what she thought about him.

His phone beeped and he flashed it under my nose. 'Fuck, man. She's hot. Well played, Geordie Al.'

I looked at the photo, and figured this was as good a time as any to try and say something about the Wall of Shame. About how off I thought it was.

I tried to sound casual: 'By the way, I never told you. I was out a few nights back and this girl said something about the Wall of Shame stuff. Like, how she'd heard rumours about it.'

Will's face tightened. 'You didn't say anything, did you?'

'No . . .'

His face relaxed back into a smile, which made me feel sort of dirty and complicit somehow. As if I'd told that lie out of team loyalty, rather than just panicking under the pressure and shame, and blurting it out.

'Some girls are so fucking uptight, honestly.' Will shook his head. 'I mean, people take pictures of people all the time. It's just banter.'

I nodded. But it really didn't feel like banter.

'I'd better go,' I said.

I sprinted all the way across campus, hoping I'd get to the lecture early enough to get a seat next to Phoebe. But in the end I was still five minutes late. I took a deep breath and pushed the doors as gently as possible, but they squeaked ridiculously loudly, and about a hundred heads turned to look at me.

'Ah . . . There's always one, isn't there?' said the lecturer, peering up over his glasses. 'In you come, quick as possible.'

There was only one free seat – in the middle of a packed row near the back. I squeezed my way through, apologizing to the muttering people who had to stand up. Finally, I sat down, massively relieved not to be the centre of attention any more.

And then my phone went off.

And a hundred heads turned. Again.

'There's always one, isn't there?' said the lecturer. 'Although, it's not usually the same one.' The muttering had now blossomed into full-blown laughter.

'Right . . .' said the lecturer, sternly, as I put my phone on silent and took out my copy of *Modern Romantic Poetry*. 'Let's get back to it. Now then, by 1542, Henry VIII's alliance with the Holy Roman Emperor Charles V causes him to intervene in the Italian War . . .'

I stopped unpacking my bag and looked around the hall. I

couldn't see Phoebe. In fact, I couldn't see a single person I recognized, apart from the massive *Game of Thrones* bloke who'd walked out of the football initiation. And he'd definitely not been in any of my other lectures. He was sat two seats down, scribbling notes and scratching his stubbly rust-coloured beard. He looked across at my poetry book, and wrote something on his phone. He slid it over to me: 'WRONG ROOM PAL'.

I slumped forward on to the desk as he tried to stifle his laughter.

An hour later, I had a decent – if ultimately useless – grasp of Henry VIII's foreign policy, and me and the giant shuffled out of the hall and introduced ourselves properly. He was called Ed, and since he was in Gildas College – where the quidditch thing was happening – we ended up walking in the same direction. He was so tall that his dirty blond afro nearly brushed the top of the covered walkway.

'How was the rest of that initiation, then?' he asked.

'Your walkout was probably the highlight.'

He smiled. 'That Dempers seemed like a right knobhead.'

'Yeah. He is a bit. But the rest of them are cool. Mostly.'

Ed just shrugged.

'Do you really not drink, then?' I asked him.

'Nah, never,' he said. 'Tried it once. Had five pints of lager. It had no effect whatsoever. Must be my size, I suppose. So I don't bother with it now. Just stick to the pineapple juice. Much tastier.'

'But didn't you think about drinking just for that night? So you could get on the team?'

'Not really. I mean, I like football and that, but if being on the team means putting up with all that lads-lads-lads bullshit, then I'm best off out of it, I reckon. Plenty of other stuff to do here.'

We crossed the Stephanie Stevens bridge, and something stopped me in my tracks.

'Fuck. I know that smell . . .'

Rita and Arthur were lying on the grass, both leafing through massive books while Arthur ate a wedge of brie like a pizza slice. He almost choked on it when he spotted Ed. 'Jesus, look at the size of him,' he sputtered.

Ed sniffed deeply. 'That's good-quality brie, is that. Very nice.'

'Exactly.' Arthur snapped his book shut. 'I wish you were on our corridor. I'm surrounded by fucking savages. No offence, Luke.'

'None taken,' I said. 'Ed, this is Arthur and Rita. Arthur and Rita, Ed.'

'Where are you guys off to?' Rita asked.

'I'm going to this quidditch thing. You lot should come if you want.'

Rita's lips twitched. 'Ah . . . Accidental Text Girl?'

'Who's Accidental Text Girl?' Ed asked.

'No one. It's too long to explain. Look, are you lot coming or not?' I checked my phone. 'I'm late as it is. And it could be quite fun. It's just a friendly match, I think. There'll probably be free food. And free pineapple juice.'

'I've got a seminar,' Rita said, but Arthur stood up and

dusted his coat off. 'Yeah, fuck it, I'm in.'

Ed shrugged. 'Me too. Though if anyone tries to handcuff me, I'm straight out the door.'

PHOEBE

'Sorry, but if he bails this time, none of us are speaking to him again. Ever. The end.' Frankie didn't look angry, she looked upset.

Negin nodded and sipped her cream-soda-and-syrup butterbeer. 'Me and you haven't even spoken to him anyway. But yeah, to do this twice, he'd have to be either mentally unhinged or genuinely evil.'

'Or dead,' I said, hopefully. 'I mean, why did he miss the lecture? This is so gutting it's tragic. I kept telling people I was saving his seat, and then I had to sit with an empty space next to me for the whole hour.' I really, really thought he'd come. 'He's such a *dick*,' I added.

'Scrap that, no he's not.' Frankie squeezed my arm. 'And, sorry, but who the *hell* is that with him?'

We all looked over at the entrance to the hall. Luke was walking towards us, smiling, with two other boys next to him. I didn't even realize I was smiling back until Negin whispered: 'Look how cute you are. It's disgusting.'

Frankie still had a tight grip on my arm. 'Sorry but I think I might actually die. Look. How. Tall. He. Is.'

She squeezed harder with each syllable.

'Sorry I'm late,' Luke said. 'Went to the wrong lecture.'

'I can vouch for that, he did.' The tall boy nodded.

'Nothing's started yet.' I tried to sound offhand, but seeing Luke in the flesh was weird; because I spent so much time intensely thinking about him when he wasn't there, it was like dreams and real life muddling together.

'I'm Luke.' He smiled at Frankie and Negin.

'Arthur,' the boy next to him added. 'First time quidditcher. Or is it quiditchee?'

'Quidditcher, I reckon,' said the ridiculously tall boy, who had a strong northern accent. 'If you're doing the quidditch, you'd be a quidditcher. Like if you're doing a murder, you're a murderer.' Then he smiled at us. 'I'm Ed, by the way.'

'So, it's Ed and Arthur,' I repeated.

'And you're . . . Luke, was it?' Frankie said 'Luke' as if it was a strange foreign name that she was hearing for the first time. 'Yes, I think Phoebe's mentioned you.'

I made a mental note to kick her later in her sleep.

'You have to go and sign up.' Negin nodded over to the table where Brandon and Misty were sitting, and the boys wandered off to join the queue.

Frankie slipped her arms around us as she watched them go: 'He's tall and fit and he knows about grammar and quidditch and murder. He's literally the perfect man. He—' She broke off as Luke came back. When she'd turned to Negin, I whispered, 'Does Ed have a girlfriend?'

Luke smirked at me. 'I don't know, why, are you interested?' Our eyes met for a second.

'No . . .' I said slowly. He was still smiling his fit smile at me, and I willed myself not to go red. 'I was asking for Frankie. She's

204

been looking for a tall man since the first night of Freshers'.'

'Noted. Let's make it happen.' He looked around the hall at people warming up and comparing broomsticks. 'So what goes on at this thing, then?'

'Right, well –' I pointed at Brandon, who was bobbing up and down excitedly – 'that's Brandon. He's the jolly one. And that –' I pointed at Misty, who was wearing a dark-red camouflage hoody and looking pissed off – 'That's Misty. She's the not-jolly one.'

He looked at me. 'Misty?'

I nodded. 'I know, I know. Me and Negin and Frankie have already discussed it.' We both laughed, and then Brandon gathered us all together in a little circle.

'Right, thanks for coming, gang,' he said. 'I'm seeing some new faces here tonight, which is super exciting, isn't it, Mist?'

Misty was looking at us like she wanted to kill us, but she still agreed that it was super exciting.

Brandon carried on: 'Competitive matches start next week, so today will just be a bit of fun. We'll play a few friendlies among ourselves. Right, grab some brooms, people,' he shouted. 'Let's do this!'

I realized I was going to have to actually do physical exercise in front of Luke Taylor. I tried to sneak a look at him in a non-bait way. And when I did, he was looking right back at me.

LUKE

The Brandon bloke was the most excitable person I'd ever seen. He was like someone had trapped a rabbit in a human body then wrapped it in a Gryffindor robe.

'OK, so for the friendlies, we usually divide up into houses,' he yelled. 'So, let's just see if we have anything even resembling equal numbers . . .' He looked around the circle, and his gaze rested on Arthur. 'How about you, mate? Didn't see you at our first meeting. What's your name?'

'Arthur.'

'Great. And what house are you in?'

Arthur shrugged. 'No idea. I don't really care about Harry Potter, to be honest.'

Brandon smiled, completely unoffended. 'OK, cool, well let's put you in Hufflepuff, then.'

Arthur snorted. 'Fuck off. No *way* am I Hufflepuff.'

Frankie let out a yelp of laughter so loud it echoed round the hall.

Misty stepped forward and clapped Arthur on the shoulder, proudly. 'Yeah, you're right. Hot-headed, fiery, passionate . . . You're Gryffindor through and through, aren't you?'

Arthur sniffed and tried to regain some of his composure. 'Yeah, I guess. Maybe. Whatever. I mean, it's not like I care either way.'

'Oh, well, in that case,' said Brandon, 'if you don't mind being Hufflepuff . . .'

'No, we've *said* I'm Gryffindor now, haven't we,' Arthur snapped. 'So I might as well definitely be Gryffindor. Definitely.'

We split up into two groups. I got put in Ravenclaw with Ed and Negin. We were playing Hufflepuff, who had Phoebe and Frankie on their team.

'I've been given a fucking mop!' I heard Arthur yell from across the hall, where Gryffindor were getting ready to take on Slytherin. 'I'm supposed to be a wizard, not a caretaker!'

Somebody blew a whistle, and even though half of us had no clue what to do, we started playing.

One of the first years chucked me the ball straight away, and I saw Phoebe sprinting towards me. For half a second I had the mad idea to just keep hold of it, and see if she would crash right into me.

But I didn't. I chucked it to Ed, and Phoebe pulled up an inch from my chest.

She hitched an eyebrow and smiled. 'So nearly.' Then she sprinted off again, and I suddenly wondered whether I was the first person in history to feel horny on a quidditch pitch.

Ed was legging it down the wing, the ball clamped under his arm. He stopped short in front of the goal hoop things. Frankie went galloping madly towards him, but he chucked the ball right past her into the top hoop.

Our team all went mental, and even Frankie started clapping, until one of the Hufflepuffs shouted: 'You're not on their team!'

The Hufflepuff keeper immediately started scanning for a decent pass. I drifted over to Phoebe, and stood right behind her.

'Right, I'm marking you, Bennet,' I said. 'There's no way you're getting past me.'

She stepped backwards into me gently, scraping the inside of my leg with her broomstick. 'This isn't football, Luke Taylor.' She turned to look at me, her cheeks flushed. 'This is a proper sport, yeah? You're out of your depth.'

I was finding it pretty hard to concentrate on anything except Phoebe, but I tried to get my head back in the game as the Hufflepuffs were jogging out of their area.

Someone shouted, 'Mark up!' and I yelled, 'Got Phoebe!'

'No one's marking me,' Frankie bellowed, looking directly at Ed. 'I mean, someone should be marking me, shouldn't they?' Ed was totally oblivious to this; he was just watching the ball.

One of the Hufflepuffs tried a long pass, but Ed plucked it out of the air with his tree trunk arm. He chucked it to Negin, who stared at it blankly for a second and then burst off down the wing.

It stopped everyone dead. 'Negin,' hissed Frankie. 'Are you joking?'

Negin was unbelievably quick. The Hufflepuff beaters launched three 'bludgers' (flat volleyballs) at her, but she dodged them all. Without slowing down, she sent the ball straight through the top hoop, and our team went mad again.

Misty stood up and shouted from the sidelines at Ed and Negin: 'You and you – what are your names?'

They told her and she started scribbling furiously on her notepad.

It was weird: that same edge that comes out in me on the football pitch suddenly came out here, too. I really wanted to win.

Hufflepuff got a goal back, but me and Ed passed it about neatly, then I sent Negin off on another blazing run. Again, she slammed the ball through the hoop, and the three of us high-tenned.

Brandon jostled about among the chaos, slapping people on the back and randomly shouting encouragement. He'd grin at you if you did something right, and he'd grin more brightly if you did something wrong. When Frankie nearly decapitated him by swinging her broom at the ball, he just fell about laughing and started calling her 'Belinda Broomswing'.

Eventually, when we were 14–10 up, another whistle blew, and the Ravenclaws all cheered and collapsed on to the floor. I felt sweaty and knackered and the happiest I had done in ages.

Misty asked me and Phoebe if we'd mind putting the goal hoops away, and I could feel Frankie and Negin's eyes on us as we wheeled them out into the corridor. We found the store room and propped the hoops up against an old table tennis table. And then we were just stood there, still red-faced and a bit out of breath, looking at each other. Realizing that we were completely alone in a dusty back room. Just smiling and breathing and not saying anything. We both knew it was gonna happen, and it was sort of exciting and excruciating at the same time.

Phoebe mumbled, 'OK, then . . .' and we both laughed, awkwardly. I felt my heartbeat up its pace, and just as thoughts of Abbey were starting to tumble into my head, she leant forward, and then I leant forward, and then she closed her eyes.

And then it was like I stopped thinking altogether.

I put my arms around her, and we were suddenly right up against each other, sticky with sweat, and kissing harder and harder.

CHAPTER 15

PHOEBE

Frankie took her full-to-the-brim Shreddies and hot milk out of the microwave and pigeon-stepped to the table so they didn't spill. Negin and me were eating honey on toast.

'I'm gonna leave it to dry for a bit,' Frankie said. 'I only like it when it's turned into a kind of paste.' She picked up a bag of sugar and started shaking it out over the top of the gloopy brown mixture. Negin wrinkled her nose slightly.

'So, would you say Luke Taylor is your official boyfriend now?' Frankie took an un-offered bite of Negin's toast.

I shook my head. 'As if. Would you say random-Freshers'-pull is *your* boyfriend? We've kissed. Once.'

Negin shook her head. 'Come on, it's different. You've had this *really* long build-up.'

Since it had happened I had felt permanently giddy. I had never had this feeling, about anything, ever. The closest was when I was so bored in GCSE study leave that I entered an

211

online competition and won a luxury holiday to Disneyland, Florida for my whole family. It was the same kind of initial quake and then tremors of fuzzy, giggly aftershock that made me feel like some kind of epic hero.

'Did you tell Flora?' Negin asked.

'Yup. She literally started hyperventilating. She acted as if we had achieved it together. Like a joint Oscar win.' She had just kept saying, 'You've fucking *kissed* Luke Taylor. You *did* it,' over and over again. Which was pretty much what was going through my head, even in real time as it was actually happening. Like my subconscious was yelling, *'What the hell? This is cracked out. Is this even real?'*

Frankie started to eat the congealed sugar crust on her Shreddies. 'He obviously likes you. I mean, he messaged you *"goodnight"*. "Goodnight" is the most meaningful message you can send someone. It's more than "I love you". "Goodnight" actually incorporates "I love you". Because you only message people you *love* "goodnight". No one has ever messaged me "goodnight". Literally, no one.'

'I just really want to know what happened with him and Abbey,' I said. 'But it's impossible to find out.'

'Is there any way you could like . . . bring it up casually?' Negin suggested.

'No, because that will instantly make me seem like a crazy person who wants to marry him.'

'Fair. Both ways. I mean, you do.' Frankie poured another layer of sugar into her bowl. 'I was telling my mum about it last night. Do you know the woman from Abba married her stalker?'

I snorted into my tea. 'OK, stop saying stuff like that out loud. Although, you know, I only have about four memories before I saw Luke Taylor. I know because I counted them recently.'

Negin looked up from her toast. 'You specifically counted the number of memories you have before you first saw him? That's quite weird. No offence, but that is a bit stalkerish.'

'I think it's romantic,' said Frankie. 'But I have a really bad memory, so I don't have a lot of memories pre the first time I met Ed yesterday.'

'I didn't specifically count them in relation to him. We're doing memory on my course. Like how memory is what makes literature. How you can't have the written word without memory.'

'I have no clue what we do in Archaeology,' Frankie yawned. 'They keep talking about science. No one ever told me it had anything to do with science. I'm absolutely crap at science.' She took another mouthful of Shreddies paste. 'So, what *is* the deal with this Abbey, then?'

'I can't find anything out about her,' I said. 'As in she used to be social media obsessed and she has, like . . . disappeared.'

'Oh my god, do you think Luke Taylor killed her?' Frankie said.

'He does play sport.' Negin nodded. 'More testosterone.'

'*You* play sport,' I said.

'Negin's killed mad amounts of people,' Frankie shouted. 'With her resting bitch face alone.'

I got up and put more bread in the toaster. 'Seriously,

though, Abbey has vanished. Literally vanished. And now I have absolutely no way at all of finding out what happened between her and Luke.'

'Except asking Luke . . .' Negin shrugged. 'Which would be fairly straightforward.'

'Obviously, I'm not gonna do that.'

Becky walked in wrapped in a massive coat, carrying a pile of parcels.

'Beckster,' Frankie shouted, even though she was about a metre away from her. She held up her hand and Becky put the parcels on the table and very gently high-fived her. 'How come you're back?'

Becky tucked her hair behind her ears. 'Me and Aaron had a fight so I got an earlier train.' I looked at her more closely. Her eyes were ever so slightly red.

I jumped up and pulled out a chair for her. 'Are you OK?'

She nodded. 'Yeah, I just . . . it'll be fine. I'm gonna call him in a bit.' She sounded tired. 'I might go home again on Tuesday.'

Frankie shook her head. 'Tuesday is Halloween. You have to come to the 999 thing. Pre's here first. I'm making cocktails inspired by everyone's personalities. You say vodka and Fanta to me, with a dash of green syrup.' She picked her bowl up and tipped the last of the milk into her mouth.

'All we have currently is vodka, Fanta and some green syrup,' Negin said.

Frankie picked up one of the parcels and started unwrapping it. 'Speaking of the 999 party . . .' She tore open the plastic packaging with force and emptied the contents on to the table.

A weird white plasticky dress with a red cross on it fell out. We all looked at the cardboard insert with a stripper-type woman on that said 'Sexy Nurse Costume'. Frankie sniffed it. 'It smells really weird. Like marker pen. Shall we try them on?'

We traipsed back to my room and she immediately started flinging her clothes off. Becky zipped her up in the costume, and she turned around and threw her arms in the air like she was opening a show in Vegas.

'It weirdly makes you look even taller,' I said. 'I think it's because the dress is so tiny. Your legs look insanely long. Like they are three quarters of your body.'

'Like a daddy-long-legs? Bitch.' Frankie scowled, and changed model pose. 'What am I supposed to do? Go to the giant's costume emporium?'

'If someone spills their drink on you, at least you can just wipe it off.' Negin squinted at her. 'Is it made of pencil-case material?'

'No, Negin, I just look like an actual pencil.' She tried to pull the suspender things up but they only reached a bit over her knees. 'I thought the only people who actually wore suspenders were Victoria's Secret models, so why are they so short?'

'I'll have the opposite problem,' I said. 'I bet mine are too long and go right up to my bum.'

'And there is this gap for my boobs, but I have no boobs to put in it.' Frankie swung round to Becky, who was sitting on my bed. 'Becky, you aren't a bitch like these two. Be honest, if you were Ed, would you find me in any way sexual in this outfit?'

Becky looked a bit overwhelmed by the question. 'Um . . .'

215

Me and Negin burst out laughing. 'Sorry, you are sexual,'
I said. 'It was just Becky's face . . . And the way you said
"sexual".'

'Fuck you all,' Frankie said, and one of the suspenders fell
around her ankles. She plonked down next to Becky. 'Do you
know my mum is actually a nurse? And they don't even wear
this shit. They wear tunics like women on beauty counters.
Maybe I should have got the £23.99 one. Did you get the £23.99
one? Come on, I want to see yours.'

Usually I would have felt a bit self-conscious showing people
my body, but Frankie seemed so at home with hers that it kind
of made me want to feel at home in mine. Even if I didn't.

I think, in my whole life, Frankie was the only girl apart
from Mum I had seen completely naked. In PE at school, everyone was so careful, wriggling around inside their Aertex tops.
Even when I had been away with Flora, we had put our biki-
nis on in the bathroom. But the first night Frankie had stayed
in my room, she had just stripped off, and it had kind of
mesmerized me. Partly just seeing another person's naked
body and partly because she didn't think it was weird. Like
she had never got the memo about squirming around in your
T-shirt to take your bra off at a sleepover.

I opened the plastic packet and started to get changed, trying
to affect Frankie's give-a-shit vibe.

'You look way more like an actual nurse than Frankie does,'
Negin said. 'I think the green colour helps.'

'I feel like one of the fairies from Cinderella. It really poofs
out at the waist.'

I sat on the bed and tried to work out how to put the suspenders on. In the end we had to watch a YouTube video to figure it out. I stood up and looked at myself. 'They kind of funnel all my fat upwards and then it spills over the top of them. Like I'm a cupcake and my fat is buttercream icing.'

'Why are blokes so into them?' Frankie said. 'Can you ask Luke? Let's get a picture. Do a nurse face.'

I stood up straight and did a sort of stern-but-kind face. Negin shook her head as she took the picture.

'I think the suspender thing is because of olden-day prostitutes.' Frankie undid her other stocking. 'And maybe they fancy nurses because they're . . . kind?'

'I find boys really weird sometimes.' I looked at myself in the mirror. 'I will definitely sweat shitloads in this fabric. Fuck it. I'm not gonna wear it. It's a joke. Who am I?'

Frankie flopped down on the bed. 'Well if you're not gonna wear it, then I'll feel even more ridiculous. Do you think we can get the £12.99 back?'

'Let's just both not wear it. In fact, let's just agree to never wear suspenders, ever. I'm not a prostitute from the olden days. Or any kind of health worker. So it would be false advertising.'

'Agreed,' said Frankie. 'Let's shake on it.'

'Just wear scrubs like me and Becky.' Negin shrugged. 'We're gonna steal them from M Block tomorrow. We'll steal you some, too.'

My phone started flashing on the bed. I looked at the screen, then looked up. 'Fuck.'

'Who is it?' Negin frowned. 'Why do you look so scared?'

'Oh my god, is it ISIS?' Frankie yelled.

'Yes, it's ISIS,' Negin yelled back. 'They always phone Phoebe before they strike.'

Becky laughed. The phone was still flashing and I didn't know what to do. 'It's Luke,' I said.

'Shut. Up.' Before I could stop her, Frankie snatched it out of my hand.

'Don't be a twat, Frankie!' I screamed. 'This is my life.'

'"This is my life,"' Negin repeated, and she and Becky cracked up again. Frankie shushed them and hit answer. 'Hi, Luke Taylor.' She jumped up on to the bed and held the phone so high I couldn't reach it.

'Oh my god,' I whisper-groaned and jumped on to the bed next to her, elbowing her in the stomach to try and get the phone back.

'Yes, it's Frankie. It was delightful to meet you yesterday. Top, top quidditching on your part . . . What . . . Oh, right . . . Oh, really?'

I mouthed, 'What's he saying?' Her face changed and she nodded frantically at the window.

Standing on the grass outside, looking up at us with a slightly bemused expression, was Luke.

LUKE

'Is that how you always dress for breakfast, then?'

Her mouth twitched, like she was trying to pin back a smile. 'Yeah. Obviously. It's D Block tradition. We wake up, put on our latex nurse outfits, have some Shreddies . . .'

218

I looked back at D Block as we headed up the walkway to our lecture. Frankie was still wearing the costume and dancing at us through the kitchen window.

'So, were they for the 999 thing?' I asked.

She tilted her head at me. 'No, Luke, I just randomly bowl about the place dressed like a sexy nurse.'

I tilted back. 'Well, you might do.' I was slightly disappointed she hadn't come downstairs still wearing it. I wondered how long I should wait before trying to kiss her again. It was pretty much all I'd thought about since we'd left the hall yesterday.

'What are you going as?' she asked.

I shrugged. 'I'll probably just borrow a lab coat off one of the chemists. Go as a doctor.'

She buttoned her jacket up against the wind. 'It's weird how people consider doctors and nurses inherently sexy. Like, why?'

'Well . . . They do spend a lot of time around naked people.'

'Yeah, but naked people who are either ill or dead.'

'True. And no one finds undertakers sexy. To be honest, I reckon blokes just like any outfit that shows a lot of bare flesh.' I put my hands up. 'I apologize for my gender.'

She nodded. 'Apology accepted. I should warn you that me and Frankie have decided to fuck the whole sexy nurse thing off, anyway. We're just gonna wear scrubs with Negin and Becky.'

'Good plan.'

'Is your mate Ed gonna come? Frankie's obsessed with him.' She stopped and slapped her hand across her mouth. 'Don't

219

tell Ed that, obviously. Unless he's obsessed with her, too. Is he obsessed with her, too?'

We kept walking. 'No idea. I'll pump him for info next time I see him.'

'No, Luke. You have to be subtle.'

I looked at her, mock-offended. 'I am subtle, Phoebe. I'm super subtle. Don't worry about that.'

She half glanced at me, her mouth twitching again.

We got to the lecture and found seats near the back of the hall. It was so packed that everyone was bunched right up together, like sardines on ridiculously uncomfortable folding seats. Because me and Phoebe were sat so close, our legs kept brushing under the desk, and after a while it became a sort of game. One of us would nudge the other, the other would nudge back harder, with both of us trying – not very successfully – to keep a straight face.

Because of all this, by the time the lecture finished, I had learnt literally nothing. I wondered as we walked out if I was ever going to take on *any* new knowledge during my three years here. If my parents knew my loan was being spent on nudging legs and obsessing over text messages, they'd be fucking furious.

We traipsed up the hill to the library and got the books we needed for the next seminar. When we were back outside, I suddenly realized that we had no more legitimate, scheduled reasons to keep hanging out.

'Do you fancy a cup of tea, or something?' I asked, hopefully.

'Yeah, that'd be nice.'

We went into the vaguely litigious library cafe, 'Starcups' – which was half-heartedly decked out with rubber skeletons and pumpkins – and got teas and M&M cookies. Then we went and sat underneath the massive tree by the edge of the lake. It was jacket-and-gloves cold, but the air was fresh and the sky was clear blue. The ground was covered in conkers, and Phoebe picked one up. 'I used to love playing conkers with my brother.'

A memory bumped me out of nowhere. 'Hey, do you re-member when Tom Gale got suspended for whacking Dhiraj on the head with a conker? When was that? Year Eight?'

'Oh yeah. We had a whole assembly on "conker safety" the day after. But I thought it was Dhiraj who conkered Tom, after Tom shot him with a BB gun? Tom Gale was definitely a bit of a psycho.'

'I still find it so weird that we have all these memories in common, but we didn't even know each other until the start of this month.' I handed her the biggest, glossiest conker I could see. 'Here, this will definitely win any conker clash you'll ever enter. You'd be able to knock Tom Gale out cold with this one.'

She smiled and put it in her jacket pocket, and I suddenly couldn't wait any longer. I leant over and we were kissing again.

It felt even better than yesterday, but we definitely weren't at that point yet where we could go straight back into post-kiss normal conversation. As soon as we broke apart, a slightly awkward silence settled.

I glanced across the lake and noticed a big group of people milling about on the other side. One of them broke away, and it seemed like he was looking at us, but he was too far away to tell. Suddenly, he stuck up a hand and waved, and I realized it was Will. We both waved back. It was impossible to read his expression. The silence felt heavier suddenly.

'I might live with Will next year, actually,' I said, without really knowing why. Just to break the silence, I guess. 'I mean, it's not definite, or anything . . .'

'Oh, right.' Phoebe nodded. 'Cool.' She picked up another conker.

I wondered again what she thought about Will. How serious their Freshers' Week thing had actually been. I didn't care that they'd probably hooked up, but I did care that he might have taken a photo of her. That she might be up there somewhere, on the Wall of Shame, with Dempers and everyone posting comments about her. Since I could only see the group from the day I'd been added, there was literally no way of knowing.

'I'm freaking out about the whole house thing, to be honest,' Phoebe said.

'Surely you'll live with Frankie and Negin?'

She shrugged and stared down at the conker. 'We haven't talked about it yet. Negin's got loads of mates on her course, and Frankie knows literally everyone on campus. So, I dunno.'

'Yeah, the whole thing's really stressful.'

I looked across the lake and watched Will a second longer as he walked away.

PART 4

CHAPTER 16

PHOEBE

Turned out I did *not* look sexy in scrubs.

They were enormous on me and smelt like toilet cleaner. But it was kind of awesome. Like being in a club wearing an invisibility cloak. Usually I spend all night checking out how much the humidity is making my hair frizz in the mirrors, but I just didn't care this time. And, collectively, it made us all go mental.

At one point, I took a running jump and launched myself into Josh. He was dressed as a fireman and had literally not left the dance floor since we'd arrived. He managed to catch me but the force sent us both crashing into the speaker.

'Bennet, you are crazy tonight,' he shouted at me.

'It's always there,' I yelled. 'It just pops out into the world every so often.'

The song changed, and he closed his eyes and started to do such exaggerated ravey hand moves that people had to step back to give him space.

I felt someone's arms around my waist and a kiss on my cheek. 'Ed is here,' Frankie yelled in my ear. 'Like, here. Not here. But near. Near here. In the club. I feel sick.'

'Do you need to go to the toilet?'

'No, sick with *love*. I just need to dance. Dance it out.' She kissed me again. Even Negin and Becky were going for it. Becky had let a boy dressed as a policeman carry her to the DJ booth to request a song and Negin was introducing some of her Medicine mates to the quidditch lot.

Luke waved his stethoscope at me from across the room, where he was talking to Ed and Arthur. I'd become sort of addicted to him. I liked being alone so I could think about him uninterrupted. I liked re-reading his messages and smiling to myself and thinking again and again about things he had said or moments that had passed between us. I had become one of *those* people. I had become obsessed with memory and had started collecting stuff. Serviettes from cafes we had been to and notes he had written me in the library after we had been told to shut up. It had been less than a week, but I was in it so deep. I missed him as soon as he left. I wanted him to message me straight away. But in the club it was perfect. Like we both knew the other one was there, and that we would go home together, so we could just relax and have fun until then. Every so often we would catch eyes across the dance floor and it felt amazing. Like he was addicted to me, too.

Negin squeezed through the crowd and mouthed: 'Do you want a drink?'

We walked over to the bar. 'Is it weird being sober when everyone else is pissed?' I asked her.

She smiled. 'The most annoying thing is that everyone constantly repeats themselves.'

I nodded. 'Is it weird being sober when everyone else is pissed?'

She rolled her eyes, and waved the barman over. 'Phoebs, I just heard something . . . A girl on my course told me this thing about the football team.' She looked down like she was debating how to say whatever it was she wanted to say. 'She said they do this gross thing. They take pictures of girls they've . . .' She made a face. 'Anyway, they take pictures of them asleep and then rate them on the group chat.'

I shook my head. 'It's totally fine, I've heard this whole thing already. Honestly, it's totally not true. You can tell her she doesn't have to worry. It's just a stupid rumour someone made up.'

Negin smiled weakly. 'Are you sure? She sounded really upset about it.'

'Honestly, Negin, one hundred per cent. Someone asked Luke about it at Bowl-Cut's gig. He said it's bullshit. And he is, like, their star player, so he would know, right?'

Negin picked up her bottle of water and handed me my gin and tonic. She took a breath and almost said something else.

'Thank you for worrying, though,' I shouted. I almost added that I had been worried about Will when I'd heard about it. But I didn't.

At just gone midnight I said goodbye to the girls and me

and Luke left.

We bought chips and walked home slowly and then sneaked back into D Block and made tea.

In my room, we lay next to each other, staring at the ceiling.

'I wonder who has slept in this room before,' I said. 'These halls were built sixty years ago. So at least sixty people have laid in this exact same place, staring at the ceiling.'

I pulled a bit of the duvet back and climbed underneath. He did the same. I reached over and switched the lamp off. And then wondered what he was thinking about me doing it. It was a sign that I knew he was staying.

He lifted his arm up. 'Tuck in.'

Neither of us had talked about when we were going to have sex. He had slept in my bed for the past few nights, and we had done stuff, but not gone all the way. But this didn't feel like the past few nights.

We just lay there, saying random things until we both fell asleep. When I woke up we were detangled. It was still dark outside, and condensation was trickling down the window. Luke put an arm over me and pulled me closer to him. I wriggled round. We were facing each other. He leant a tiny bit further in and opened his eyes and then closed them again and we were kissing. We kissed for ages, and then, bit by bit, we were both undressed.

I kissed him on the stomach, and then wondered if I should go down on him. I get so nervous about blow jobs. It's like this thing that you can be bad at. You can't really be bad at someone putting their willy inside you. Unless it won't go in. But as long as that happens, it's sort of deemed a success. Flora gave a blow job to a boy in Majorca and he fell asleep while she was doing it, so she was obviously messing it up somehow.

I kissed him again and then did it. Just for a few seconds. Long enough to say I had done it but not long enough to mess it up in any way. Unless only doing it for a few seconds *was* messing it up. He made a noise as if he liked it. And then he threw the duvet back and cold air hit me and I shivered a bit.

'Have you got a condom?' I whispered. And then it hit me: the complete, total, bonkers surrealness of me, naked, asking Luke Taylor, naked, if he had a condom. I had to physically strain to stop from laughing. Or grabbing my phone to text Flora.

I tried to look at the ceiling politely while he put it on and then wondered if I should pat him on the back or something to keep some kind of connection going.

He turned around and kissed me. And then he pulled back a bit. In movies people just put it in easily. Like it's not complicated to get it in the right place. Like it will just happen automatically without some kind of mapwork. I held it and put it in me a tiny bit.

And then he was inside me. And it actually felt good. Really good. The surrealness resurfaced and I giggled by accident.

'Are you laughing at me?' he said, smiling. 'This is not the moment you really want a girl to start laughing uncontrollably.'

None of it felt awkward. I wouldn't say I totally lost myself in the moment. I still wondered about what I looked like and if I should be doing some porn star thing I have no idea how to do. But it was the closest I had ever felt to being myself while having sex.

Afterwards, I needed to wee, but the toilets felt so far away.

'Erm, Phoebe?' Luke sat up suddenly. I was too tired to open my eyes and look at him.

'Hmmmm?'

He paused. 'Where's the condom?'

CHAPTER 17

LUKE

'Shit! Fuck! No! What?!'

Phoebe was hopping around the room in circles, pulling her pyjama bottoms on and hissing random swear words.

I rubbed my eyes. I couldn't quite get my head around it. This seemed like way too much to handle at three o'clock in the morning. Though, to be fair, it probably would've been too much to handle at any time of the day. The cold, clammy feeling that something very, very bad was happening started to unfurl in my stomach.

'Fuck . . . Phoebe . . . I'm so sorry. What can we do? What happens now?'

'I don't know, Luke,' she snapped. 'Funnily enough, this has never happened to me before. I don't usually just walk around the place with condoms stuck inside me.'

'OK. Well . . . I'm sure we can figure this out.'

She yanked open the door. 'OK, great. That's very

reassuring. I'm going to the loo.' She checked the corridor was empty, and then she was gone. I heard her socks padding quickly along the corridor.

I pulled on my boxers, edged my way out and knocked gently on the toilet door. 'Phoebe? Is everything OK?'

'Not really,' she hissed through the door. I could hear her breathing heavily.

'What . . . should I do?'

'Can you go get Frankie and Negin?'

'Er . . . OK. Will they be up?'

'I don't know! Just get them!'

I went to the door I was fairly sure was Negin's and paused outside it. My phone said it was 3.07 a.m.

I knocked softly, and I heard Negin murmur what sounded like 'Not dead'. I thought she might be talking in her sleep, until Frankie's much louder murmur added: 'Not dead, Phoebs, both not dead. Go away, Phoebs.'

I knocked again and heard them both groan simultaneously. Then there was lots of shuffling, and Frankie's voice getting progressively louder as she approached the door. 'I don't know what the fuck you are doing knocking us up at three in the morning. You should be letting Luke Taylor knock you up. Ooh, Luke, knock me up, you're so good, Luke, oooh—'

She opened the door and blinked at me. She was wearing a duvet like a toga, and her hair was sticking up all over the place. 'Luke Taylor. I was literally just talking about you.'

'Er, yeah, sorry to wake you, Frankie. It's just Phoebe . . . She needs you. She's in the toilet.'

232

She made a face. 'Is she puking? Can't you deal with the puke? You *are* her boyfriend.'

'Well . . . not technically . . .'

Frankie narrowed her eyes. 'Not technically puking or not technically boyfriend?'

'Frankie, can this wait? Phoebe actually, genuinely needs you. Like, now.'

She sighed and swung the door fully open to reveal Negin under another duvet in the bed. 'Fine. Negin, let's go. The sisterhood calls.' Then she turned back to me: 'So, what's actually wrong with her?'

PHOEBE

I could hear people talking in the kitchen.

I could smell the toasties they were eating. I couldn't think properly knowing they were so close. I should have brought my phone. I couldn't really go back and get it now. I just had to get this over with.

I started speaking to myself in my head, like before A Level exams. Everything is going to be OK. You can do this. I rolled my shoulders back like I was about to start an Olympic sprint. Fuck. The longer you wait the more freaked out you're going to get.

I took a deep breath and pushed my fingers inside myself. I tried to move them around, but I couldn't feel anything. I sat back down on the toilet seat and then pulled my bottoms fully off. I put my leg up on the toilet, the same way Flora taught me when I put a tampon in for the first time. I pushed my fingers inside again and for a second I thought I felt it. Every time I tried I felt a bit more nauseous. It was definitely there, I just couldn't get hold of it. Oh god.

I tried to breathe deeply and then I realized I was rocking back and forth like a lunatic. My face was so boiling. I put my cheek against the cold wall and a hot tear squeezed out. Maybe I should call Mum? Or Flora? Or NHS Direct?

There was a soft knock on the door. 'Phoebe.' Negin sounded totally calm. 'Are you OK?'

'Phoebs,' Frankie hissed. 'Luke told us what happened. Don't panic. Negin is a doctor.'

'Negin is not yet a doctor,' Negin corrected her.

'I am freaking out,' I whispered. I sounded crazy. It came out like a wail.

I heard the kitchen door open and people tumble out. I shut my eyes.

There was a wallop on the door, and I heard Negin say: 'Phoebe's in there.' Then Connor bellowed: 'Phoebs, you chunder legend! I had a tactical chunder earlier and carried on.'

I heard him and the others bundling off down the corridor, and then slamming their doors. As I opened the toilet door, I realized I was actually crying. 'I don't want to go to hospital.'

Frankie was holding a toastie and Negin was wearing her fleece pyjamas. They hugged me, and we walked quickly across the hall to Negin's room.

'Where's Luke?' I whispered.

'In your room,' Negin said. 'I told him we would get him when you wanted him.'

'When you no longer had his condom womping around up your cavities.' Frankie took a bite of toastie and Negin gave her a look. 'Sorry.' She reached over and held my hand. 'It's gonna be OK.'

'Have you tried to get it out?' Negin said gently.

'Yes, I've been trying for, like, ten minutes.'

Frankie yanked her hand out of mine. 'You've just put your minge juice on me.'

'I've washed my hands, obviously.'

'There will still be minge juice traces. I don't even want to eat this toastie now. Cheese and marmite and minge.' She took a bite of the toastie and then threw it in the bin. 'I suppose people eat minge juice all the time, but still . . .'

'What am I going to do?' I put my hands over my face.

'Have you googled it?' Negin pulled her phone out of its charger. 'You google it, too,' she barked at Frankie.

'My phone is the kitchen,' she said, and walked out.

'It will be fine, I promise.' Negin's voice was really calm and comforting. 'It's in Google predict. So it obviously, you know . . . happens.'

Frankie came back in holding a jam sandwich and her phone. We all sat on the bed in silence while they googled.

'Mate, have you really like . . . got in there and tried?' Frankie said. 'Cos people on here seem to think you can definitely get in there.'

'People on where?'

'The internet. Cosmopolitan.'

'I don't know if that is . . . reputable.' Negin was scrolling

235

down her phone. 'But I can't find it on the NHS website.'

'There are loads of Yahoo answers.' Frankie shook her head. 'Mate, some of these people . . . I get why people ask the questions but who goes around answering them? Smileyturtle underscore happydayz, with a z, says: "Dude, sex before marriage is against God." He's written it in capitals: "AGAINST GOD."'

'Why do you think it's not on the NHS?' I looked at Negin.

'Because maybe it's too . . . impolite.'

'I actually love Luke Taylor.' Frankie flopped back on to the duvet. 'His little face was so confused. He looked like a newborn otter. What is going on with you and Luke Taylor anyway?'

'Frankie, there is a condom lodged in her vagina,' Negin said. 'This is not the time for relationship analysis.'

Frankie sighed melodramatically: 'Luke Taylor's so dreamy, he got a condom lodged in my vagina.'

'Is that supposed to be my voice?' I said. 'I'm not Welsh.'

'What kind of moves was LT pulling, then, eh?' Frankie took a bite of her jam sandwich and thrust her crotch forward.

I started laughing, and then I literally couldn't stop. I really hoped that Luke couldn't hear across the hall.

'Just a friendly reminder that you still have a condom stuck in you.' Negin flicked my cheek with her finger. 'Are you still drunk?'

'No,' I gasped. 'I think I'm in medical shock and now it's making me hysterical.'

Frankie leapt up. 'Have you tried jumping up and down to make it fall out?'

She started jumping and the whole room began to shake. I stood up and jumped in the air a couple of times.

'Anything going on down there?' Frankie asked, as she came to a stop.

'No. What am I going to do? I literally have no idea what to do.'

'I know what to do.' Frankie grabbed her phone.

'Are you calling an ambulance?' Negin wrinkled her brow. 'Because this is not an emergency situation.'

'It fucking is,' Frankie said.

'I don't need an ambulance,' I shouted.

'Mummy,' Frankie barked into the phone. 'Mummy, wake up, I need you. It's an emergency.'

There was no sound at all at the other end. 'Mummy?' Frankie said again. She put her phone on speaker.

'Sorry, darling,' the voice crackled. 'I've come into the conservatory and shut the door. Are you OK, Francesca?' Frankie's mum sounded like a radio announcer from the war.

'Basically, Mummy, in a nutshell, you know Phoebs, well, basically she had sex with this boy Luke Taylor . . .'

'Oh, well done, Phoebe,' her mum interrupted, cheerfully. 'Yummy Luke from school.'

'Are you joking?' I mouthed at Frankie, but she held up a hand to stop me.

'Anyway, Mummy, they had the sex, and now the condom is stuck up her fanny.'

'Oh Christ,' Frankie's mum sighed. 'Is she there with you?'

I nodded.

'She is, Mummy, but she's too embarrassed to speak. She's just nodding.'

'It's not embarrassing at all, Phoebe, darling,' Frankie's mum's boomed. 'I have seen all sorts of things up there in my time. Even a bottle of Tippex.'

'Mummy is a nurse, remember.' Frankie frowned. 'She doesn't just look up people's fannies for jokes.'

'Do we need to go to A&E?' Negin mouthed at her.

'Do we need to go to hospital, Mummy?'

'I shouldn't think so,' the voice crackled. 'If you keep calm I can tell you what to do. Wash your hands, Frankie, darling. You're going to have to try and get it out.'

Frankie recoiled. 'Mummy, that is absolutely gross. I am not putting my hand up her minge.' She looked at Negin. 'Can't you do it? You want to be a doctor.'

'Darling, it's going to be absolutely fine. Phoebe, lie down and put a cushion underneath your bottom. Frankie, try and find a light and go and wash your hands.'

There was a frantic little silence where I moved Negin's toy elephant off the pillow and lay on the bed, staring at the ceiling. Just as I was plucking up the courage to speak to Frankie's mum, Frankie hoved back into view above me wearing some sort of miner's torch on her head.

'See, I'm using my gap-year kit, Mummy. I've got the head torch on.'

'Oh, darling, well done,' the impossibly posh voice chimed. 'You just need to approach this rationally. It's probably got stuck on the side, near the top, OK?'

238

I couldn't see Negin's or Frankie's faces and they'd gone completely quiet.

'Mate, you're going to have to crack out your minge,' Frankie told me. 'We can't do it through your Minnie Mouse pyjamas.'

I wriggled out of my PJs. Frankie whistled. 'Very neat. Perfectly trimmed lawn you've got there. You clearly knew Mr Taylor was going to be—'

'Frankie.' Frankie's mum and Negin said it at the exact same time.

'This is literally the worst thing that's ever happened,' I groaned.

'Don't be ridiculous, Phoebe,' the posh voice tutted. 'There are people in camps in Syria.'

'Oh god . . .'

'Phoebe, just relax, she won't be able to do it unless you are relaxed.'

'Just imagine I'm Luke,' Frankie cooed.

'Shut up.'

'Mummy, I can't see anything, even with the torch,' she whined.

'You need to get closer and really look. Then just slide your finger in and do a sweep.'

'What the fuck are you talking about, Mummy? Phoebs, I can't do this, we'll have to go to hospital.'

'Let me look.' Negin sounded almost angry. 'Don't speak for a second, Frankie.'

I flinched as her fingers went inside me and I felt it

being pulled out.

'Negin, you fucking legend!' Frankie shouted it so loudly it must have woken the entire block.

I stood up and we all stared at the shrivelled condom lying on Negin's navy blue sheet.

'It's a boy!' Frankie shouted. And Negin laughed harder than I had literally ever seen her laugh. Even Frankie's mum was laughing on the phone.

'Mission accomplished.' Frankie grinned, and then threw her arms around me.

CHAPTER 18

LUKE

'So . . .' I said. 'This is not how my nights out usually end.'

'Or begin, I hope,' Phoebe added.

'No, exactly. At no point in the beginning, middle *or* end of my average night out do I normally end up in the family planning clinic. I swear.'

We both laughed awkwardly, and shuffled on the hard, uncomfortable, bright-orange chairs. It had been a pretty restless night's sleep, and now, at the rarely experienced hour of 8 a.m., we were sat in the waiting area of the uni sexual health centre, which was all the way across campus.

'Seriously, Phoebe. I'm really sorry. This is obviously quite, *quite* shit.' I reached down to squeeze her hand: 'Hope you're OK?'

She squeezed back: 'Yeah, 'course, it'll be all right. It's not like we didn't use protection. It's just that the protection didn't end up being as . . . protective as we'd have liked. I might get, y'know, tested, though. Just to be sure.'

'What, for . . . if you're pregnant?'

'No, they give you the morning-after pill for that. I mean for, y'know . . .' She lowered her voice. 'STIs.'

'Oh, right. Yeah, definitely. But I mean, that should be OK, shouldn't it? I've only slept with one other person. And we were both each other's first.'

What with all the condom terror, I hadn't really had time to process what had actually happened last night. I had slept with someone else. Someone who wasn't Abbey. It's not like I didn't know it was going to happen eventually, but now that it had, it still felt massive. Like things had changed permanently, and there was no going back.

There was a pause, while Phoebe studied – or pretended to study – a brochure called *TEN THINGS YOU DIDN'T KNOW ABOUT CHLAMYDIA*. Finally, she said: 'Oh, right, so really? Abbey Baker's the only girl you ever . . .?'

'Well, yeah.' I shrugged. 'We went out more than three years. Started going out when I was fifteen.'

Phoebe nodded. It felt weird talking to her about Abbey. It felt weird even thinking about Abbey, to be fair. I'd been try-ing not to think about her at all over the past week. Which had actually been surprisingly easy. Worryingly easy. Every time she popped into my head, it was like my brain automatically chucked her straight back out again.

I knew I should tell her what was going on. Especially now me and Phoebe had actually slept together. But telling Abbey the truth hadn't exactly worked out over the past few weeks.

Telling Abbey the truth had done nothing but cause us both fuckloads of misery. So telling Abbey the truth didn't really seem like a viable option.

Phoebe was flicking absently through the Chlamydia brochure. Or not 'brochure'. Leaflet, I guess. 'Brochure' makes it sound like Chlamydia is a holiday resort.

'How about you, then?' I asked. 'Y'know, since we're being honest.'

She dropped the leaflet, and held up two fingers. Then she said, 'Well, actually, now, it's . . .' She added another finger.

'Oh yeah? Who are the other lucky guys, then, eh?'

She blushed, smiling. 'Do you remember Adam Kramer? And Max Fulda?'

'Er . . .' For a second I could only focus on the fact she hadn't said Will's name. I had to make a conscious effort to actually respond. 'Don't remember Adam, but I had Art with Max in Year Eleven, He was seriously good.'

'Yeah.' She nodded. 'He's at Goldsmith's now. We sort of went out for a couple of months just before school ended.'

'You didn't think about trying to make it work long-distance?'

'Not really. I guess we both thought it would be better to meet some new people.'

'Well, you've done a great job there,' I said, and we both laughed, drawing irritated glances from the other people in the waiting room.

A lady with a clipboard bounded in and called, 'Phoebe Bennet?' I gave Phoebe another hand-squeeze, and she got up

243

and followed her out. I sat there reading about Chlamydia and wondering whether I should try to call Abbey at some point. Or at least message her. Just to make sure she was OK. The thought suddenly occurred to me that, if I didn't, we might never speak to each other again. Would I be all right with that? It's like, you go through all this stuff with somebody – grow up together, basically – and then, one day, they're out of your life for ever. There's nothing else that goes from a hundred to zero that quickly. With mates, you just drift apart slowly, or whatever: you never actually say, 'We're not friends any more' or 'Our friendship's over'. But with girlfriends it's like it's everything and then, suddenly, it's nothing. Is that how it always happens? In three years' time would Phoebe just be another person I never spoke to any more?

Finally, Phoebe came back into the waiting area. 'She gave me the morning-after pill, and I took the test,' she said. 'So, hopefully, all good.'

We walked out into the sharp, cold, morning sunlight to see Will heading straight towards us. I felt a little spasm of panic, but it was way too late to try and avoid him. He was with his housemate: that Josh bloke who worked in Bettys with Phoebe.

Josh was smiling. Will wasn't.

'All right, you two,' Josh said brightly. 'Top night last night. I thought we did the emergency services proud.' I noticed him and Will were both staring down at my hands, which I thought was a bit weird until I realized I was still holding the Chlamydia leaflet. I stuffed it into my pocket, and Josh hitched an eyebrow: 'Having an eventful morning?'

Phoebe shuffled her feet, and laughed. I stayed silent and so did Will, so Josh filled the awkwardness by murmuring: 'Ooookay then.'

I could feel Will's eyes on me, but he didn't say anything.

'Where are you lot off to, then?' I asked, trying to sound casual.

'Library.' Josh grimaced. 'Got essays in for tomorrow, and we can't work at ours because the boiler's fucked and it's freezing.' He half-smiled at Will. 'And the landlord here won't sort it, so . . .'

Will shot him a half-smile back, but the annoyance in it was obvious. I realized I hadn't actually chatted to Will about the house stuff since he'd first mentioned it. I needed to get that sorted. My corridor chemists had literally already found their place for next year, and signed the contract.

Another chasm of awkwardness opened up, and Josh scratched his head and chucked one more 'Oooookay then' into it. I'd only met him a couple of times, when we were out and pissed, but he seemed like a really good bloke. I was massively glad he was here right now, anyway. Just me, Will and Phoebe would have been genuinely unbearable. Josh grinned at Phoebe: 'You working Friday, Bennet?'

'Ten to four.' She nodded.

'Cool. Well, see you both later, then,'

'See you at three, right?' I said to Will. He nodded without making eye contact, and they both walked off.

'Have you got a match this afternoon, then?' Phoebe asked,

as we headed back towards Jutland.

'Yeah. Leeds. Apparently they're pretty good.'

'Right . . .'

I wondered if we were ever actually going to talk about Will directly. But then, maybe there was nothing to talk about. Maybe there was no awkwardness. Maybe I was just being paranoid.

Coming off the pitch later, after Leeds had effortlessly battered us 6–1, I tried to catch up to Will, but he marched straight off into the changing rooms.

Trev fell into step alongside me. 'He's not exactly a good loser, is he?'

'Guess not.'

'Their third goal was his fault, to be fair.'

That was definitely true, but I wasn't convinced that was what was bothering him.

'Dunno why we even turned up today, to be honest,' Trev sighed, wiping his forehead with his sleeve. 'It was pretty demoralizing.'

'I dunno. I still enjoy it, actually, even when we get beaten.'

'You're weird, Taylor.'

'Thanks, mate. Your goal was good, at least.'

He ruffled his sweaty hair. 'Yeah, cheers. When you're five foot six you get an added buzz off scoring a header. You out tonight, then?'

'Probably, yeah.' I shrugged.

He grinned at me. 'Try not to sound too excited, mate.'

246

Wednesday night was Sports Night, which basically meant the whole squad went into town together, got shitfaced, and ended up in some kebab shop, where Dempers would invariably get us chucked out by performing a lewd act with the condiments.

I'd usually arrive at every match with some bulletproof excuse about why I wouldn't be able to come out afterwards, but when it came down to it, I never had the guts to bail out. I always secretly suspected that Trev knew how I felt. Because I secretly suspected he felt it, too.

Back in the changing room, Will was already stuffing his kit into his rucksack while Dempers banged on about some photo on the group chat.

'Wicks should be banned for life for that one,' he yelled, hurling his water bottle across the room.

'It's true, she was a fucking munter, Wicks,' said Geordie Al. 'I'm surprised your camera didn't break.'

Wicks – a tall, blond, extremely self-satisfied second year – held his hands up and said, 'Her face was ropey, but trust me, boys, the tits were amazing.'

'Well, next time, let's have a shot of her tits, then,' said Dempers.

Will zipped his bag up and his eyes fell on me. 'Have you checked the Wall today, Taylor?'

'No, haven't seen it,' I said.

Geordie Al leant across and showed me the photo on his phone. Another girl lying asleep in a messy bedroom. Not knowing she was having her picture taken. Not knowing she

247

was being passed around a changing room.

I nodded and said, 'Huh,' which I'm pretty sure wasn't the desired reaction, but was the only thing I could think of.

Geordie Al cocked an eyebrow at me. 'Swifty obviously doesn't think she's that bad.'

'He's a fresher,' bellowed Dempers. 'He'll fuck anything that moves!'

Everyone laughed again, but Will was still looking at me, with a weird, cold smile on his face. When the laughter died down, he said: 'No, seriously, though, Taylor. Now that you and Phoebe Bennet are a thing, you've got to get a photo up on the Wall. Bit unacceptable to still be on zero pictures six weeks into first term.'

I felt my face heating up as everyone turned to look at me.

'Told you that girlfriend-from-home thing wouldn't last, didn't I?' Will smirked.

'No, no, it's not like that,' I said. 'Honestly, me and Phoebe are just . . . mates.'

'Oh, really,' Will scoffed. 'Cos, obviously, I go to the sex clinic with all my mates.'

'Mate, nice one,' cackled Dempers. 'Pregnant or herpes? Or both?'

Will ignored this and turned back to me. 'Seriously though, Luke, mate. When's the Phoebe photo going up?'

Trev caught my eye, and then looked away. Me and him were pretty much the only ones who didn't comment on the photos.

'Honestly, man, it isn't like that,' I stuttered. 'I'm still with

Abbey. From home.'

'Stick up a photo of Abbey From Home, then,' said Geordie Al, and everyone cracked up. I laughed along with them, hating them, but hating myself slightly more.

Will shrugged, like he was bored of the whole conversation now. He pulled his rucksack over his shoulder. 'Oh, well, whatever. I'm sure Phoebe Bennet will find her way on to the Wall somehow.'

And before I could process that properly, he yelled: 'Hurry up, then, you fucking girls. Taxis into town!'

CHAPTER 19

PHOEBE

'How are you dancing? I can't walk properly.' I squeezed the mop in the bucket.

'You are shit at mopping,' Josh laughed. 'You do weird show-mopping, have you mopped a star?'

'It's a snowflake.'

'Have you just chucked all the water on the floor? Do you ever wanna leave here? It's like you want to sleep the night in Bettys kitchen.'

'Well, at least I wouldn't have to walk anywhere.'

Josh picked up the mop and started systematically working it round the floor. 'Phoebe Bennet: too posh to mop. Too tired to dance. Too full to eat another vanilla slice.'

'I've had two. I'm sorry. My back aches.'

'I thought it was your feet, you shirker. Go and start doing the stocktake in the freezer.'

I was about to tell him about how the freezer reminded me

of *The Shining*, and every time I went in there I freaked out, but I thought that might be a step too far. I pulled the incredibly heavy door open and walked in. It was completely silent. I took my shoes off and put my feet on to the freezing floor and padded about, letting the cold soothe them.

I took the clipboard off its hook. I was completely alone. I tried to remember the last time I had actually been by myself and I couldn't. Apart from being in the toilet, every second of my day was spent with other people. Even at night, I shared a single bed with either Frankie or Luke. I sat down on the floor and leant against the wall at the back of the freezer. The cold crept through my bun and right to my head. The buzzing ache in my feet spread through my body.

I took my phone out of my pocket. My mum had messaged me a picture of Fat Cat asleep on my Turtles pillowcase. Seeing it made me feel lost and kind of disconnected. I tried to call Mum but there was no reception. I hadn't been home at all. Becky went home every weekend. Maybe I should go back for my birthday, just do a family thing. For no reason at all I started crying.

It was ridiculous. Nothing had happened. I shut my eyes and let it wash over me for a second.

'Bennet?' Josh was standing at the door. 'Are you OK?'

I nodded. 'Yeah. I am, just . . .' I didn't know what to say. I didn't really know what was going on. 'Just leave me for a minute, honestly. I'm embarrassed. I'm a shambles of a person.' Trying to speak was making me more tearful. I sniffed in a disgusting attempt to try and pull myself together and wiped my eyes. 'Honestly, just give me a second.'

He nodded and walked out. But as soon as he did I wished he hadn't. I scanned the clipboard and told myself I would get up and start counting in exactly three minutes. I felt like I could fall asleep. It was like the tears had drained me, left me totally exhausted.

The door creaked again and Josh was peeking back into the empty kitchen. 'OK, coast is clear.' He pulled the door shut. He was holding two steaming cups in one hand.

He crouched down next to me. 'Do you want the tea or the hot chocolate?'

I reached out and took the tea.

'Budge up.' He sat down.

'Imagine if we got trapped in here. This is how they killed people in the Cold War.' I leant my head against his shoulder.

'Bennet, you do know that's not why it's called the Cold War?'

'It's in a Bond film. They kill the man in a freezer. Or it might be a sauna, actually.'

I closed my eyes and neither of us said anything. The silence just rolled over us.

'Are you OK?' he said softly after a while. 'I've never seen you upset. It's horrible. You're such a smiley person usually.'

I nodded against his shoulder. He smelt like chocolate and fabric softener. 'Yeah. I really do think I'm just tired. I miss my mum today. It's the first time I have, properly. I'm nineteen soon. It'll be the first birthday I won't be with my family.'

'Well, you could go home for it?'

I shook my head. 'Nah, I don't want to, and the girls are organizing something, I think.'

'What do you want to do in your twentieth year then, Bennet? If me and you are sitting on the floor in this freezer one year from today, what one thing do you want to have done?'

The steam off the tea was dissolving the ice on the shelf and making it drip. 'I dunno.'

'Come on, it can be anything. So you can say "The year I was nineteen I . . ."' He scooped his finger round the edge of his mug to get all the foam.

'I feel really boring. Can I get back to you?'

He tilted his head on top of mine. 'Yup. This freezer is actually warmer than my house.'

'Has Will still not fixed the boiler? Are you definitely moving out next year?'

'I think so. It'll just be . . . easier.'

He took two Bettys biscuits out of his pocket and gave one to me. 'So, how's your ever-eventful love life, then?'

I elbowed him. 'I told you I don't have chlamydia.'

He laughed softly. 'You get in some scrapes, Bennet, I swear.'

'All right. We don't need to list them.' If he knew about the condom he'd probably die laughing right here in the freezer.

'But you and Luke are solid, right?' he asked. 'It's not him making you sad?'

'No. He is one of the really, really good things. Well, I think he is. I just wish I knew what was actually going on between

253

us. As in, I am in it, living it and I don't really know. Like, we see each other every day. We spend most nights together. We message each other. We cook together. Don't those things, added up, mean that we are a couple?'

'Well, it sounds pretty couply.'

'But I don't exactly know what happened with his ex and he never talks about it. And he was a bit off about Frankie taking a picture of me and him together at the 999 thing. I dunno . . . I hate this stuff. Like, how you never know what the status is. What the status of your own life is. I mean, is there an amount of time that passes, and then you just kind of are a couple, whether you've said it out loud or not?'

Josh shrugged. 'If you're worried about it, just ask him. What are you scared of?'

LUKE

For a moment, I thought she was Abbey.

It was just a few seconds, in that weird, fuzzy state between sleep and waking, but, still, I could have sworn it was Abbey's head resting softly on my chest. Then my phone buzzed on the bedside table, and reality came sliding back into focus.

It was the morning after yet another night before; another night where we'd both gone out separately, got pissed, then ended up back in bed together.

I woke up the same way I always seemed to wake up these days; with a throbbing head, and a tongue that felt like the top of a snooker table. I tried to swallow, but my mouth didn't have enough moisture, so I ended up making a weird sort of clicking noise at the back of my throat, like a radiator coming on.

Through the door, I could hear the chemists having an unnecessarily loud conversation while smashing saucepans about. Eventually, they headed off to labs and I lay there, listening to the soft flutter of Phoebe's breathing, and thinking about Abbey. I thought about how *I'd* feel if *she* slept with someone else. Like, I *really* thought about it. Hard. I tried to imagine her telling me, and exactly how I would react. I decided that, honestly, I'd be happy. I just wanted her to be OK. I wanted us both to get on with our lives.

But, then, was I really getting on with *my* life? I still wasn't totally sure if I was ready to start something new. Something *official*. I liked Phoebe – a lot – but the idea of getting into something serious seemed so much riskier now. What if things ended with her the same way they had with Abbey? What if I was destined to go through life just screwing stuff up and hurting people? What if I was *never* brave enough to start another relationship because I was so sure it'd all turn to shit?

Truth was, I'd spent all this time worrying that I'd fucked Abbey up, but I never really considered that maybe she'd fucked me up a bit, too.

My phone buzzed three times in quick succession, and Phoebe snuffled and shifted under the duvet. I couldn't reach the phone without lifting her head off my arm. She scratched her nose, blinked a couple of times, then grabbed my phone, and passed it to me.

'Was that your alarm?' she mumbled.

Four new messages on the football group flickered open. A photo of a girl I vaguely recognized from somewhere, with Will's and Dempers' and Wicks' increasingly grim comments underneath.

I switched the phone to silent, and locked it. 'It's just the football group.'

Phoebe rolled over, still half asleep. 'Mm. What're they saying?'

'Just about training later.'

I pushed the duvet back, and then suddenly remembered I was completely naked. Being naked with Phoebe when we were pissed in the middle of the night felt like the most natural thing in the world, but I still wasn't quite ready for it in daylight.

I wriggled my foot out of the bed and used it to blindly sweep the floor for my boxers. I connected with something and reached down to grab it, only to find that it was just my T-shirt. My boxers were, for some reason I couldn't quite remember, all the way across the room.

'I just need to grab my, erm . . .' Instead of finishing the sentence, I put my shirt on and stood up, tugging it as far down my arse as it would go, and waddling to the door like a penguin in a cocktail dress.

I put my boxers on, and when I came back from the loo, Phoebe was sat up in bed, putting her bra on.

'Do you want some breakfast?' I asked.

She frowned. 'Well, yeah. But your kitchen smells so, *so* bad.'

'It's all right, I've got a system now. I just open all the windows.'

'But it's *November*. It's freezing.'

'Yeah, so then I turn the oven on full and leave the door open.'

She wrinkled her nose. 'Still not sure.'

'All right. One sec.'

I went and knocked at Arthur's and a muffled zombie-moan told me he was still in bed.

'I'm putting your cheese in the bath,' I shouted through the door. 'Just for half an hour.'

There was another moan, which I took to mean, 'Please, go right ahead.'

When I'd moved the cheese and aired the kitchen, Phoebe ventured in wearing my tracksuit bottoms and T-shirt, and we sat munching toast.

'Hey, who's that girl Ed's always with?' she asked, putting two more slices in the toaster.

'Which one?'

'You know. The blonde girl who looks like she's in a Wes Anderson film.'

'Oh, right. Sarah, or Sophie, or something. From his halls.'

'Are they together?'

I shrugged. 'Dunno. Don't think so.' I got the jam out of the fridge. 'I have tried to pump him for information, honestly. But Ed doesn't exactly talk much about his feelings.'

She rolled her eyes. 'Well, can you try harder? Frankie's eternal happiness basically depends on you.'

257

Arthur's door swung open and he emerged, scruffy-haired, wearing his duvet like a massive coat.

'Here they are,' he yawned. 'The lovebirds.'

We both forced a laugh.

'What we saying, then?' He peered at my plate and scratched his chin. 'Toast?'

'Yes, Arthur. That's what this is.'

He picked up one of my pieces, which I'd just coated with jam, and walked back to his room.

'Right, I'm back to bed for a spliff and some Schopenhauer. If you need me, you know where I am.'

He slammed his door. Phoebe smiled at me. 'I remember you saying on that first night how your corridor weren't that great. But Arthur is really nice.'

I nodded. 'Yeah, he is. I do feel a bit better here now. It's just that I'm not that similar to most of them, and I guess that freaked me out at first.'

She took a sip of tea. 'Are you still gonna live with Will next year?'

'Er . . . Maybe.' The atmosphere tightened slightly. I'd barely even spoken to Will in the past few days. He hadn't messaged me all week. 'I need to chat to him about it properly.'

We finished breakfast and she headed off back to D Block. Even saying goodbye was weird nowadays. Full on lip-kissing always felt way too couply in the mornings, so I just went for a kind of half-arsed cheek kiss that morphed uncomfortably into a semi-hug.

'See you later,' she said.

Back in my room, I found my phone humming with Wall of Shame comments, but I didn't even look at them. Instead, without thinking too much about it, I wrote Abbey a message:

'Hey. Long time . . . How are you? Really hope you're ok.'

I didn't hesitate, just pressed send. Then I lay back on my bed and tried to wrap my head around the impossible-to-understand medieval literature we were supposed to read for next week's seminar.

A few minutes later, she replied:

'Hey. I'm good. Much better anyway. I miss you.'

CHAPTER 20

PHOEBE

The library was the most distracting place I'd ever tried to work. We'd been there for two hours but all I had done was wander round the English section twice and watch who was going up and down the stairs. My phone was already in my hand when Frankie messaged us. I looked up at her. She was sat on the other side of the huge room, accidentally-on-purpose right next to the Renaissance History section, with her hair arranged into a just-got-out-of-bed messy bun to complement her casually chic grey cashmere jumper and matching slate eyeliner.

Her message said: 'The OTHER woman is here – wearing a fishing coat – her face looks like one of those toys babies push shapes through.'

Ed's possible love interest, Sophie or Sarah, was walking across the floor to the Sociology section. She was wearing a yellow anorak and had a perfectly normal face. I gently nudged

Negin. We both looked at her and she smiled slightly awkwardly, like she wasn't sure if she was supposed to know us. My phone flashed again: 'OK this is horrendous, we now have to leave.'

We wandered out into the cold and trudged down the hill.

'I don't know why I bother, honestly.' Frankie's bottom lip jutted out as she unpinned her hair and kicked a can off the path, huffily. 'Ed never comes in the library anyway. I think he's so intelligent he doesn't need to.'

Negin nodded. 'Yup, that makes perfect sense.'

Frankie squealed and jabbed her finger at the Starcups window display. 'Oh my god, free hat with every gingerbread par-*tay* la-*tte*.' She broke out into a sort of canter. 'Holidays are coming,' she chanted as she tumbled down the hill and into the cafe.

We followed her inside. 'Look! The mice are here.' She waved enthusiastically at a group in the corner. 'Roomies!' she yelled, and threw a clenched fist in the air.

'When was the last time you actually went back to your corridor?' Negin asked.

'When Fiona helped me with my first essay and made macaroni cheese. I go back there for archaeology chat and food. They are the greatest. I hope to be exactly like them when I am old.'

'What are they? Like twenty two?' Negin whispered.

'Fiona's twenty-*three*.' Frankie pouted.

We sat down with our red cups. 'I actually feel Christmassy now,' I said. 'Even though it's not for ages yet.'

Frankie pulled on her free, synthetic red bobble hat and sniffed her drink. 'My mum actually won't let me come home before Christmas. In case I change my mind and won't leave.'

'My mum is the opposite,' Negin said. 'Every day she texts me and is like, "It's your brother's birthday, come home", or "We're having chicken, come home", or "Your father can't work Netflix, come home".'

'This tastes like a warmed-up almond croissant,' I said, sipping my latte.

'Guys.' Frankie readjusted her bobble hat. 'Deep and meaningful. The reason I bought your drinks is because I'm trying to bribe you. I've actually been super uptight about this.' She took an exaggerated deep breath. For a split second I wondered if it was about Luke. 'I don't know how to say this.' She pulled the hat down fully over her entire face and let out a warbled groan. I whacked the table and she jumped.

'Do-you-guys-wanna-live-with-me?' She yelped it so quickly it sounded like one word.

Everyone in Starcups turned and looked at us. It made me laugh involuntarily with sheer joy and relief.

Me and Negin both nodded.

'Awkward.' Frankie pulled the hat up to reveal one eye. 'Why aren't you guys saying anything?'

'We both nodded,' Negin laughed. 'Assertively nodded.'

'OK, well I couldn't see that so I felt really sad. But now I'm super happy. I was also thinking we should ask Becky.' Frankie took a massive gulp of par-tay la-tte and I could see Negin was relieved.

'Definitely,' I said. I couldn't stop smiling. 'We'll need two doctors with the amount of disasters we have.'

'*You* have.' They said it at exactly the same time. Then Frankie downed her latte. 'Let's go home and celebrate.'

We linked arms as we walked home and showed each other Pinterest boards with cushions and photo walls and brightly coloured kettles.

'Let's go and ask Becky,' Frankie said as we pushed open the doors of D Block.

We walked past our own rooms and stood outside Becky's door. Frankie looked at us both and then knocked. But as she did it swung open. We all stood looking in.

It was totally empty. Nothing on the walls. The bed stripped. The curtains still closed. It looked exactly the same as the day we had moved in.

'Do you think we can go in?' I asked.

'Well, she's not here.' Negin stepped inside and me and Frankie followed her. With us three in the room it felt full, but still completely empty.

Frankie sat on the bed. 'I don't understand. We saw her yesterday.'

'Maybe she's just moved rooms,' Negin said. 'Let's message her before we jump to conclusions.'

Frankie opened the desk drawers and the sink cupboard. 'It's all just . . . empty.'

All the jolliness of the last hour had disappeared. We walked silently back down the corridor and pushed the kitchen door open. *Everyone* was in there. It was completely packed and boiling hot. They were all stood at the table, gathered round something.

'Oooo . . . that one is bad.' I could hear Liberty in the centre but I couldn't see her. I watched Frankie's face change. She could see something I couldn't over the top of the crowd.

'I've got that pillowcase,' Liberty shouted. 'Exact same one. It's from Dunelm. Can't believe it.'

I pushed past Nathan and Phillip and the others. Connor was sat in the middle of them all, at a laptop. On the screen there was a picture of a girl. Well, half a girl's face, slumped on a pillow. She had brown hair and freckles.

'I know that girl,' Connor said. It was the quietest and most serious he'd ever sounded. It was actually scary. 'I swear she's on my course.'

'She looks like she's having a dream. She's kind of smiling in her sleep.' Liberty said it like she was cooing over a baby.

Connor scrolled up and another girl's face appeared, her red hair pressed against the pillow and her mouth gaping slightly open. My hands started to feel tingly and all the blood rushed to my ears. I felt like I was going to vomit.

'Fuck, is this actually real?' Frankie said.

'Where did you get these?' Negin asked, and Connor turned to her.

'Someone leaked them to The Tab. They're everywhere.'

Liberty squinted at the screen and read out one of the comments underneath. '"Ginny Weasley's rank sister".' She laughed and then covered her mouth straight away. 'Sorry, that's horrible.'

'This is just grim, man,' Connor muttered.

I felt dazed. I wasn't sure if anyone else had noticed it, but the comment underneath it was from 'Luke Taylor'. I peered closer at the screen. It wasn't about the girl; it was just him asking what time everyone was meeting for practice. But it *was* from Luke Taylor.

I thought about the Fit Sister gig; the way he had sounded when he said it wasn't true. I didn't want to look at Negin or Frankie. I let Liberty and Nathan crowd me out as they huddled closer towards the screen. I shut my eyes for a second and took a deep breath.

And then Connor flicked to another screenshot and the whole room went silent. I couldn't see the screen properly, but I knew what was on it. Deep down, I must have known Will had done it. I didn't want to cry in front of them all. I would have to try and pretend like I didn't give a shit. Liberty took a step back and looked at me. I tried to arrange my face to look normal and pushed in front of Nathan.

But the girl in the photo wasn't me. It was Becky.

LUKE

'Man, you lot are fucking rubbish,' said Arthur, high-fiving Rita triumphantly. 'One more game?'

Ed shook his head and finished his pineapple juice. 'Got an essay to write. Plus, y'know, getting battered six games in a row isn't exactly doing wonders for my self-esteem.'

We were in Wulfstan Bar, killing time between lectures, seminars and essays by playing table football. Which had been fun at first until me and Ed had realized that Arthur and Rita were basically an unstoppable dream team; she was rock-like in defence, he was insanely quick-flicking in attack.

'Me and Reets *are* a bit good, there's no denying it,' Arthur admitted, digging into his pocket for another 50p.

Rita shook her head. 'The amount of time we wasted on this table last year.'

Arthur waggled the coin at Ed. 'Come on, Edward, don't be a dick. You can write your essay later.'

'I'm not being a dick,' said Ed. 'And it's Mund.'

'You what?'

'It's Ed*mund*, not Edward.'

Arthur nearly spat his pint out. 'Are you fucking *kidding* me? Your name's *Edmund*? Are you literally from the Middle Ages? Is that why you're doing Renaissance History? Because it's *when* you were born?'

'The Middle Ages and the Renaissance are different periods,' Ed said drily. 'And I'm Edmund cos of Edmund Hillary. My dad's into mountain climbing, and that. Anyway, I'll see you lot later.'

'Later, Ed,' I said.

'I bid you farewell, good Edmund,' Arthur shouted after him.

I watched him go, slightly annoyed he hadn't stayed longer. Over the past few days, as I'd seen less and less of Will, I'd started to form this stupid, probably over-optimistic idea that me, Ed, Arthur and Rita could live together next year. I wanted to sound Ed out on it first, but for all I knew, the three of them already had houses sorted.

The idea of being the one person on campus without anyone to live with was too fucking terrifying to think about.

Arthur turned back to me: 'Come on, Luke, one more game. Cheeky little one-on-one. I'll even play left-handed.'

'You *are* left-handed.' I grabbed my bag. 'And I've got a seminar in, like, ten minutes, which I've done literally no reading for.'

'What's it on?' Rita asked.

'Medieval literature. This book called *Sir Gawain and the Green Knight*.'

'Should've asked Edmund about it,' muttered Arthur. 'He probably wrote the fucking thing.'

'I am genuinely quite worried. Like, if I get asked anything I will be totally screwed.'

Arthur leant in, conspiratorially. 'OK, look, if you promise to play one more game, I'll let you in on my foolproof, works-every-time, haven't-done-the-reading seminar trick.'

Rita frowned. 'What trick?'

'You know – Arthur's Law. I discovered it, that's why it's named after me. It's a simple yet effective rule to be employed whenever you haven't done the reading for a seminar.'

'Sounds ideal,' I said.

'Sounds like bullshit,' Rita said.

Arthur ignored her: 'Basically, Arthur's Law states that the first person to speak in a seminar will not get asked to speak again. If you step up straight away, the tutor forgets you're there – they try and get everyone else involved *except* you.'

'OK . . . But what do I say?'

Arthur shrugged. 'Doesn't matter. It can be the most meaningless, obvious, pointless thing in the world. Any old bollocks off Wikipedia. Just say it first, and you're in the clear for the rest of the seminar. Trust me. Get on Wikipedia now, then let's play.'

'Can't. My phone's dead.'

'Fuck's sake. Use mine.'

I quickly memorized an appropriate comment off the *Gawain* Wikipedia page, and then we played one more game, which Arthur won, 8–2.

When I got to the seminar, Phoebe was already there. But she hadn't saved the seat next to her, like she normally did. Katie and Scouse Paul were sat either side of her.

I said, 'Hey,' but she literally didn't even look up from her book. A couple of people giggled awkwardly, and Scouse Paul saved me from total humiliation by saying 'Hey' back, which was pretty nice of him considering we'd only spoken twice.

Feeling a bit flushed and confused, I went and sat on the other side of the room, next to Mary. Our tutor – a short, curly-haired man called Hugh – came in and started speaking straight away, which left me trying desperately to make eye contact with Phoebe, and wondering what the hell was up with her.

'So, what did everyone think of Gawain?' Hugh was saying. 'And don't say that he's basically a medieval James Bond. Even though, to some extent, that's true.'

There was a split-second pause, so I dived right in: 'I thought it was interesting how the pentangle on Gawain's shield came to represent the five virtues of medieval knights: chastity, generosity, courtesy, piety and friendship.'

A suitably awestruck silence followed this, and Hugh smiled. 'Yes, that's a good point, Luke.'

Mary gave me a shit-that-was-impressive grin, but Phoebe still wasn't looking up from the desk. I wondered if something had happened between her and Negin or Frankie. But then, why would she be taking it out on me?

'What did everyone else think?' Hugh asked, looking round the room as people shuffled in their seats. 'Picking up on what Luke said, some critics see the book as a satire on chivalry. What do you make of that?'

No one piped up, and I sat there smugly, wondering who he would pick on. He swivelled his chair back to me. 'How about you, Luke? You seem to have really got to grips with this text. Did you see it as a satire?'

All eyes were back on me. Except Phoebe's.

'Er . . . yeah,' I mumbled. 'I mean, sort of. I guess.'

Another silence followed this. It was noticeably less awestruck than the first one. Mary was biting her lip and staring up at the ceiling.

'Right,' said Hugh, dragging the word out to last about five seconds. He swivelled back to the group. 'I mean, what was everyone's take on the meaning of the Green Girdle?'

No one seemed to have any particularly strong thoughts on the Green Girdle, so he turned back to me again. 'Luke – the Green Girdle?'

I felt myself starting to go red. 'Erm, well, I was more . . . I actually thought the pentangle was more interesting, actually, as it represented—'

'The five virtues, yes, you said.' Hugh nodded. 'Right. Maybe we should all read the first part of the text together, as a group, and see what we can get out of it. Mary, can you kick us off?'

Mary started reading, and I sat there next to her, feeling my cheeks burn and trying to figure out the most painful way to murder Arthur.

When the seminar finally ended, Phoebe was up and out of the room quicker than the accidental text day. I ran and caught up with her in the corridor, trying my best to be casual. 'Hey. So, if Arthur ever tries to give you advice about seminars, trust me—'

She didn't stop, just kept walking.

'Phoebe!'

'Fuck off, Luke.' She didn't even turn around to say it. I caught up with her again. 'Phoebe, what's up? Are you OK? What's wrong?'

She finally spun around and looked at me. Her face was hard, and her green-blue eyes were shining with anger.

'Did you take any of me?' she said. I noticed the strap of her rucksack was trembling, and then realized it was because *she* was trembling.

'Did I . . . What are you on about?'

'Come on. Let me see your phone. Did you take any of me?'

'My phone's dead. Seriously, what is going on?'

She shook her head, bitterly: 'Oh, that's a coincidence.' Then all the hardness went out of her face suddenly and she just looked . . . tired. 'You're such a prick, Luke. You lied, right to my face.'

My first thought was Abbey. But while I was turning to ice on the inside, I kept up the performance on the outside: 'Lied about what? Phoebe, what's going on?'

'For fuck's sake, Luke! You can stop pretending now.' People were streaming out of another lecture room, slowing down to watch us.

'Pretending about what?'

Phoebe looked close to tears. 'The . . . "Wall of Shame"? Isn't that what you all call it? And don't fucking *lie* again, Luke. I *saw* you on it. And now Becky's gone. She's left uni. Not that any of you give a shit. So, don't fucking speak to me any more. I don't want to know you.'

The streams of people had passed now, and in the silence I could hear the soft hum of the vending machines.

Phoebe turned to go. 'I don't know why I thought . . . Fuck it. You're exactly what you were at school. A dumb fucking footballer.'

I stood there numbly for a few seconds, watching her walk off, not knowing what to do or what to think. Then I felt a tweak on my shoulder and looked round to see Mary strolling past.

'Cheer up, Pentangle.' She smiled. 'It's not the end of the world.'

CHAPTER 21

PHOEBE

To everyone else I acted like I was furious with Luke. Like I hated him. And in part that was true.

But other things were true too. That I was lonely. That I felt paranoid that no one liked me any more. That maybe people were suspicious that I had known. That I was guilty by association.

I went to bed earlier than everyone else and imagined them talking about me in the kitchen: saying that maybe things could have been different with Becky if I hadn't been some lovesick moron. I felt like some vital part of me had suddenly become unsteady. My foundations had cracked. I hadn't seen Luke as he really was. I had been having sex with – falling in love with, even – a person who wasn't really there and I couldn't even figure out if it was my fault or not.

And like a clichéd, pathetic dick, I missed him. He had kind of seeped in and distorted everything on the inside of me, and everything on the outside of me too.

I slipped off to the library alone to do my reading. It crossed my mind that I might see Luke. I had a random fantasy where he explained how it was all a terrible mistake and we kissed in front of everyone and another concurrent one where I punched him in the face.

I had crossed my arms on the desk, and was almost asleep on them when Frankie and Negin found me.

'Phoebs,' Frankie whispered, her face right next to mine. She laid something wrapped in a piece of A4 lined paper in front of me. The paper unfurled to reveal a quite-squashed cloud-shaped fairy sandwich.

'Josh popped in to see you,' Frankie said. 'And you weren't there, so we made these and kept you one.'

'Don't know how the fried egg will taste cold,' Negin added. 'But it's the thought that counts.'

They sat down opposite me and I bit into the cold congealed egg and icing. It still tasted quite good.

'Do you wanna get a coffee?' Negin asked. I nodded and started to collect up my things.

'I need to photocopy stuff first.' We wandered down the stairs and into the weird little room filled with whirring photocopiers. We waited in the line and watched a boy copy page after page of a book called *Why Do Buses Come in Threes?*

I noticed a group of girls swing through the security gates and walk past us. And then one of them turned on her heel and started back towards the photocopy room. Two of her mates broke away and followed her. I realized the first girl was

Sequin Skirt from the Fit Sister gig. And Bowl-Cut Mary and Wedding Veil were behind her.

'So.' Sequin Skirt girl chucked her bag on the floor and looked right at me. 'Your boyfriend is a fucking lying *arsehole*.' She shouted it into the silence of the library and the quiet whirring of the photocopying. The boy stared straight ahead like he hadn't heard, but he tensed. My whole body shook with adrenalin. I didn't know what to say.

'Are you still with him, cos fucking hell—'

'Jen, you're acting like a *pyscho*.' Mary put a hand on the girl's shoulder, and shot me an apologetic look. 'Phoebe is my mate and it's not her fault she shagged a guy who turned out to be a twat.' She shrugged. 'I mean, we've all done it.'

Jen's face softened slightly and she half-glanced at me. 'OK, sorry. This whole thing's just utterly rancid. You're not still with him, are you?'

I shook my head, and looked at the floor like I was being told off.

'This is *so* not Phoebe's fault,' Frankie snapped. 'Like, come on, how *can* it be? Luke lied to her, too.'

'And Becky, the girl who left, is our friend,' Negin said gently.

Mary's eyes widened. 'Is she OK?'

'We don't know,' I said. 'She won't reply to any of our messages or calls. She's just disappeared.'

The boy at the photocopier collected up his pages quickly and edged out. Jen stood in front of the door. 'OK, so what the fuck are we gonna do about this? The pictures are literally *all* over campus. This is the time to annihilate those bastards.'

A middle-aged man carrying a pile of books tried to walk into the room but Jen held her hand out. 'We're having a meeting in here, sorry.'

'We need to do something to humiliate them,' Mary said. 'To make them get how cruel and disgusting they are. To make them understand that it's not a joke.'

'That Becky is a real person,' Negin said, and Jen nodded: 'Exactly.'

Becky had become sort of famous. The girl who left uni because she was so ashamed. It was awful. We had talked about it non-stop: when she might have slept with that football bloke, whether her boyfriend knew, why she hadn't told us at the time. Why she hadn't told us she was leaving. Even Connor felt bad about it. He said if he saw the boy who posted the picture he would knock him out.

'It's their last game of term next week,' Jen said.

'Yeah, that is the moment.' Mary nodded.

'Laxatives?' Wedding Veil suggested. 'In their water bottles?'

'I think we should graffiti the pitch,' Frankie said.

'Yeah, but how would we actually do that, without someone seeing before and getting rid of it?' Jen shook her head.

'I've got an idea,' I said. They all looked at me, and I felt scared and excited at the same time.

LUKE

The only sound was the echoey *clack-clack-clack* of Will's studs on the tiles.

It was ten minutes before kick-off, but no one seemed

particularly pumped. They were all either checking their phones or lacing their boots or just staring down at the changing-room floor.

One of the freshers, Murf, suddenly piped up. 'The girls on my corridor have literally stopped speaking to me,' he said. 'Like, I'll go in the kitchen and they just literally pretend I'm not there.' He laughed. 'It's like . . . fuck's sake. Chill out.'

'People are so fucking touchy, honestly,' Geordie Al said. 'It's not even *that* bad.'

Will stopped pacing, and looked at him. 'It was blatantly Louise who took those screenshots,' he told him. 'She must've known you were fucking around on her. She was probably trying to get you back.'

Al scratched at his stubble. 'Maybe . . .'

'It could have been a lot of people, to be fair,' Wicks said.

'Whoever did it, did it anonymously,' snapped Dempers. 'So we aren't gonna find out, are we?'

'Yeah, well . . .' Will started pacing again.

Over the past few days, all anyone had talked about was who might have leaked the screenshots. To be quite honest, I didn't give a shit. It was literally the last thing on my mind.

Phoebe had basically cut me out of her life. She wasn't returning my calls or messages. Rita and Arthur had barely spoken to me, too. Worst of all, though, a girl had left uni. Her whole life had been ripped down the middle, and it was all our fault. My fault. I could have stopped it. First Abbey, now Becky. It was like everything I touched turned to shit.

I glanced over at Trev, who was just staring down blankly at his unlaced boots. I wondered if he was thinking what I'd been thinking all week: that it wasn't worth it. That being friendless and houseless and alone for the next three years was still much, much better than being part of all this.

There was this Sylvia Plath poem we'd done that I couldn't get out of my head lately. It was about her keeping this box of bees in her house, and being half-terrified, half-fascinated by it. By the chaos that would come if she opened it. The last few nights, lying awake, I kept thinking: that's me. It's me and the Wall of Shame. Until last week, it had been something I'd just done my best to try and ignore. But now it was like the bees had busted out and they were swarming through the house, stinging people, and I couldn't just sit there, pretending they didn't exist any more. I had to actually *do* something.

'What's gonna happen, do you reckon?' asked Wicks, nervously. 'Like, do you think we'll all get in shit for this?'

Will exhaled, bored. 'How can we get in shit for it? It was just fucking banter. The girls weren't naked or anything, were they?'

'That Becky girl did drop out, though,' said another second year, quietly. 'I mean, that's quite . . . serious, isn't it?'

Dempers finished lacing his boots and glared at Geordie Al. 'If you hadn't nailed that Becky in the first place . . .'

'I don't even know why you did,' Will muttered. 'She's rank.'

'Yeah, well, why d'you think it's called the Wall of *Shame*?' said Geordie Al, trying to lighten the mood, and failing quite spectacularly.

Will looked up at the clock. 'Anyway, come on,' he murmured.

We all trooped out on to the pitch. The Manchester team were already out there, and it slightly freaked me out to see that we had the biggest crowd we'd had all term. Not that they looked particularly supportive. There was no cheering or applause as we came out; just odd little pockets of nervous chatter. I had the sudden feeling people had turned up to see more than just a game of football.

The whistle blew, and we kicked off. I tried to focus on the game, but I kept noticing commotion in the crowd – ripples of movement that stopped as soon as I turned to look at them.

I'd just fed Will the ball, and he was tearing off down the wing, when the commotion suddenly exploded into something else.

About thirty girls streamed on to the grass around us, shouting and screaming. At first, I thought they were all wearing brightly coloured clown suits, or something, but after a second I realized it was pyjamas. They were all dressed in pyjamas.

Our team and the Manchester lot just stood there, frozen, as the pyjama-clad girls stormed the pitch around us. I spotted Phoebe, Frankie, Negin, Mary, and some of the girls from the Fit Sister night.

The crowd were going even more mental than the girls themselves; they were laughing, clapping, cheering, whooping, shouting. I stayed there, glued to the spot, with absolutely zero clue what was going on.

Suddenly, as quickly as it had started, it was over. The girls dropped in unison down on to the muddy grass, and lay there, totally still, like a load of weirdly dressed dead bodies.

The Manchester team and the ref looked even more confused than we did. The bloke who'd been marking me leant in and whispered: 'Does this normally happen, mate?'

Will had been frozen like the rest of us, watching all this with his mouth hanging open, but now he finally managed to get himself together. He strode across to Mary and Frankie, who were both lying on their backs in front of him. The crowd was so loud he had to yell down.

'OK . . .' he shouted. 'What the fuck?'

'What d'you mean?' Frankie shot back. 'I thought you liked looking at sleeping girls?'

Then Mary sat up, and glared around at me, and the rest of the team. 'Yeah, come on! What's wrong with you? Get your fucking phones out!'

Will sighed, and bent down towards her, his hands on his knees like he was talking to a naughty little kid.

'Yeah, OK, you've made your point. Can you fuck off now, please? We are actually trying to play a match here.'

My eyes found Phoebe among all the madness. She was lying on the centre circle in her blue pyjamas with whales on, but I couldn't see her face. Like everyone else, she was watching Mary and Will.

Will stood up: 'You lot are so fucking lame.' Then he chipped the ball over to me. 'Taylor.' He nodded. 'Let's just keep playing.'

I looked at him, then at the crowd. I couldn't see a single face in there – it was just a sea of phones pointed straight at me. I thought about Becky again, and the idea suddenly occurred to me that if this was a cheesy American film, I'd probably pick the ball up, walk over and punch Will in the face.

But it wasn't, and I didn't. Instead, I just kicked the ball gently back to him and started walking off.

'Where you going, Taylor?' he shouted. 'I said keep playing.'

I turned back round to look at him. 'You can keep playing,' I said. 'I'm done.'

For some reason, he smiled at this, and then nodded. 'Yeah. I fucking *knew* it was you, wasn't it, Taylor?' he said.

Before I could say anything back, Frankie shouted something at him – something I didn't hear, because of the wind and the noise of the crowd. Will looked down, and his whole face crinkled with scorn.

And then, suddenly, he booted the ball at her.

For a split second, the whole crowd went silent. It was like all the air had been sucked out of them. There was just the dull thud of the ball hitting Frankie's chest, and then her strangled sort of half-gasp-half-scream.

I didn't think; I just reacted. I was suddenly sprinting towards Will, with no plan for what I'd do when I got to him. Out of the corner of my eye, I saw Trev had had the exact same idea – he was streaking out ahead of me, aiming straight for Will.

But somehow, Ed got there first.

He bolted out of the crowd, threw himself at Will and just *flattened* him. I expected him to start hitting him, or something, but he didn't. He just shifted his weight and sat there calmly, on top of him.

'Frankie,' he said. 'Are you all right?'

Frankie stood up and dusted herself off. 'Yeah, I'm fine.' She stared down at Will with her hands on her hips. 'What is *wrong* with you?'

'Get the fuck off me, you fat fuck!' Will was screaming at Ed.

'It's not fat, mate,' I heard Ed say. 'It's muscle, thank you very much.'

Dempers stomped over, but Ed just smiled up at him and he shrank backwards, and suddenly Frankie was dancing about madly in her *Adventure Time* pyjamas, and the crowd was roaring with laughter and Mary and Negin and the others were cheering and taking photos of Will as he wriggled out from under Ed and stormed back to the changing rooms.

And I was just stood there, on the edge of the pitch, wishing I could celebrate with them.

CHAPTER 22

PHOEBE

None of us took our pyjamas off.

We did a sort of victory lap of Jutland. For Frankie, it was an *actual* victory lap. She ran in a circle around each college, clapping her hands at the bemused-looking people in the windows, like she had just won the Olympic 100m.

Bowl-Cut Mary did a backflip. She just casually did it, as if before she came to uni she had been a professional gymnast, as well as a singer in an electro band and a tattooed, pastel-haired siren.

'I *love* Bowl-Cut,' said Frankie, flopping down on the grass outside D Block.

'She's *so* hot,' I sighed. 'But still, she's just a person. An unobtainably cool one, obviously, but still, a person.'

We watched her dancing by the lake with Jen and Wedding Veil and the rest of them. Her oversized nightie said 'My Marxist feminist dialectic brings all the boys to the yard' on it, and she was wearing leggings with cartoon David Bowies riding unicorns.

'I kind of just want to admire her from a distance,' Frankie said. 'I'm worried if we get *too* close to her, the illusion will be shattered. It's like, my mum used to be obsessed with Colin Firth – like, *obsessed* – and then she saw him in Peter Jones buying scales – kitchen ones not weight ones – and she spoke to him, and he was polite and everything, but he clearly just wanted her to fuck off. And I just feel like if I *really* get to know Bowl-Cut Mary she might not be everything I hoped and dreamt, you know.'

The sky cracked and it started to rain – big, heavy droplets – so all of us piled up into D Block, our pyjamas and hair dripping like crazy as we ran up the stairs.

Connor, Liberty, Nathan and Phillip were doing pre's in the kitchen, and Connor marched straight up to me, Frankie and Negin and bundled us into a group hug.

'Were you at the match?' Negin laughed.

'Course I was.' He broke out of the hug, grinning broadly. 'Never been so proud to be D Block. You lot were fucking amazing.' He held up his vodka and Coke. 'For the Beckster.'

'The Beckster,' Frankie shouted.

Liberty leant in to me: 'God, I hope she's OK.'

I nodded. 'Me too. I just wish she'd reply to our messages.'

'I've got an appointment to see her personal tutor this week,' Negin said. 'And I'm saving all her lecture notes.'

Connor put on some incredibly loud hip hop, and started pouring drinks for Bowl-Cut and the rest of the girls. The kitchen was already heaving, and the noise was so loud we were soon attracting people from all over Jutland. It was like a celebration. Within half an hour, it seemed like everyone on campus was stuffed into our corridor – every room was packed with people I'd never seen before. There were even randoms sat in the shower, drinking.

Connor waved his phone at us. 'You know you're famous? Everyone's Story is just videos of you lot storming the pitch.'

It was raining so hard that you could hear it above the music, but it was so hot inside that the windows had steamed up. Liberty had made a kind of dance floor in the middle of the kitchen and was madly showing off routines she had invented to various Justin Bieber songs. Everyone seemed like they had been wound up and set off.

I went to the loo and saw I had a message from Flora: 'What are your bday plans BEST ONE?'

I wrote back straight away: 'I haven't seen you in for ever. Can you come up for it next week? It's the day before our Christmas Ball, but we can still GET ON IT'. She sent back: 'YES YES YES!'

I came out to see Connor hauling his mattress off his bed and shoving Nathan and Phillip's skateboards underneath it.

'Right, clear the corridor,' he shouted. 'D Block chariot, coming through.'

Negin grabbed Liberty, Nathan and Frankie, and all of us ran as fast as we could and jumped on to the mattress, whooping like mad as it sped down the corridor, faster and faster and faster. People came out of their rooms and showered us with beer as we flew by.

The mattress crashed into the kitchen door, and we all fell off, screaming with laughter. 'Again, again,' Frankie was yelling. Then she looked up, and suddenly went pale.

'Bagsy us next.' Ed was there, scratching his damp curly hair and grinning down at us. And Luke Taylor was stood right beside him.

Ed hugged all of us, but Luke just nodded and leant awkwardly against the kitchen counter.

'We could hear you lot from B Block,' Ed said. 'Although, to be fair, they can probably hear you in Scotland.'

I snuck a look at Luke, his hair still wet from the rain, and wondered if I would *ever* stop feeling stuff for him. Like, when I am fifty, will I still look at him and feel scared and excited and on edge? I feel like it will never go away. It got written into my DNA so long ago that my body doesn't know how to undo it. If Luke Taylor murdered someone I'd probably end up marrying him in prison.

If Connor sensed any awkwardness, he didn't show it. He just thumped beers into Ed and Luke's hands, and then started dragging the mattress back up the corridor.

'So, Luke Taylor . . .' Negin said. 'What are you actually doing here?'

Frankie nearly choked on her cocktail, and even Ed winced and clenched his teeth.

Luke shuffled against the counter, and took a swig of his beer. 'I just wanted to say sorry, I guess. Because I really *am* sorry. I've felt so shit about it all term. So guilty. It's not an

285

excuse, or anything, I know. But it's the truth.'

Everyone was looking at him, but he was looking at me. 'I've been such a dickhead. I don't know what else to say. I don't know why I didn't do anything earlier, but then when Becky left, it was just . . .' He took another sip of his beer, and looked around at everyone this time – Negin and Frankie and Ed, and then back to me. 'I'm so, so sorry,' he said again, and I could feel how much he meant it.

Connor came smashing into the door again, with a whole new mattress-load of randoms falling off behind him. He stood up, dusted himself off and shouted: 'Right . . . I Have Never.'

Suddenly there was only the scream of chairs scraping and glasses clinking and people cramming themselves frantically round the table.

'Sorry, Luke Taylor,' Frankie shouted, pouring herself another drink. 'We'll have to return to your soul-searching later. I Have Never takes priority.'

Luke looked quite relieved. He unwrinkled his brow and ran a hand through his hair. I saw Ed punch him on the arm, and grin.

'I have never been in love,' Liberty shouted. And I looked at Luke. I didn't mean to; it was an insane, drunk, instantaneous reaction. He looked at me. And then we both looked away.

'I have never vomited blue sick,' Connor shouted, and he and Frankie both drank.

'I have never sleepwalked,' Liberty squealed.

Frankie held her glass up and looked around the table. 'I have never lied about wanking.' Then she drank. Everyone burst out laughing. 'I literally don't know why I lied about it before,' she said.

And then, one by one, all the girls drank. And everyone was thumping the table and cheering.

Connor stood up on his chair. 'To everyone wanking,' he boomed. 'We are *all* wankers. Everyone in D Block is a wanker!'

Ed frowned. 'I'm not *in* D Block.'

'It's all right, mate.' Connor smiled. 'You're still a wanker to me.'

Ed squeezed his shoulder. 'Thanks, man. That means a lot.'

'Let's play Sardines,' Liberty squealed, and suddenly every-one was charging down the stairs, out into the driving rain. It was pitch black and freezing, but it felt amazing to be out in the cold after how boiling hot the kitchen had been.

We ran to the clearing behind the blocks that was flanked by massive, manicured trees. It was *so* muddy. Loads of us had fallen on the way and looked like we had just swum through a bog. There was a trail of shoes that people had discarded in favour of going barefoot.

'Phoebs is *it*,' Liberty shouted, so I ran off, and they all started counting. I kept falling over and by the time I'd found a decent hiding place, inside a bush, my entire face was caked in mud. I sat there quietly, thinking how I wanted and really *didn't* want Luke to be the first one to find me. But then Negin's face poked through the leaves.

'Fuck, you're good at Sardines,' I whispered. 'Sardines and quidditch. Your two major life skills.'

287

She settled down beside me. 'It's *so* cold.'

'I think my beer jacket's wearing off,' I moaned.

'I don't even *have* one of those,' she said, wiping the wet mud off her forehead.

'I'm so excited about our house,' I said. 'I'm so, so glad we all met.' And because I was drunk I just threw my arms around her. 'Sorry,' I whispered. 'I know you're not a hugger.'

'I think I've become *more* of a hugger.' She smiled. 'What can I say? Uni's changed me. I still don't like puke, though.'

Then Connor, Frankie and Liberty emerged through the leaves. 'We could hear you lot laughing from three trees down,' Connor hissed. 'You might be good at feminism, but you're shit at hiding.'

'"Good at feminism",' Negin repeated. 'I might get a T-shirt with that on.'

'You could put "Shit at hiding" on the back,' Connor suggested.

'Can you lot shut up, I don't want Ed to find us,' Frankie whispered.

'Why not?' I said. 'He's your knight in shining armour.'

'I know. But I'm too nervous to speak to him.'

'You need to get over it, Frankie. He's not gonna Colin Firth you, I promise.'

'What's Colin Firthing?' whispered Connor. 'Is that, like, a sex thing?'

Frankie shrieked, and suddenly Ed was clambering into the bush, too. 'All right, who's screaming in here?' He was so big that his knees stuck out through the leaves. 'I'm guessing that was you, Connor?'

Everybody got hysterical, and then suddenly Luke was peering into the bush, too.

'Luke Taylor,' said Frankie. 'I'm not sure there's room in this shrub for the likes of you.'

'I'm not sure there's room in this shrub for the likes of *anyone*,' said Negin.

Luke looked uncomfortable. Almost shy, like we were at primary school and he was trying to join in our game, but not sure if we would let him. He took a step backwards and nodded, accepting that he wasn't welcome. I scooched closer to Negin, and gestured at the little patch of mud beside me. Neither of us said anything as he smiled and sat down.

PART 5

CHAPTER 23

LUKE

Rita looked down at the book. 'I feel like it's too precious to actually touch. How much was it?'

'Fifty-five quid,' I said, and she whistled: '*Luke*. Going all out.'

We were drinking Oreo milkshakes on the bus back from town, where I'd spent a good half-hour rifling through various dusty bookshops until I'd finally found it. An early edition of *Ariel*.

'I hope she likes it,' I said.

Rita handed it back. 'She will.'

The present had been her idea. Well, not the book itself, but the idea of getting Phoebe something special for her birthday.

But the extra thing – the surprise – had been all me. It had come to me on that mad night in D Block, right after I'd made my garbled apology to everyone. I suddenly knew what I needed to do. I hadn't even told Rita about it yet. I hadn't told anyone.

A week had gone by since the Sardines craziness, and it had quietly, inexplicably, turned into the best week of term so far. Not because everything was suddenly perfect: it wasn't. Random girls still gave me evils as I walked through campus, and the D Block lot were as frosty as ever, but at least it was all out in the open now; not some shadowy, guilt-ridden secret that I had to carry around on my own.

Me and Phoebe definitely weren't back to whatever we had been before Becky left, but we were edging closer. We'd spent most days together in the library, whispering and laughing and people-watching, when we should have been working on our essays. We hadn't even kissed again yet, but in a weird way it felt like we were closer than before. Like, now that everything had been knocked down, we could actually start to build something new.

Will had gone home the day after the match. No one even knew if he was coming back. All football stuff was on a sort of hiatus. The morning after Sardines I'd gone and spoken to Arthur and Rita about it all. The Wall of Shame; everything. Just laid it all out and told them how awful I felt. And how I knew saying sorry didn't make it better, but I was still really, really sorry.

Rita had told me: 'You know, Luke, for someone who's not a dick, you can be *such* a dick.' But then Arthur had thumped me gently on the arm, and they'd both told me how much they'd hated the first term, too.

A buzz in my pocket shook me out of the memory, but before I could check it, Rita said: 'So, are you and Phoebe actually a thing again now?'

'I don't know, really. I feel like tomorrow, at her birthday thing, maybe . . .' I took a sip of my drink and stared out of the bus window. 'I don't know. It's still kind of awkward. I want us to be a thing again, but I'm not sure whether she wants it. I don't really feel like she's properly forgiven me—'

'Which, let's be honest, is fair enough,' Rita cut in sharply, and I could tell she was only half-joking.

I nodded. 'I know, I know. I really fucked up. Shit, man. Why do things have to be so messy?'

'They don't.' She shrugged. 'I mean, we're not sixteen any more, Luke. It is possible to sleep with someone a few times and for things not to be awkward afterwards.'

'Not sure about that.'

'Well . . . Me and Arthur.'

I nearly choked on my milkshake. 'What? Seriously?'

She smiled. 'Yeah, seriously. We had a little thing in the first term. I was still rebounding pretty hard from Jack. And me and Arth just got on so well. We were spending loads of time together, and . . . it just happened.'

'Shit. Then what?'

'Well . . . I think he wanted it to turn into something more serious, but I wasn't sure. I mean, I'd literally just split up with Jack. So I suggested that maybe we should just be mates for a bit and see what happened. And a year later, we still are mates. Really good mates.' She pushed the bell for the next stop, and stood up. 'And who knows what'll happen in the future? In spite of my good taste, and his many, many shortcomings, there is still something about that boy . . .'

I lifted my knees to let her past. 'I can't believe it. You and Arthur. I've always thought you'd make an amazing couple.'

'Ha! Maybe. Who knows, I'll probably end up marrying him.' This idea made her snort into her milkshake for a good five seconds.

She got off the bus outside her house, and I stayed on till campus: the end of the line. I walked the long way back, around the lake, towards Jutland. It was properly, bitterly cold, and I could feel the book bumping against my back through my rucksack. I thought about giving it to Phoebe at her birthday dinner tomorrow, and how she might react. And then I thought about how she would react to the surprise.

As I passed the library, I remembered that buzz in my pocket. The message was from Reece. It said: 'Shit man, you OK? You seen Abbey's Instagram . . .?'

A little quiver of shock ran through me – mostly at the fact that Abbey literally hadn't even crossed my mind in the past week. I checked her Instagram and saw that she'd posted a new photo, just a few hours ago. She was smiling brightly in it, and weirdly my first thought was to wonder how long it had been since I saw her smile properly like that.

My second thought was: Who the fuck is the guy kissing her?

By the time I got back to B Block, I'd tried her five times. No answer. I unlocked my room and kept trying. Nothing. Just the first two seconds of her voicemail, over and over again: 'Hi, it's Abb—'. Hang up. Redial.

The guy in the picture had glasses, black hair and a full beard, like a proper adult, even though he couldn't have been more than a couple of years older than us. They were stood on a beach somewhere, wrapped up in scarves and jumpers, Abbey's hair billowing out sideways in the wind. He had his eyes closed, and was kissing the side of her mouth, while she half-kissed him back and half-grinned at the camera. At me.

I tried her again. No answer. I felt panicked suddenly. On edge. What the fuck was wrong with me? Why was I reacting like this? I thought back to that morning in bed with Phoebe a few weeks ago, when I'd wondered how I'd feel if Abbey met someone else. I'd really thought I'd be OK with it. Relieved, even. Happy.

But clearly, Hypothetical Me was much more stable and mature than Actual Me. Actual Me, as it turned out, was a fucking pathetic dick. Actual Me was suddenly wondering if breaking up with Abbey had been a huge mistake.

But then, were we *really* broken up? That night after the initiation, I'd said, 'I'm not over you,' and she'd said, 'I'm not over you either.' What the *fuck* did that actually *mean*?

After an hour or so, sick of feeling this cold, gathering panic, I gave up and went for a walk across campus. I purposely left my phone in the room, picturing it swollen with messages and missed calls by the time I got back. In the end, I was out of the block for all of about six minutes I basically jogged to the munchie machines and back – and the phone was just as Abbeyless as it was when I left.

I picked it up and tried her again. No answer. Arthur

knocked on my door, and poked his head round: 'Yo. What you up to?'

'Nothing.'

'Who were you calling?'

'No one.'

'Cheeky spliff?'

'No, you're all right.'

'Bit of cheese?'

'No.'

He shrugged. 'Suit yourself.'

As soon as he'd closed the door, my phone buzzed. I leapt on it, but it was just a message from Phoebe, asking if I wanted to have coffee with her and Flora before the dinner tomorrow.

I chucked the phone back on to the bed, but it burst straight back into life again. It was ringing now, and Abbey's name was flashing across the screen. I felt my heart kick into double-time.

'Abbey?'

There was silence, and for a horrible second I thought she'd hung up. Then she spoke, really softly.

'Hey Luke . . . Are you OK?'

A weird sense of calm came over me. Like, now I'd finally got through to her, everything was going to be all right.

'I just needed to speak to you. Where've you been? I've been calling for ages.'

'We've been driving back from Sussex. I've been down there quite a bit lately, staying with my gran.'

'Cool. How was it?'

Another pause. 'Yeah, it was good.'

I couldn't dance around the subject of the photo any longer. 'So . . . what's his name?'

She sighed, heavily. 'Luke . . .'

'Oh, his name's Luke, too? That's a coincidence.' I was being a twat, and I knew it. But then, as we've established, Actual Me is – and probably always will be – an utter twat.

She sighed again. 'He's called Marcus.'

'*Marcus*?'

'You don't need to say it like that.'

'Who the fuck is called *Marcus*?'

'He is.'

'Right. So, is he . . .?' I ran out of words. 'Who is he?'

I listened as she explained how they'd met. How his family had rented a cottage next to her gran's. How they'd spent most of the past few weeks hanging out together, going for walks by the sea. How he'd just finished uni – he was twenty-two, he'd got a first in Classics at Oxford – and was now trying to figure out what to do with his life. How they'd bonded over both being in what Marcus referred to as 'a transitory stage' of their lives.

If I'd disliked the bloke after seeing that photo, I absolutely *hated* him now.

'Are you together, then?' I asked, when she'd finally finished talking about Marcus and all his incredible achievements. 'Like, is he your boyfriend?'

'No, Luke. Of course not.'

'Well, you look pretty cosy in that picture.' I was reaching new, previously unexplored levels of twattishness.

She half-sighed-half-tutted. 'Look, I'm sorry if I embarrassed you, or whatever, by putting that photo up, but—'

'I'm not embarrassed, Abbey,' I snapped. 'I don't care what other people think – I never did. I just care about what *I* think and what *you* think.'

'Well, what do you think?'

'I think . . .' What *did* I think? 'I think it's really weird seeing you with someone else. Not just weird. Horrible.'

There was silence again. Then she said: 'Luke, you need to figure out what you want.'

'I don't know what I want,' I said, lamely.

'Well, you said you didn't want me any more,' she said. '*You* broke up with *me*, remember?'

'I said I wasn't over you.'

She groaned. 'You only said that when you were pissed and lonely and . . . confused, or whatever.'

'Well, I didn't know you were going to run off straight into the arms of some posh knobhead called *Marcus*.'

'He's not posh.'

'So you're not disputing the knobhead bit?'

She ignored this. 'Look, I didn't *know* I was going to run straight off to Marcus. I *didn't* run straight off to Marcus. I didn't plan any of this. I'm sorry. But isn't this what you wanted? I'm *OK* now, Luke. At least, I think I'm on the way to OK. Aren't you happy about that?'

'Yeah. Of course.'

'Luke . . .' Her voice wavered, and sounded heavier suddenly. 'Trying to get over you has been the hardest, most awful thing I've ever had to do.'

I didn't know what to say to this. I felt like the conversation was snowballing out of control. I was saying things I wasn't sure I meant. I felt knackered.

'What are you saying, then?' she said, finally. 'Are you saying you want to get back together?'

'No. Or . . . maybe. I don't know.'

'Great,' she snapped. 'Well, your decisiveness is really reassuring.'

'Sorry.'

I heard her click her tongue, irritably. 'Shit, we can't talk like this. I hate not being able to see you. It's crazy talking about this stuff over the phone.'

'I know. It feels like years since I last saw you.'

'Yeah. I know.' She exhaled, heavily. 'Shall we just talk tomorrow? I'm tired, we've been driving for ages.'

'Yeah, OK. Speak to you tomorrow.'

I knew I should try to think properly about what I really wanted. Try to get everything straight in my head. I messaged Phoebe back and told her I couldn't meet tomorrow in the daytime, as I had to work.

Then I looked down at the *Ariel* book, poking out the top of my rucksack, and wondered what the fuck I was going to do.

CHAPTER 24

PHOEBE

Seeing Flora tumble out of the carriage and on to the platform made me unexpectedly tearful. I sprinted over to her like she was my long-lost love. In a way she kind of is, I suppose. She is the memory stick that carries anything that has ever happened to me that meant something. The sight of her is like a jolt connecting me to every version of myself I have ever been, all at once.

She was wearing the old red duffle coat that was her dad's in the eighties. It was sort of falling off her shoulders because she was carrying so many random bags. Underneath, she was wearing a knitted jumper and the lime-green flares she had bought from an Etsy shop that had been too small so we had hacked the waistband off.

'Best one.' She cuddled me hard. 'Happy birthday. I thought you would look different but you look exactly the same. Are you *crying*? I *joked* to my mum you would cry but now you actually *are*.'

'You know what I'm like. Why do you have so many small bags? You look like a crazy bag lady.'

'Because I didn't bring a small suitcase to uni, only one massive one.'

I slung three of them over my shoulder and then linked arms with her.

It was a weirdly warm day for the first of December, and the sun made York look quaint and picturesque. We wandered through the cobbled streets and took a photo by the wall. Flora reached out and ran her fingers across a block. 'It's weird that an actual medieval person stood right here . . .'

'I find stuff like that totally crazy. Do you remember when Mr Gillcrest told us that if you stood on a star and looked at the world you would be looking at it in Tudor times? And I still don't get that thing about the human race fitting in a sugar cube.' I reached out and put both my palms on one stone.

'You remember the weirdest things.' She put her hands next to mine. 'I am so excited to see you with Luke Taylor. Like, *beyond*.'

'OK, well. Just know that it isn't going to happen until I have laid down some ground rules.'

Flora started pigeon-footing her way along a crack in the pavement, and held her arms out like she was on a trapeze. She looked at me and winked. 'What's it worth? Cos I have *material*.'

I jumped in front of her. 'I mean it. However drunk you get, whatever happens, you cannot say . . . anything. I mean, I feel like it's best if you don't ever speak to him.'

'What, so you'll be married and I'll be godmother to your kids but I'll never have spoken to him?'

'Yup.'

She put her arms down. 'OK, I'm obviously going to play it perfectly. I'll be like "Oh yeah, Luke, I couldn't picture you when Phoebe mentioned you, but actually, yeah, now I recognize you."'

'You're over-acting. It's not panto.'

'I'm not, you're paranoid. Who won the drama cup?' She took a bow at a random man walking past.

'Look. I just . . . I'm nervous. This week has been really weird.'

It was weird because suddenly the gap between who I was on the inside and who I was on the outside had become like a crater. Outside there was the casual, confident me who agreed with Negin and Frankie that maybe Luke didn't deserve to be forgiven, and that I could do better. And inside was the real me, who was spending way more time with him than I was letting on, and was getting deeper into it than ever. And now Flora was dive-bombing right into the middle of it all and I was going to have to negotiate it.

'We have been together every day,' I told her, 'but we haven't even kissed yet.'

'Romantic. Like a weird Amish dating trial.'

'No. I just think he wants us to get it right this time. He said he wants tonight to be amazing.'

'Maybe he'll flamenco dance in the middle of the restaurant.'

Flora snorted. 'Anyway, is this real? Like, actually *real*? Like, *Luke Taylor*. Marauder's Map Luke Taylor? Love potion Luke Taylor—'

I jumped on her back and she screamed. 'This is exactly what I am talking about. You have to *shut up*.'

She nodded. 'OK, OK. Promise.'

'Do you actually?'

She held my hand. 'Obviously.' She squeezed it. 'I'm messing with you. I would rather die than fuck it up. I feel like this is happening to me, too. It's happening to us.'

We walked into the main bit of town, to the huge glass windows of Bettys.

'Oh my god.' Flora walked right up to the window where an elderly couple were eating strawberry meringues and cupped her hands and peered in. 'Bettys is *fan*-cy. It looks like the kind of place Daisy Buchanan goes for tea.' She started to Charleston.

The couple stared disapprovingly at her and she smiled at them and backed away. 'There is a full-on queue to get in. Like a club. Are you joking me?'

She walked into the main door for people who only want to buy things over the counter. I followed her in and scanned the room but Josh wasn't there. I felt a bit disappointed.

Sandra appeared. 'Josh isn't here, love. He's on his break. Do you want something to take home with you? Is this your friend?'

Flora bowed slightly. 'Yup. Friend-from-home. Best friend, in fact.'

We picked a cake each and Sandra put them in a box and tied it with ribbon.

'He's probably at the pasty shop,' she said, as she handed them to me. 'And he's already had four French fancies.'

Him not being there made me realize how much I wanted Flora to meet him.

And then, as we wandered back down the street, something pushed between us and linked both our arms. 'Now then, Birthday Girl.' Josh was still holding half a pasty in his hand, which he took a chomp out of. 'Do you want one? I've got two more. It's not your *real* present, obviously.'

'Two more?' Flora said, disapprovingly. 'And you've already had four French fancies.'

'Spying on me when you don't even know me?' Josh shook his head. 'I'm Josh.' He held out his Greggs bag as greeting.

Flora shook the bag. 'Flora.'

Josh and Flora are those kind of people who have that easy confidence that means they can make friends with anyone in about thirty-five seconds.

'Are you coming out tonight?' she asked.

Josh shook his head. 'I'm working.'

'He's actually working my shift, so I don't have to work my birthday.'

'I'm gonna come out afterwards, though. Would never let Miss Bennet's birthday go uncelebrated.' He held out his arms and gave me a massive hug. 'Happy birthday.' He picked me up as he said it and then waved us goodbye whilst shoving the rest of his pasty in his mouth.

'Well, he is attractive,' Flora said. 'Apparently, York Met is full of eligible bachelors.'

We walked back to campus, and I started to feel weird about Flora being there. Like she was an anachronism that didn't belong in Jutland D Block, but in my bedroom or the sixth-form common room or Finnegan's on a Friday night.

When we got back to the corridor it felt like a bit of an anticlimax, because no one was there. I showed Flora my birthday present from Frankie and Negin – a set of big wooden letters to decoupage for our house next year. They were in all our initials, including Becky's. Then we went into the kitchen, made Oats So Simple and crumbled a Crunchie bar over the top.

'Shall we have a nap?' Flora ran her finger round the bowl and ate the last bits of Crunchie-flavoured porridge.

We got into our pyjamas and climbed into opposite ends of the bed.

'Luke Taylor has slept in this bed,' Flora mumbled. 'That's fucking weird.' I checked my phone. Luke still hadn't messaged since telling me happy birthday at 10 a.m. It was making me nervous. Of all the days to not be in touch. But maybe he was busy, sorting my present, or something. I wondered if it was a surprise party in halls, or decorating the restaurant or something?

And then Flora fell asleep and I lay there imagining how the night would be. I thought about Luke hugging Flora and then, when I wasn't there, telling her how much he liked me. How they would get on and Flora would ask us both to go and see her in Leeds. I wanted to look really good, because tonight did feel like something I would remember for ever.

I woke up to faint knocking on the door. 'You in, Phoebe?' It was Negin.

'Yeah, we were just napping,' I called gently. Flora wriggled around. I opened the curtain up a bit. Negin pushed the door and craned her head in.

'Hey, I'm Negin. Do you guys want a cup of tea?'

'That would be amazing.' Negin wanting to be nice to Flora made a wave of happiness wash over me.

Flora wriggled around to face Negin. 'That would be *legit* amazing.'

By the time Frankie came over all we had achieved was making room for Negin on the bed and drinking another cup of tea and eating the other two Crunchies in the pack. Frankie had brought a seaside bucket and spade with donkeys on them to use as a punch vessel and stirrer.

'Er, we're not leaving for another three hours,' I said.

'It's your birthday, Phoebster. That means we're getting on it, and we're getting on it *hard*.'

She sat down on my floor and started filling it with brightly coloured juice and then vodka. She opened a bottle of Coke and poured it in and started mixing it with the spade. 'I feel like a witch making a brew.' She peered into the bowl. 'Make Ed want to kiss me,' she muttered in a slow zombie voice as she stirred.

We started getting ready, but the longer Luke didn't text me, the more anxious I got. I tried to be as breezy as possible and only allowed myself to check my phone every four songs.

'Have you seen Luke today?' I tried to sound casual. Frankie and Negin shook their heads. They didn't look like they were acting.

'Haven't you?' Frankie asked.

'No, no, I mean, he knows I'm with Flora so . . .'

They all nodded.

'So, what do you think of Luke Taylor?' Flora said conspiratorially. 'I mean, I don't *know* him, you guys do.'

Neither Frankie or Negin said anything immediately and then they both nodded exaggeratedly. 'Yeah, he's really nice. Really, really nice.' The way Negin said it made me nervous. I didn't want to get into all the Wall of Shame stuff. To be honest, I'd given Flora a slightly rose-tinted version of it all, playing up Luke's walk-off at the match and almost making him out to be the hero of the whole thing. I turned the music up but Flora kept talking.

'I mean, you must understand how mental this is for me. Like, I spent seven years of my life investing in Phoebe's Luke Taylor chat, and it's like, now her and Luke Taylor are an *actual thing*.'

Negin and Frankie nodded again.

'You guys know about the Marauder's Map, right?' Flora asked.

'Flora, shut up.' I hit her on the knee. 'This is exactly what I was talking about earlier.'

'Oh come on, I can tell Frankie and Negin.'

I rolled my eyes. 'OK . . .'

Flora shuffled up on to her knees and leant forward,

swishing the spade like a wand. 'Basically, in Year Nine we found a copy of Luke's timetable in the library and hand-drew a Luke Taylor Marauder's Map so we knew exactly where he was at all times.'

Frankie whistled, and Negin said: 'We could do with that now, to be honest.' I laughed along with them, but my stomach was tenser than ever.

Connor and Liberty and the others met us in the kitchen and we took pictures and played Ring of Fire. I kept going to the toilet to look at my phone, but nothing. He said he would come. He *knew* Flora was coming. When I came back into the kitchen, Flora, Negin and Frankie all exchanged a look.

'Have you heard from Luke?' Flora asked casually. 'Why don't you message him?'

'Yeah, I'll see where he's at.' I shrugged like it was no big deal as I got my phone out, and wrote: 'Are you coming for pre's? If not, see you at browns at 8?'

I put my phone in my pocket and made myself not look at it for the rest of the game. I pretended to have forgotten my lip gloss and ran back to my room just so I could check my phone without them seeing. He had *seen* the message. I took a deep breath. I only sent it half an hour ago. He might be doing anything, really. But, what?

As I walked back to the kitchen I could hear them all talking through the door, but when I opened it, they went quiet suddenly.

'What did Luke say?' Negin asked.

'Oh, nothing yet. I think he's finishing his essay.'

She smiled, and Frankie said: 'Luke Taylor . . . What an enigma.'

I laughed. 'What do you mean?'

'No, nothing. Just . . .' She tailed off, and looked at Negin, like she was tagging her into the conversation.

'I just wonder if he has . . . issues,' Negin said quietly, and Flora handed me a massive drink.

LUKE

I was leaving the library when I got Phoebe's message. I checked my phone and saw she was getting ready to go to Brown's with Flora and everyone.

I wandered around campus aimlessly, and thought about calling her, or even heading over to D Block, but I didn't. Eventually, I just sent her a message that said: 'Sorry, been so hectic today, see you at dinner later x.' Which basically translated as, *Sorry, I'm a massive wanker*, but at that moment I couldn't think of anything better.

I hadn't even had time to sort the surprise out. It was supposed to be the big thing for tonight – bigger than the *Ariel* book, even – but I'd been so weighed down with Abbey thoughts all day, I'd forgotten all about it.

I got back to B Block, fully intending to flop down on to my bed and try to get my head straight before I headed out to the dinner. But when I opened the kitchen door, I thought I was hallucinating. Like, maybe the half-spliff I'd had earlier with Arthur was making me see things. But there was no way Arthur's rubbish weed could cause such a heart-stoppingly

311

realistic apparition.

'Hey,' Abbey said.

'Hey,' I heard myself say back.

She stood up and I thought she was coming over to give me a hug or something, but she just stayed on the other side of the table, scratching her elbow awkwardly.

'This girl let me in,' she said. 'Hope that's OK.'

'What the hell are you doing here?' I meant to say. But instead I said: 'Yeah, of course.'

She wrinkled her nose. 'It smells quite bad in here.'

'That's the cheese,' I said, flicking Barney's latest note on the fridge.

I was having serious trouble coming to terms with the fact that she was *actually* here. Here in York. Here in B Block. She looked healthy and happy – or maybe just healthier and happier than the last time I'd seen her. She was wearing her long, dark-blue coat and she must have just got here because her cheeks were still pink from the cold. It felt like so long since I'd last seen her.

In the end, she answered the question without me even asking it.

'I know this is a bit out of the blue, but after yesterday, I just thought it would be better to talk properly,' she said. 'Face to face.'

'Yeah, definitely.' I nodded. 'It's good to see you.' And it really was. I felt the sudden urge to go and hug her, to hold her tight and feel her pressed right up against me, with her head tucked neatly under my chin. She used to say that's how she knew we were meant to be together; because we clicked into each other perfectly, like a jigsaw puzzle.

'Can we go somewhere the smell can't get us?' she asked, frowning. I unlocked my room and she followed me inside.

'So . . . This is where it all happens?'

'Yeah, I guess. If by "where it all happens", you mean "where I try to understand what the fuck Ted Hughes is going on about."'

She sat down on the bed, and cracked a smile. 'I bet you haven't changed your sheets once yet, have you?'

I smiled back. 'Good guess.'

'And I bet your mum put these on for you.'

'Yeah, yeah. You know me so well.'

It was meant as an off-the-cuff comment, but I felt the air tighten around it. She really *did* know me well. We were together nearly three and a half years. That had to mean something, right?

I sat down on the bed next to her. 'So . . . what's going on, then?' I asked.

She smoothed a crease in the duvet. 'I don't know. I just . . . after we spoke yesterday, I wanted to see you. To talk about stuff properly. About what's happening. Or what's going to happen.'

'OK.' I had no idea what was going to happen, but even more worryingly, I had no idea what I really *wanted* to happen.

Earlier, getting stoned with Arthur, I'd tried to think about what I'd do if Abbey told me she wanted us to get back together. I eventually concluded that my head would say no, but my gut – or was it my heart? – would say yes. Why can't bodies think as a *whole*? Or was it just *my* body?

There was a knock on the door. The handle swivelled, and Arthur's head appeared.

'I will have a cup of tea, then, if you're mak—' He clocked Abbey and stopped. 'Oh. Hi.'

'Hey,' Abbey smiled.

'Abbey, this is Arthur. Arthur, Abbey.'

'All right? Just seeing if you fancied some Scrabble action, Luke, but no worries. I'll see you later. Nice to meet you, Abbey.'

'You too.'

When he'd left, she looked around the room: 'It's so cool, this. It's like living in a big block of flats with all your friends.'

'I'm so sorry about you not going to Cardiff,' I said. 'I can't believe I haven't even told you that yet.'

'It's OK.' She nodded. 'I really think it was for the best. I think if I'd gone this year, I would have ended up dropping out in, like, two weeks. I just know I wasn't in the right place for it.'

'But you're going next year?'

'Yeah. My mum and Miss Sawyer sorted it.'

She stood up and started flicking distractedly through the books on my desk. She picked up the *Ariel* book – Phoebe's present – and murmured, 'This is pretty,' and I thought about how my life was starting to become so messy I might never untangle it.

She put the book back on the desk. 'Sorry, Luke. I don't

know what's up with me at the moment. It's quite random to just get on a train and come up to see you.'

'No, it's not random. I mean, it is a *bit* random. But good random.'

'I just thought it would be better if we actually *saw* each other. That it might help us both figure out what we wanted.'

'Yeah. Definitely.' There was a pause while she stared down idly at my *Modern Romantic Poetry* anthology. Then I said: 'Do you fancy a cup of tea?'

I went back out into the kitchen, and checked my phone. I had two missed calls from Phoebe. I checked her Story: they were on the bus into town. In the picture, she was smiling brightly, wearing an 'IT'S MY BIRTHDAY, BITCH' badge that I assumed was Frankie's doing. Using every bit of mental strength, I forced out all traces of guilt, and concentrated on boiling the kettle.

We drank our teas, and then I cooked us some gloopy, slightly burnt tuna mayonnaise pasta, which Abbey actually seemed quite impressed with, mainly because it was the first meal I'd ever made her that didn't involve a microwave or my mum. We ate it at my tiny desk, sat so close that our plates overlapped at the edges, and laughed about stupid stuff: what people from school were doing on their gap years, how her ultra-posh mate Veronica had converted to Buddhism within forty-eight hours of arriving in Thailand. It almost felt like the beginning again; the early days of Year Ten, when we were just getting together, realizing how much we fancied each other, how well we seemed to fit.

But there was also this weird, nagging sense of unreality about it all. Like we both knew deep down that this was an odd sort of flashback that couldn't possibly sustain itself in the long run. At some point, we had to talk about the future.

When we'd finished eating, I went and washed up, and checked the pictures of Phoebe and the rest of them in Brown's. I told myself I could think about all that later. I just had to get through whatever was going to happen with Abbey, and then I could make the world's biggest apology to Phoebe tomorrow. I went back into the room and said: 'So, what do you fancy doing?'

She shrugged. 'Well, I was sat on a train for three hours, so it'd be nice to go out for a bit. You could show me York.'

'There's not much to show.'

'Erm, excuse me. I'm sure your mum told us York was the UK's second most popular tourist destination?'

'Yes, I think she only mentioned that 700 times over the summer.'

She laughed. 'Well, then.'

We walked off campus and followed the little leafy back streets into town. Even though I was purposely aiming us at the exact opposite side of the city to where Brown's was, I still felt a constant thrum of terror as I imagined Phoebe or Frankie or Negin stepping around every corner.

We'd just turned on to the main road, which was lined with identical red-brick terraced houses, when I heard a sudden burst of music and shouting.

'Oi! Taylor!' I looked up to see Trev leaning casually out

of a top-floor window, waving a can of lager at me. The room behind him was packed with people, dancing and shouting and drinking.

'Yes, Trev,' I shouted up at him. 'Is this where you live?'

He shook his head. 'No idea whose house this is. But I'm sure everyone's welcome. You coming in?'

I looked at Abbey. 'Er, no, I don't think so.'

Abbey shrugged. 'I wouldn't mind. It'd be nice to meet some of your friends.'

'No, I really think—'

'Luke Taylor! Get the fuck inside!' Drunk Toby had materialized next to Trev at the window, brandishing a half-empty bottle of vodka.

'We could just say hello.' Abbey smiled.

'I'll let you in!' Trev yelled, disappearing back into the room.

Feeling the panic in my chest step up a few gears, I pushed the broken gate open. Trev ushered us into the living room and I realized I recognized nearly every single person inside it. Misty and Brandon and the quidditch lot were all here. Hot Mary was chatting to Scouse Paul on the sofa. Even Caribbean Jeremy was sat on the carpet, inexpertly rolling a stupidly big spliff.

Drunk Toby came galloping down the stairs and whacked me on the back. He handed me a can of Stella, and then started introducing himself to Abbey. Trev turned to me: 'What's going on with Will, then? Do you think he's actually gone for good?'

'Dunno,' I said. 'I haven't heard anything.'

'I heard he had to see the Provost. They might disband the team.'

'Shit, really?'

He took a swig of beer. 'I was thinking, you know, if they do, we should just start our own thing next term. No initiations, no dickheads, no Dempers. Just playing football and having a laugh.'

'That's actually a really good idea,' I said.

'I've already told Toby,' Trev said proudly. 'He's on board.'

'I reckon Ed would be into it, too.'

We clinked cans and he staggered off towards Jeremy, who was now attempting to light his precarious spliff. I looked past them, over at the doorway, to see that Negin and Frankie had appeared, and their eyes were shooting daggers at me.

And next to them, Abbey was talking to Phoebe.

CHAPTER 25

PHOEBE

Abbey Baker looked as neat and perfectly groomed as she always had.

She has that Kate Middleton-type hair that no one really has in real life; long and bouncy and perfectly blow-dried. She was wearing an impossibly white cotton vest top with little purple strawberries embroidered on it, tucked into her jeans. Her white Converse didn't have a single mark on them. Her nails were painted pale lilac to match the strawberries. She had hugged me like we had been mates at school. Not a cold, I-don't-really-give-a-shit hug, but a warm, genuine one.

'Phoebe, I want to know *everything*,' she said. 'It's so rubbish being on a gap year. I keep seeing photos of people going out every night and I'm just sat with my mum and dad watching *Countryfile*.' She laughed gently. Everything she did was sort of reserved.

I was trying so hard to keep smiling that it was difficult to concentrate on what she was saying. I felt like if I pretended it was just me and her in the room I might be able to get through.

I couldn't look at Flora next to me, or over at Frankie and Negin. Flora was deliberately not looking at one corner of the room, so I knew that's where Luke was. The nerves in my tummy were mostly because of Flora. Because she is an unknown quantity. She could say anything at any moment.

'I love your trousers. We match.' Abbey took a sip of her drink and smiled at Flora. 'I want to be able to wear vintage stuff but I just don't know where to start. You always look amazing. You need to give me some tips.'

Abbey was *nice*. I had never heard a bad word about her. She had always been in the popular group but she was one of the ones that everyone knew was actually OK. She was sweet to everyone. She ran homework club with Year Seven in the Sixth Form. She was the full package, really. *Girlfriend* material.

Flora looked down at her seventies flares, which were covered in psychedelic pineapples and strawberries. It wasn't Abbey's fault. I looked at Flora. She must feel it. That Abbey didn't deserve to be hurt. That she hadn't done anything. I willed her to be nice.

'Strawberries are clearly the thing. Phoebs, here . . .' Flora unpinned her strawberry brooch and leant over and jabbed it into my vest. It dug into me.

'Ouch.'

'Oops, sorry.' She fastened it. 'Strawberry crew.'

Abbey got out her phone. I smiled as she took the picture. She showed it to us. I didn't look like myself. Or maybe I

320

did but I just felt so weird that nothing seemed normal. Flora was half smiling. A kind of non-committal smile. Like she didn't want to give anything away one way or another. Abbey was doing a perfect off-duty model smile. Warm and accessible and polished.

I looked across the room by accident and saw Frankie and Negin. Frankie's face looked different, too. She was usually so animated that I had never really stopped and realized that she was actually quite beautiful in a statuesque, almost old-fashioned way. When she wasn't scoffing and gurning she looked like a woman from a Victorian painting. The kind of face people used to call handsome. She was expressionless almost. She looked grown-up.

'I need the loo,' I said, and didn't look at Flora but just crossed the room. In my side gaze I thought I saw Luke's shape but I made myself keep moving forward.

There was someone in the bathroom. I could hear footsteps behind me. Neither Frankie or Negin spoke. We just stood outside the toilet, all waiting together. Hot Quidditch Marco walked out carrying a pint of blue liquid. None of us said anything.

He smiled. 'You look serious.' The way his Italian accent said the word 'serious' would usually have made Frankie burst into an impression. But she didn't. He held the blue drink out. We all shook our heads in a way that said 'not now'.

We crammed in, and locked the door. You could tell boys lived here. It was functional with a grimy edge. I sat on the toilet and Frankie and Negin sat on the edge of the bath. None of us spoke. And the longer none of us said anything the harder it got to break the silence. I felt like it should be me. Like they were waiting for my cue. To see whether I was angry or sad or confused. They didn't want to jump in any direction until I had.

'I just . . . I don't know . . . I hope Flora is OK.' It was empty. Of course it was. Flora would be OK on Mars, psychedelic flares and all.

'She'll be fine. She knows her . . . kind of.' Frankie was serious.

'I don't want her to feel like I've left her.'

Negin shook her head. 'She won't.'

'I don't want her to make anything . . . weird.' This was closer to the truth. I couldn't bear for her to make me endure some public scene.

'I don't think she'll say anything to Abbey,' Negin said gently. 'If she was going to she would have done it by now.'

I nodded. I wasn't going to cry. I wasn't angry. I just wanted to evaporate. To not have to live through what was coming. There was a knock on the door. My stomach lurched intensely. It must be Luke.

'You all right, ladies?' It was Josh's voice.

'Phoebe isn't very well,' Frankie said to the door.

'I'll get you some water,' he called back and we heard his feet thud down the stairs.

The silence continued until he knocked on the door again. Negin opened it and he handed her a pint of water. 'Classic Bennet, peaking too early.' None of us responded and he seemed to catch that something was going on. 'Hope you're OK.' He leant over and touched me really gently on the shoulder and then left, shutting the door behind him.

'Shall we just go?' Frankie said. 'There's no point sitting in here for hours.'

'I'll go. Flora will come with me. You two should definitely stay. I mean, Ed might be coming . . . I don't want you guys to . . .'

'To be honest I think this evening is a bit cursed,' Frankie said. 'I don't think I want tonight to be me and Ed's night anyway. I think tomorrow will be a better day for . . . everything.'

I just needed to get from the bathroom to the front door. It was, like, fifteen steps. As soon as I was out I would be OK.

'I don't want to say goodbye to anyone,' I said.

'We'll just say you are really ill.' Negin put her arm around my shoulder. It was so unlike her that for a split second I felt tears prick. 'Ten seconds and we'll be out of here.'

'I'll go and tell Flora,' Frankie said.

Negin held my hand as she unlocked the door. She squeezed it. We walked out. I could hear everyone in the living room and in the kitchen. A couple I had never seen before were getting off with each other in the hall.

'My coat's in the living room,' I whispered to Negin.

She nodded. 'OK, wait here, I'll get it.' She walked in just as Flora walked out. She was shaking her head like she was slightly pissed off. She looked up and saw me. She threw her arms around me. 'Let's get the fuck out of here.'

Negin came out holding my coat. I put it on and shuffled

towards the front door. As we passed the living room I heard my name.

'Phoebe?' I looked up. It was Abbey. 'Are you leaving?' She looked so earnest.

I nodded. 'I don't feel very well.'

'Luke!' Abbey shouted. 'Phoebe Bennet is leaving.'

Flora shook her head. 'Fuck's sake.' She said it under her breath and Abbey's face flickered momentarily.

Luke appeared beside Abbey. I made myself not look at him.

'I don't have my bag,' I said to no one in particular.

'I'll get it.' Abbey turned and went back into the living room.

'Hope you feel better.' Luke's voice sounded tiny.

'You're a fucking arsehole,' Flora said it plainly and clearly but low enough that only we could hear it.

'Flora, please.' I reached down for her hand but she shook it away from me.

'No, Phoebs. Don't try and make it better for him.'

'Stop. I don't want—'

'Fine.' She looked at Luke. 'Go and enjoy the party, Luke. It's Phoebe's birthday after all, so it's important we all really go for it.' She handed him her glass of punch and smiled a huge fake smile. 'Enjoy.'

Abbey was standing behind Luke holding my bag. She reached over and handed it to me. I knew she had heard. And I knew that she knew. She looked the same as she had twenty minutes ago, perfectly coiffed, but her face couldn't hide it. She was broken. She looked at me and something in her eyes triggered something in me. I knew I was going to cry and that

324

there was nothing I could do to stop it.

'Thank you,' I said, and put the bag over my shoulder.

'Fuck. My stuff is in the bedroom.' Flora turned and bounded upstairs. And I ran out of the door.

The cold felt so good. I ran to the top of the street and turned the corner. I was right in front of the city walls that me and Flora had touched only a few hours ago. It felt so weird. So much had changed. How could it all have changed so quickly?

I let myself start crying.

'Phoebe.' I turned around. Josh was there. I let him hold me. And then I was physically shaking.

It was weirdly violent. Like my whole body was part of it, these long convulsions that I couldn't stop. I couldn't breathe and I couldn't control myself. It was so loud. Not tears, but huge gasping wails. Every time I tried to stop they sounded more strangled and desperate.

The force of his hold steadied me. I let him hold me so tight that all the sounds were buried in him. It went on and on until the gulps slowed to every ten seconds or so. He just held me and held me. Rocked me gently in a kind of rhythm that matched how I was crying until it was soothing. I didn't want him to let me go. I couldn't speak and he didn't speak. I stepped away and the cold air hit me and I gulped an after-shock of a cry. Josh didn't seem to need to say anything. It was like he would have stood next to me endlessly not needing any kind of explanation or movement. I opened my mouth to speak and breathed in but I didn't know what I wanted to come out. I wiped my nose with my sleeve.

Finally, I said: 'I feel sick.' I didn't know if I did. I didn't even feel like I was connected to myself, like I was in my own body. I just said it because I felt like maybe it could be true.

He nodded. 'Do you have a hair tie?'

I took mine off my wrist and he took it off me and tied my hair into a ponytail. 'You'll be fine now. Nothing worse than sick in hair. Just feel free to really chunder your guts out now if you need to.'

A rasped laugh came out of me. 'OK. Thanks.' I stared at the pavement. 'What a *shit* birthday.'

'Well . . .' He took his rucksack off his back. 'OK, Bennet, it hasn't been ideal, I get that. I mean, I'm sure other birthdays have been better. But, you haven't had *my* birthday present on other birthdays.'

He pulled out an extremely crumpled package with Thomas the Tank Engine wrapping paper.

I smiled weakly as he handed it to me and unwrapped it slowly. They were cookie cutters. A cupcake, a ladybird, a cactus and a train. I held them all cupped in my hands. 'Thank you. I love them. Especially the train.'

He nodded. 'I told you, I knew you were a train person.'

'It's really weird.' I held it up and looked at him through the middle of the train outline. 'I told Flora today, and I was going to tell you.'

'Tell me what?'

'I decided what I want to do with my twentieth year.'

'Indeed, Miss Bennet?' He picked the cactus up and looked at me through it. 'Well, what is it then?'

'I want to go travelling. Like round Europe. Inter-*railing*. You know –' I held up the train – 'on trains.'

We looked at each other through our cookie cutters.

'Well,' he said, casually looking to the side. 'Are you going on your own, you know, just training it about on your own or—'

'Well, I might ask some people, you know, I don't know. I'll have to see, if anyone . . . wants to come.'

He looped his arm through mine and pulled me in towards him. 'Let's get you home.'

But I didn't want to go home. I wanted to be close to him. I pulled back and looked at him and took a step forward. And then I kissed him on the cheek, gently, near his mouth, and then moved across and kissed him again, closer this time. He cupped my face in his hands and made a sort of quiet, frustrated moan.

'Phoebe . . .' He took a step away and put his hands in his pockets. 'Let's get you home.' He sounded upset. Almost angry. I had never seen him even vaguely angry before.

I could feel myself going red. I got my phone out and ordered a cab. He walked away a bit and stood with his back to me.

'Phoebe—'

'Don't say anything. Like, please. I just can't face any more tonight.'

'Phoebe, I just . . . Listen. You know what I want in my twenty-first year?'

'What?' I almost shouted it.

'To know that I will know you for the rest of my life. For forever.'

'Yup.' I shook my head as I said it and turned and started to walk up the road. 'Whatever.' I could hear his paces behind me. 'Will you at least leave me to feel humiliated alone?'

His paces stopped. We had only walked about five metres. The cab slowed down and I got into it, keeping my eyes fixed on the floor.

'Are you getting in?' the driver asked, and Josh must have shaken his head because he shrugged and wound the window up.

He glanced in the mirror and it made me do the same. He had clearly assessed the situation in one bored flick of the eye: *drunk student*. My mascara had run all down my face and my eyes were still red and swollen. Neither of us spoke. I looked at my phone just in time to see I had seventeen messages before it died. So I just peered into the darkness and tried to block everything out.

Finally, we slowed to a stop. 'Mind how you go, love. They're never worth it.'

It made me smile. 'That's what my mum says. She says you shouldn't trust anyone with a Y chromosome between the age of fourteen and thirty-seven.'

He nodded. 'Sounds about right.'

I slammed the door shut and looked up at D Block. The kitchens were lit up but all the rooms were dark. I was glad no one was there to have to explain it all to. Music was still playing in the bar and I could see some people playing table football.

It was sort of comforting to see life going on as normal.

And then I saw him.

He was standing alone at the bar, swaying ever so slightly from side to side, drinking a pint. It was the first time I had actually seen him since the football match. I didn't want him to see me so I started to walk quickly, but I heard the doors swing open as I passed.

'Phoebe,' Will shouted.

I kept walking.

'Phoebe.'

I stopped and turned to look at him. That confident swagger had completely disappeared. He just looked lost and a bit desperate.

'Can I talk to you?' he said. 'There is something I just really, really need to say . . .'

LUKE

By the time I caught up to Abbey, she was almost halfway into town. But she wouldn't even stop to look at me.

'Abbey, please . . .'

She just carried on storming forward into the freezing night. 'Please let me explain,' I said. 'I'm so sorry. I'm a fucking idiot.'

'Fuck. You. Luke.'

'Where are you going?'

'Train station.'

'Abbey, don't be crazy. There won't be another train back now.'

She spun round and looked me straight in the eyes. 'Oh, OK,

329

fine. So, what? Shall we just go back to the party, then?'

'Well, no, obviously not, but—'

'Why the *fuck* did you even take me in there?' she hissed.

'Because you wanted to go,' I said, pathetically.

'Yeah. That was before I knew the girl you've been secretly shagging would be there, too.'

I looked down at the pavement.

'So you have?' she said.

I looked back up at her but didn't speak. She closed her eyes and nodded.

'Right,' she said, with her eyes still closed. 'Did you know she would be there?'

'Of course not,' I muttered.

'So, how long were you thinking you could keep this up?'

I almost laughed. 'How long . . . Abbey, you're talking like I'm some fucking criminal mastermind, or, like, serial playboy. It should be pretty obvious that I *wasn't* thinking. About anything. It's like I haven't been thinking all term. I've just been . . . blindly moving forward, smashing into stuff as I go.'

Abbey was shaking her head, staring down at her feet. I kept going, feeling a strange lightness at finally telling the truth. 'I've been trying to fit in and make friends, but everything keeps falling apart. It's like, school was so . . . easy. With you and Reece and football and everything, it all just slotted into place. But here, it's different. It's like nothing fits properly.' I exhaled, and watched my smoky breath mushroom out like a speech bubble above our heads. 'This thing with Phoebe,' I said, quietly. 'It was the first thing here that seemed to fit.'

Abbey looked up at me, tears glinting in her eyes. 'Why didn't you tell me about her, Luke?' she shouted. Like, *literally*, shouted. I saw a light go on in the house nearest us.

I shrugged. 'Same reason you didn't tell me about Marcus?'

She turned round again and started walking.

'Abbey, I'm sorry.'

'Fuck off.'

'Seriously, please. There won't be any trains now.'

'I don't care.'

'And even if there are, it'll be ridiculously expensive at the last minute.'

She stopped suddenly, and spun around furiously to face me. 'I'VE GOT A YOUNG PERSON'S FUCKING RAILCARD, LUKE!' she screamed.

It was so loud that two blokes in the chippy across the road popped their heads out.

I couldn't help it. It was like something just snapped inside me.

'Are you actually fucking *laughing*?' Abbey whispered.

'I'm sorry . . .'

'You're such a . . .' But then she was laughing, too. Laughing and crying at the same time. Big gulping laughs sloshing into big groaning sobs.

We stood there for a few seconds like that; barking like mad seals, while the chip-shop blokes just stared at us.

Then she wiped her eyes with her sleeve and sat down on the wall of the house we were outside. 'Oh, fucking hell, Luke.' She took a deep breath and blew it back out. She sniffed and stared down at the pavement. 'Phoebe Bennet,' she said, blankly. 'From school.'

I shook my head. 'No . . . Well, yeah, but we're not *together*, or anything . . . We sort of were, though. I don't know what we are, really.' I paused. 'I'm so sorry, Abbs.'

She looked up at me, eyes glistening. 'No, it's all right, I suppose. I mean . . . we were broken up. We *are* broken up.'

'Yeah, but still. I should have told you.'

She shrugged. 'I should have told you about Marcus.'

'Well, yeah. Fucking *Reece* told me about Marcus. Or, at least, he told me to check Instagram.'

'Yeah. Sorry. I shouldn't have put that picture up.'

'Why did you?'

She opened her mouth to answer and then stopped. Then she suddenly burst out laughing again. 'I wanted you to see it,' she said, shaking her head. 'I don't know what's wrong with me.'

'It's all right. I don't know what's wrong with me either. At least we're confused together.'

She dried her eyes on her sleeve again, and took a couple more wobbly deep breaths.

'Why did you come up, Abbey?' I asked. 'I mean, do you want us to get back together?'

'No, I don't think so,' she sighed. 'I don't know what I want, really. I just wanted to see you. I've missed you.'

'Yeah, I've missed you, too. Still, you've got old Marcus now, haven't you . . .'

She snickered. 'Marcus is a *dick*, Luke. His Instagram is like

332

ninety per cent Latin proverbs.'

This made me lose it again: 'I *suspected* he was a dick, but I didn't want to say anything.'

When we'd both stopped laughing, she said: 'But I guess he did make me feel better.'

'Well, maybe he's not a *total* dick, then.'

She looked at me. 'Does Phoebe Bennet make you feel like that?'

'Like what?'

'Better?'

I didn't really know the answer to that. To be quite honest, the idea that Phoebe would ever even want to be in the same room with me again seemed pretty unlikely, so it was hard to try and properly assess my feelings for her. But, still, I gave it a go.

'I really like her, yeah. I like being with her.' Abbey smiled sadly and nodded. I shifted closer to her along the wall. 'I really want you to be OK, Abbs.'

'I think I am now,' she said softly. 'But it's weird, you know? Like, half my bedroom wall is pictures of me and you. And now . . . what am I supposed to do with them? Put them up in the attic and forget about them? Or just chuck them away? I don't want that. I don't want to forget that we ever happened.'

'Me neither. But why do we have to? I wouldn't ever change what we had. I was so happy with you. Maybe it's the right thing that it's over, but that doesn't mean it shouldn't have happened. I'm glad it did.'

'I'm glad too,' she said, smiling. 'But maybe we shouldn't

see each other for a bit, though. After tomorrow, I mean. It might be a good thing. It might mean that we *can* see each other in the long run.'

'Yeah. I really, really want that.'

She reached into her bag and handed me an envelope. 'Here. I forgot to give you this. Early Christmas card.'

I opened it. It had a picture of some golf clubs and a pint of beer on the front, and said: 'TO A WONDERFUL STEP DAD ON FATHER'S DAY'.

'Shit,' I said. 'That's good. That's really good.'

Inside the card she'd written: 'Luke – whatever happens, you made me the happiest I've ever been.'

We walked back to Jutland arm in arm. Back in my room, I made tea and gave her the bed, even though she insisted it wouldn't be weird if we both slept in it. But it really felt like we'd got past something tonight – something we never properly got past in the summer – and it seemed stupid to risk going back a step.

I laid out three pairs of jeans and a jacket on the floor beside her, and tried unsuccessfully to get comfy. I thought about Phoebe. About how our relationship – or whatever the hell it was – really had been the one thing here that had actually made me happy.

'You sure you're all right down there?' Abbey murmured in the darkness.

'Yeah, I'm all right. Night, Abbs.'

'Night, Luke.'

And I really *was* all right.

At least, I was all right until about 4.30 a.m., when a piercing electronic scream burst down the corridor and zapped me awake.

'Mmmph . . .' Abbey sat up suddenly, her hair over her eyes. 'Whassat?'

'It's the fire alarm,' I groaned over the noise. 'Come on, we'd best go down. It won't be a drill at this time of night.'

I shrugged on my jacket and handed Abbey my old parka, and we wandered downstairs, where half of Jutland was already shivering outside in their coats and pyjama bottoms.

Arthur bumbled over, barefoot and wrapped in two zip-up hoodies, looking extremely worried. 'Fuck, man, I think this was me, you know,' he whispered. 'I had a dream that I was making cheese on toast. Maybe I actually *did* make cheese on toast. Maybe I was sleep-toasting.'

'You can't sleep-toast, Arthur. It's impossible. Also, for someone who smokes as much weed as you do, your dreams are surprisingly boring.'

He wasn't listening. 'If this turns out to be my fault, I'll be out on my ear, man. I set the alarm off last year, too. Trying to light a spliff off Rita's hair straighteners.'

I nodded across to D Block, which was also leaking pissed-off, half-asleep people. 'I wouldn't worry about it. They're evacuating the other blocks, too. It was probably someone in there.'

Negin, Frankie and Flora were already outside the entrance,

shivering together, wrapped in a duvet. They all turned at the same time to look at the main staircase, where Phoebe was shuffling down the steps, sheepishly.

With Will right behind her.

CHAPTER 26

PHOEBE

I didn't look up but I knew everyone was staring at us.

Will had already started to walk away, but as he did he shook his head and almost laughed to himself. 'Whatever,' he muttered, pushing past me. 'You're a fucking bitch.'

Before I was even sure I'd heard him right, he disappeared down the walkway, back towards the bar. I looked around for someone to acknowledge what had happened but there was no one. I scanned the crowd but the only person who met my gaze was Abbey. Luke was next to her, his eyes on his feet. I smiled at her and she smiled back. A watery acknowledgement of something that I couldn't decipher.

Negin, Frankie and Flora were outside the other entrance. Porters were counting us and holding clipboards and yelling for people to keep still and be quiet. I tried to walk over but one of them told me in no uncertain terms that was not allowed. The girls just stood, huddled together, not speaking. It was like they genuinely had no idea I was there, but I knew that couldn't be true.

People had duvets and blankets wrapped round them. Some were starting to make loud jokes and a few were even singing. But this vacuum surrounded random little circles of people scattered across the grass. One where Luke and Abbey stood completely still, not looking at each other; one where Frankie, Negin and Flora were avoiding even glancing in my direction.

Finally, we were allowed back in. I trudged slowly back up the stairs. Not even Connor really acknowledged me as he shuffled past me to his room.

Negin's door was already shut. I knew I should be brave: knock and explain everything to them, so that bit of my life, at least, was OK again. But I was too scared I would mess that up too, and end the night with less than nothing. So I didn't.

I pushed my door open and looked at my phone. I stared at the picture of a cake Mum had sent earlier. It had my name on it. In the message she'd written: 'Celebrating in your honour xx'.

Climbing into bed, my whole body felt heavy, but my brain was whirring like mad. I curled myself up into a ball under the duvet and stared out through the window at the silent little church outside. I closed my eyes and tried to rock myself shut like a seashell, to block out every single thought. How could every part of my life have unravelled within three hours? I thought I would never sleep, but I went from being awake to completely unconscious in one single beat. I didn't wake up to do that weird alcohol wee you do in the night when you've been drinking. I didn't dream. I didn't even move.

I woke up to Flora picking her stuff up around me.

'My train is in an hour.' She didn't look at me as she said it, just kept gathering her make-up off the floor and chucking it randomly into her array of canvas shoppers. She seemed calm but underneath I knew her heart was beating really fast. The classic girl freeze-out. I'm angry at you, but there is no way I'm going to come right out and say it.

She sighed as she scrunched up her pyjamas and shoved them in.

'I slept in Negin's room.' She said it like I had asked the question first.

'Sorry . . . You could have—'

She rolled her eyes. 'Yup.'

'I'm sorry I left you at the party.'

She didn't look at me. 'It's totally fine. Honestly, I actually had a really good night after you left.' I couldn't tell if she was taking the piss or not. Her voice was so even.

'I was just really upset and I wanted to get out of there.'

She nodded but still didn't look up. 'Yup . . . last night was certainly full of the drama.' It was belittling, like she was making out I had loved every minute. Like I was some attention-seeking drain.

I laughed to try and defuse it. 'Just so you know, nothing happened with me and Will. It was actually really weird. As he left, he called me a bitch.'

She picked up her little pot of confetti stars that she sometimes stuck underneath her eyes, but she did it so forcefully they all scattered across the room. Tiny gold and silver stars wafted to the floor.

'He called you a bitch, did he?' she snapped as she started trying to pick up the stars. '*Poor you*, Phoebs. Do you want a cuddle? Do you want everyone to stick up for you? Do you want a special party just for you? Like, what is it you want?'

'I'm sorry. I really . . . I know it looks weird he was in my room. He's the boy that—'

'I know who he is.' It was almost mocking. 'I just don't know who *you* are.' She turned and actually, properly looked at me for the first time. 'Like, Phoebe, I came to see you. I paid money and spent a week making you a photo scrapbook. I was excited yesterday. I have *missed* you. And you just spend the whole time talking about, or being treated like shit by, Luke fucking Taylor. I mean, I don't give a shit what happened with Luke, or this Will person. I care about the fact you are my mate. You are my best friend, Phoebe. But who are you? I was worried about you. Really, *really* worried. I called you a million times, but you just ignored me. You just left that party, left me on my own.'

She gave up on the stars and carried on packing her bags. 'I don't know. D'you remember in summer how we talked and talked about going to uni? Like, how we couldn't wait for our lives to actually start? *You* were the one who saw uni as this whole new beginning, but all you've done is come here and act like it's still Year Nine, and the only thing in your life is fantasizing about Luke Taylor. Who, by the way, in real life, is a twat. You're confusing *our* Luke Taylor with the real one.'

She picked up her phone and looked at it. 'My taxi's here.'

And she walked out. Just like that. I hadn't even got out of bed.

I could hear Frankie and Negin in the kitchen with the others. Drinking tea and laughing as if life was normal. I went to my door three times and couldn't get up the courage to open it. I got dressed really slowly and meticulously and brushed my hair section by section.

When I finally managed to walk to the kitchen and push the door open it was almost midday. Frankie, Negin and Liberty were all sitting at the kitchen table. 'All right, Phoebs?' Liberty smiled and then walked out, clearly feeling the tension.

Neither of them spoke.

'Hey,' I said and shuffled over. I didn't even feel like I had permission to sit down. Connor appeared at the door and then quickly disappeared again. Frankie took a sip of her tea.

'How are you both feeling?' I tried to keep my voice even.

'I just . . .' Frankie stared at her empty cup. 'The thing with Will. I just found that really strange.'

'After what happened with Becky . . .' Negin added. I felt like it was a line she had rehearsed, something she had wanted to get out before I even came in.

It was like this tangled spaghetti mess. Everything in my life was twisted together so tightly that it was impossible to separate. If one bit of it went wrong, everything else did, too. I almost didn't have the energy to try and explain it all. 'OK . . .' I started. 'Look. *Nothing* happened with Will. When I got back, he was in the bar.'

They both looked down at their cups. What if they didn't

believe me?

'He saw me, and he came out and just kept repeating himself again and again and saying he was in so much trouble. That he was already failing his course and now he was gonna get chucked out of uni, and that he was a good person and that people had to realize that he was a good person. He told me his dad hates him, which was fucking strange, and I just didn't know what to say. He was just so pissed. So, I made him a cup of tea and—'

Negin put a hand up to stop me. 'You made *Will* a cup of tea?' She sounded disgusted.

'I know, it sounds weird. It *is* weird. But he seemed so desperate. He was in such a state. And then he told me that he had been called to see the Provost and that he needed to sort things out or the football team would get disbanded and he would get chucked out.'

'Good, he should get chucked out.' Frankie shrugged. 'That was the whole point of the protest.'

I nodded. 'I know, I know.'

'Did you tell him that?'

'I just said that it was a mess. He asked me to come and see the Provost with him today. As, like, a character witness. Someone who was in the protest but didn't want him to get chucked out. Who could vouch for him and say he was a decent guy.' Frankie laughed sharply at that. 'I told him no, obviously,' I continued. 'But he kept asking and he got more and more upset that I wouldn't do it. Like, he was almost crying. And then the fire alarm went off.'

Frankie and Negin looked at each other. 'Right.'

'Do you want a cup of tea?' Negin said quietly. I nodded.

'Honestly . . . I really, really know that last night was a fucked-up mess and that I acted—'

'Yeah it was,' Frankie said. 'But not really because of you.' She smiled at me, softly. 'The Abbey thing was awful, Phoebs.'

'Yeah. It feels like this domino effect of fucking awfulness piling up around me. Like I'm drowning in it. The last thing I need is to go to a *ball*. I need to go to a mental institution.'

'There's no milk,' Negin groaned.

We trudged downstairs to buy some. Frankie hadn't bothered to change out of her pyjamas and still had her duvet wrapped round her. We walked into the shop and some people looked at us and exchanged glances. We bought the milk in a slightly tense, exhausted silence. As we walked back we noticed a group of people staring at the noticeboard outside the bar. We slowed down and it took me a second to compute what I was seeing.

It was right in the middle, pinned on top of loads of other sheets. In grainy but all too clear black and white. Asleep, head tilted back on the pillow, hair frizzing in all directions, mouth lolling wide open: a photo of me.

LUKE

I watched Abbey's train shrink until it was a tiny speck on the horizon. Then I found a bench and just sat there pointlessly for a bit, looking up at the display board and listening to the announcer's dreary voice echoing around the walls.

It was weird to think that this time tomorrow, I'd be heading home. Seeing mum and dad again. Seeing Reece and everyone. Spending the whole Christmas holiday summing up Freshers' to various relatives in short, socially acceptable soundbites. 'Yeah, it was good. Tiring, but really good.' That's probably what I'd go with. I mean, how can you *actually* describe the first term to anyone? How can you possibly express the confusion and awkwardness and freedom and fun and terror and just general batshit mentalness of it all? You can't. You just have to live through it.

I got up and started trudging slowly back down the platform. For some reason, something Arthur had said last week kept circling round and round in my head. It had been about three in the morning, when we were stoned watching Netflix, and he'd started going on about this philosophy book he was reading. He said the bloke who wrote it, some Russian-sounding guy, had this theory about how human beings aren't just one single, unified 'I' – they are actually billions of separate, tiny 'I's, all pulling in different directions to try and get what they want.

At the time, I'd just told him to shut up so I could concentrate on *Iron Man 3*. But now, after Abbey and Marcus, and Phoebe and Will, and everything else that had happened this term, the whole concept suddenly made sense to me. Walking through this freezing station, I didn't feel like a proper, unified person; I felt like a swarm of stupid, confused, jealous 'I's, all stuffed into the same body.

At least things with Abbey finally felt OK. Or on their way to being OK in the long run. But things with Phoebe . . . Seeing her come down those stairs last night with Will had been grim. *Really* grim. I hated the idea of them together, but did it actually change the way I felt about her? It was weird; the more I thought about it, the only thing that all my 'I's seemed to agree on was Phoebe.

That was when it hit me. Maybe it wasn't too late for the surprise.

A lot had changed in the last twenty-four hours – Abbey had come to my room, Will had come out of Phoebe's – but it didn't really make any difference. The truth was, I'd been acting all week like this whole thing was just about me and Phoebe, when really that was obviously bollocks. It was way more important than that.

I looked up at the display board again and dithered for a few seconds, wondering whether this actually was or was not a good idea. Stood here, in what was quite literally the cold light of day, it could very easily be considered a *bad* idea.

But, no. It had seemed like a good idea last week, when Ed had told me about Jamila. And it had seemed like a good idea every day since, as I sat in the library with Phoebe, and thought about what it would mean to her.

So, it still felt like a good idea now. Or, at least, I had to *make* it a good idea.

PHOEBE

The door was bright red with an over-the-top eagle door-knocker in the centre.

It didn't match the front garden, which was full of dead

plants and a few black bin bags. There wasn't a doorbell. I lifted the eagle's wings and knocked. The knocks sounded much clearer and more sure of themselves than I did. I could hear footsteps padding towards the door and felt a shudder of nerves.

'Wait a second, I can't find the keys.' It was Will's voice. I looked at the gate. I could still run away.

A key turned in the lock and it opened. Will was wearing brushed cotton pyjama bottoms and a T-shirt with Michelangelo eating pizza that had a speech bubble that said 'I'm a party dude'. And he was wearing glasses. He just stood there.

'I didn't know you wore glasses.' I don't know how I thought I would start it. But not like that. Not in a small talk, I've-just-bumped-into-you-at-the-optician's sort of way.

'Yeah, only for watching TV and . . . stuff.'

There was a silence. I looked down at the floor, which was still covered in takeaway leaflets and unopened letters.

'Josh isn't . . .' He ruffled his hair. For a second I thought he was trying to suppress a yawn.

'I wanted to talk to you, actually.' My voice didn't shake. I was impressed by how level it sounded.

He looked behind him. Hoping for someone to come and save him, maybe.

'Come in.' He extended his arm, welcoming me. 'Would you like a cup of tea?'

'Yeah. OK. Thanks.' Accepting tea felt like I was coming in peace. I was supposed to be confronting him, and he was ruining it with his boarding school manners.

He shut the front door behind me, and our mutual uneasiness made the seconds slow down.

I cleared a patch on the sofa and thought about the last time I'd sat here. I listened to him put the kettle on. He popped his head round the door. 'We haven't got any milk. Or tea bags. Do you want hot squash? Or Josh has got some Fanta?'

'Fanta would be great, thanks.'

I had to say something as soon as he came back in or I would just end up having a polite glass of Fanta and leaving, like a surreal interlude to this whole fucked-up thing.

He handed me a dirty-looking glass and I took a sip. It was completely flat, like drinking sugared water. I wondered what Will's family home looked like. Some massive country estate with welly-boot scrapers and an Aga and a dog named after a Greek philosopher. I wondered if his dad really did hate him, and if he even remembered telling me that.

He had left the kitchen door open. I could see right through to his bedroom. To the bed with its burgundy duvet cover and still bare mattress. I almost made a joke about him still not having put a sheet on. How sick am I?

If I let any more small talk happen, I wouldn't do it. I stared into the Fanta, took a deep breath and then looked straight at him. 'Why did you put that picture up on the noticeboard?' My voice was louder and angrier than I had expected.

His face tightened for a second, then relaxed. 'Phoebe, I didn't,' he said, slowly. 'The boys on the team reckon it was Taylor. I mean, you did . . .'

He left it there. But I didn't. It was so ridiculous I actually laughed. He was like a little kid.

'Will, I *know* it was you. You were angry when you left. You called me a bitch.'

He shook his head. 'No, I didn't.'

'At least admit it. This is a joke. What's the point when we were both *there*? Luke Taylor might be a complete twat in many, many respects, but I know for a fact that he wouldn't . . .'

I couldn't think of the words to make him understand. *Were* there even words that could describe all this?

'He wouldn't do something to deliberately make someone . . . To humiliate someone on purpose.'

He ruffled his hair again and laughed awkwardly, shifting his weight from leg to leg. 'OK, I hold my hands up.' And then he actually, literally, held his hands up, like he was saying he'd eaten the last Quality Street at Christmas. 'I am a *massive* wanker. And I was really wrecked. I just thought you could maybe do me that *one* little favour, which would basically mean I wouldn't get kicked out of uni. But, obviously, that was too much of a hassle . . .'

'Are you being serious? Will, the whole thing is completely disgusting. It's rank. Becky *left* university. A girl *left* because she felt so bad about it.' I didn't shout. I just let the words fall plainly between us.

He sighed. 'Yeah, but come on, Phoebe. Like, she probably had issues anyway. If *that* is gonna make you leave uni, then . . . Come on. That is just ridiculous.' He snorted slightly. 'I mean, the photos thing . . . It was just supposed to be a laugh between us lot. And now, honestly, people are acting like it was some gross, creepy, terrible thing.'

'Yeah,' I said. 'Because it is.'

He took his glasses off and started cleaning them on his T-shirt. 'Just so you know, I didn't start that stuff. Like, god, that was actually nothing to do with me. Just cos I'm the captain, people are making out like I invented the whole thing.'

'You still took *my* picture. And then you printed it out and put it on the noticeboard . . .' He didn't say anything. He looked out of the window. I wondered if he was thinking about that night. The night we *didn't* have sex.

He picked up his phone and looked at it. Like he was bored. 'Look, I'm probably gonna get kicked out for it anyway. Like I say, I hold my hands up. I am a bad person.'

But I knew from the way he said it that he didn't really believe it. That he thought saying sorry made everything better. That he actually thought he was a great person underneath it all.

'I don't know why Josh was ever friends with you,' I said quietly. 'I don't know why anyone is friends with you.'

He laughed again, nervously. 'Me neither, what a douche. Phoebs, I hope things are OK between us now anyway, like, thanks for coming to clear the air.'

'It's not clear.' I thought about telling him about my own appointment with the Provost, but I didn't. I got up. 'I just wanted to see what you would say.'

Neither of us knew how we were supposed to say goodbye. I should have marched out and slammed the door behind me but I just picked up my bag and then fumbled about checking if I had everything. Then I made a kind of awkward face and walked to the door. He politely followed me, his autopilot charm kicking in. The unopened mail scrunched underneath my boots. I put my hand on the lock to open it.

'See you at the ball,' he said, quite brightly, really.

I half turned back at him. 'Honestly, you just don't get it. And even being chucked out of uni won't make you get it. I'm going to tell the Provost that you actually spent time finding that picture, and printing it out, and taking it to the board, and finding pins so you could put it there so that people would wake up and laugh at me. But nobody did. Everybody just thought you were gross and said, "I hope he gets chucked out". Honestly, I really hope you *do*.'

I didn't walk out feeling any kind of triumph. I didn't feel any better about it all. Just a tiny bit better about myself.

Later, as we all wandered over to Central Hall, I sort of wished I hadn't worn Flora's dress. She had lent it to me before everything had happened, when everything we owned was still joint. As we were getting ready, I'd sent her a picture of me wearing it and written that I missed her. She still hadn't messaged back.

The dress wasn't even a *dress*, really. It was a nightie from the 1930s. It was ivory silk and had initials embroidered on the front that said *EWR*. We had spent ages wondering what names they stood for.

'I can't even talk to you normally,' Frankie said to Negin, as we headed up the walkway. 'You're *so* different in evening wear.'

Negin looked like Audrey Hepburn in *Breakfast at Tiffany's*. She was wearing a plain black dress with a high neckline. With the dress and her bob and her small diamond earrings, she made everyone else look like they had tried too hard.

Frankie was in plain red silk, and Liberty was wearing a white floor-length dress with a slit. She had stepped up her usual glitter game to include a single, hand-painted-by-Negin silver glitter snowflake on her shoulder.

The spaceship building looked amazing. Totally different from the safety briefing day. All the chairs had been folded down into the floor to make a giant wooden dance floor, and the walls were covered in tinsel and fairy lights and holly. A massive Christmas tree loomed right at the back of the hall, throwing its shadow over the DJ stage. I tried to pick out Luke among the swarms of tux-wearing boys, but I couldn't see him.

We waited patiently in the line to have our photo taken. An arch of silver and white balloons had been put up specially for the occasion.

'I want to take my shoes off already,' Frankie groaned. 'And eat. I wish I had brought those Mini Cheddars with me.'

'Come on then,' the photographer shouted, and we all crammed in under the arch. I adjusted the fake-fur shrug thing Liberty had lent me, and smiled as brightly as I could into the lens.

'Any couples come into the middle,' the photographer said.

'No couples here, mate,' Connor bellowed. 'Single and ready to mingle: D Block middle floor.'

'Have you seen Ed?' Negin whispered to Frankie.

351

She shook her head. 'Do you think if I had seen him I would have just kept that information to myself?'

The photographer walked along the line manually adjusting our poses before saying: 'OK, best Christmas smiles.'

'Last day of ter—' Connor's yell cut out suddenly. He burst out of the formation and sprinted across the hall. Our eyes all followed him and found Becky at the entrance.

She was standing in a long blue dress, smiling. And standing next to her was Luke.

CHAPTER 27

LUKE

Connor was charging madly towards us and my first thought was: He's going to punch me. He is literally going to punch me in the face.

But he didn't. He just picked Becky up and carried her victoriously back to her screaming corridor, who swallowed her in a wild scrum of hugs and kisses and war whoops.

I just stood there, by myself, watching it all happen and feeling simultaneously really pleased and slightly awkward. All week I'd had this picture in my head of me turning up to Phoebe's birthday dinner with Becky in tow, and the two of us being given this hero's welcome. Obviously that plan had completely gone to shit over the past twenty-four hours, but still . . . At least something good had come out of it.

Phoebe broke away from the Becky bundle, and looked over at me. She was wearing this long, white dress, and it brushed the hall floor gently as she crossed to me. I couldn't read the look on her face. But, then, I never really can.

All she said was: 'How did you find her?'

'This girl on Ed's corridor, Jamila, used to go to school with her,' I said. 'She gave me her address.'

Her eyes widened a little bit. 'What, you actually went and physically *got* her?'

I nodded. 'She only lives, like, an hour away.'

'That . . .' She fiddled with the weird fur scarf thing she was wearing. It was like she was trying to find the right words hidden somewhere inside it. 'That was an amazing thing to do,' she said, finally. 'You have a weird ability, Luke Taylor, to be the hero and the villain at the same time. Like, concurrently.'

'Right . . .' I shoved my hands into the pockets of my dad's too-big tuxedo jacket. 'Is that a compliment, or . . .?'

She rolled her eyes, but she was smiling. 'No, it's definitely *not* a compliment. But it's still impressive. It's like, just when we are all going to sentence you to death for doing something terrible and unforgivable, you go and do some miraculous thing that saves you at the eleventh hour. I mean . . . how did you convince her to come back?'

I shrugged. 'To be honest, I think she was already convinced. She said she'd told her boyfriend about the photos and everything, but they'd made up and they were back together now. So I think she would've come back next term anyway. All I did was convince her to come back for *tonight*.'

'What did you say?'

'Just that I was so sorry about everything that happened,

and that no one, literally *no one*, had fucked up this first term more than me. But *I* was still coming back. I told her we should both look at it like first term didn't happen. Like, next term we were starting again from scratch.'

We looked over at Becky, who was still being joyously manhandled by Frankie, Negin and the rest of them. She caught my eye for a second – or maybe it was Phoebe's eye – but whoever's it was, she looked happy. Definitely the happiest I had ever seen her.

I turned back to Phoebe. 'This is gonna sound weird, but can we go outside for one second? I've got to give you something.'

'That sounds ominous . . .'

'Please, just one sec.'

I grabbed my bag and she grabbed her coat and we walked out of the hall and started following the edge of the lake round to Wulfstan.

'So, look . . .' I started. 'I know it's awkward to mention your birthday . . .'

She cut me off with a humourless snort-laugh. 'Last night was pretty much a disaster from start to finish.'

'Because of me.' I nodded.

She didn't look at me. 'Well . . . At least eighty per cent because of you, yeah.'

We got to the First Night Bridge and both automatically sat down on it, with our legs dangling out over the edge. The hum of music and laughter from the hall carried across the lake towards us. Earlier, on the train back with Becky, I'd tried to rehearse this whole big speech in my head, but like everything else this term, I ended up just bumbling straight into it without thinking.

'Phoebe, listen,' I said. 'I know that everything that happened with Abbey yesterday makes me out to be a complete arsehole. And obviously the reason for that is because I *am* a complete arsehole. But you have to know: I barely spoke to her all term. Yesterday she literally came up here out of the blue. And I know it was awful, and I'm so sorry, but it was also good because we finally sorted everything out. We just needed to see each other and say the last things we had to say, and properly say goodbye. And we've done that. And the truth is . . . I told her how much I like you. Because I really, *really* like you. And I want us to be a couple. Like, an *actual* couple. You have been the best thing about uni. The *only* good thing.'

I stopped to catch my breath, but Phoebe didn't say anything. She was just watching the water lapping softly at the bank below her. I reached into my rucksack.

'I should have given you this yesterday. And it's not wrapped because I am a twat. And, y'know, also because I was busy heroically bringing Becky back . . .'

She gave me a pretty hefty eye-roll for that, which, to be fair, I deserved.

'But, anyway . . . happy birthday.'

I handed her the *Ariel* book, and she just stared down at it blankly, like I'd given her a bus ticket, or something. Finally, she said: 'It's beautiful.'

'Do you really like it?'

She turned to look at me. 'Of course. Thank you. It will

be on my shelf for ever.' She touched the yellowy, frayed corner of the cover, gently. 'I love things like this. Like, when you look at them it reminds you suddenly of some really specific memory. Something you thought was buried, but then you touch this kind of emotional portkey and it all comes back to you.'

'Yeah.' I nodded, even though I wasn't entirely sure what she was on about. I was mainly wondering if and when she was going to respond to my declaration of . . . not *love*, exactly, but pretty serious *like*.

Suddenly, she said: 'Why were you crying on that first night?' and I must have flinched or something because she added: 'I saw you in the computer room.'

I exhaled. 'Well . . . Me and Abbey had had this awful summer and I just couldn't take it any more. We broke up that night. Or . . . started breaking up. I don't know. It feels so long ago. But I felt like there was all this pressure welling up inside me, and it just got too much . . . I can't really describe it.' I shook my head. 'I can't really describe *anything*. I think about that a lot. I feel like the words that can explain what is actually happening inside me don't exist.'

She looked at me, and almost laughed. 'Listen . . . this is cringe but I really don't care any more.' She took a deep breath. 'I fancied you at school. I feel like I'm on a TV show doing some big reveal, but whatever, there it is. Secret's out.'

I didn't really know how to respond to that. I was more interested in whether she fancied me *now*. So I just said: 'Well, that's nice . . . thanks,' which for some reason made her laugh so hard that her fur thing fell off and nearly dropped in the water.

I grabbed it before it could tumble over the edge. 'Hang on, do you mean even in Year Eleven when I had that ridiculous, shaved-at-the-sides haircut?'

She laughed again. 'Well, it lessened then, obviously. That was when I turned my attentions to Adam Kramer.'

'Thank god. I would have lost all respect for you.'

She wrapped the fur back around her neck, and I wondered if maybe I should try to kiss her.

She stretched her legs out over the water and sighed and then looked me dead in the eyes. 'To be honest, Luke, and obviously I may live to regret this, but . . . I just don't think I want to be with you.'

PHOEBE

He opened his mouth to respond, but I kept talking.

'I want us to be friends,' I said. 'Proper, *real* friends who would be there for each other whether we were getting with each other or not.'

He closed his mouth, and then nodded. He looked out across the lake.

'And right now,' I said, 'don't you need a *proper* friend more than you need a girlfriend?'

He smiled sadly. 'Well, yeah. I haven't got too many proper friends at the moment.'

'That's not true.'

He straightened his back and reached over to hold my hand.

'Phoebe, seriously, I know things have been really messy, honestly, I know that, but—'

I shook my head to cut him off. '*Things* haven't been really messy, Luke. *You've* been really messy. And your mess has started to mess me up, too. So, if you really do like me, then be a good friend and don't let that happen.'

He breathed out slowly, like he'd just been deflated. But he kept hold of my hand. Finally, he said, 'If friends is your final offer, Phoebe, I guess I'll have to take it.'

I wriggled my fingers round his, into a handshake position: 'To friendship.' He laughed and we shook. He was really handsome in a tux. Clean cut and broad and grown-up. He looked like he was born to wear it, and walk down a red carpet having his picture taken.

We clambered to our feet and started to walk back round the lake. When we got to the hall I said: 'I'm just going to put the book back in my room. Don't think Sylvia would forgive me if I got Jägerbomb all over it.'

He nodded. 'See you in there.'

I watched him walk off into the madness of the ball, where Ed and Arthur and a few others were cheering and waving him over. And that was it. I had rejected Luke Taylor. Year Nine me would have died from shock at that sentence. It actually made me laugh out loud, to myself, like a lunatic. And then I wanted to tell Flora. I got out my phone and saw she had texted back:

'You look awesome, best one. If you ruin that dress I will kill you xxx'

I went back to my room and squeezed the *Ariel* book on to the little bookshelf. Who knows, maybe Luke Taylor *would* turn out to be the love of my life, but in order to ascertain that I would have to actually get to know him first, and properly pay attention this time.

I wandered back down the deserted Jutland walkway, and as I crossed the car park I could see Josh was near the entrance to the hall. As I came in, he turned and smiled and I felt a bit nervous. He started walking towards me, and I wondered what we would say.

'What time you heading home tomorrow?' he asked. There was a tension in his voice I had never heard before.

'Think my mum's coming at midday.'

Neither of us knew what to say next. I replayed the moment I had tried to kiss him in my head. It was almost unbearable.

Just as I was about to make an excuse and walk off, he threw his arms around me. And I hugged him back. And we both just stayed there in the hug. The words we'd said had felt all strange and wrong and not what we meant, but the hug felt right and not weird and how things really were.

We broke away and looked at each other and I didn't un-derstand what was happening between us. What he felt and what I felt and what everything meant. But there was loads of time to figure that out.

'I'll see you later, Bennet.' He smiled.

I found Frankie and Negin at the edge of the dance floor, watching Becky get frantically waltzed about by Connor. Luke was on the other side of the hall, dancing with Arthur and Rita and everyone. There was still no sign of Will, or any of the other football boys.

'So . . .' Frankie took a sip of her drink. 'Glad you and Luke Taylor are love's young dream because my life as the nun of York Met is continuing without my consent.'

Negin gave me a look that said: *Things are not good.*

'Shape-Face Girl and Ed are over there,' she whispered. I followed her glance to where Ed and Sophie-or-Sarah were kissing, right in the middle of the dance floor.

'Oh, shit,' I groaned.

Frankie huffed. 'Maybe if *I* had a banana mouth and perfectly circular eyes *I* could bag an attractive tall man, too.'

'Well, I'm not with Luke Taylor, either,' I said. 'So you can also sign me up to the York Met nunnery.'

'Me, too,' Negin sighed. 'Interesting Thought Boy is getting with some random.'

'What?' We followed her gaze. I didn't recognize ITB at first without his holey jumper. He looked less philosophical in a tux. But there he was, his tongue down the throat of some rand—

'That's not a random!' I yelled. 'That's *Stephanie Stevens*.'

'Who?' Negin and Frankie said in unison.

I shook my head. 'I should never have saved her life. I should have let her choke on her own vomit.'

We stood in a row, my head leaning on Frankie, and Negin's head leaning on me. We just watched Stephanie Stevens and ITB, and Ed and Sophie-or-Sarah like we were watching late night QVC.

'Oh well . . .' Frankie sighed. 'I think we should just get Becky, dance our arses off, then go back and decoupage our letters and competitively eat cheese toasties until one of us dies from a cheddar overdose.'

'Sounds good.' I looped an arm around each of them. 'I mean, you know loads of people die in Freshers', right? Like, *millions*.'

ACKNOWLEDGEMENTS

We owe *at least* one round of Jägerbombs to all the following people:

Everyone at Chicken House for being amazing as always. Our fantastic editor Rachel Leyshon, who suggested so many of the best twists and turns and various other things in this novel: we bloody love you, Rachel. Huge, huge thank yous also to Barry, Rachel H, Elinor, Jazz, Esther, Kesia and Laura for being brilliant and for doing so much for us. We really appreciate it.

Our incredible agent Kirsty McLachlan for being a constant source of advice, support and highly reassuring phone chats throughout the entire writing process.

All our mates who either experienced the stuff in this book alongside us, or generously donated their stories, or just sat in various pubs with us over the past two years, reminiscing about all aspects of uni life. Most notably: Laura Allsop, James Amos, Kate Baker, Max Baldwin, Jonathan Bray, Chris Carroll, Alexie Cottam, Jonathan Driscoll, Christina Heaps, Harvey Horner, Louise Gaskell, Yasmina Green, Ryan Kohn, Tim Lee, Michael Lindall, Robin Pasricha, Jodie Peake, Neil Redford, Matthew Sharkey, Ed Shirley, Jeremy Stubbings, Ella Sunyer, Peter Todd and Alex Trotter.

Shauna Kavanagh for WAY too much to mention, really, but here goes: reading countless drafts, offering phenomenal (and vitally useful) feedback, explaining to us what the hell

Snapchat is (even though we still don't really get it), and providing us with high-quality tea and biscuits on our recce in York. You were a massive part of this book, Shauna, and we owe you big time. You are a truly amazing and inspirational person. THANK YOU.

Vanessa Long for very kindly having us to stay and buying us Bettys treats when we went back to York to illegally break into Derwent halls and relive our youth.

Holly Bourne and Anna McCleery for reading early drafts, and giving us invaluable feedback. You are both proper legends.

Families Ellen and Ivison for being a great bunch of lads and giving us so much love and support.

Diana, Rosey and Jessyka Battle for cups of tea and teen angst.

Everybody in the ridiculously supportive and amazing UKYA and UKMG communities, most notably: Emma Shevah, Non Pratt, Lisa Williamson, Juno Dawson, Liz Hyder, Maura Brickell, Nina Douglas, bloggers extraordinaire Jim and Debbie, Peter Bunzl, Honor and Perdita Cargill, and Abi Elphinstone.

Kate Sullivan, Allison Hellegers and Myrthe Spiteri for their fantastic support from the US and the Netherlands, and generally just for being awesome.

Tom would also like to thank Anna Hards and Laura Yogasundram for their friendship and general greatness over the past fifteen years, and also for kindly donating Interesting Thought Boy (and so, so much more . . .)

And Lucy would like to thank Richard for sacking off Cambridge to come to York and sit on bridges with me. As well as reminding me of a million ways we were in the autumn of 2001.

Plus, Frankie Colborne-Malpas for being Frankie. I am writing this just as you are (supposed to be) revising for your A levels and have all of the freshers experience to come. I can't wait to hear about how the real Frankie lollops through it all. You are an extremely special, talented and hilarious person and I will always, always want to know what you are up to so don't forget who your librarian is when you make it to the big time . . .

And to Negin Tellaie for being inspirationally brave and brilliantly witty. Thank you for letting me borrow you as my inspiration for *Freshers* Negin. I hope you like her.

The Francis Holland class of 2017 for telling me their university hopes and dreams. Most notably – Lily Carr-Gomm for being a first draft reader, Bella, Alice, Issey, Renata, Marina, Lydia, Phoebe, Andrea and, of course, the best library prefects a gal could wish for: Alix Sharp and Lily Sayre.

The staff at Francis Holland who are the most supportive and lovely people that anyone could wish to work with. I am so lucky to be a person who never wakes up and doesn't want to go to work, even when I've been writing all weekend. Your constant support and cake provision keeps me going. Tally, Cat, Pip, Jo, Dorian, Tash and my 11+ sisters Raff and Caroline all made writing this book a little bit more fun. I would also like to formally acknowledge my head teacher

Lucy Elphinstone, who has always supported me as a writer as well as a librarian. I wouldn't be able to pursue both of my passions without her help and understanding.

And, lastly, from both of us, to all our Derwent College friends from 2001 to 2005. This one is for you . . .

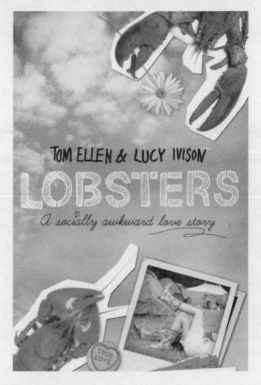

TOM ELLEN & LUCY IVISON

LOBSTERS

A socially awkward love story

LOBSTERS by TOM ELLEN & LUCY IVISON

Sam and Hannah have just the summer before uni to find 'The One'. Their lobster.

But fate works against them, with awkward misunderstandings, the plotting of friends and their own fears of being virgins for ever.

In the end though, it all boils down to love...

'...frank, funny and honest.'
THE OBSERVER

'...will make you laugh and cringe.'
THE TELEGRAPH

Paperback, ISBN 978-1-909489-33-2, £7.99 • ebook, ISBN 978-1-909489-57-8, £7.99

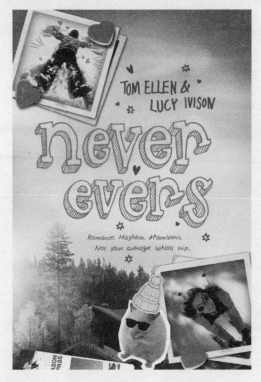

NEVER EVERS by TOM ELLEN & LUCY IVISON

The school ski trip isn't going to plan. Mouse has fallen out with her friends and Jack's totally clueless about girls. But when a French pop star – who Jack's a dead ringer for – arrives in the resort, the snowy slopes begin to get a bit more interesting...

'This book perfectly captures the highs and lows of the early teenage years.'
THE SUN

'I gobbled it whole in a day. Everyone who likes enjoying life should read it.'
HOLLY BOURNE

Paperback, ISBN: 978-1-910002-36-0, £6.99 • ebook, ISBN 978-1-910655-36-8, £6.99

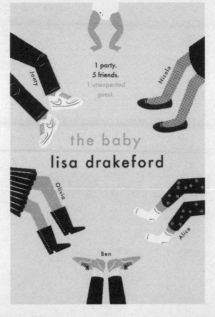

THE BABY by LISA DRAKEFORD

Five friends. A party. One unexpected guest.

When Olivia opens the bathroom door, the last thing she expects to see is her best friend Nicola giving birth on the floor – and to say Nicola is shocked is an understatement. She's not ready to be a mum, and she needs Olivia's help. But Olivia has her own problems – specifically her bullying boyfriend, Jonty, and keeping an eye on younger sister Alice. And then there's Nicola's friend Ben, who's struggling with secrets of his own . . .

> 'I read it in a day and couldn't do anything else until it was finished.'
> THE SUN

> 'Written with urgency and style, this is good stuff . . .'
> THE SUN

Paperback, ISBN 978-1-910002-23-0, £7.99 • ebook, ISBN 978-1-910002-24-7, £7.99

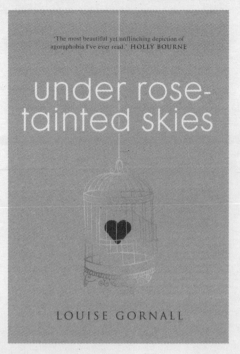

UNDER ROSE-TAINTED SKIES by LOUISE GORNALL

I'm Norah, and my life happens within the walls of my house, where I live with my mom, and this evil overlord called Agoraphobia.

Everything's under control. It's not rosy – I'm not going to win any prizes for Most Exciting Life or anything, but at least I'm safe from the outside world, right?

Wrong. This new boy, Luke, just moved in next door, and suddenly staying safe isn't enough. If I don't take risks, how will I ever get out – or let anyone in?

'. . . the most beautiful, yet unflinching, depiction of agoraphobia I've ever read.'
HOLLY BOURNE

Paperback, ISBN 978-1-910655-86-3, £7.99 • ebook, ISBN 978-1-910655-87-0, £7.99